BY ALLISON SAFT

A FAR WILDER MAGIC
DOWN COMES THE NIGHT
A FRAGILE ENCHANTMENT
A DARK AND DROWNING TIDE

A Dark and Drowning Tide

A Dark and Drowning Tide

A NOVEL

ALLISON SAFT

NEW YORK

A Del Rey Trade Paperback Original

Copyright © 2024 by Allison Saft

Published in the United States by Del Rey, an imprint of Random House, a division of Penguin Random House LLC, New York.

Del Rey and the Circle colophon are registered trademarks of Penguin Random House LLC.

ISBN 978-0-593-72234-3
Ebook ISBN 978-0-593-72235-0

Printed in the United States of America on acid-free paper

randomhousebooks.com

9 8 7 6 5 4

Book design by Simon M. Sullivan

FOR MOSES, GILBERT, AND ALEXANDER

PART I

The Yeva in Thorns

ONE

SYLVIA WAS IN THE RIVER AGAIN. Lorelei didn't need to see her to be certain of it. Crowds, after all, were the smoke to Sylvia's fire.

Lorelei stood with her shoulders hunched against the wind, trying and failing to contain her mounting disgust. In the span of an hour, the entire student population of Ruhigburg University had spilled onto the banks of the Vereist. They clamored and shoved and jostled one another as they fought for a better view of the water—or, perhaps more accurately, the spectacle they'd been promised. Most of them, predictably, were nursing a bottle of wine.

As she approached the edge of the crowds, she saw silver glittering on throats and iron chains jangling on wrists. They wore their jackets inside out and strung horseshoes around their necks. A few—Sylvia's most avid devotees, no doubt—had crowned themselves with rowan branches and braided clover into their hair. They clearly expected blood. Lorelei had never seen so many protective wards in her life.

Utterly ridiculous. If they truly wanted to guard themselves against fairy magic, they should have stayed well away from the river instead of gawping at it like nitwits. She supposed she shouldn't be surprised. Good sense tended to flee wherever Sylvia von Wolff went.

Apparently, some poor fool had nearly drowned an hour ago— lured into the abyssal depths of the river by an errant nixie's song.

It was almost impressive, considering a nixie hadn't been spotted this close to the city in ten years. She'd overheard a girl regaling her friends with the gruesome details—and then, nauseatingly starry-eyed: "Did you hear Sylvia von Wolff has promised to tame the nixie?"

Lorelei had nearly combusted then and there.

Professor Ziegler had asked Lorelei and Sylvia to meet her fifteen minutes ago. Tonight, the king of Brunnestaad himself was hosting a send-off ball in honor of the expedition, and the three of them were meant to make a grand entrance: the esteemed professor and her two star students. If they made Ziegler late . . .

No, she could not even think of it.

Lorelei shoved into the crowd. "Move."

The effect was instantaneous. One man dropped his opera glasses as he leapt out of her path. Another yelped when the hem of her black greatcoat brushed his leg. Another less fortunate soul stumbled forward as Lorelei's shoulder clipped hers.

As she passed, someone behind her muttered, "*Viper.*"

If she had any time to spare, she might have risen to the bait. Every now and again, people needed to be reminded of exactly how she'd earned that name.

She elbowed her way to the front of the crowd and scanned the riverbank. Even beneath the pale light of dusk, the waters of the Vereist remained an eerie, lightless black. It cut straight through campus like an ink stain that wouldn't lift. And there, shrouded in the branches of a weeping willow, was Sylvia.

From this angle, Lorelei couldn't see her face, but she could see her hair. Even after five years of knowing her, it always shocked her—the stark, deathlike white of it. She'd knotted the unruly waves at the nape of her neck with a ribbon of blood-red silk, but a few stubborn strands had managed to escape. In Lorelei's weaker moments, she imagined that grabbing hold of it would feel like plunging her hands into cold water.

She stalked toward Sylvia, and with as much acid as she could muster in two syllables, she said, "Von Wolff."

Sylvia gasped, whirling around to face her. As soon as their gazes met, Sylvia's face paled to the enchanting color of soured milk. Lorelei allowed herself one moment to delight in that glimpse of startled dread before Sylvia's perfectly pleasant mask slotted back into place. Somehow, after all this time, Sylvia had never grown accustomed to being hated.

And oh, how Lorelei despised her.

"Lorelei!" Her pained smile dimpled the dueling scar slashed across her cheek. "What a pleasant surprise."

Sylvia sat on the riverbank, her feet dangling in the water and the skirts of her damask gown puddled around her. Her mud-caked slippers lay abandoned beside her, and she cradled—of all things—a guitar in her lap.

The beginnings of a tension headache pounded in Lorelei's temples. She felt as though she'd suddenly lost her grasp of the Brunnisch language—or perhaps been transported to some stranger realm where one could reasonably face down one of Brunnestaad's deadliest creatures in full dress. Then again, Sylvia looked as though she'd gotten ready in a great hurry and then gone traipsing through the woods. She very well might have, if the stray petals tangled in her hair were anything to go by. Cherry blossoms, Lorelei noted absently. Spring had come early this year, but a damp cold lingered like a fever that wouldn't break.

"You're late."

Sylvia had the good sense to wince, but she continued tuning her guitar. "I am sure Ziegler will understand. You've heard about the nixie attack, haven't you? Someone had to do something about it."

Lorelei felt her entire body seize with murderous intent. "That doesn't mean it had to be *you*, you arrogant fool."

Sylvia reeled back, affronted. "Excuse me? Arrogant?"

Lorelei glanced pointedly at the crowds behind them—at the hundreds of eyes trained on Sylvia. Lorelei could nearly taste their hunger in the air. Whether they truly wanted to see Sylvia work her strange magic or to watch her blood run into the water, Lorelei did not know. She supposed it didn't matter. Either way, they'd have gotten what they came for.

"Insatiable, then." She sneered. "You'll have a legion of well-wishers to fend off in a matter of hours, and yet you're starved for attention."

Bitterness crept unbidden into her voice. Six months ago, Ziegler promised to name one of her students the co-leader of the Ruhigburg Expedition, and tonight, she would finally announce her selection at the send-off ball. Lorelei had never harbored any expectation that she'd be chosen. At twenty-five years old, Sylvia was one of the most famous and beloved naturalists in the country. And Lorelei was no one, a cobbler's daughter plucked from the Yevanverte.

Even so, she dreamed.

With that kind of renown, any publisher would leap at the opportunity to print her research. Even better, it would force the king to acknowledge her. Past rulers had only kept Yevani in their court as bankers and financiers, but King Wilhelm surrounded himself with artists and scholars. Lorelei was not beautiful enough to whisper her heart's desires into the king's ear and believe he would listen. There was no charm she had, no power she possessed to make her persecutors throw themselves at her feet. All she had was her mind. If she co-led the expedition he'd commissioned, she'd have the sway to ask him to appoint her a shutzyeva: a Yeva under the direct protection of the king.

She'd learned to survive the viper pit of Ruhigburg University by becoming the worst of them. But outside the university, her reputation meant nothing. As a shutzyeva, she would be granted the full rights of a citizen. She could exist, unbothered and untouchable, outside the walls of the Yevanverte. With a direct line to the king, she could advocate for her people. But her most secret, selfish desire was simple. As a citizen, she could purchase a passport, her ticket to a world she'd only ever read about. It was all she'd ever wanted, the only thing she'd ever allowed herself to want: the freedom to be a real naturalist.

Wilhelm had not appointed any shutzyevan during his brief reign. But it was an exceedingly rare honor—one she was certain she could earn.

"I am not doing this for *attention*." Sylvia looked flustered. "I'm doing this for—"

"What you're doing is wasting everyone's time," Lorelei said brusquely. She had endured far too many speeches about *noblesse oblige* over the years to let Sylvia continue uninterrupted. "Mine, Ziegler's—and His Majesty's, for that matter. You've spent far too long playing knight-errant with your own research. It's high time you took your responsibility to the expedition seriously."

Sylvia's face flushed, and her pale eyes filled with fire. It made Lorelei's blood quicken with anticipation and her mouth go dry. "Accuse me of neglecting my duties to Wilhelm again, and I will pitch you into the Vereist."

Lorelei knew she'd touched a nerve. Most provinces had resisted the unification of their patchwork Kingdom of Brunnestaad— and none fought more valiantly than Sylvia's homeland of Albe. Even twenty years after their annexation, they agitated for their independence. Lorelei supposed she could sympathize. They practiced their own religion, spoke their own dialect, and by land mass rivaled the rest of Brunnestaad combined. The rest of the kingdom believed them heretical, mountain-dwelling yokels, ready to turn and bite at a moment's notice. Sylvia, naturally, was the heir apparent to its ducal seat.

"Besides," Sylvia continued huffily, "this will be fast. I know exactly how to deal with nixies by now."

Lorelei had never seen a nixie before, but as the expedition's folklorist, she had recorded countless tales of the wildeleute over the years. Most commoners she'd interviewed thought them monsters, sometimes even gods. In truth, most species of wildeleute were nothing but a nuisance. The more bearable sort sequestered themselves in far-flung places and amused themselves by leading travelers astray. Others ran amok in the countryside, stirring up mischief in villages and trading petty enchantments for bread crusts or jars of cream.

And then, there were creatures like nixies. Facing one armed with only a guitar and three kilos of silk seemed to Lorelei a regrettable idea. "And how, exactly, do you plan to deal with it? Bludgeon it? Perhaps invite it to tea?"

"Don't be ridiculous," Sylvia replied crossly. "I am going to sing to her. I've been practicing my technique for months now."

"*Sing* to it?" Lorelei spluttered. "That is the most ridiculous thing I've ever heard."

Sylvia canted her chin. "And how many books have you published on the subject of nixies?"

A frigid silence descended. Both of them knew very well that Lorelei had not published a word.

"Mock me all you'd like," said Sylvia, "but my research suggests that nixies congregate around sources of magic. Learning to communicate with them could prove invaluable on the expedition."

Lorelei very much doubted that. Debates still raged in the halls of the university about the exact origin and nature of magic, but the most widely accepted theory posited that it was aether, a natural substance found only in water. Thaumatologists, specialists in the study of magic, had already developed instruments to measure it, and those were far less deadly and far more precise than *nixies*, of all things.

Feeling spiteful, she gestured at the empty expanse of the river. "Well, then, let us see your groundbreaking research in action. Or have nixies learned to cloak themselves as well as alps?"

The crowd was growing restless. Farther upriver, she spied a group of boys shouting and jeering as they hefted one of their friends into the air. Clearly, they meant to throw him into the river. Lorelei rolled her eyes. There was a reason no one swam in the Vereist. Once you sank beneath the surface, there was no way to orient yourself in the total darkness. Nixie or not, someone was going to die today.

Sylvia flushed with indignation. "She will come."

"Go on, then. Far be it from me to distract you."

Sylvia smiled beatifically. "Wonderful! Then please be quiet."

Lorelei had half a mind to shove her into the river, but she complied.

Sylvia plucked an off-key little arpeggio, and then began to sing. Lorelei watched her from the corner of her eye. The evening light filtered through the branches overhead, casting lacelike shadows across Sylvia's face. She grinned as her fingers clumsily shaped the chords. Never in Lorelei's life had she encountered anyone so *demonstrative*. She'd spent most of her life around northerners and had grown accustomed to their cold, clipped efficiency. But in Albe, people did strange things like sing in public and—worse—hug one another in greeting. Most of the time, Sylvia's easy warmth and excitability infuriated Lorelei. Other times, it reminded her too much of all the things she'd left behind.

She tore her gaze away and tightened the stranglehold on her own homesickness. Out in front of her, the Vereist shone like a sheet of black glass. It had always unsettled her, but it was far from the strangest river in Brunnestaad. To the north, there was the Salz, where you could step onto its churning surface and walk straight across from bank to bank. To the west, you could wade into the Heilen and your every wound would close. And somewhere in this treacherous, sprawling kingdom lay the aim of the Ruhigburg Expedition: the Ursprung, the fabled source of all magic and King Wilhelm's current obsession.

Sylvia grabbed her arm. "Look!"

Before Lorelei could twist out of her grasp, the water rippled. Slowly, something emerged from the darkness of the river. The mist parted, and a gaunt face stared out at them, as gray and lustrous as a full moon against the clouds.

Gasps and shouts rang out from the crowds behind them. Lorelei couldn't find it in herself to be annoyed. There was, admittedly, a certain provincial novelty in seeing one of the wildeleute here in the city, as if some folktale or quaint landscape painting had come to life. All of the engravings in the travel narratives she'd read paled in comparison to the sight of her, real and solid and terrible. The nixie's skin glistened, and her dark hair fanned out atop the river like a spill of ink. But her eyes struck Lorelei with a cold, instinctual dread. They were a solid black as depthless as the Vereist— and uncannily reptilian; a thin, translucent film slid over them as she blinked.

"Look at her," Sylvia said with true wonder in her voice. "Isn't she magnificent?"

No, Lorelei wanted to say. *She's dreadful.*

A glittery sound caught Lorelei's attention. A tangle of pendants rested against Sylvia's collarbone, each one engraved with the icon of a saint. Lorelei could not recall the last time she'd seen her without them; they'd always struck her as unusual. Here in the province of Neide, non-Yevani tended to be more restrained in their faith. But Sylvia, Albisch through and through, prayed as ostentatiously as she did anything else. She unclasped them one by one until they lay in a heap beside her. Just like that, she carried no wards that might whittle the edges of the nixie's magic.

Despite herself, Lorelei understood the morbid fascination of the crowd. She'd never watched Sylvia work before. Admittedly, there was a sick sort of thrill that came from watching someone hurl themselves headlong into danger. In recent years, Sylvia had made a name for herself due to her . . . unusual methodology. She published trivial little stories of her adventures with the wildeleute, ones in which she purposefully ensnared herself in fairy magic in order to record the experience. Her travelogues enraptured her readers—bamboozled them into calling her a visionary.

But there was no scientific merit to them whatsoever. They were an affront to empiricism, based on threadbare anecdotal data and—worse—*whimsy*. Lorelei knew by now that Sylvia was only exceptionally lucky—and incredibly stupid. A nixie's song held a powerful hypnotic magic; countless had drowned under their spell.

The nixie eased herself onto a smooth rock jutting from the river's surface, and Lorelei did her best not to recoil. The nixie's hair was tangled with lotus flowers and as slick as a knot of cattails. It cascaded over her bony shoulders and pooled in her lap. Where a human's legs would begin, her hips were covered in iridescent scales and tapered into a long, serpentine tail. Her blue lips parted just enough to reveal the barest glimpse of her serrated teeth. It was a smile that sent a bolt of fear straight through Lorelei.

"Von Wolff," Lorelei warned.

"Peace, Lorelei." The fact Sylvia *sang* it only added insult to injury. "She's just curious."

She hardly saw how that was reassuring. A clamor went up behind them. Lorelei glanced over her shoulder to see that their audience had grown in number—and grown bolder. They pressed in closer, chattering excitedly and pointing.

Idiots, all of them.

"Get back," Lorelei snapped, "unless you want to drown today."

A *hiss* pulled her attention back to the water. As the nixie drew in a breath, the membranous gills on her rib cage rippled and flared. Then she began to sing, and all the world went perfectly still.

It was a song like the sea—the sweetest song Lorelei had ever heard. It swelled and crested, inexorable and irresistible as it wove around Sylvia's in perfect harmony. One moment, Lorelei had her feet planted solidly on the earth. The next, she felt weightless, soaring. Never before had she felt so . . . complete, as though she breathed in tandem with every being on earth. For one glorious, incandescent moment, she saw it: the vibrant, wild beauty of the world. Aether was within all of them—within *everything*. It glimmered in the mist, and the Vereist sparkled with a thousand different colors, so bright it nearly brought tears to her eyes. How had she ever thought it so dark?

She took one step toward the water, then another. Just as she toed the edge of the riverbank, the iron chain around her neck singed her, as though she'd touched a white-hot brand. With a gasp, Lorelei snapped back to her senses. The river—once again black and dull as iron—churned winkingly below her. She nearly swore aloud. If she didn't get herself together, she was going to drown in shallow water like a doddering fool.

Focus, damn you.

She bit down on the inside of her lip. As the tang of copper coated her tongue, the nixie's magic dissipated completely. A horrid keening cut through the haze of her thoughts and set her blood to ice.

So *that* was the true sound of its song.

Sylvia, however, remained under its enchantment. She stood perfectly still, with a strange and shining look of rapture in her eyes. It was a rare thing to examine her up close, when she was always in motion. Her eyes were a shade of gray so pale they were almost violet. Like most of the nobility, she had a fine latticework of dueling scars across her temples: each one a dubious badge of honor for enduring a blow to the face. The thickest one, gashed across her cheek, shone like a sheet of sunlit ice. Sylvia set down her guitar, still humming her eerie, tuneless song. The noise of the crowd swelled once again.

Somewhere in the din, Lorelei could make out someone shouting, "She's doing it!"

A bolt of alarm shot through Lorelei. "What are you doing?"

Sylvia ignored her as she walked toward the river. The loose ends of her hair danced in the wind, the last red glare of the day illuminating it like white fire. The nixie extended a webbed hand to her. As Sylvia waded toward her, it was all too easy to imagine her slipping under. Her fine plum gown would bloom around her like a rose. Her silver hair would be stark as bone against the deep black of the river. Alas, Ziegler would never forgive Lorelei if she sat idly by while their naturalist waded to her death. She would have to intervene.

As a rule, Lorelei didn't use her magic where anyone might see. But over the years, she'd grown adept at concealing it. Inhaling deeply, she called on her magic. Power unfurled through her chest and flowed down to the tips of her fingers. She imagined closing her fist around the aether rushing through the water, and—there. There was a brief moment of overwhelm, when her will pulled uselessly against the river. But then the connection snapped into place, and she felt the Vereist like an extension of herself, a phantom limb. Its current roared in her ears like the flow of her own blood. Sweat beaded on her brow. She didn't have long before she lost her hold on it entirely, but she didn't need much.

With an exhale, she sent the water skipping off its course—just enough to sweep the nixie from her perch. Sylvia jerked like her strings had been cut. At last, Lorelei let go of her magic. Relief and exhaustion settled heavily over her.

The nixie shot out of the water a moment later, fixing Lorelei with a look almost like indignation. With a toss of her hair, the nixie slipped back beneath the surface and disappeared. It was so startlingly human, it left Lorelei dumbfounded.

"Wait!" Sylvia called helplessly.

So help her, if Sylvia tried to pursue that beast . . .

Before she could think better of it, Lorelei closed the gap between them and took hold of her elbow. "Have you lost your mind? Get back here *now*."

Sylvia rounded on her with her mouth hinged open, no doubt to say something petulant and irritating, but Lorelei didn't get a chance to hear it. Sylvia wrenched her arm away so vehemently, she lost her footing—and took Lorelei with her. For one horrible moment, time seemed to grind to a halt. The sounds of shrieks reached her from a thousand kilometers away.

Then, they toppled into the water.

Blackness enveloped her, so complete she couldn't see her own hand in front of her face. The cold greedily snatched her breath away. Lorelei kicked her way to the surface and gasped in a lungful of air.

Sylvia had already crawled onto the shore, looking very much like a wet cat. She bristled, her dress clinging to her skin, her hair limp around her shoulders. The gathered masses had already begun to scatter, disappointment plain on their faces.

"Look what you've done now," Sylvia said accusingly. "She was speaking to me."

"What *I've* done?" It was hard to feel especially righteous with her hair plastered to her face. Her mouth tasted like river water and silt. She somehow managed to overcome the weight of her sodden greatcoat and hauled herself onto the riverbank. "That was entirely your fault."

Sylvia jabbed a finger at Lorelei's face. How absurd, that someone a full head shorter than Lorelei was attempting to menace her. "I was perfectly in control of the situation. You've made me look like a fool."

"You do a good enough job of that on your own." Lorelei pulled her watch from her breast pocket. "We need to hurry if . . ."

The second hand *tick, tick, ticked* feebly in place, broken. The minute hand had met its untimely demise, fixed eternally at five minutes past their scheduled departure time.

They were going to be late, and Ziegler was going to murder them.

TWO

WHEN THEY FINALLY ARRIVED at the meeting point, there was nothing left to say. Lorelei had wrung every ounce of vitriol she could from the Brunnisch language and then some in Yevanisch. Sylvia had endured it all with a spitefully martyred expression and now kept her sullen silence.

Ziegler leaned against the carriage, radiating palpable malcontent. As they approached, she fixed them with a flat, unimpressed stare.

"Get in," Ziegler said, and climbed into the carriage.

Obediently, they followed her. Lorelei took the seat opposite Ziegler. Sylvia, infuriatingly, settled in beside Lorelei and adjusted the sodden train of her gown. Lorelei clenched her jaw to keep her teeth from chattering.

The river had washed the starch out of her shirt, and somehow, that enraged her as much as their tardiness. She could not afford vanity, but this was a matter of respectability—of *order*. She had fastidiously knotted her cravat, and her collar points had once cut a strong, sharp line across her jaw. Both, now, were limp and sad. Worse still was the awful sensation of wet fabric against her skin. Sylvia, meanwhile . . . Even half-drowned in a mud-stained gown, she managed to look fairy-tale beautiful, as perfect as a princess in a glass coffin. When Lorelei looked at her, she felt sick with an emotion she preferred not to name.

Long ago, a seed of bitterness had taken root within Lorelei.

Over the years, it had grown wild and sprouted thorns that coiled around her heart. She didn't envy Sylvia, exactly; she had never wanted to be beautiful. Still, it sometimes stung that she couldn't even claim to be conventionally handsome—or at least classically Brunnisch, with fair hair and pale blue eyes. She'd cut her dark curls short, save for an unruly spill over her forehead, the style fashionable with most gentlemen. But with her sharp cheekbones and aquiline nose, she looked severe and dour rather than rakish, an effect that wasn't softened when she spoke.

At last, as the carriage began to move, Ziegler opened fire. "Do you care to explain why you're late?"

Oh, would she ever. Lorelei sat up straighter. "I—"

"Or why you look like drowned rats?"

Sylvia wilted. "Well—"

"Or why you've chosen to spite me on today of all days?" With every question, her voice grew more strident, her words quicker.

"If you'd just—"

"What part of 'all of our careers depend on the expedition's success' was difficult for you to understand?" It took a moment for Lorelei to process she'd begun speaking in Javenish. Ziegler had spent most of her adult life in Javenor before the previous king summoned her home some fifteen years ago. She'd returned bitterly, but in many ways—her affected Javenish accent, her disdain for all things Brunnisch—she acted as though she'd never left. "Do I need to put it more plainly?"

When neither of them answered, she said, "Well?"

"No?" Sylvia tried.

"No? Then why are you trying to sabotage it? Showing up this late—and with you two in such a state—is a complete and utter embarrassment!"

"He and I are old friends," Sylvia said miserably. "He has seen far worse, I assure you."

"And I've been advising politicians longer than you've been alive," Ziegler countered. "This event is meant to communicate stability. Unity. *Confidence.* How do you think it will look when his most credible political rival strolls in as though it's a joke to her?"

"I am not interested in being his puppet!"

"Too bad. Tonight, we all are." Ziegler slouched deeper into her seat and crossed her arms. She looked somewhere between defeated and disgusted, with her steely glare fixed out the window. "I don't care how long you've known the man or how good-natured he is. None of that means a thing if he feels the stability of his reign is in jeopardy."

It was a fair point. No man secure in his reign would waste resources seeking the Ursprung. Few people believed it existed outside the realm of fairy tale.

Most people had some ability to wield magic. The most skilled practitioners could pull moisture from the air or freeze the surface of a pond with a wave of their hand. But the Ursprung—if you were willing to pay the price, of course—granted incredible power. The folktales Lorelei had compiled over the years could never seem to agree on how exactly it worked or what horrible fate awaited whoever sought its power.

"Fifteen years," Ziegler said with palpable resentment. "Fifteen *years* the royal family has kept me in the palace on a gilded chain. Finding this damn spring is the very last service I owe him."

Once, Ziegler had undertaken years-long expeditions and spent her off-time in a well-appointed flat in the most fashionable city in Javenor. Now she served as Wilhelm's chamberlain, a role she resented but could not escape. He called her his walking encyclopedia.

More like his dancing monkey, Ziegler often groused.

"I need open air. I need interesting people," she continued. "I have worked far too hard on this for you two upstarts to ruin it for me."

Upstarts. It stung more than Lorelei expected. Of course, Ziegler did not truly mean it; she often lashed out in a temper.

Even so, Lorelei could not help feeling like the broken twelve-year-old girl she'd been when Ziegler first took her under her wing: as desperate to please as she was to escape.

"This is entirely von Wolff's fault." Lorelei hated the petulance of her own voice, but she could not stop herself. "I was on time."

Sylvia shot her a mutinous look. "I was testing a theory that will prove invaluable—"

"Enough. You're giving me a headache." Ziegler pinched the bridge of her nose and heaved a long, exasperated sigh. "I can't bear to look at either of you right now."

A hot rush of shame struck Lorelei first. But as she stared at Sylvia, it was consumed by a steady, burning hatred. Nothing was safe. Not her pride, not her position, not even the affection of their mentor. By the time they graduated, Sylvia von Wolff would take everything from her.

Lorelei angled herself sharply toward the window and stared out at the passing city. As the sun settled like a banked coal on the horizon, it occurred to her that it was the eve of the day of rest. Her parents and younger sister, Rahel, would soon be making their way to the evening service. Lorelei couldn't remember the last time she'd prayed, or when exactly she'd stopped feeling guilty about it. Even so, she couldn't tamp down the longing that rose within her when she saw the temple's spires reaching out of the gloom.

She missed the bustling hours before sundown, how her family would cook and clean as if about to welcome the king himself to their home. She missed the soothing rhythm of her father's voice as he blessed their wine at dinner, the sweet scent of braided bread. Sometimes, she even missed the interminable morning services. Lorelei didn't mourn her faith, only the girl she was before she met Ingrid Ziegler—the girl who still belonged in the Yevanverte. Every night, she returned to her family more a stranger than the last: more Brunnestaader than Yevanisch.

They never *said* anything, of course, but Lorelei was not oblivious. She saw how it pained them when she spoke to them in Brunnisch without thinking, or when she couldn't recall which of their neighbors' children had gotten married last month, or when she burned another candle down to nothing, working long after everyone had gone to sleep. Still, she awoke each morning to tea and a slice of apple cake on the table. She came home every night to a place set for her at the dinner table. She endured all of their needling about her well-being and happiness and marriage prospects. Even if they no longer understood her, they loved her. If only she could say she was doing all of this for them.

Someday, maybe, they'd benefit from her selfishness.

Soon, the royal palace rose before them. She had only ever seen it from a distance: a pale smear on the other side of Ziegler's lonely office window. Up close, it was an ostentatious sprawl of white stone crowned with a dome of copper. The moon seemed to balance on its tallest peak, silvering the gardens with a soft hand. The air was thick and sweet with the scent of roses. Thanks to the king's veritable army of royal botanists, they blossomed in every imaginable color, from dusky gold to purest white. But it was their thorns that Lorelei most admired, each one a bolt of silver in the dark.

The coachman brought them to a stop at the end of a line of carriages. A footman rushed to help Sylvia down from the carriage. Rolling her eyes, Lorelei shoved open her own door.

Another footman appeared at her side. Before he could open his mouth, she snapped, "Don't touch me."

Together, the three of them ascended the palace's marble staircase. The doors looming over them might have been awe-inspiring were they not so utterly tasteless. The wood paneling was inlaid with gold, and the lintel was ornately carved with—of all things—*nixies* rising from sea-foam. Sylvia, to her credit, said nothing of it.

When she'd imagined herself walking through those doors tonight, it was a triumph: the end of a long and brutal road. She would've been greeted by the king himself. She would've been introduced to the most esteemed naturalists in the country. The reality was worse than anything she could've conjured herself.

Without a word, Ziegler thrust their invitations toward the doorman, who scanned first the invitations, then their faces, with something resembling judgment. "Welcome."

When he opened the doors, the sounds of conversation and laughter spilled out. Clearing his throat, he called, "Herr Professor Ingrid Ziegler, leader of the Ruhigburg Expedition; Miss Sylvia von Wolff, naturalist of the Ruhigburg Expedition; and Lorelei Kaskel, folklorist of the Ruhigburg Expedition."

It was as though he'd dropped a bell jar over them. Every sound suddenly grew muffled and indistinct. Some were amused, others clearly suffered from secondhand embarrassment, and still others were deeply unimpressed. Lorelei felt like a specimen pinned on a naturalist's table, open for dissection.

She must have been scowling, because Sylvia leaned in and jammed an elbow into her ribs. Lorelei managed a rictus of a smile, which caused the nobleman closest to them to shrink back as though she'd thrown hot oil at his feet.

"Good evening!" Sylvia said, too sunnily to be entirely convincing. "Thank you so much for coming tonight."

Just like that, the spell broke. Conversation resumed, the music soared high above them, and Lorelei took the opportunity to vanish into the crowds.

The dazzle of the chandeliers and the incessant drone of the crowd plucked at the headache she hadn't quite shaken. A good night's sleep would set her straight, but she couldn't help feeling irritated with herself. She shouldn't have used magic so frivolously—or recklessly, for that matter. Magic always drained its channeler; how much depended on the volume and speed of the water, as well as the channeler's proficiency. By all accounts, she shouldn't have attempted what she did, but that hungry, dangerous look in the nixie's eyes had awakened some selfless impulse within her. Lorelei bit down on a furious groan.

Next time, she'd let Sylvia wade to her own pointless death.

She kept her chin lifted as she navigated through the press of bodies. Among all this finery, she was remarkable in her unremarkableness. She had dressed, as she usually did, in black. Her mother had insisted on taking the jacket to the tailor, who had embroidered the lapels and cuffs with roses in glossy black thread. Lorelei now wished she hadn't given in. The ruined extravagance of it embarrassed her even more than her dishevelment—and it wasn't as though she had anything to celebrate tonight.

It took her no more than a minute to locate the far-flung corner where the rest of the unsociables lurked. She had gotten this far. She had no dignity or expectations left to shatter. All there was to do now was survive until the end of the night. When a servant passed with a silver platter of wine flutes, she took one and immediately swilled it.

"Kaskel," said a familiar voice.

As if her evening hadn't been ruined enough.

She turned to find Johann zu Wittelsbach, the expedition's medic and future duke of Herzin, standing there in full military dress. Half his hair was pulled back from his face, and the rest tumbled down to his shoulders in a spill of gold. He wore a ceremonial saber and an expression that suggested he was both surprised and affronted to find her here.

The feeling was quite mutual.

"Johann," she said curtly. "You've obviously come here for some good reason. What is it?"

"Hostile," he noted. "I'm here to keep an eye on you."

"And what have I done to warrant scrutiny?"

He drew near enough that he loomed over her, but Lorelei held her ground. This close, she could smell liquor on his breath. It made her skin crawl with half-remembered dread. Alcohol and men like Johann never mixed well. It emboldened them.

Beneath his spectacles, his eyes were a flat, glacial blue. "You're here."

She understood very clearly what he left unsaid: *And you shouldn't be, filthy Yeva.* Tamping down her anger as best she could, Lorelei said, "By His Majesty's invitation."

A flicker of annoyance passed over his face. "An oversight on his part. Wilhelm has always had the unfortunate tendency to see the best in others."

Lorelei supposed he would know. He and the rest of the expedition crew—the Ruhigburg Five, as they were known around campus—had spent their childhood summers together, running wild in these very halls. They had all the squabbles and half-buried resentments real siblings did. All of them were in their mid-twenties, but she'd come to understand Johann had taken on the role of the oldest: a bully or a protector, depending on his mood.

No good would come from provoking him. But she'd been worked into too much of a temper to stop herself. "How fortunate he is to have such a well-trained guard dog."

His eyes grew flinty as he registered her mockery. "I know how you intend to repay his hospitality."

"And how is that?" she hissed.

He gave her an unkind smile of his own. That was answer enough.

As if on instinct, her gaze dropped to the chain around his neck. From it hung a roggenwolf's fang cast in silver: the symbol of a now-defunct holy order known as the Hounds. They'd gotten their start hundreds of years ago, hunting dangerous wildeleute (or demons, as they called them) with blessed silver. But a few decades back, they'd aimed to cleanse Herzin of "vermin": people like Lorelei—and people like Sylvia, whose aberrant religious practices corrupted the spiritual purity of their territory. When Johann took power from his father, she did not imagine it would take them long to return.

"I've been watching you for a long time, Kaskel. I've seen the extent of your scheming, grasping ambition." He bent down and murmured, "I look forward to seeing it thwarted tonight."

With that, he walked away.

Lorelei could only watch him go with impotent rage boiling within her. Nothing about his behavior surprised her. She'd once checked out Johann's first book from the library—and promptly returned it after reading the phrase "those from a superior branch of humanity are morphologically better adapted for channeling aether" halfway down the first page.

Since then, she'd never taken him seriously as a scholar. Contrary to the ridiculous taxa of humanity he and his ilk had developed, Yevani could use magic.

The first time Lorelei had done it, her father had struck her. It was the very first time he'd done so—and the last. For a moment, she'd only been able to stare up at him with her ears ringing. He gazed back at her in horror, pale and trembling. When he'd finished apologizing and dried both of their tears, he knelt at her feet and cradled her face in his hands.

You must never do that, he said, *where any of them can see. They believe us powerless. It upsets them to see proof otherwise. Do you understand?*

Even then, she did. Now she only wondered if her obedience had cost Aaron his life.

The way the candles' flames refracted through the crystal chandeliers gave the whole room the impression of being underwater. From her vantage point, she could see all the hollow splendor laid out before her. Partygoers chilled their drinks with an absent touch and wicked sweat from their brows with a thoughtless flick of their fingers. Beads of ice glittered cold as stars on the hems of their jackets, and mist billowed around the trains of their gowns. Magic truly meant nothing to these people.

Past the glittery whirl of skirts and tailcoats, Lorelei spied Ziegler speaking with Sylvia's mother, Anja von Wolff. Unlike her daughter, the duchess was a slip of a woman: frail-boned, hollow-eyed, and deathly pale. There was no resemblance between them but the determined set of their jaws; it seemed Sylvia had not inherited the bone white of her hair from her mother.

What business could they possibly have with each other? Ziegler often advised politicians on matters of land conservation and colonization, of which she was a strong and vocal opponent, but Anja von Wolff was known for her military strategy, not her curious mind.

Lorelei's curiosity outweighed her self-preservation enough to watch. As they spoke—or perhaps argued—Anja jabbed a finger at Ziegler. Despite herself, Lorelei felt a twinge of sympathy at how familiar that gesture was. Sylvia had inherited something from her mother, after all.

Her message clearly delivered, Anja turned on her heel and slipped into the crowds. Ziegler stood dumbfounded for a moment. Then, as if Lorelei had called her name, she met her gaze from across the room. Her surprise melted into something entirely unreadable. After a moment, she looked pointedly away, as if they were no more than strangers.

Before disappointment could truly sink in, tinkling laughter sounded from beside her. "Poor Lori. You're like a spaniel that's still surprised when it's kicked."

Heike van der Kaas: the expedition's astronomer, the cosseted heiress of the seaside province of Sorvig, and widely rumored to be the most beautiful woman in Brunnestaad. When confronted with her deep-red hair and striking green eyes, it was difficult to dispute. Lorelei, however, had never been able to look past her petty cruelty.

"I don't know what you're talking about," she said.

"There's no need to be strong for my sake." Heike fluttered an ivory-boned fan in front of her face. "If Ziegler's upset with you, that doesn't bode well for the announcement, does it?"

"What does it matter to me?" Lorelei asked coolly. "It was never a competition."

Not one she ever expected to win, at any rate.

"Well," Heike said, clearly disappointed she had not gotten a rise out of her. "*I'm* still holding out hope for you, if only to see the look on Sylvia's face."

By now, the genuine spite in Heike's voice did not surprise Lorelei. Over the months the crew had been preparing for the expedition, Lorelei had watched countless rifts form and mend among the group almost day by day. But whatever tension simmered between Heike and Sylvia had the air of something old and unforgiven, like a bone that had never set quite right.

After a pause, Heike leaned in conspiratorially. "And Johann's, for that matter. Could you imagine *him* taking orders from *you?* How I'd laugh."

Lorelei had endured far too many insults today to let it go unpunished. Before she could think better of it, she said, "I'm holding out hope for you as well."

Heike's coy smile faltered. With venom, she said, "How sweet of you."

For almost two years, each member of the crew had been conducting their own expeditions in order to collect data for Ziegler—data she'd use to pinpoint the general location of the Ursprung. After twelve years of knowing her, Lorelei understood the theory well enough. The density and types of flora, the behavior of the wildeleute, even the number of magic users in a given population . . . All of it was correlated with the concentration of aether in nearby bodies of water. If the Ursprung was indeed the source of all magic, all they had to do was follow the data like a breadcrumb trail through the woods. Ziegler hadn't shared her findings with any of them—except Heike, who she'd conscripted to chart their course a few weeks ago. Ever since then, Heike had been in a foul, vengeful mood. Lorelei could hazard a guess as to why.

Wilhelm had promised to marry someone from the province where the Ursprung was found, and Heike had made no secret of her aspirations: Wilhelm's hand and the throne at his side. Clearly, the Ursprung was not in Sorvig.

A voice cut through the chilly silence: "I beg your pardon. Miss van der Kaas?"

A young man—one of Heike's countless suitors, judging by his hopeful expression and the sweating glass of punch in his hand—sidled up to them.

"Ah, my drink!" She accepted the glass from him. "Thank you, Walter."

"Werner," he amended.

"Right." Heike stared at him as though mystified he hadn't already disappeared. "Did you still need something?"

He shifted on his feet. "You'd promised me your next dance."

"Did I?" she said with mock surprise. "I'm afraid I'm dreadfully tired. Ah, but Miss Kaskel hasn't danced all evening."

"Nor do I intend to," Lorelei said.

Predictably, the lordling recoiled. Try as she might to hide it, her accent exposed her for what she was. Fifty years ago, Yevani had stitched rings onto their cloaks with golden thread, but there was no point to it now. She was branded by her tongue as surely as she was by her government-issued surname.

"She's just being demure." Heike's smile turned predatory. "Go on. Ask her."

"If I do," he managed, "people will talk."

"Ask," she repeated, all sweet pretense draining from her voice. "If you're gallant enough, perhaps I'll find a second wind."

Now Lorelei understood what game Heike was playing. She'd almost feel a scrap of kinship—or at least pity—for the poor bastard if he weren't eyeing her as though she were about to play some devilish trick on him. With grim resignation, he extended a hand to her. Lorelei could only stare at it in numb surprise.

Heike inspected her nails. "Is that all the grace you can muster?"

He met Lorelei's eyes, his gaze smoldering with furious, humiliated resentment. "Miss Kaskel, would you do me the great honor of this dance?"

Indignation rose up within her. "I will not."

Heike laughed. "All right, enough. You've convinced me. I will give you your dance, sir."

Werner all but wilted in relief. As she tucked her hand into his elbow, Heike winked at Lorelei. "Good luck."

She did not need luck. She needed another drink.

Just before the orchestra struck up a new song, a herald's clarion voice cut through the chatter: "His Imperial Majesty King Wilhelm II."

The crowd fell into a breathless hush. The doors of the balcony above the dance floor opened. King Wilhelm himself stepped into the wash of the chandeliers' light. He was dressed, as he always was for his public appearances, in a scarlet military frock coat adorned with shining golden medals. Evidently, he'd earned every one of them. When he renewed his father's war of unification at the beginning of his reign, he'd led his armies into battle himself, and it was said he'd had no less than three horses shot out from under him before he began taming dragonlings instead. He cut an impressive figure: tall and broad, with dark brown hair neatly combed back from his face.

No one dared move as he surveyed the crowd.

"Good evening, everyone." A wide smile broke across his face. It was always a strange transformation, to watch a king become a man. "Thank you so much for coming tonight. Now, I know most of you are here for the food, but if you'll indulge me, I want to talk about a dream. My father's dream, really."

Someone good-naturedly jeered in the audience, and Wilhelm's smile turned almost bashful.

A dream was certainly one word for it. Wilhelm's father, King Friedrich II, had set out to unite every Brunnisch-speaking territory under one banner: his own. Lorelei had to admire his ruthless efficiency. Before his death, Friedrich annexed nearly all of them in an ambitious military campaign, then executed anyone who refused to swear fealty to him. Once the streets ran red with the blood of traitors, he seized their lands and redistributed them to those he deemed more loyal—or at least more biddable.

At eighteen, Wilhelm had inherited both the crown and his father's dream. By twenty, he'd seized the last free territories. Five years later, here he stood before them: the king of a tenuously united Brunnestaad.

"What unifying our kingdom has taught me is this: every Brunnestaader, no matter which province we hail from, no matter our class or creed, has a warrior's spirit. We're stubborn as hell. Few more so than my friends, which is more than half the reason I've chosen them to carry out this expedition. None of them needs introduction, of course, but for ceremony's sake, I'd like to embarrass them.

"First, we have the lovely Heike van der Kaas, the expedition's astronomer and navigator." Wilhelm winked and extended a hand to her. "Join me up here, will you?"

Heike made a show of her ascent, tossing her hair over one bare shoulder and sliding her gloved fingers sensually along the banister. When at last she arrived at Wilhelm's side, he took her hand and pressed a kiss to her knuckles. Bracing herself with one hand on his arm, she stood on her toes and whispered something in his ear. He smothered a laugh and all but shoved her away.

Once he recovered, he continued, "Adelheid de Mohl, our thaumatologist."

Wilhelm spoke Adelheid's name with a startling, wide-open yearning. It was foolish, Lorelei thought, for a man like him to display a weakness so plainly. Adelheid, for her part, met his gaze with cool indifference.

When she strode forward, the crowd shifted as if making way for a queen. She was a statuesque woman, not quite as tall as Lorelei but built along strong, decisive lines: broad shoulders, thick muscles, and sharp, cut-stone features. Her hair, the yellow of a bleak summer afternoon, was woven into a coronet around her temples. Adelheid was pragmatic in a way none of the others were, from her simple white gown to her plainspoken manner. Growing up in the province Ebul, where little but the hardiest things grew, toughened even a noblewoman. As soon as Adelheid reached the balcony, Heike looped her arm in Adelheid's.

"Johann zu Wittelsbach, hero of the Battle of Neide and our medic."

Johann skulked up the stairs, his shadow cutting harshly across the marble. Wilhelm clapped him on the shoulder and squeezed—whether fond or possessive or both, Lorelei could not tell. Johann did not move until the king released him.

Johann went to stand at Adelheid's right-hand side. He rested one hand on the hilt of his saber as though ready to draw it at the first sign of danger. The two of them were nearly inseparable, with Johann trailing after Adelheid like her shadow.

"Ludwig von Meyer, our botanist."

Ludwig emerged from the crowd dressed like a poisonous species: noxiously, clashingly bright. Or, perhaps more accurately, like a man with something to prove. After greeting the king with a handshake, he wedged himself beside Heike. He whispered something in her ear, and she pinched him in what seemed to be retaliation. Adelheid stared repressively at them both.

"And last but certainly not least, our naturalist, Sylvia von Wolff." As she made her way toward the balcony, Wilhelm raised an eyebrow at her. "Who is joining us directly from the field, I see."

The crowd tittered.

Lorelei recognized the irritated look on Sylvia's face. Clearly, the rest of the group did, too. They looked on with matching expressions of dread. Sylvia, however, gathered her waterlogged skirts in both hands and curtsied to him. It seemed even she had the good sense to refrain from bickering with His Majesty in front of an audience.

When she rose, she strode past the others with her chin held high. Johann leered at her with a strange, predatory smile that made Lorelei's skin crawl. Sylvia pointedly ignored him and stationed herself beside Ludwig. He nudged her shoulder encouragingly with his own.

An awed hush descended over the ballroom. Even Lorelei could not find it in herself to feel bitter. It was, admittedly, an arresting sight. All of them were as strange and luminous as distant stars. When Lorelei first arrived at the university, its glittering splendor was entirely foreign to her. But the most striking of everything on campus were the Ruhigburg Five.

They were one year older than her, drifting through campus as a single entity—like a hydra with warring heads—or else a group of heroes stepped right out of a myth. Rumors about them abounded, from the laughably mundane to the wildly improbable. That they'd all fought in the war together (true, save Ludwig and Heike); that Johann was the sole survivor of the Battle of Neide (questionable); that Adelheid had gotten no fewer than ten students expelled for cheating (plausible); that Sylvia had once, impromptu, taken the place of a lead soprano who'd injured herself minutes before curtain call (God willing, false).

Until last year, when Ziegler had brought Lorelei onto the team, she'd never imagined they'd deign to speak to her.

"Our people are many," Wilhelm continued. "But no matter which province we hail from, whether we're of noble or common blood, we're bound together by an invisible thread. Our magic, our language, and most importantly, our stories. Who among us hasn't grown up on the tale of the Ursprung?"

He paused for effect, and murmurs rippled through the ballroom.

"Let it be known that it is no longer just a story. We've found it."

His voice rose above the swelling noise of the crowd. "Claiming its power will establish Brunnestaad as a unified kingdom—and an unassailable one. Nothing shall tear us apart again, either inside or outside our borders."

The air seemed to thicken with tension. Lorelei scanned the crowd. For as many gazing hungrily up at Wilhelm, others had clearly taken his words for the threat they were.

"Tonight is just the beginning." His voice softened again. "But before we dance and make merry, I'd like to give the floor to the leader of the expedition and my personal walking encyclopedia, Professor Ingrid Ziegler."

Her smile was tight as she climbed the stairs and took her place on the balcony. For the first time tonight, Lorelei truly saw her. Even though she knew, mathematically speaking, that Ziegler was forty-seven, she looked somehow ageless with her unlined face and overbright expression. Ziegler credited it to how much she walked. Lorelei had her doubts, although she could offer no other explanation. She was a stout, ruddy woman with graying chestnut hair and clear, blue eyes. She wore a gown in bold red satin, trimmed with ribbons and pearls. Although the Brunnisch court had caught on to the latest fashion trends, they were still woefully behind the rest of the continent. Standing above them, Ziegler looked like an exotic bird.

"Good evening," she said. "I want to extend my deepest gratitude to King Wilhelm for being a patron of the arts and sciences over the course of his reign—and for generously relieving me of my courtly duties for this venture. It is my great honor to represent Ruhigburg University tonight. Now I want to introduce the co-leader of the expedition. She will serve as my right hand in the field."

This was it: the moment Lorelei had been dreading for months. She didn't know if she could bear to watch Sylvia basking in the light of their adoration. She couldn't bear spending another night as her shadow, wallowing just outside her brilliance.

She couldn't bear it.

"She is adept in the sciences," Ziegler continued, "respected as a scholar, and she demonstrates an excellence of character and constitution, and a generosity of spirit and mind, that are requisite for this project. It is my great pleasure to introduce her to all of you."

Sylvia seemed light as air, ready to take flight.

"Lorelei Kaskel," Ziegler said, "will you please join me and say a few words?"

"What?" she and Sylvia said in unison.

It carried over the fragile hush in the room. Every eye was on her. Murmurs rippled through the crowd, but from somewhere outside herself, all she could hear was the same accusation echoing through her skull again and again.

Yevanisch viper.

Yevanisch thief.

THREE

DARKNESS SETTLED HEAVY between the walls of the Yevanverte.

Lorelei sat on the roof of her parents' house, nursing a cup of
coffee. Sleep eluded her so often, it had become something of a
habit at this point: to keep watch as the moon poured its light
over the single narrow street she called home. The coffee had
dulled the sharpest edges of her headache—although it had done
nothing at all for her fraying nerves. In no more than an hour, she
would board a ship and leave this city for the first time in her life.

She had wanted this. That was the worst part about it. She had
wanted this so desperately, yet she couldn't find a shred of happiness.

Yevanisch viper.

She'd never regretted her reputation before. It made her life
easier to encourage what they said about her. No one bothered
her when they knew how sharp her tongue was. Few were openly
hostile to her when there were rumors—false, regrettably—of
how she had the power to tear a man's blood from his veins. For so
long, she'd believed her thorns would protect her. That if she
spoke their language and rose in their ranks, she would be safe,
maybe even accepted. How naïve she'd been.

Yevanisch thief.

With shaking hands, she took a gulp of coffee. It sat like venom
on her tongue. Before she could think better of it, she dashed her
mug on the ground. It rang out, brittle and harsh against her

nerves. Somewhere down the street, a dog howled. Lorelei squeezed her eyes shut and blew out a breath. She needed to . . . Well, first she needed to clean up this mess and dispose of the evidence. After that, she needed to compose herself. Someone would be arriving at any moment to escort her to the harbor.

And yet, she could not let it go.

Why had Ziegler done this to her? Her dreams realized suddenly felt like a terrible curse, indeed. She'd transcribed enough folktales to know that happy endings were for girls like Sylvia. Ones in pretty stories about peasant girls who kiss frog-princes, whose tree-mothers give them slippers embroidered with moonlight, who defeat their most wicked tormentors with wit and sweetness and grace. Then, there were stories for girls like Lorelei. The worst of them went like this.

Back in the days when wishes still held power, there was a boy, the most loyal and clever of his master's servants, who met an elf in the woods. In exchange for the three ducats the boy had saved, the elf gave him a fiddle that compelled anyone who heard it to dance, a blowpipe that never missed its mark, and the power to be granted any favor he asked. Later that day, the servant stumbled upon a Yeva admiring a bird perched above a bramble thicket, its feathers as vibrant as flame, as brilliant as diamond.

If only I had a voice so beautiful, the Yeva sighed. *If only I had a coat so fine.*

If that's truly all you want, said the servant, *why don't you go and get it?*

He shot the bird with his blowpipe. Just as the Yeva crawled into the brambles to fetch her prize, the servant said, *You have bled people dry long enough. Now the thicket shall do the same to you.*

He began to play his fiddle. Ensorcelled by its magic, the Yeva danced among the thorns until her blood painted the thicket red, until she offered her entire purse of gold in exchange for mercy. But as soon as the servant took her money and freed her from the enchantment, she coldly plotted her vengeance. She went to the nearest town and prostrated herself before the judge.

Oh, anguish! she cried. *I have been attacked. My skin is cut to ribbons, my clothes are in tatters, and what precious little I own has been stolen from me.*

When the judge had the servant brought before him, the servant protested that the Yeva gave him her gold of her own free will.

You must think me daft, replied the judge. *No Yeva would ever do such a thing.*

As the servant was led to the executioner's block, he asked for his dying wish to be granted: to play his fiddle one more time. Despite the Yeva's protests, the judge, compelled by the elf's magic, granted him his last request. As the clever servant struck up a tune, the entire town began to tremble like water in a struck glass. As the servant's song soared higher, they danced, whirling and leaping like marionettes, until they were breathless, until the judge offered the servant his life in exchange for mercy. The servant accepted the bargain—on the condition that the Yeva tell the judge where she got her purse of gold.

I stole it, the Yeva said, *while you have honestly earned it.*

And with that, she was hanged as a thief.

Lorelei almost admired the cruel, stark justice of those fairy-tale worlds. There was good, and there was evil. Those who were rewarded and those who were punished. But she would never be the pitiable girl in the blood-red cape or the golden-haired orphan who charms a prince with her fragile beauty. She would always be the goblin forcing maidens to spin straw into gold. She would always be the Yeva in thorns.

The moment she let down her guard, everything she'd fought for would be taken from her. This place had made Lorelei into a viper, and if she should go down, she would go down hissing like one. Until that day when they inevitably turned on her, she would guard what was hers, no matter who she had to bring down with her.

"Lorelei?"

She nearly fell off the roof from shock. When she opened her eyes, there was Sylvia, peering up at her from outside the front door.

She looked more like herself than she had at the ball. Her hair was incorrigibly wild as ever, but she'd traded her gown for a loose linen shirt tucked into trousers. She wore no cravat, no waistcoat, not even a jacket. But, of course, her saber was strapped to her hip. The basket handle was a coil of serpents engraved in a fine filigree pattern. The blade gleamed in the dark, as sleek and pale as a blade of moonlight—and just as impractical, too. It was made of pure silver. Effective against the wildeleute, perhaps, but it was virtually useless against any human opponent's steel.

Lorelei reminded herself to stop staring, but her mind refused to process it. Sylvia von Wolff, *here*, witnessing the bare facts of her life. She wanted to throw herself from the roof and tear the protective scroll from the doorpost. She wanted to set her father's starveling herb garden aflame.

"What," she hissed, "are you doing here?"

Sylvia glanced over her shoulder, as though Lorelei must have addressed someone else so rudely. "I've come to return the favor of fetching you." She paused, and a smile tugged at the corner of her lips. "Although I confess, I didn't expect I'd have to scale a wall to do it."

Lorelei glared at her. How anyone could be in such a jolly mood at this hour was beyond her. She'd expected Ludwig, maybe even Adelheid, to be saddled with the burden of fetching her. Really, she resented that it had to be anyone at all. By law, all Yevani had to be within the gates of the Yevanverte between sundown and sunrise, unless accompanied by a citizen of Brunnestaad.

"Keep your voice down—and don't climb anything, for God's sake. I will be . . ." She trailed off. Sylvia was already climbing the rickety old trellis. With any luck, it would collapse beneath her. "...with you in a moment."

Lorelei considered the wreckage of her mug and decided, for expediency's sake, to sweep the shards into a neat pile. As long as Sylvia—and her mother—did not see it, no harm done.

Sylvia swung herself onto the roof and settled beside Lorelei. She gazed out over the Yevanverte, with its haphazardly stacked houses and cramped alleyways. Lorelei expected pity or disgust. But Sylvia only smiled softly and said, "What a lovely view you have."

She tried not to let her surprise show. Lorelei could see little of note from here, apart from the wall—and an occasional glimpse into her neighbors' windows, which was not what she would call *lovely*. She didn't have any polite responses for her, so she held her silence. The starlight found Sylvia, even in a place like this. She had an infuriating knack for looking utterly at home or at peace anywhere she went.

"So, did you draw the short straw, or have you come on Ziegler's orders?" Lorelei asked.

"Actually, I volunteered."

"And why would you do that?"

Sylvia had the nerve to look offended. "I wanted to congratulate you. You ran off before I got the chance."

"I did not *run off.*"

Sylvia gave her a meaningful look, which Lorelei decided to ignore. In all fairness, she had hidden on a balcony until Ludwig coaxed her into his carriage at the end of the night, but she would not concede the point.

"Congratulations, then."

Lorelei braced herself for a caveat or a challenge, but none came. Very suspiciously, she said, "Thank you."

"You worked hard for it," Sylvia continued. "I confess, you inspired me to push myself, even—"

"Flattery, von Wolff?"

"No!" she protested. "I do mean it. Truly."

Lorelei averted her eyes. "I find myself skeptical that you'd need any encouragement to push yourself. You're relentless."

Sylvia smiled uncertainly at her. "I will choose to take that as a compliment."

"As you like," Lorelei said, feeling oddly flustered. "That's really why you came? To exchange pleasantries?"

Sylvia hesitated. "No, I suppose it isn't."

Of course not. Lorelei hated that she felt even a pang of disappointment. She never should have expected anything different. "Out with it, then."

Sylvia cast a fretful look at the edge of the roof. "Perhaps we should get moving first. I will meet you outside."

"Oh," Lorelei said darkly, "this should be good."

With that, she climbed back through her bedroom window. A candle still burned low on her writing desk, the flame whispering just above a pool of wax. By its guttering light, Lorelei collected her traveling cases. Her family would have wanted her to wake them, but it was far easier to vanish. She could stomach neither tears nor the prospect of her two worlds colliding.

Sylvia leapt to attention as soon as Lorelei shut the front door behind her.

"Allow me." Before Lorelei could protest, Sylvia snatched one of her traveling cases from her hands. She made a surprised little sound as she hefted it. "Saints, Lorelei, this is heavy! What have you got in here?"

"Nothing," Lorelei snapped automatically. "Put that down at once."

"Why?" Sylvia looked alarmed. "Is it something dangerous?"

"Of course not." Lorelei paused, pretending to consider it. "Just don't make any sudden movements."

She did not like to be separated from her valuables: a set of ivory-handled pens her mother had gotten her for her eighteenth birthday; a collection of leather-bound notebooks filled with her folktale transcriptions and illustrations; a sedative in the strongest dose Johann was willing to compound for her; and her battered copy of *Tales of the Tropics*, the one sentimental indulgence she allowed herself.

As a child, she had run wild through the streets of the Yevanverte. She'd collected vials of water from the river for study, stuffed her pockets full of clippings from the neighbors' gardens. She'd collected insects, tucking beetles into her mouth for safekeeping—until one had secreted acid onto her tongue and put an end to that. She had sat on the roof and watched ships in the harbor, a black forest of masts and sails bobbing and shifting in the wind. She'd driven her parents mad filling the house with her collections, until one day, her father came home with a book: *Tales of the Tropics* by Ingrid Ziegler. A book, he said, written by the most famous woman in Brunnestaad.

She had lain awake deep into the night, devouring every word until the candle went out, puddled on her windowsill. It painted a picture so exquisite, she'd wept from longing. Now, having read Ziegler's later works, Lorelei knew it was a piece of juvenilia. But that book had cracked her world open like an egg. It was a place full of wonder, of adventure. And for the first time, her yearning had a name: naturalism. That far-off dream contented her at first. But as she grew older, she realized that girls from the Yevanverte didn't get to leave it.

She had no money to buy equipment. No influence to persuade anyone to finance an expedition. No legal documents that would allow her to travel. It had been an impossible dream until Ziegler answered her silly, girlish letter. Training as a folklorist had been her ticket into the university. But without the king's favor, come graduation, she would be cast out of this world again. She would be nothing and no one.

Sylvia adjusted the case in her arms very carefully. Then she set off down the street. Lorelei took one long stride forward and fell into step with her. They followed the narrow street to the northern gate, a rotting wooden door set into a low archway. The stone walls enclosing the Yevanverte were unadorned and overgrown with moss. They reminded Lorelei of gravestones slumped together. Sylvia set down Lorelei's trunk just long enough to unlatch the gate and let them through. Lorelei breathed in the damp air, marveling at the silence. The storefronts lay dark, the construction sites empty. At this hour, the city still dreamed.

It never failed to strike her just how simple it was to leave. There were no guards, no complicated locks or wards, no dogs primed to chase them down. No one who lived here would willingly walk into the dangers outside these walls, and no one in Ruhigburg particularly cared if anyone snuck in.

They certainly did not care what happened once they did.

Lorelei closed her fist around that familiar rush of anger. "So. What is it you wanted?"

"Right." Sylvia sighed fretfully. "I have come to ask you to reconsider accepting the position. I worry that Ziegler's decision was shortsighted."

Lorelei stiffened. "Is that so?"

"Please, listen before you immolate me," Sylvia protested. "Wilhelm is in over his head. In title, he is a king, but at heart, he is a soldier. He has a brilliant mind for strategy but no stomach for policy. He has done what his father set out to do, but he has no real vision from here.

"His ancestral lands are small and sparsely populated. The administrative burden of acquiring so much land in such a short period of time is—well, I shall not bore you with the finer points of governance. What matters is that there has been a great deal of upheaval over the past few decades, and it is the common people who pay the price."

"Yes, yes, I understand your point," Lorelei said impatiently. She was admittedly surprised to find she hadn't disagreed with Sylvia outright—and that Sylvia spared a thought for commoners beyond an abstract sense of duty. "Where are you going with this?"

A small measure of relief softened Sylvia's expression. Pressing her advantage, she went on. "Wilhelm is ill-prepared to rule during peacetime. I, however, have prepared my whole life to manage a vast territory. After the success of the expedition, I'd intended to ask to be appointed to his retinue."

Now Lorelei saw the shape of it. Sylvia's bruised ego was masquerading as noblesse oblige. And yet, the passion in her voice . . . She spoke as though she believed every word. In the end, that was what rankled Lorelei the most. What did Sylvia of all people have to prove? She and Wilhelm were friends—and there were other methods a noblewoman could employ to ensure her place in court.

"You will be. Perhaps you'll be heartened to know that the Ursprung isn't in Sorvig. He may marry you yet."

Sylvia sighed exasperatedly. "I have no interest in marrying Wilhelm."

"No? You already bicker as if you're wed."

"Healthy rivalry is, by his own philosophy, the instrument of progress."

"Is that right?" Lorelei asked dryly.

"It's different when it's between equals," she huffed. "Wilhelm needs to be challenged. But you slink and scrape for him like a beaten hound, just as you do for Ziegler. How can you ever hope to be of use to him that way?"

Her words struck like a slap to the face. So that was it. Sylvia didn't think Lorelei deserved it. Perhaps she did not have a grasp on the finer points of governance, but Wilhelm had a veritable army of advisers to steer him true. Perhaps she was not bold enough to challenge him, but Sylvia would never understand what it meant to make yourself less than you were. If she had nothing else, she would always have her name—and all her stupid pride.

There was nothing else to do. Lorelei laughed. By now, she knew it was not a pleasant sound, low and what Heike had once described as *sinister*. A shiver, barely perceptible, passed through Sylvia.

"What's so funny?" Sylvia asked, clearly distressed.

What's funny is that you've been given everything, and you can't even see it. It would be so simple to say it, to watch Sylvia's temper go up like a wildfire. But for once, Lorelei found she had no will to pick a fight—at least not at five in the morning.

Instead, she said, "Why, nothing at all," and contented herself with Sylvia's visible disappointment.

When they arrived at the harbor, the riverboat loomed above them: a three-tiered monstrosity carving a black silhouette into the mist seething at the waterline. The vessel's name was painted on a placard above the paddle wheel in decisive crimson lines: *Prinzessin.* Beneath it was the motto of Ruhigburg University: *amoenitate veritas.* In beauty, truth. It took every ounce of Lorelei's strength not to roll her eyes.

Moments after they boarded, a footman materialized to take Lorelei's trunk from Sylvia. Sailors bustled around them, loading the last of their supplies into the boat. It boggled the mind, just how much *stuff* they had. There were barometers and thermometers, microscopes and telescopes, sextants and compasses, vials for seeds and soil, all of them tucked into velvet-lined boxes. Someone's poor footman was struggling with a stack of them. They teetered dangerously in his arms. A scroll of paper fell off the top and went sprawling across the docks, unraveling like the long train of a wedding gown.

"Be careful," Lorelei snapped. "Those instruments are worth more than your life."

It was hardly an exaggeration. If any of them broke, they couldn't afford to fix them, with the expedition's limited funding. The footman gave her an anguished look. "Yes, sir! Sorry, sir!"

"You cannot hope to win respect through fear," Sylvia chided. "A good leader—"

"Surely you have something more important to do than follow me around."

"Why, yes," Sylvia said, as if it had just dawned on her. "I should finish setting up the wards."

And with that, Lorelei was blissfully alone.

Ash curled from smokestacks as if from the mouth of a pipe, twinkling orange against the dark stretch of sky. The cinders rained softly onto the deck and tangled in Lorelei's curls like snowfall. It made her feel ill at ease, inhaling the smell of burning wood mixing with the damp, silty smell of the river. Most smaller ships these days were propelled by magic—and for good reason. Steam engines were the most efficient and least expensive form of travel, but their boilers often burst from the pressure. She didn't care to think of how many ships lay sleeping beneath the void-like depths of the river. Their budget, however, hadn't allowed for a crew large enough to propel the ship with magic, and Ziegler did not have the patience to accommodate rest stops.

"Lorelei!"

Lorelei glanced up to see Ludwig, the expedition's botanist, waving at her—and leaning out over the railing of the promenade deck two stories above her. Her stomach bottomed out at the sight of him.

"Be careful, you dolt," she called. "I'll be right there."

By the time she reached him, he'd perched himself more comfortably on the railing. He flashed her a sly smile. "Hello, Captain."

Lorelei grimaced. "Hello."

Ludwig von Meyer was the only one of the Ruhigburg Five who treated her cordially. After he'd returned from his most recent expedition, he talked to her persistently enough that she'd been forced to concede they were friends. They'd spent hours holed up in the warren of offices in the natural sciences department, turning their haphazard notes into something resembling manuscripts—and, of course, trading gossip. The amount of knowledge he'd compiled on both aetheric plants and who was courting whom on campus frightened her.

He was a delicate sprite of a man with foxlike features, a placid smile permanently affixed to his face, and brown hair she'd once heard a moony classmate describe as *artfully tousled*. Today, he wore a green cravat and a silk waistcoat hand-painted with a pink-and-yellow water lily motif. Rings glittered on all his fingers, and a fat sapphire dangled from one earlobe. Even on an expedition, it seemed, he could not abandon his pretensions.

"Well?" he asked. "Are you excited?"

"Are *you?*"

"Of course I am." Mischief glittered in his eyes. "I get to spend time with my dearest, oldest friends. What more could I want in this life?"

She scoffed. "A great deal, I imagine. Surely you will miss . . . what is his name again? Hans? Or have your irreconcilable differences reared their heads once again?"

"Oh, come now," he chided. He'd conspicuously ignored her barb. "They're not so bad once they warm up to you. Half the stories about them aren't even true."

Lorelei bristled. He meant well, she knew, but she resented the reminder that she was and always would be an outsider. "And how long did it take for them to warm up to you?"

Ludwig, after all, hadn't a drop of noble blood in his veins. His father had earned a small fortune as a merchant, and with it, he purchased himself a title and made generous donations to Friedrich's war efforts. His loyalty had landed him a place in court—and his son a friendship with the crown prince. Still, Lorelei couldn't imagine they'd ever treated him as an equal.

If she'd offended him, it didn't show. His placid smile remained fixed in place. "Some advice, Lorelei? Keep them wrong-footed enough to forget why they hated you in the first place. You might try being nice for a change."

"Thank you for your wise counsel," she said witheringly.

"Anytime," he said breezily. "Why not practice now? We're going to be stuck on a boat together for God knows how long, and you know I don't like to get in the middle of things, but you and Sylvia . . ."

"Oh, spare me. Does meddling ever get exhausting?"

"Never," he said. "You know, I hear she likes the tall and gloomy type."

Lorelei choked on her own saliva. Pounding on her chest, she barely managed to splutter, "You're disgusting. I'm leaving."

He laughed into his sleeve as though covering a sneeze. It was the one weakness she'd ever been able to find in him: an insecurity about the gap between his front teeth. "I'll see you at the meeting. It should be fun."

Ziegler had asked them all to meet at seven—fifteen minutes from now—to go over some logistics and to finally share where they were headed.

"Until then."

Lorelei made her way to the stern of the ship, watching as they pulled away from the docks. The spokes of the paddle wheel restlessly churned the water into froth, and the engine whirred. Past the prow cutting up the water, she swore she could see pale faces—nixies or the ghosts of the drowned—staring up at her. Her stomach turning, Lorelei fixed her gaze on the horizon.

Bit by bit, the city slipped by and the world outside its walls unfolded before her. The wind carded through her hair and sent her coattails billowing. No joy swelled within her at the landscape before her, no awe. Until they left Neide province behind—assuming they were leaving it behind at all—there would be little to see but meadows and marshes. The kingdom seemed to her nothing but a vast, bleak expanse of mud.

Nothing was going as she dreamed it would.

A low *caw* pulled her from her thoughts. Lorelei glanced over, then quickly averted her eyes with a muffled swear. A nachtkrapp perched on the rail, preening its sharp black feathers. It looked harmless enough, nearly identical to a common raven, but Lorelei knew better.

It was a bad omen.

A few years ago, Ziegler had acquired a specimen to stuff and mount in her office. Lorelei had helped her prepare it. When she'd pinned back its serrated wings on her worktable, it revealed the red eyes set into each wing like fat rubies in the black velvet of a jewelry box. The luckiest who met those horrible eyes were struck dead immediately. The less fortunate suffered a wasting sickness that rotted them slowly from the inside out.

Lorelei shooed it, but it only hopped a few paces down the railing and ruffled its feathers indignantly. It occurred to her that Sylvia would likely have some elegant way of getting rid of it. The thought darkened her mood even more.

"Begone, damn you!" She waved her arms more insistently.

The nachtkrapp let out a deafening *scraw* before taking flight. Lorelei slumped bonelessly against the railing, grateful no one else had witnessed her humiliation.

"Well done," said Adelheid.

Lorelei startled at the sound of her voice. Adelheid sat on the deck a few meters away from her, seemingly engrossed in whatever she was doing. With mechanical precision, she measured out long coils of wire and snipped them with a pair of iron scissors. In her wide, steady hands, the blades looked almost fragile. Up close, Lorelei could see the sunburn dusting the bridge of her nose and the premature creases on her forehead and around her eyes.

"How long have you been there?" Lorelei asked.

"Long enough." Adelheid began to twist the wires together in a complicated-looking pattern. "I was just setting up my equipment. I didn't mean to disturb you."

Her tone was so polite, it verged on cold. She still had not looked up from her work. Over months of working with her, Lorelei had noticed that she spoke to everyone with the same meted-out distance. She'd chosen not to take Adelheid's indifference personally. Adelheid worked hard and did not suffer nonsense. Lorelei could respect that.

"What are the wires for?" she asked.

Adelheid raised her eyebrows. "I did not realize you had any interest in thaumatology."

Lorelei heard the unspoken insult: how surprising that a Yeva would have any interest in magic. She smiled thinly. "Everything that happens on this ship is of interest to me."

"Of course." At last, Adelheid raised her dull green eyes to Lorelei's. "Congratulations are in order."

Lorelei sensed she was being mocked. Drawing herself up taller, she said, "Whatever it is you're doing, wrap it up. They're expecting us."

Displeasure twitched at the corner of Adelheid's lips, but she collected her things. Clearly, she did not appreciate being told what to do.

They made their way to the door of the expedition crew's quarters—one accessible only by magic, thanks to the needlessly complex aetheric lock. Only someone as paranoid as Ziegler could have contrived such a method of torture. Adelheid closed her eyes, her brow furrowed in concentration as she manipulated the water within the mechanism. Her mouth twitched with irritation as she struggled with it. Then, at last, it gave way.

No one would be interfering with their work—or stealing it.

A hallway stretched out before them. The *Prinzessin* was something pulled from Lorelei's nightmares, which was to say, tasteless and excessive. But upon closer inspection, it was terribly worn. The delicate splinters in the woodwork, the uneven seams in the damask wallpaper, the way the tiles of marble on the floor fit together like crooked teeth. It was a splendor she could slide her fingers beneath, like a loose tile or a strip of rain-swollen bark. Some superstitious part of her feared what rot she'd find if she peeled it back.

A row of chandeliers illuminated their path, their crystals scattering light onto the floor like handfuls of broken glass. Lorelei led them briskly past their bedrooms and through the double doors to what they'd taken to calling the war room.

Its centerpiece was a massive table, a polished cross section of some ancient redwood imported from across the ocean. Sunlight fell over it in latticed patterns, let in by the narrow windows. The air smelled faintly of chamomile and ginger. Ludwig and Sylvia's doing, she assumed. The two of them were flitting about busily—and bickering, by the looks of it. Sylvia was gesticulating with a teaspoon.

Heike sat with her head resting on the table. Johann was slumped disconcertingly in his chair. His glasses had slid down the bridge of his nose and settled at a jaunty angle, but he made no effort to adjust them.

Lorelei refrained from commenting as she took her seat at the head of the table. Unfortunately, it happened to be right next to one of Ziegler's favorite pets, an elwedritsche she had taken during her very first expedition. It sat preening on its perch, a fowl-like creature with the horns of a goat and the iridescent scales of a serpent. It cocked its head and regarded Lorelei with one beady yellow eye. "Hello. Good girl?"

No, she wanted to reply. *Demonic beast.*

Johann startled at the sound of its voice, glaring at it with a mixture of horror and disgust. His hand twitched toward the sword on his belt.

On this one point, they were agreed.

Adelheid pinched the bridge of her nose as she drank in the scene before them. "What is this?"

Ludwig poured boiling water into a teacup. "They're dying, I'm afraid."

"Johann is seasick," Sylvia said exasperatedly.

Adelheid glanced at Heike. "And her?"

"Also seasick," Heike said, at the same time Ludwig said, "Hungover."

Heike lifted her head to glare at him but accepted the cup of tea he set in front of her. After taking a sip, she flashed a sly smile at Adelheid. "It was a long night."

Adelheid looked deeply unimpressed, but the faintest shade of red dusted her cheeks. Lorelei resisted the urge to roll her eyes.

It was the first time they'd all been together without the weight of planning bearing down on them. The folklorist, the naturalist, the botanist, the medic, the thaumatologist, and the astronomer. It sounded like the setup of an elaborate fairy tale—or else a terrible joke.

The doors flung open, and in walked Ziegler. "Good. You're all here."

Today, she wore a simple black coat, but her collar frothed with layers upon layers of lace ruffles. It was ostentatious, Javenish in sensibility, and quintessentially Ziegler. The thought almost made Lorelei smile.

Ziegler took stock of them, her hands planted on her hips. "You're suspiciously quiet. Is something the matter?"

"We're only eager to begin," said Sylvia, clearly trying to muster enough cheer for all six of them.

"As am I!" Ziegler clapped her hands together. "Lorelei, why don't you start us off?"

Every eye in the room snapped to her, all of them but Ludwig's burning with suspicion or hostility. Heat clawed its way up her neck. She had not prepared for this, but if she showed even a glimmer of weakness, they would never take her seriously.

Slowly, Lorelei stood. "I want to begin by thanking each of you for your work these past few years. Each of you has contributed a piece of the greater whole and made this expedition possible.

"As you know, I have spent the last year developing a categorization system for various Ursprung types." She surveyed the room. "Ludwig, your notes on the distribution of plant species across Brunnestaad have proven invaluable, as have Adelheid's measurements of where aether is concentrated in our water system."

Lorelei's gaze landed on Sylvia. As civilly as she could, she said, "And your interactions with the wildeleute, von Wolff, have provided much-needed color."

Sylvia looked ready to argue, but Ludwig laid a hand over hers. "This expedition was King Wilhelm's idea, of course, but it has far more important scientific value than he imagined or intended. Over the course of her long and storied career, Professor Ziegler has been working toward a radical new idea of the natural world. Everything is connected, and nothing can be considered in isolation. As she wrote in the first installment of *Kosmos:* 'Every plant, every human, every wildeleute, every drop of water, is a thread. Together, they make up the great tapestry of life. If even one stitch is pulled loose, the whole thing will unravel.'"

She glanced at Ziegler from the corner of her eye. The professor was beaming with something like pride. Emboldened, Lorelei continued, "Magic exists in everything, and all of it points directly to its source."

At last, Sylvia broke her silence. "Where is it?"

"I am so glad you asked," Lorelei replied flatly. "Heike?"

Heike looked irked, but she did not argue as she hefted a scroll onto the table. She unfastened the knot binding it shut, then carefully unrolled it. Her delicate fingers were ink-stained and glittering with rings as she smoothed the parchment out, and they were trembling. She gazed down at her handiwork with something like regret.

It was a painstakingly illustrated map of Brunnestaad—and a work of art. Their young kingdom was vast and wheel-shaped, cradled between two mountain ranges and bisected vertically by the River Vereist. Heike had rendered it in shimmering black ink, with its vast network of tributaries frittering off in shades of pale blue.

In the center was the province of Neide, the drab, waterlogged seat of the kingdom. Heike had sketched it with as little effort as possible. Wilhelm's gaudy palace, the university, and Ludwig's properties—a charming townhouse in downtown Ruhigburg and his country estate, both doodled with absent fondness, as though her hand had traced the shape of them many times before—were the only landmarks she had bothered to fill in.

To the west was Herzin, its jagged borders like a weapon in the right hand of the capital. Dark, treacherous forests covered almost the entirety of it; eyes blinked out of a tangle of briars. To the north was Heike's homeland of Sorvig, a thin strip of land reaching out almost longingly across the sea to their northern neighbor, Gansland. In the water, Lorelei spied a lindworm slipping beneath the waves, curling sinuously around the ships bobbing in the bay.

The easternmost province of Ebul, which was often relegated to an afterthought on most maps, was rendered here in loving detail. She had carefully penciled in the fields of tulips it had once been known for, long before the Wars of Unification, and the fertile valleys and vineyards. All the lines were hazy and soft, more a memory of a place than a depiction of one. Last, spanning almost the entirety of the south, was Albe in bold, angry lines. Between mountain ranges and dark swatches of woods, castles jutted from the countryside like rib bones pushing up through carrion.

The detail—and the feeling behind it all—astounded Lorelei. She was still admiring it when Ziegler jammed a pin directly into the map. It marked a spot somewhere in the frost-backed chain of mountains on the kingdom's southern border.

"It's in Albe," Ziegler said.

Albe? Lorelei frowned, unable to keep the confusion off her face. Based on her own research, that was among the last places she would have placed it.

Heike and Adelheid exchanged a look across the table. Sylvia's expression, meanwhile, was frozen in horror. She darted her gaze wildly about, as if searching for some salvation, some escape. "That can't be right."

"Agreed." Johann's voice was tight with barely restrained fury. "I refuse to believe the Ursprung is in some backward—"

Sylvia rounded on him. "Bite your tongue!"

"Johann," Adelheid said warningly.

"Oh, but it is," Ziegler said, a little peevishly. "Lorelei had made her case quite clearly."

Her case? She had only been introducing Ziegler's methodology, but both of them took the bait. Johann turned his glare on Lorelei. Sylvia had the nerve to look betrayed.

I didn't know, you fool, she wanted to say.

Then she remembered she'd mocked Sylvia only hours before. *Perhaps you'll be heartened to know that the Ursprung isn't in Sorvig. He may marry you yet.*

"Upon reflection, I suppose it makes sense." Sylvia laughed, an airy, forced sound if Lorelei had ever heard one. "The von Wolff line boasts some of the most talented magic users in the kingdom. The proximity to the Ursprung must explain it. Now, if you'll excuse me for just a moment."

With that, she fled the room. Lorelei wanted to find her dramatics ridiculous, but the words *that can't be right* rang incessantly in her skull. Hadn't Lorelei thought the same?

"How can you all sit idly by?" Johann slammed his palm flat on the table. "Yevani commanding the nobility—and soon we'll have an Albisch queen! What next? What will be left for us? Wilhelm is leading this kingdom into degeneracy."

Heike looked positively delighted by his outburst. "Why don't you write to him? Your frothing rants are always *so* compelling."

Johann rose unsteadily to his feet. As he stalked out of the war room, he muttered, "This is a farce."

"And why," Adelheid asked flatly, "did you think provoking him was wise?"

"Oh, relax," Heike cooed. "It's good for the two of them to be humbled every now and again. It builds resilience."

Adelheid stared at her with exasperated disbelief. "Fine. I will deal with them myself."

When she left, the doors slammed shut behind her. After a few moments of silence, Heike and Ludwig looked at each other, clearly doing their very best not to burst out laughing.

"Good girl?" Ziegler's infernal bird chirped.

Lorelei placed her head on the table. No more than two hours in the field, and already she had completely lost control of the expedition.

FOUR

*T*HAT CAN'T BE RIGHT.

Hours later, Sylvia's plain shock still haunted Lorelei. Alone in her room, she turned over the image again and again: Sylvia's slack expression, all the light and exuberance drained from her in an instant—then how quickly she'd papered it over with an empty smile.

Lorelei could not decide if she envied Wilhelm for his ability to inspire such despair in her or if she resented Sylvia for turning her nose up at the prospect of marrying a king. By all accounts, her reaction defied all reason. If she became queen of Brunnestaad, she could advocate for whatever fanciful policies she wished. She could even ensure Lorelei's ruin if she saw fit to deprive her of her place in court out of spite. But she did not seem to believe that the Ursprung was in Albe, and infuriatingly, Lorelei agreed with her.

It felt treasonous to even entertain it. This expedition was the culmination of decades of Ziegler's work. And yet, Lorelei had spent the last hour filled with doubt and leafing through her own notes.

Ludwig had once called them "deranged," but she took pride in the system she had developed. Order was essential in identifying patterns in a project of this scope. She'd loosely indexed the tales she'd collected by motif and basic plot structure. For each one, she included a transcription of her conversation with the storyteller, her notes on the tale (primarily composed of snippy commentary), and the final version, cobbled together from all her sources.

Over the past year, Ziegler had brought in people from all over the kingdom for Lorelei to interview. Each province—each *village*, no less—had their own version of the Ursprung legend. The general sketch of the tale always followed the same beats, but they never agreed exactly on who the protagonist was, what trials he faced on his journey, what he lost by its bitter end, or even what power it granted. In a kingdom as large as Brunnestaad, variants were to be expected. But not one variant placed the Ursprung in the Albisch mountains.

Lorelei had spent months agonizing over how to present the definitive version. Which details to cut, which textures to flatten, what moral to emphasize. In the end, she'd decided on this:

Back in the days when wishes still held power, there lived a king whose realm had fallen on hard times. But no matter how poor the harvest or how hostile his enemies, he had one boon: all the waters in his land contained a strange and powerful magic. Of all those waters, the king's greatest treasure was a pool that answered one question of each person who asked. It did not speak, but like a dark mirror, images swam on its surface. He built a chamber around it in his castle, with a skylight that let in the moon's silver rays.

It so happened that one day, the king asked the pool where he might find power enough to save his people from those who sought to destroy them. In reply, an image took shape in the water. It showed him a spring he had never seen before, hidden in the swamplands from which mankind had first emerged. To the one it deemed worthy, it granted incredible power. But those who had been found wanting could take its power by force—at a cost.

The king ventured forth and, of course, faced three tedious challenges along the way to prove his mettle. At the end of his journey, he found a vast lake that looked to be made of starlight. But when he approached it, it did not awaken. He had been found wanting.

Enraged, the king dove in, and when he emerged again, he

knew he possessed all that he wanted. He could sweep whole villages off the coastline. He could flood his enemies' farmlands. He could rain hail the size of fists on their armies. But he soon learned that stolen power came at too high a price. Every time he wielded it, it drained his life force a little more.

Before he drew his last breath, he sealed away the knowledge of both the pool and the spring. No one, he vowed, would suffer or cause suffering as he had ever again.

Some versions suggested he died by slow and painful exsanguination. Evidently, a village a few days' ride from Ruhigburg had kept his blood in a reliquary. She knew this only because she overheard Heike complaining that Wilhelm had brought it back to the palace and insisted on carrying it around. The man had either a morbid sense of humor or a flair for the dramatic.

A knock sounded on her door. Lorelei slammed her notebook shut with a flash of irritation. "Enter."

As the door swung open, the string of warding bells Sylvia had installed jangled merrily. The sound grated against her, but she supposed it beat an untimely death at the hands of the wildeleute.

She was surprised to see Ziegler standing in the threshold. In the morning light, she looked soft and unruffled, with a fur-lined coat drawn tightly around her shoulders. Her hair—had there always been so much gray creeping into it?—tangled gently in the breeze coming through the open window. It wasn't until now that Lorelei fully appreciated what the years in Ruhigburg had done to Ziegler. Before they began preparing for the expedition, she'd moved through the world like a lion in a cage. But now she was aglow. She looked almost like the woman Lorelei had met for the first time twelve years ago: a swashbuckler in her mid-thirties, hot off the runaway success of her first publication.

Ziegler's ready smile faltered. "What's the matter?"

"Nothing," Lorelei said automatically. At the skeptical look on Ziegler's face, she added, "Nothing important."

Ziegler settled on the edge of Lorelei's bed. "Tell me."

"I have been thinking since our meeting." Under the probing intensity of Ziegler's stare, it suddenly felt difficult to speak. How ridiculous. She cleared her throat and pressed onward. "I am curious how, specifically, you arrived at your conclusion."

Ziegler's expression grew remote. "You doubt me as well."

Lorelei's gaze darted to the open window as she half willed the river to rise up and pull her under. Oblivion seemed preferable to this, but it was not in her nature to turn back once she'd set down a path. When the silence stretched on too long to bear, she said, "It's not the conclusion I would have drawn, based on my own findings."

"Do you trust me?"

Of course she did. For better or for worse, Ziegler had made her who she was.

Sometime after her thirtieth reread of *Tales*, Lorelei had, against her parents' counsel, written a letter to Ziegler. The memory embarrassed her too much to examine closely. It had been all frills and wide-eyed praise. But to her astonishment, Ziegler had replied. More astonishing yet, she had promised to come visit her in the Yevanverte. Only, the girl Ziegler finally met wasn't the same one who had written her the letter.

In truth, Lorelei couldn't remember much from that time in her life. The days after Ziegler's letter arrived had been a giddy blur. And then, a week later, Aaron died.

When Ziegler herself arrived, in the height of Lorelei's grief-fueled stupor, she'd been both nothing like and exactly as Lorelei had envisioned. She was stocky and fast-talking, generous in spirit and mind. But she was also refreshingly brusque and ungentle. She'd grilled Lorelei on what she'd observed of nature in the Yevanverte. She'd asked her which languages she'd studied and what folktales she knew. She'd even demanded—despite Lorelei's parents' insistence that she could not move even a droplet of water—a demonstration of her magical ability. Ziegler had sat silently through it all, taking notes with an alarming speed and volume.

And then she'd left.

Two days later, another letter arrived, inviting Lorelei to be tutored in the natural sciences. Lorelei could still recite the entire thing word for word, but she'd clung to two lines so fervently, they were all but branded on her heart. *It seems to me you've far too much potential to waste it making shoes and moping. How would you like to be extraordinary?*

Lorelei had clung to that promise ever since. Her patience—her devotion, her trust—had been rewarded. Ziegler had earned it a thousand times over. But her evasiveness set Lorelei on edge. It was entirely unlike her, and it ill-suited her.

"With all due respect," Lorelei replied, colder than she'd intended, "I don't see how trust factors into it."

Ziegler paused, then sat up straighter. "You're right, of course. The data point to—"

"A very significant concentration of aether," Lorelei said. The more she spoke, the more her certainty grew. "But there are, of course, a great many scattered across Brunnestaad. Relying on only one source is irresponsible. It's—"

"You've done well."

Why, then, did it feel like a dismissal? Lorelei hesitated. "I have always hoped to be of use to you."

"And you have been. My brilliant Lorelei." Ziegler crossed the room and rested her hands on Lorelei's shoulders. When, Lorelei wondered absently, had she grown so much taller than Ziegler? She'd once loomed as large as a giant. "You're tired. You've been too close to your work these last few months."

It took a moment for Lorelei to register her meaning. "You think I'm mistaken."

"I think," she said before Lorelei could interject, her voice more forceful than it had been, "you have misinterpreted your data.

However, I still made good use of your journals, if not your theory. Rest assured, I'm very certain about our destination."

The finality of those words brooked no further discussion. Lorelei could say nothing but "Yes. Of course."

Ziegler patted her shoulders, visibly relieved. It had been a long while since she'd extended any gesture of maternal fondness. It made Lorelei's stomach twist violently with—what, exactly, longing? She felt vaguely disgusted with herself. Somehow, all she could think of was the barely leashed fire in Sylvia's voice. *You slink and scrape for him like a beaten hound, just as you do for Ziegler.*

"I'll give you a moment," Ziegler said. "Come find me when you're ready to discuss logistics."

When the door latched shut behind her, Lorelei flung open her journal again. She did not know what she was looking for. Her own handwriting seemed an entirely foreign language to her. She slammed it shut and reached for the cold comfort of anger. She had been given one task. One simple task. How could she have misinterpreted—

Clarity doused her like a bucket of cold water. Folklore was not a science that depended on calculations, and Lorelei did not make careless mistakes. Neither did Ziegler. Her conclusion was sound, surely; she just had not seen fit to explain how she'd arrived at it.

And so, she'd lied.

Surprise came first, then an aching sort of confusion that settled heavy as a stone in Lorelei's breast. It felt the same way it had when her father had struck her. Absently, she touched the phantom bruise on her cheek with gloved fingertips.

How strange, she thought. Ziegler had never lied to her before.

Lorelei slept fitfully. In her dreams, a sound pursued her, soft and eerie, as elusive as wind through winter-bare trees. With every step, it shivered and chimed, drawing closer and closer until—

She shot upright. The sedative she'd taken made molasses of

her thoughts, and she could not be certain what was real or not. Then that incessant twinkling sound came again. *The warding bells,* she realized.

Someone was outside her room.

Throwing off the covers, she fumbled to turn on the gas lantern resting on her bedside table. The flame flickered to life, but the darkness was a thick veil she could not push through. The whole room swayed and shifted, and the floorboards had a sickly gleam, like fevered sweat. Outside her window, there was nothing but the jagged dark of the water, restlessly churning. The window bloomed with condensation at her touch, the glass streaked with rainwater. The sun still had not risen.

Who would be awake at this hour, to have roused her?

Plenty of people, you paranoid fool.

Prinzessin had a staff of roughly fifteen charged with stoking the boiler, steering the ship, and otherwise ensuring they didn't starve. All of them worked early mornings, some all through the night. If not them, perhaps one of the expedition crew had risen early and nudged the string of bells as they passed. Whatever she'd heard wasn't a wildeleute; the iron chain around her neck was cool and inert against her skin.

It could not hurt to check. If nothing else, perhaps venting her spleen on someone would make her feel better. Lorelei retrieved her gloves from the nightstand's drawer and pulled them on, then grabbed the coat slung over the back of her desk chair. Lantern in hand, she stepped into the hallway.

The darkness yawned open. She swore she heard the faint echoes of laughter, the shattering of glass. Her breath quickened.

Damn you, get ahold of yourself.

Even after twelve years, the one weakness she'd not beaten out of herself was this childish fear of the dark. As it always did, her mind spun shadows into monsters who wore the faces of men. Blood running slick on the floor. The specter of Aaron with bone gleaming through his matted hair. Lorelei dug the heel of her palm into one eye, trying to blink away the memories overlaid on the world.

None of this was real. The dead were dead.

Prinzessin rocked against her anchor. The water churned softly. Lorelei made her way down the hall by the lantern's glow. As she passed a window, the moon punched through the fog. Its light hemorrhaged onto the floor and sloshed against the toes of her boots. Her heart thudded louder in her ears.

The doors to the war room listed open. Lamplight fell like a blade through the threshold. Some small, fanciful part of her re-membered wandering the halls of Ziegler's home as a girl. Some-times, she stayed overnight when their lessons went long, and when the nightmares frightened her awake, she found Ziegler in her office. She'd drone on about whatever she was working on that day until Lorelei dozed off in an armchair.

Quietly, Lorelei called out to her, "Ziegler."

No response.

Lorelei moved farther down the hall and stopped just outside the door. More tentatively, she said, "Ziegler?"

Still, nothing.

Maybe she'd gone back to bed without extinguishing the lights, or perhaps she had fallen asleep, her manuscript as her pillow. She could be so absent-minded when she was immersed in a project. Lorelei pushed open the door. It groaned on its hinges.

Inside the war room, a dying oil lamp cast harsh shadows across the wall. A dark shape slumped over the table. Water dripped rhythmically from its fingers, which hung loose at its side. It ran off the table and spread across the floorboards like rot.

No, not water—blood.

"Ziegler!"

The scope of Lorelei's world narrowed to a pinprick as she ap-proached the figure. No breath stirred it. Lorelei grabbed it by the shoulder and turned it over. Its head lolled at a grotesque angle, and its skin glowed with a horrible, waxen sheen. There was a stab wound in its chest, leaking sluggishly with blood. For a moment, Lorelei couldn't make sense of it. What lay before her scrambled itself into meaninglessness.

Ziegler's eyes stared unseeingly into Lorelei's.

She choked on a scream; it burned in her throat like acid. Her breaths came shallow and frantic.

"No," she murmured. "No, no, no."

She was dead.

Ziegler's pale blue lips were flecked with froth and parted in an unspoken accusation. Just over her shoulder, the wintry glow of a specter rose from the floorboards.

Aaron.

His eyes were as black as the Vereist boring into her, flung wide and sightless with fear. Blood trailed from his skull like a ribbon caught in the wind.

You abandoned me, he said. *You killed me.*

Her breaths came harder. "No, I—"

You killed her.

Lorelei couldn't stop it then, and she couldn't stop it now. Death followed her relentlessly. No matter how far she ran or how high she climbed, no matter how desperately she tried to steel herself against it, it would find her. What could she ever say to make him understand? "I'm sorry! Please forgive me, sheifale, please . . ."

Behind her, the floorboards moaned.

It's in your head, she told herself. *It's all in your head.*

But they didn't stop. The footsteps slowing to a stop outside the war room were real.

The door creaked open and a soft voice called, "Lorelei?"

FIVE

A WOMAN STOOD IN THE DOORWAY with a delicate iron candlestick clutched in her hand. The flame dancing on its wick cast her face in a sallow glow. With her thin white shift and long white hair, she looked like something out of Lorelei's most tormented dreams. Another ghost—or else a wiedergänger had found her. When they scented death or grief in the air, they swarmed like sharks to a spill of blood, wearing the faces of the dead.

"Get out." Lorelei staggered toward her and filled the doorway with her height. Ghost or not, no one could come into this room. No one could lay eyes on Ziegler in this state. She needed *time* to think, to process. She needed . . .

With clinical detachment, Lorelei registered that she was being pulled out of the war room and lowered to the ground. She slid to a heap on the hallway floor, folding in on herself. It felt as though she were trapped behind glass with no way to break free. On the other side, the world was strangely distorted, something she could see but not touch. The ghost's lips were moving, but Lorelei couldn't make sense of what she was saying.

"Lorelei!" The sound of her name jolted her back to her senses. "Breathe."

She did—or at least she tried. Every rattling breath she drew was agony. Through her delirium, Lorelei at last recognized that it was Sylvia holding her shoulders steady. Shame, hot and relentless, seared through her. Of all people to see her like this, to witness how humiliatingly fragile she truly was, of course it was *her*. Her own death would be a blessing now. She wanted to drive her fist through the wall, to dip her power into the river and overturn the entire boat with the force of her rage. All those years ago, she had been too much of a coward to protect the ones she loved. This time, she had been too late.

Nothing would ever change.

"Close the door," Lorelei snapped. "She'll hear you."

The dead's souls lingered. To speak of their passing where they could hear was the highest form of disrespect she could imagine. She felt hysterical clinging to Yevanisch tradition now, but it was all she had to hold on to.

Sylvia did as she was asked without fuss. When she returned, she knelt in front of Lorelei and procured a handkerchief from somewhere on her person. Lorelei took it from her with trembling fingers and dabbed at the tears drying on her face. It was a tidily folded slip of plum silk trimmed in lace, as excessively frilly as Sylvia's nightgown. It smelled—like Sylvia did, *of course*—of rose water and lemon cake. That one ridiculous detail managed to ground Lorelei. She breathed in steadily until the fog in her mind began to dissipate and the world around her felt more solid.

There were no ghosts here tonight.

When she dared to look up at Sylvia again, the concern glimmering in Sylvia's pale eyes stunned her. The thick band of scar tissue on her cheek seemed to shine with fresh blood in the candlelight. "Lorelei, will you tell me what happened?"

A part of her wanted to close her eyes and pretend the last ten minutes had never happened. Another more animal part of her wanted to snatch the candlestick sitting beside them and bash in Sylvia's skull, to replace one problem with another. But there was no escape from this nightmare. Ziegler was dead, and Lorelei had been found alone with her body. There was no explanation she could offer Sylvia that would incriminate her less.

"I fear I am not in my right mind," she rasped. "I don't want to talk."

"You're never in your right mind," Sylvia said, not unkindly. "Tell me."

"Ziegler is . . ." Saying it aloud would make it real; she didn't know if she could bear it. "Ziegler is dead."

"What do you mean she's dead?" Sylvia's voice was as loud as glass shattering in the quiet of the hallway.

"*Dead*, von Wolff. For God's sake." Her voice sounded broken. Lorelei buried her face in her hands. Somehow, she couldn't even muster the energy to be furious with Sylvia. "There is no hidden meaning."

It did not seem possible.

Ziegler had survived everything her adventures had thrown at her. She had summited mountains in the thick of a blizzard and cut through jungles with jaguars stalking her at every turn. She had crossed deserts with a single canteen of water and all of her equipment strapped to her back. To Lorelei, she had been a god, untouchable and unimpeachable. But she had seen her broken body. She'd touched it.

She was really gone.

It felt like a star had winked out. What a banal death. What a waste. The pitiless brutality of it—the sheer *injustice* of it—stole Lorelei's breath away. Not twelve hours ago, Ziegler had been incandescently alive, and had lied to her. Lorelei couldn't even remember the last words she'd said to her. All she could remember now were all the things she wanted to accuse her of.

"What a tragedy." Sylvia's expression crumpled. "I'm so sorry you were the one to . . ."

The thorns around her heart tightened until she could scarcely see through her anger. After all these years, after every insult they'd traded, how *dare* Sylvia pretend to care about her? Lorelei wanted to throttle her. She wanted to repay her sympathy with cruelty. Anger, at least, was a balm to the rawness of her grief. But she was too tired to sharpen it into a blade, so she wound it around herself like armor.

As cold as a winter night, she replied, "Thank you."

Sylvia hesitated. "You should get some rest. I can wake the others. They'll want to know."

A bolt of panic shot through her. Without thinking, she seized Sylvia by the elbow. "No!"

Both of them stared down at her hand. Lorelei slowly let go of her, flexing her fingers as though trying to work out a cramp. Sylvia, meanwhile, looked as though she'd been struck with a blunt object.

"I, ah, of course want to give you space to grieve," Sylvia said weakly. "But I don't think this is something we can keep from them for long."

"Of course not. But you can't tell them yet, and you certainly can't do it on your own. Think for a moment, will you? If we don't present a unified front, they'll be suspicious."

"Are you suggesting they'll think one of *us* killed her?" As if something more fundamental dawned on her, she paled. "You're suggesting one of our friends killed her."

Our friends was perhaps an overstatement, but Lorelei would not press the point. "She was stabbed."

"*What?*" Sylvia went deathly pale. "Why would someone do such a thing?"

"Wilhelm wants the Ursprung to secure his reign. The heir of every major province is here on this ship. Not everyone believes a unified Brunnestaad should exist—or that Wilhelm should be the one to rule it." The righteous anger unspooling through her was intoxicating, a sweet poison chasing away her despair. "He'll now also choose a queen from Albe—which will almost certainly be you. Perhaps someone resented that."

Johann and Heike certainly did.

"As I recall," Lorelei continued, "you weren't thrilled at the prospect yourself."

"No, but I would never—" An edge of desperate, affronted panic knifed into Sylvia's voice. "What are you suggesting? You're the one who found her. That means *you're* the most suspicious of us."

Lorelei had nothing to say to that. It was damningly true, but they were at a stalemate. "Calm yourself. I'm not accusing you of anything."

"I cannot *believe* even now you would be so . . . !" When Sylvia realized what Lorelei had said, all the fire bled out of her. "Huh?"

"I don't believe it was you." She was almost disappointed to admit it. But when she had turned Ziegler's body over, it was still warm. Lorelei fought the panic that threatened to unmoor her from reality again.

Think, she scolded herself.

If the body was warm, the timing didn't make sense. It seemed unlikely that Sylvia would murder Ziegler, return to her room, change her clothes, and return to the scene of the crime looking for all the world like she had just rolled out of bed. And even if she did, why circle back to confront Lorelei? Sylvia was smarter than that.

But it wasn't just that. Lorelei knew, deep as marrow, that Sylvia was innocent. Her conviction needed no logic, only years of observing her. She *knew* Sylvia. Her tells and her fears. The way she wrote and how it exactly mirrored the overexuberant way she spoke. The way she took her tea—with a teeth-rotting amount of sugar—and her favorite color—amethyst, not purple—and the tenderest spots to dig the knife of her words. She was irritatingly forthright. When she was happy, she laughed. When she was sad, she wept. She wouldn't know subtlety if it threw a dueling gauntlet at her feet.

No, Sylvia was not made for cold-blooded calculation. She was too loud, too earnest, too *heroic*. She had been a soldier, but Lorelei imagined she had done her duty romantically. Riding into battle astride a warhorse in gleaming armor. Dragging her comrades off the battlefield. Perhaps taking down an entire battalion with nothing but her saber and an improvised soliloquy about the inevitable tragedy of war. But the thought of her killing someone like this, in such an ignoble way . . .

It simply wasn't in her nature.

"You're not capable of it," Lorelei said reluctantly.

"Neither are you, as much as you'd like people to believe otherwise." Sylvia's lips curled in an almost-fond smile. "I've seen what true monsters look like."

To know Sylvia saw through her was almost too mortifying to bear. That old, petty part of Lorelei wanted to loom over her, to threaten her, to do anything and everything in her power to prove her wrong. But she was too exhausted to argue anymore. All she wanted was to be alone and to sleep for a decade. "Then I believe it's in our best interests to vouch for each other."

"Yes, you're right." She drew in a deep breath, as though steeling herself. "Just this once, I can find it in myself to speak to the quality of your character. It will take some effort, but I believe with enough preparation I can—"

"What are you talking about? No speeches will be necessary. We simply need to tell them we found her body together."

"But that's a lie!" Sylvia protested. "And frankly a difficult one to believe. What would you and I be doing together in the middle of the night?"

No, she would not dignify that with an answer. Something so horrible did not bear consideration. "A little white lie in the interest of protecting each other. It will be our secret. Surely your honor can withstand that."

After a brief eternity, Sylvia threw up her hands. "Fine."

"Fine."

It sunk in then exactly what Lorelei had done. If anyone found out they were covering for each other, it would be far worse than the alternative. With this tenuous pact, she had put her life in Sylvia's hands. And Sylvia had given hers to Lorelei in turn.

In the pale moonlight, with the fog pressing its fingers longingly against the glass, Sylvia still looked like a specter. Like something that might slip through Lorelei's fingers if she held too tight.

Lorelei and Sylvia had gone door to door, collecting the rest of the crew until they stumbled out into the hallway, bleary-eyed and still in their nightshirts. Once she delivered the news, there fell a silence so complete, Lorelei wondered if they'd heard her at all.

And then chaos erupted.

"How?"

"When did this happen?"

"Where is she?"

Lorelei let their questions wash over her with a cool, cultivated detachment. Gas lamps burned dully in their sconces, softening the edges of the darkness. Dawn had only just begun to spread cautiously across the sky, like a pearl of blood dropped into water.

"We don't have any answers yet," Lorelei said, firmly enough to slice through the noise. "Von Wolff and I found her together ten minutes ago."

Sylvia looked physically pained. Lorelei's heart skipped as though she had missed a stair in the dark. For a moment, she wondered if she would back down and let Lorelei be caught in the lie. A thousand horrible futures spun out before her, all of them ending with her swinging on a gallows rope.

If Sylvia truly wanted to ruin her, it would take so little.

"Indeed," Sylvia said. Lorelei nearly crumpled to the floor with relief. "We thought it would be best if we all discussed it together. It seems there was, ah . . . foul play involved."

"Foul play?" Johann asked, interest clear in his voice. "You believe she was murdered?"

"There is a stab wound on the body," Lorelei replied stiffly.

A tense hush fell over the group. Ludwig looked ill, but the others' faces were entirely unreadable.

"Well, then," Johann said. "Let me take a look."

He fetched his medical case from his room. Once Johann rejoined them in the hall, Lorelei led them to the war room. In the hazy smear of daylight, the walk felt almost dreamlike. Inside, everything was exactly as she had left it. Ziegler's body lay perfectly still, her skin beginning to swell and discolor where the fluids collected. Her eyes stared into vast emptiness. The spilled water lay glasslike on her desk and floorboards, mottled with blood. Lorelei found herself staring at the teacup on Ziegler's desk—the one with the inlaid seashell and the handle fashioned in the shape of a coral. Ziegler had always chosen it because its gaudiness amused her. Distantly, Lorelei noted the damp breeze sighing through the open window—and Ziegler's elwedritsche missing from its perch. It must have flown off after Ziegler died, the disloyal beast.

Good riddance.

No one spoke. She felt the horror spread through their group like winter's chill unfurling. Heike, clinging to Adelheid's arm, buried her face in her shoulder with a choked sob.

Lorelei thought she understood what grief was. That night twelve years ago had torn something out of her, something she'd never managed to sew shut. Through that wound, pieces of Aaron had slipped in. His fear of blood. The ripple of his shadow always stalking her through darkness. The echoing laughter of his murderers. By now, she was used to living with ghosts. And so, she hadn't expected seeing Ziegler again to feel like nothing.

Johann's expression didn't change as he crouched beside Ziegler's body. Closing his eyes, he extended his hands over the body. His fingers twitched, just barely, as though he were maneuvering a puppet on gossamer-fine strings. While most people possessed some aptitude for magic, only a rare few—those with the utmost precision of technique—could become medics. They studied for years, mastering the art of detecting any anomalies in the body's fluids. Lorelei could not fathom it herself. The human body was primarily water; it all seemed an undifferentiated mass to her untrained senses.

"I'd estimate the time of death was around two in the morning." Johann opened his eyes. A strange light filled them—something like intrigue. Disgust curdled Lorelei's stomach. "There is fluid in her lungs. Blood, I suspect. The stab wound appears to be the cause of death. It is a clean cut, likely inflicted by a knife."

"Human, then." Adelheid's lips pressed together in a bloodless line. "But the staff don't have access to these rooms."

Heike made an admirable effort to keep her voice disinterested. "What, are you suggesting one of *us* killed her?"

"That would be the most reasonable explanation," said Johann.

"Now, let's not be rash." Ludwig held up his hands placatingly. "I'm sure there's at least one other reasonable explanation."

"Such as?" Johann asked. He fished a scalpel from his medical case and made a thin incision in Ziegler's arm. Blood welled lazily to the surface, and he pressed a vial to the wound to collect it. Lorelei steadied herself against the wall at a sudden rush of light-headedness.

"You can't be serious." Heike laughed humorlessly. "I've known all of you since you were as high as my knee. No one here is a murderer."

"Well," Ludwig said weakly, "technically, that isn't true."

Sometimes, it was easy to forget that half of them—Adelheid, Johann, and Sylvia—had taken up arms for Wilhelm's cause. Ludwig, a commoner by birth if not by title, had not been expected to fight. Heike had abstained "on principle." Lorelei suspected that principle was self-preservation rather than any true pacifist senti-ment. They did not train their children for battle in Sorvig like they did in Herzin or Ebul. It was a tiny, wealthy territory that valued a rapier wit over swordplay.

Neither Johann nor Adelheid flinched at Ludwig's quibble, but

Sylvia reacted bodily. Her shoulders bowed, and for a moment, her silver eyes went vacant. Lorelei hated it. The swift change—like a candle extinguished—discomfited her.

"Is it really *murder* if it's war?" Heike jabbed a finger at him. "You be quiet. You're not helping. And you"—here, she rounded on Johann—"are provoking people. Stop it."

Johann corked the vial of blood and rose to his full height. His shadow cut the room in half. "Believe what you want to believe, but you can't hide from the truth. You've been sheltered and spoiled in your lonely castle by the sea. You always have been."

"Johann," Adelheid hissed.

"How dare you." Heike's voice trembled with barely leashed anger. "You know that isn't true."

"The reality is," he continued, undeterred, "everyone here had a reason to want Ingrid Ziegler dead."

Sylvia bristled, her eyes ablaze with fury. "Be that as it may, only one of us has the capacity to act on it."

At last, the cruel amusement drained from Johann's eyes. The muscles in his jaw flexed as he leveled her with a flat stare.

Lorelei could not bear to listen to them discuss *murder* so callously any longer. A headache bloomed in her temples, and she felt dangerously on the brink of losing control of her power. "Enough!"

Everyone stopped talking at once. Slowly, Lorelei forced her fists to unclench.

Something bothered her about the scene—something she had not been able to place until now. "Ziegler wasn't a particularly talented magic user. Why would someone stab her when they could drown her? It seems a more difficult way to go about it."

Johann met Lorelei's gaze with clear intent. "Perhaps they couldn't."

Lorelei felt the attention in the room shift to her. "Be careful of what you're implying."

"Johann," Sylvia cut in, "I don't want to accuse you of lying, but you and I both know this does not look like a stabbing."

"There are some anomalies," he said lowly, "but it is the simplest explanation."

Adelheid's expression darkened with understanding. "There's hardly any blood—not in the room or on her body."

"What are you all talking about?" Heike demanded, looking vaguely nauseated.

"Stabbing is . . . messy." Sylvia winced. "The wound was likely inflicted after her heart stopped beating." She approached the body and lifted her hand. Ziegler's fingers were a mottled, bruise-like blue. "This pattern of discoloration typically indicates oxygen deprivation. Isn't that right?"

"Yes," Johann gritted out. "That's correct. I hadn't noticed that."

"Of course you didn't," Lorelei said dryly. Had he been *trying* to frame her? "So she drowned."

"Perhaps," Johann said begrudgingly. "I can't determine exactly how she was killed yet. There are no contusions on the body, no signs of struggle. If she drowned, she didn't fight it. People don't surrender to death so easily."

"The ward is missing from her door." Adelheid ran her fingers along the wooden lintel. "If one of the wildeleute ensorcelled her, that would explain the lack of struggle."

At the mention of her precious creatures, Sylvia perked up. "To my knowledge, there's no wildeleute that could have done this. If it were a nixie, there would be no body. And alps suffocate their victims, but with their weight, not water. Besides, none of them would carry a knife."

There was no doubt, then. Someone in this room had murdered Ingrid Ziegler.

"Then what are we doing standing here?" Heike cried. "One of us could be next! We need to get off this ship and go back home. Now."

"No," Lorelei snapped. "What we must do is act rationally, *calmly*. With Ziegler gone, I am the leader of the Ruhigburg Expedition. I will write to Wilhelm to seek his counsel. In the meantime, Johann, I want a thorough autopsy performed. Ludwig, I want analyses performed on blood samples to look for poisons. Heike and Adelheid, keep us on course. And von Wolff, replace the wards."

For a moment, they stood gawping at her.

"You have your orders," she said, surprising herself with the cold conviction in her voice. "Now *go*."

SIX

THE FOLLOWING NIGHT, the messenger raven fluttered in through the war room's open window.

Its feathers were nearly indigo, gleaming with the same oily sheen as the lacquer on the writing desk. Fresh air sighed into the room, along with a nip of cold against Lorelei's cheeks. Another thick fog had rolled in today, creeping through the woods like candlelight leaking beneath a locked door. From here, she could hear the whirring of the engine and the steady churn of the water. It settled into her like a second pulse.

She tugged loose the knot of twine from its leg and retrieved a letter emblazoned with Wilhelm's seal, a dragon stamped in dark and vivid blue. Behind it was a loose leaf of paper folded into neat squares. With shaking hands, she unfurled the parchment and began to read.

Lorelei,

I wish I could thank you for your letter, but given its grave contents, I cannot. I do, however, appreciate your candidness and brevity, and I will, as much as I'm capable, extend you the same courtesy. In short: Stay the course. If word got out that this project was unpopular even among my closest friends, my enemies would seize upon me. I cannot afford to show them any weakness.

I know each member of the group well, and while I want to say none of them is capable of such an atrocity, it would be dis-

ingenuous. If one of them is determined to sabotage my expedition, then I will not give them the satisfaction. I suspect the guilt or the pressure will reveal whoever it is.

I've enclosed another sealed letter addressed to the group, expressing my wishes: for the expedition to proceed—and for you to continue leading it. Ziegler—God rest her soul—always spoke highly of you, and I will honor the decision she made before her death.

What I remember most is her praise of your keen eye for details and analysis. I ask that you put them to use for the Crown. I would like to know who is responsible before you return to Ruhigburg. If you cannot give me that, then I hope you understand that someone must answer for Ziegler's murder. Unity requires sacrifice. If you succeed, however, I would gladly have you as an adviser.

Burn this letter after reading. Find the Ursprung. As for the body, do with it what you will.

Yours,
Wilhelm

"You son of a bitch," Lorelei muttered.

She read the letter twice more before she threw it onto her desk in disgust.

Wilhelm might look like a charming fop, but his heart was colder than hers. His was a desolate, far-reaching cold, like a long winter's night. She could almost admire it, if it weren't for the terror simmering just beneath the surface.

Unity requires sacrifice.

Wilhelm's plan was simple and ruthless, one she was intimately familiar with: create a common enemy. The Yevani had been Brunnestaad's favorite scapegoat for centuries and had taken the blame for most of the kingdom's misfortune, from plague to insurrection. Even though Ziegler had handed her everything she'd ever wanted on a silver platter, even though they believed Lorelei entirely unable to wield magic—if it really came down to it, hatred would choke out logic like a weed.

Unless, of course, she discovered the true murderer.

As far as she was concerned, there were only two viable suspects. Johann: a soldier and zealot who despised her enough to frame her, refused to acknowledge an Albisch queen, and disagreed with Wilhelm's relative tolerance. If he truly believed Brunnestaad would be overrun with people he deemed lesser beings, then of course he would fight to preserve what was his.

And then there was Heike. Less convincing, certainly, but Lorelei could see a motive. She'd quarreled with Sylvia for years—and had been left to simmer with her jilted, thwarted ambition. If she wanted to prevent Sylvia's ascension—or spite Wilhelm for overlooking her—then sabotaging the expedition was certainly one way to do it.

She could not accuse either of them without proof, of course, but investigating could very well get her killed. The moment they suspected she was on their trail would be the moment she made a target of herself.

And yet, she couldn't deny her own curiosity any more than she could deny the spirit of justice rising up within her. Ziegler had chosen her for a reason. To escape death, she would have to think like Ziegler: holistically. Everything was connected. Just as magic pointed back to its source, so did everything the killer had done. More importantly, she would have to think like a folklorist. This group was nothing more than a collection of folktales she had to catalogue and dissect. She would pry them open slowly—and she would do it with them being none the wiser.

All to serve a king who would scapegoat her without a second thought.

He claimed he wanted the Ursprung to stabilize Brunnestaad, but now she wasn't so sure. With the power of the Ursprung, Wilhelm could drown whole armies of men where they stood. He could flood their enemies' farmlands and starve them slowly. He would use it freely to get whatever he wanted.

Does it even matter? Wilhelm was a tolerant enough king. He had incited no pogroms against the Yevani. He had not expelled them. She would take him over an unknown any day. Once this was over, she would have his ear and her freedom.

Everything else came after.

She could do this. Under the right pressure, one of them would snap. They'd confess, or else make a fatal mistake. Or maybe they already had—something she'd overlooked. She tugged on the knob of a drawer, only to find it locked. The next one rattled uselessly, too, and the one after that.

No matter. Lorelei uncorked a flask she kept in her pocket. Drawing in a steadying breath, she focused on the water inside until she felt her awareness expand. With a wave of her hand, it rose serpentine from its prison and coiled around the lock. Lorelei squeezed her fist, and frost bloomed over the metal. She rifled through the sheer number of *things* piled on Ziegler's desk until she found a letter opener with a delicately engraved pearl handle. Before she could talk herself out of it, she bashed in the lock with the butt of the handle. The metal dropped to the ground with a brittle *clink*. Shards of ice skittered across the floor.

The drawer was completely empty.

She thumbed at her lip. Whoever had done this intended to keep them from moving forward. No one but Lorelei knew how Ziegler organized her files, which was . . . under no system that made sense. The killer had likely taken them to peruse at their leisure. She tucked that observation away for later. For now, she knew what to do. Wilhelm had handed her a knife. It was time to turn it on the others.

They gathered in the war room. Tension hung as thick as fog in the air as she surveyed each of them. No one dared to look at her, as if the truth would shine out of their eyes. Lorelei very much doubted it.

There was a popular folktale that Lorelei had transcribed many times over, one about a murdered Yeva. He'd been carting his wares back to the city when a tailor, down on his luck, hatched a wicked scheme: to kill the Yeva and steal the money he surely had. With his dying breath, the Yeva cursed the tailor: *the bright sun shall bring all to light.*

When life faded from his black eyes, the tailor was dismayed to find he hadn't a single coin on him. Grousing at his rotten luck, the tailor buried the Yeva beneath a juniper tree and left his cart to rot.

Years later, the tailor's fortunes had changed. His home was filled with beautiful things and tended by his beautiful wife. He sat on his porch with a cup of coffee, and as the sun rose to its full height, its rays glanced off his coffee and cast coins of golden light onto the ceiling. As he watched them gleam and waver, it reminded him of the Yeva he'd murdered so long ago. He laughed and laughed.

When his wife came to ask what was so funny, the tailor said, *Ah, the bright sun would very much like to bring all to light, but it cannot.*

When his wife pressed him on what he meant and gave him sweet assurances that she would tell no one else, he confessed all that he'd done to her—along with the Yeva's curse. Within hours, of course, the entire neighborhood knew of his crime, and when he stood trial the next day, the tailor was condemned to death.

Lorelei had never drawn any satisfaction in that tale. What comfort could be found in a warning about the folly of lonely, gossiping wives? At twelve years old, she'd learned there was no real justice in this world.

Lorelei threw the sealed letter onto the table. "We've received a response from the king."

Each of them read it in strained silence. When Heike finished, she tore the parchment in half and buried her face in her hands. "Why would he leave us here?"

"He's trying to prevent a civil war," Adelheid said coolly. "It's a calculated risk."

"I agree." Lorelei folded her hands beneath her chin. "Ziegler was an outsider to your group—as am I. I imagine he assumes you won't turn on each other."

"Of course we wouldn't," Ludwig said wanly. "We promised, after all."

Lorelei sensed there was a story. "A promise?"

At first, no one spoke.

"Our territories were annexed in the First War of Unification," Sylvia offered. "The negotiations in the wake of that campaign were bitter, and our parents were often in Ruhigburg on official business. But while our parents tore each other apart in court, the six of us played together. I remember those days fondly."

Ludwig raised his eyebrows. "Even the day we left you stranded at the lake?"

The others snickered. Even Adelheid cracked a thin smile.

"Except that day," she said sharply, clearly flustered. "At any rate! Wilhelm made us all promise that when we were in power, we would never allow the kind of violence we grew up with. We would never turn on each other or let each other suffer."

It was such a romantic, whimsical notion: exactly the sort of thing only Wilhelm would propose and only children could believe. And yet, none of them mocked her. None of them, she realized, wanted the others to know they'd strayed in their loyalty to him.

Curious. So they genuinely liked him.

"Then I expect you to hold to it," she said briskly. "In the meantime, shall we discuss the matter at hand?"

"The official cause of death is fluid in the lungs: death by as-phyxiation," Johann said, clearly eager to move past sentimental reflections of their shared childhood.

"No botanical poisons that I could detect," Ludwig added. "But there were trace amounts of chloral hydrate in her system."

Heike yawned. "Meaning?"

"She was drugged before she was murdered." The corners of Johann's mouth twitched in a smile, full of malice. It set Lorelei's blood to ice. He did not need to speak for her to catch his meaning: *the sedative you use to sleep.*

The one *he* compounded for her.

"Whoever killed her is an adept magic user," he continued. "It is theoretically possible one of the staff could have solved the lock—"

"Highly unlikely," said Adelheid with a grimace. "It's too com-plicated."

Ludwig frowned. "Someone could have left the door open?"

"Of course," Lorelei snapped. "And they just so happened to be passing by and took that very convenient opportunity to drug and murder her."

Ludwig winced. "Right. Point taken."

"Your sarcasm is not appreciated." Sylvia shot her a look of pure reproach. "At any rate, if we are all agreed on the matter of the cause of death, that means that it could not have been Lorelei."

"She could be a witch." Johann clasped the silver fang resting against his collarbone. "Yevani can come to possess magic by un-natural means. Consorting with demons, consuming enough Brunnisch blood to absorb its power—"

"Shut up, Johann," Heike and Sylvia snapped at once.

They exchanged a startled look, as if shocked they agreed on something. Heike turned sharply away and said, "No one wants to hear it."

Johann fell silent, but he glowered at Lorelei. Nothing he said surprised her, but bracing for the blow had never once stopped it from hurting.

"It can't be me or Lud, either," Heike added. "Neither of us are as skilled with magic as any of you."

"It doesn't take finesse to drown someone," Johann said coolly.

Lorelei watched with some fascination as Heike blinked up at him with a calculated innocence. "Well, then. I'm certainly no genius like the rest of you, but if you'd just think a little, I'm sure the answer of who did it would become abundantly clear. Right, Sylvie?"

"Me?" Sylvia spluttered.

Heike's smile turned venomous. "I bet it stung to have your position taken away. Besides, your mother has been waiting for an opportunity like this for a long time, hasn't she?"

"All right, all right," Ludwig cut in. "It's true it could have been Sylvia. But consider this: it could have been me."

Adelheid let out a long-suffering sigh.

"That's just the thing, right? If the murder took place at two in the morning, none of us really has an alibi." He surveyed each of them and with offhanded lightness added, "That is, of course, assuming Johann is telling the truth about the time of death."

"Why would I lie about that?"

"You wouldn't," Ludwig said placatingly. "But if you missed one detail . . ."

Suspicion simmered in the air, coalescing into a solid thing.

"Stop this nonsense," Lorelei said. It was time to set her plan into motion. If she could convince the others to let this go—if she could assure them that the killer was no threat to them—she could conduct her own investigation unbothered. "In all likelihood, this murder was a targeted act of desperation, singular in intent: persuading us to turn around. The murderer failed. We're leaving this behind us for the sake of the expedition."

Johann watched her with some wonderment. "You'd let Ziegler go unavenged? Your kind truly have no loyalty."

The accusation stung more than she expected. It was as though he could see straight to the heart of her and all the things she so desperately wanted to hide. He was right, after all. Lorelei had abandoned Aaron in his final moments. She'd let his killers walk free. But she would not make the same mistake twice. It didn't matter how she had to lie and debase herself in the eyes of these nobles. With this scrap of power Wilhelm had given her, she would see Ziegler's murderer dragged to the gallows.

Lorelei canted her chin. "Sink Ziegler in the river and chart our course. We set off again at dawn."

"*Sink* her?" Sylvia gawped at her with genuine horror in her eyes. "I cannot believe you of all people would do her such disrespect! She deserves a proper burial."

As if Lorelei did not know that. In the Yevanverte, funeral rites were sacred, done as quickly as possible. They would have washed the body in warm water and dressed it in a plain white shroud. It would have been watched, day and night, until it was buried in a simple pine casket. They would have sat shiva, accepted guests and food. They would have let their loss bring them closer.

"She also deserved a better death," Johann said wryly.

"Make do with a ceremony if you must," Lorelei snapped, rubbing her temples. "Just make it quick."

Within the hour, they collected long coils of rope and fastened them to Ziegler's wrists and ankles. The other ends were tethered to stones. There was no elegant way to pitch her over the edge, so they placed her on a plank and lowered it onto the river with a pulley. Ludwig had found enough preserved flowers in his luggage to arrange a makeshift wreath around her head. For a moment, the six of them stood, watching her bob and float on the surface. The current lapped hungrily at her limbs.

Heike lifted her arms, and the water surged forward, sweeping Ziegler clumsily off the plank. Lorelei glared at her out of the corner of her eye. It took less than a breath for the body to slip beneath the surface.

Just like that, Ingrid Ziegler was gone.

Lorelei whispered a blessing, one that rolled over her senselessly. The only clear thought in her mind was: *I will not waste the chance you have given me.*

Lorelei found Sylvia on the promenade deck, her arms folded over the railing. In the moonlight and mist, she looked entirely otherworldly—and almost lonely. The wind gusted, blowing Lorelei's coattails back.

As if sensing her presence, Sylvia turned to face her. She twisted her lips like she was going to say something tart, but in the end, she just said, "Can we talk?"

"Come inside first. It's cold."

Lorelei led her to the war room. Sylvia hesitated at the door before coming inside.

Lorelei had straightened everything out and scrubbed the room until it no longer reeked of death. There were some of Ziegler's books here: thick, leather-bound tomes cracked and pilling with age, but everything else was manufactured to look older than it was, a cobbled-together imitation of their lives in Ruhigburg. Nothing of Ziegler truly dwelled within these walls.

Nothing but her ghost.

Lorelei shoved that thought down and locked it away where it belonged. She sat behind the writing desk and said, "Well?"

"This is . . ." Sylvia trailed off, searching for the right word. ". . . creepy, even for you. She hasn't even been dead for twenty-four hours."

Lorelei opened her notebook, determined not to rise to Sylvia's petty bait. "By all means, speak your mind. I gather you want a favor, and this is certainly endearing you to me."

Sylvia slammed the door shut behind her, a little too forcefully. Lorelei set down her pen and finally took in Sylvia's appearance. Her hair was in utter disarray—more so than usual, at least. Her cheeks were flushed, and her eyes were wild. Something about

Sylvia, full of inarticulate fury, gave Lorelei pause. "What are you doing, Lorelei?"

"I'm afraid you'll have to be more specific."

"You don't intend to investigate Ziegler's murder?"

Ah. That. Lorelei supposed she should have prepared herself for this. "That is what I said."

"Nothing," Sylvia said, clearly working herself up to a tirade. "*Nothing* is what you plan to do. What happened to your principles? Your hunger for truth?"

"Principles," she scoffed. "If we begin to make ourselves a nuisance, who do you think they'll come for next?"

"But I—"

"Is that all, then?" Lorelei asked. She had intended to sound cool and disinterested, but it came out irritable. "I'm very busy."

"Is that so?" Sylvia snatched the notebook from her, and the last of Lorelei's restraint gave way.

"I want to live to see the end of this," she hissed.

"So do I!" Sylvia slammed her hands down against the desk. She looked as though she were about to launch herself over it and throttle her. Lorelei became painfully aware of her heartbeat quickening, eager to meet her anger. "You cannot solve all your problems by pretending to be above them or—or by glaring menacingly at them!"

"Of course," Lorelei replied mockingly. "Instead, we must rush headlong at them."

Sylvia pointedly ignored her. "The greatest threat to Wilhelm's reign is Albe. What if he chooses to charge *me* with Ziegler's murder?"

Lorelei blinked hard at her. "Why would he do that?"

Sylvia stared back at her blankly, as though she was failing to grasp the urgency of the situation. "He would accuse my mother of treason and have us both imprisoned. Without us, he could install whatever toady he pleases in my place. Don't you understand? Can't you see past your own pride, or has reducing me to desperation been your aim all along? Well, you've achieved it."

Sylvia von Wolff, demanding her help. It was ludicrous. Even more so that she honestly believed Wilhelm would blame her over the obvious choice: a Yeva. "Don't be dramatic. It's unbecoming."

"I am begging you."

Something about those words sent a rush through her. Entirely against her will, Lorelei's gaze flickered down and landed on Sylvia's lips.

What depths would you sink to? Lorelei wanted to ask. *How will you convince me?*

When she met Sylvia's gaze again, she had gone deathly still. For a moment, as they stared at each other with some bewilderment, the heat of their argument fizzled.

It disturbed Lorelei that there was a part of her that enjoyed this. That some wretched, unknown desire had been waiting for this moment to make itself known: Sylvia von Wolff, entirely at her mercy. Determined to shove that thought far back into the unholy abyss it crawled from, she said, "No."

Sylvia snapped out of her stupor. "No?"

Lorelei knew the sensible thing to do was to backtrack. Sylvia could so easily turn on her. But the rush of power unfurled through her like a dram of whiskey, sweet and hot and utterly intoxicating. She could not stop herself. "I won't help you."

"How could you . . . ? Are you really so spiteful, so small?" Sylvia drew in a shaky breath, as if steeling herself. "Very well. Then if I must, I challenge you to a duel. If you lose, you will do as I ask. And you *will* lose, so save yourself the embarrassment and help me."

Lorelei laughed. Sylvia took a full step backward. "If you really believe I'm capable of such malice, do you think I care about honor? My answer is unchanged. If you want justice so desperately, you're welcome to play investigator yourself."

"How dare you talk to me this way?" Her face flushed. "I'm . . ."

She trailed off, coming to the same realization Lorelei had. For once in her miserable life, her name meant nothing.

Lorelei stood, her shadow falling over Sylvia. Slowly, she drew closer, step by step, until she could feel the heat radiating off her, until she could hear the hitch in her breath. It was moments like these that made Lorelei appreciate just how much she towered over Sylvia, who had to crane her neck to hold her gaze.

"You're what?"

Sylvia did not shy away from her. She broadened her shoulders and glared up at Lorelei as if truly seeing her for the first time. "You really are coldhearted."

"As you say. Now go."

Sylvia shoved past her and out the door.

She had gotten her to back down. Lorelei supposed she should savor this, but somehow, it felt nothing at all like she'd imagined. Suddenly exhausted, she sank back into her chair and raked her fingers through her hair. It had been a poisonous victory. In the silence of the war room, a horrible truth became clear. Until they returned to Ruhigburg, there was no one to turn to, no one to trust, but Sylvia von Wolff.

PART II

Blood
in the
Water

SEVEN

LORELEI HARDLY SLEPT. At night, the ship became a haunted place.

Her mind made ghosts of everything: the memory of Ziegler's too-loud laughter; the image of the gallows rope that awaited her; the unbridled resentment in Sylvia's pale eyes. All of them were a bitter reminder that she could not fail—not now. By the time the sun rose, she'd whittled the maudlin edge off her feelings and found clarity in her exhaustion. Wallowing would not save her, but action might.

The most sensible place to begin her investigation was with the weakest link—or at least the one most willing to talk.

Lorelei knocked on the door to the left of her own: Ludwig's. When he answered, the first thing she noticed was his rumpled hair. The next: that he hadn't finished doing up the intricate gold-wire buttons of his shirt. Clearly, he'd just woken up. It took all her strength to suppress the eldest-sister instinct to fuss at him for his dishabille. Honestly. It was the perfectly civilized hour of seven o'clock.

Ludwig looked up at her with something like pity. It made her skin crawl.

Before he offered anything as unwanted as *condolences,* she said, "I have a question for you."

"Down to business," he said. "No good mornings. I like it."

She gave him an exasperated look but entered when he moved

aside for her. As she brushed past him, the faint scent of pressed flowers washed over her.

Absently, she catalogued the room. Botanists did not require much equipment to do their work. His lacquered-iron vasculum— decorated by a landscape painter whose name she could not recall—was slung over the back of his desk chair. Equally useful for storing plant specimens and warning off wildeleute in the field, she noted. A lens with a carved mahogany handle rested atop a pile of books, alongside a veritable dragon hoard of scattered rings.

Lorelei had always suspected he felt the need to armor himself with wealth. It frustrated her endlessly. He hardly needed to prove himself to his insipid friends and their peers when his academic achievements spoke for themselves. Since he graduated two years ago, he'd identified over two hundred new species of plants, many of them with magical properties. She expected there were at least ten named after him at this point.

She made to sit on his desk chair, but he intercepted her rather urgently. "No, no. Take the bed. It's far more comfortable."

Skeptically, she perched on the edge of his bed. The springs groaned in the silence.

Ludwig put on his rings, then shuffled a haphazard pile of papers into a semblance of order. "Why do I feel like I'm in trouble?"

Lorelei hooked her ankle over her knee. "Why does Heike dislike von Wolff?"

He paused for a moment, then opened his desk drawer and tucked the papers inside. At last, he turned to her with an amused but wary smile. "You want gossip about my friends—before I've had coffee, no less? What do you take me for?"

"You don't want me to answer that," she replied wryly. "Just tell me what I want to know."

Over the months they'd known each other, she'd come to associate him with the folktale "The Wolf and the Fox." It was short but brutal, with a simple message: if you couldn't be the strongest creature in the woods, you could be the slyest. If you were agreeable enough, you could call in favors like debts. You could persuade people into revealing their weaknesses and make them feel like they'd given you a gift. That was what made Ludwig dangerous. He had a face that begged to be trusted and a smile as sharp as a knife in the back.

"You're a very intense person, you know." The drawer clicked shut. "I really shouldn't say anything."

His tone indicated he fully intended to say something. By way of prompting him, she said, "Of course not."

"But when we were about fifteen, Heike's mother proposed a marriage suit to Sylvia's mother."

Of all the things she'd expected him to tell her, it was not *that*. "What?"

"I know." His voice dropped conspiratorially. "Sylvia refused her, naturally. I still remember the letter she wrote me about it. It was like reading a novel. *Oh, injustice! My cruel mother means to sell me like a prize cow at market, but I refuse to let her use me any longer. I am writing to petition you for shelter, Ludwig, for I know you are the only one on this earth who will understand. I am running away this very evening!*"

It had the air of a well-loved joke: just rehearsed enough. How many times had he read that letter—and how many times had the others giggled over it?

"How very reassuring to know von Wolff hasn't changed at all in ten years." Lorelei scoffed. "Heike holds a grudge against her, I take it."

"She does." Ludwig slumped into his desk chair. "Although Sylvia has tried many times to make things right between them."

Lorelei frowned. "Surely, it's no great loss to Heike. They would make a terrible match."

"It was the principle of the thing. Heike . . ." He hesitated, as though he'd reached the limit of what he could share. "She has always wanted to leave home—by whatever means possible. Sylvia knew that. We all did."

Of course Heike held a grudge. Sylvia had thwarted her—twice.

"She set her sights on Wilhelm after that," Ludwig continued, "but he only has eyes for Adelheid. And surely, you've noticed—"

"Her and Adelheid." Surely, everyone had noticed the lingering looks and the way they invented excuses to touch each other. It was exhausting to watch. "Yes."

He snapped, then pointed at her as if to say *exactly*. "Needless to say, it's made things complicated. And so, all of us will be subjected to their pining forevermore. Not that you would know anything about pining."

Lorelei glowered. "I'm sure I don't know what you mean."

Before he could reply, the ship lurched as if it struck a solid wall. Both of them jolted forward. The inkwell on his desk toppled over, and a few of his field books dropped thunderously onto the floor. A cursory glance out the window revealed no obstacles in their path, and the lack of screaming meant nothing horrible had dredged itself from the bottom of the Vereist. There was no other sensible explanation than incompetence.

"What was that?" Ludwig asked.

"I don't know," she said, "but I intend to find out."

Ludwig looked vaguely alarmed at her dark tone. "Why don't I join you?"

With nothing better to redirect her frustration onto, she snapped, "You're barely dressed."

He shrugged.

Together, they made their way to the navigation room, dodging through the deckhands as they shouted at one another. She all but kicked in the door to the captain's office. "Why have we stopped?"

The captain of the *Prinzessin*, Emma, stood beside the floor-to-ceiling windows, haloed in a mantle of dreary sunlight. She had a cloud of gray hair and a certain air of mystery that made everything she said sound vaguely like a portent of doom. "Lady Heike and Lady Adelheid blew in like a storm a few minutes ago."

Of course. She should have expected as much. "Why?"

"Can't agree on our course." She took a drag of her pipe. "The river branches off just ahead. We could go straight through to Albe, or take a tributary through Herzin."

As far as Lorelei was concerned, Herzin was best avoided.

All Herzisch Ursprung legends began with a man who ventures into the woods in search of power. Inevitably, he finds himself beset by monsters: a wolf whose voice echoes in his mind. Three men who promise gifts (almost always, these turn out to be curses) in exchange for a scrap of bread. A maiden who transforms into a serpent when he stops to aid her. Naturally, he slaughters them all. Most folktale heroes tended to outwit their foes, but the Herzisch ones had never met an enemy or a problem a solid punch couldn't solve. Bloodshed and valor, of course, proved them a worthy vessel for the Ursprung's power. The undeserving who waded into its depths simply perished.

"I will speak to them. Where are they now?"

Emma pointed one gnarled finger out the window. Heike and Adelheid stood nearly nose-to-nose at the stern of the ship, clearly in the midst of some argument. Adelheid's face was frozen with the kind of calm that came from unshakable certainty. Heike had what Lorelei assumed was a map crumpled in one hand and a sextant clutched like a weapon in the other. A feeble attempt at intimidation, considering Adelheid had at least ten kilos of muscle on Heike and shoulders twice as wide.

Lorelei already felt exhausted.

Ludwig followed her out onto the deck. As they drew closer, Lorelei snapped, "Would you care to explain why my ship is stopped?"

"Oh, Lorelei! Just who I hoped to see." Heike somehow managed to purr the entire sentence. She batted her eyelashes for good measure. "Be a dear and help me settle something, will you?"

"She will not," Adelheid said, "because, unlike you, she has an ounce of sound judgment."

Ludwig perched himself atop one of Adelheid's mysterious dowsing instruments, as if settling in for a show.

Lorelei had half a mind to turn around and go back the way she came. "I will not be party to this nonsense. Fix this."

"Oh, no you don't." Heike seized Lorelei by the elbow. "I'm certain that once you hear me—"

Adelheid cut in. "I have data to support my argument."

"Data," said Ludwig. "Now, that sounds compelling."

Heike glared at the machine like she might kick it over with Ludwig still on it.

"I imagine I will regret asking," said Lorelei, "but what is the problem?" When they both opened their mouths to speak, she pinched the bridge of her nose. "One at a time, if you please."

Adelheid pursed her lips, clearly put out by having to appeal to Lorelei. "The concentration of aether along this stretch of the river is increasing at a rate that is, frankly, alarming. It would be wise to rechart our course."

Heike threw her hands up exasperatedly. "Follow the aether, find the Ursprung. Isn't that what Ziegler said? Honestly, I fail to see the issue here."

"I'd expect the increase to be more gradual if we were heading toward the Ursprung. Spikes of magical activity like this typically correlate with"—here, her expression turned grim—"anomalies."

"And what," said Lorelei, "does *that* mean?"

Ludwig perked up, which never boded well. "There already have been anomalies. Last night, Johann said he saw a deer that had a woman's face."

"What?" Adelheid looked genuinely taken aback. "That's absurd."

"Ludwig, I'm disappointed." Heike put a hand on her hip. "I

cannot believe you would give that poor man another questionable mushroom after what happened last time."

"That wasn't my fault," he protested. "I just pointed it out."

Adelheid sighed, digging her fingers into her temples. "Let us not discuss it again. Experiencing it once was enough."

"As fascinating as this conversation is . . ." Lorelei glared at them. "What anomalies?"

"Environmental changes," Adelheid said, "or—"

"We all knew this was risky," Heike said with an almost feverish insistence. "Going through Herzin will add days to our travel time. I, for one, do not want to be on this ship a moment longer than I have to be."

"You are steering us directly into the largest aetheric hot spot I have encountered in my entire career," Adelheid said lowly. "I do not know what we'll find. That is what disturbs me."

"Well, I know what we'll find in Herzin." Heike gave Lorelei a speaking gaze. It said, *People who want you dead.* She twisted a lock of hair around her finger. The dreary sunlight had washed it to the color of rust. "So, what will it be, Lorelei?"

Lorelei hesitated. "Tell Emma to keep on toward Albe."

"Yes, sir." Heike's smile was pure triumph as she sauntered off to the navigation cabin.

Adelheid gave Lorelei a speaking gaze of her own. It said, *Coward.* It stung more than she expected.

Ludwig folded his hands beneath his chin. "You two have been bickering even more than usual lately. What's that about?"

Adelheid shooed him off her machine. "You have other things to do, I trust?"

"As charming as ever." Ludwig winked at her. "Goodbye."

Adelheid did not acknowledge him. With a resigned frown, she knelt beside the machine and began to fuss with some stray wires. It was simpler than Lorelei expected it to be: a long glass tube affixed to a wooden base. Inside was a set of metal wires that forked like the branches of a tree.

Lorelei considered leaving her to her work, but she could not pass over an opportunity to speak to Adelheid without the others—especially Johann—looming.

"Will you show me how it works?" she asked.

Adelheid paused, clearly surprised, but did not glance up. "If you'd like."

Cold prickled at the back of Lorelei's neck. Then, a long shadow fell over her. Johann said, "Are you sure that's wise?"

Lorelei whirled around to face him. "How long have you been standing there?"

His cold blue eyes bored into hers. "I'm always watching, Kaskel. You would do well to remember that."

Adelheid regarded him with a touch of fond exasperation. "Peace, Johann."

With one last, lingering look at Lorelei, he nodded and slipped away. Adelheid shook her head.

"He's protective of you," Lorelei said offhandedly.

"Yes. He thinks as ill of others as he does himself." Adelheid turned a few dials without glancing up at her. "Are you well?"

"Exceedingly," Lorelei said irritably.

When she closed her eyes, she could see Ziegler's pale blue lips and the bloodshot whites of her eyes. She could still feel the boneless give of her arm when she turned her over. She drew in a long, slow breath, willing herself to stay rooted in her body. It had become too easy to desert herself, to be pulled back to the dark, close terror of that night.

Eager to divert the conversation away from her tenuous well-being, she asked, "Do *you* think ill of him?"

She winced as soon as the words were out of her mouth. Perhaps too direct.

"What a question." Amusement skittered across Adelheid's face. "But no. Not anymore. I used to despise him."

Now, *that* was a surprise. In the last five years, Lorelei could count on one hand the number of times she'd seen Adelheid without Johann at her side. He was her unwieldy, sullen shadow, darkening every doorway she passed through and lapping up every word she spoke like honey. "Why?"

Adelheid looked at her as though the answer was obvious. "Even as a boy, he was cruel and petty. I suppose with time, I came to understand him. His father did not give him much choice in the matter."

Adelheid settled onto the side of the boat. The grime on the deck seeped into her dress, and splinters in the wood snagged at the coarse weave, but she paid it no mind. She focused instead on unwinding a coil of wire and fed it slowly into the water. She had callused fingers and fine lines around her eyes from squinting into the sun. She was almost striking in her plainness: the rare kind of noblewoman who did what needed to be done herself.

"We were raised on the same tales of knights and fed the same stories about what it means to be a noble. But where I admired their chivalry, Johann was fixated on their valor. He liked the idea of slaying dragons, not protecting the people they tormented. When he was sent to war—to serve in my brother's battalion, no less—I was furious. He was in it for the wrong reasons. He was always bored as a child. He wanted something to entertain him."

War seemed an odd choice of diversion, but Lorelei refrained from commenting. "I didn't realize he knew your brother."

Adelheid brought up Alexander often enough, the same way one might evoke the name of a favored saint. Although Lorelei knew little of the specifics, she knew he had fallen in battle. Among Brunnestaaders—and especially among the nobility—it was the most honorable death there was.

"He does not like to talk about it," she said stiffly. "But, yes, they knew each other. He swore Alexander an oath to protect me. It was apparently his dying wish. When he told me that, I punched him."

"You . . . punched him."

"I did." A small smile tugged on her lips. "In any case, his protection was as unnecessary then as it is now. That is why he is here on this expedition, I suspect."

"Would you rather him be elsewhere?"

"No," Adelheid replied. "I love him dearly, and it is good for him to have something to do. He gets so restless. Now sit. I will show you how this works."

Lorelei eased herself onto the deck beside her. She found herself reluctantly interested. Adelheid traveled often for fieldwork, so Lorelei had never learned from her directly.

"When the instrument detects magic, the wires inside will nod. The meter will then give you a number." Adelheid tapped a glass circle on the base of the machine. It glinted like the face of a watch.

"That's it?" Lorelei asked skeptically.

For the second time in five minutes, she got the sense that she had gravely disappointed Adelheid. She pressed a notebook into Lorelei's hands and said witheringly, "It is a simple machine, but it requires some practice to interpret the data. Take notes."

Lorelei watched the wires bob up and down, like a ship borne on a tide. Every now and again, a glimmer of blue light would ripple through the chamber of the machine, and Adelheid would make a little disapproving sound. There seemed to be no pattern Lorelei could discern. Adelheid read out a number every few seconds, and Lorelei would dutifully transcribe it. By the end of an hour, she had almost three full pages of numbers, five columns each. It seemed unlikely that this sequence of numbers would lead them to the Ursprung.

As she worked, she turned over their conversation. Johann was hateful and cruel, yes—but also loyal enough to keep an oath he swore to his friend's dead brother. If he truly cared about things like honor and duty, would he betray Wilhelm, even if he disagreed with him? She supposed it all depended on whether he placed the demands of his god over the demands of his king.

"Johann is—"

"You have never shown any interest in us before today." Adelheid's polite tone and neutral expression betrayed nothing of her thoughts.

She knows.

Lorelei did her best not to react. "Surely I have. You are interesting people."

"I'm not a fool, Lorelei. I am not as eloquent as Sylvia is, nor am I as sensitive as Heike." She said *eloquent* and *sensitive* with the tone one might reserve for describing a wasting illness. "But I do know about loss. Grieve her, but do not let this become an obsession. It will sink you in the end."

Lorelei stood abruptly and straightened the lapels of her greatcoat. Coldly, she said, "Thank you for the advice."

Adelheid let her go without another word.

Lorelei slipped back into the cabin of the *Prinzessin*. *An obsession.* She wanted to scoff at it. But sometimes she believed she had been doomed to misery, like the victim of some fairy-tale curse. It was a devouring sort of sadness, the kind that did not grow lighter when you shared it. She had scrubbed through her life, searching for the root of it. If she spelled it out in black-and-white like one of her stories, perhaps it would all make sense.

Back in the days when wishes still held power, there was a cobbler who had three children. His youngest daughter was as joyful as daybreak after a long winter night and as warm as a summer breeze. His only son, the middle child, was the most beloved of the three: the sweetest mensch in the Ruhigburg Yevanverte, who knew everyone and their mother, too. And then, there was his irrepressible oldest daughter, who spent her days turning over stones to see what writhed beneath in the cold, dark earth.

Lorelei and her brother, Aaron, had been inseparable. He was nothing at all like her, the kind of child who begged to be allowed to tie off every box of shoes with a neat, fastidious bow. Who did everything that was asked of him with a smile. But as he grew older, he began to fear for his future. He had been apprenticed to the butcher. One day, they both watched as the butcher took the gleaming chalef and slaughtered a goat: a swift slice to the throat, blood waterfalling from its neck. Aaron had gone deathly pale as it crumpled to the ground, and Lorelei had to drag him outside when he fainted. She crouched beside him and dabbed the cold sweat from his brow until the color returned to his lips.

He'll be so disappointed, he moaned. *What am I going to do?*

After weeks of needling, Lorelei had finally convinced him to come on an "expedition" with her, to the stretch of river their parents had forbidden her from visiting alone: where the wall of the Yevanverte blocked out the rest of the city and cast its long, long shadow. They had been walking home, their pockets full of specimens, when a group of men from Ruhigburg opened the gates, laughing and slurring. They shattered the glass windows of storefronts as they passed, sending brittle, sparkling sounds like rain echoing down the alleyways.

So much of that night was a blur. But she remembered the way the looks on their faces changed when they laid eyes on Aaron's tzitzit—and again when they realized the two of them were alone. There was a hunger there, a terrifying pack-animal leer.

The look of men who realized they could do whatever they liked.

If you use magic, they'll track you down, Aaron told her, his hand clasped in hers. *Run.*

More than anything, she remembered the sound of his scream, the sound of their jeers, the sound of his skull when it split. His blood spread over the cobblestones and shone like molten steel in the moonlight. She did what he said, in the end. She ran.

It was that moment that possessed her, that moment that haunted her. The cowardice of leaving him to his murderers, to go cold alone.

After Aaron's death, Lorelei realized that there were hundreds and hundreds of ghosts in the Yevanverte. They rose from the floorboards as she stitched shoe leathers together. They pressed to the misty glass of her window as she tried to sleep. They chased her down the dark and winding alleys and leered at her from the rows and rows of stacked, colorful houses. Most of them were strangers, their eyes gleaming with cold, otherworldly light. Some of them, however, she recognized. A woman who'd lived in the house below them, walking the path toward the river every morning like a clockwork doll. A toddler who'd fallen ill some years ago, squalling through what sounded like fluid in his lungs. And worst of all: Aaron, his eyes wide, his skull concave, with blood unfurling around him like a horrible sunrise. Her parents hardly knew what to do with her, the daughter tormented by something they could not see.

And then she met Ziegler.

Day after day, for six long years, she had a carriage sent to bring Lorelei to her flat in the center of Ruhigburg. Day after day, she tutored her in the sciences and magic and sanded off the harshest edges of her accent. Day after day, Lorelei returned to the Yevanverte exhausted. And then finally, on her eighteenth birthday, Ziegler gave her a gift: a place she had secured for her at Ruhigburg University. Lorelei could still recall the shape of that joy, almost too sharp to hold on to.

She'd barely made it through her first week when she marched from campus to Ziegler's flat in the city center and told her she planned to quit. Because the moment she opened her mouth, all of her classmates knew exactly what she was. Many of them had never met someone like her before, but they had heard enough stories from their nursemaids to know exactly what kind of monster she was. The Yeva in thorns. The Yeva buried and forgotten.

A perfect villain. A perfect victim.

Ziegler stared at her as though she had spoken Yevanisch. She could not understand it at all, the idea that something as mundane as cruelty could keep Lorelei from the pursuit of knowledge.

What? she'd said. *You want to go back to your father's house and*

*make shoes for the rest of your life? Look me in the eyes and tell me
you'd be happy. No, you can't. You'd be miserable. You'd be wasting
your potential.*

Would it really have been a waste to have grown up among her
own people? To not have had to cut off pieces of herself? Those
questions tormented her now. Maybe she would have been content with the hand God dealt her, had that night twelve years
ago never happened. Maybe she would have been simply the cobbler's eldest daughter, stitching leathers and hiding her magic and
dreaming of far-off places.

But games like that were as pointless as they were punishing.
Lorelei would never know that version of herself. She would never
know how much of this bitterness within her was innate and how
much had been shaped by the inevitable cruelty of living. Her
story had been written long ago, in indelible ink and blood.

There was no hope of changing it now.

EIGHT

THAT NIGHT, Lorelei dreamed of drowning.

She sank below the surface of deep, black waters, so cold it snatched the last gasp of air from her lungs. Bubbles burst from her lips. Her hair drifted wildly around her, reaching toward the faint thread of light filtering in from above. But when she looked up, it was nothing but darkness overhead and darkness all around her.

In the distance, pale shapes came into view, beckoning her with their moonlit glow. As she swam closer, her vision rippled. She could barely make sense of what she was seeing. There were rows and rows of bodies, floating in a vast sea. One by one, their white faces turned toward her. And there, in the center, she saw them.

Ziegler, her eyes flung wide, her broken teacup in hand. Aaron, blood seeping from the wound in his head like a cloud of smoke rising.

The people she had failed to save.

Lorelei reached for them blindly. Pale hands clamped around her wrists, but she could not find it within herself to panic. After all the ways she'd failed, would it be so terrible to die? To let her limbs go lax and close her eyes for the last time. It would be sweet, after all these years of fighting, to rest.

You let us die, a voice hissed in her ear.

Lorelei jerked awake, gasping for air that would not come. Her entire body was paralyzed, save for her roving eyes. Her lungs burned as if someone had filled them up with stones. A strange, weightless sensation bloomed in her skull. No, that hadn't been a dream. She *was* drowning—this time, in open air.

Alpdrücke.

She could barely see the alp through the gloom and her own heady delirium. But she could see the glint of its sharp, yellowed teeth in the dark—and, of course, its damnable tarnkappe. The bright red cap bled through the darkness like a beacon. The alp crouched on her chest, drinking down her life force with every breath she failed to draw. She desperately tried to recall something, anything, that Sylvia had written about these creatures.

How pathetic, she thought, *that* she *would save my life.*

What was more pathetic, she decided, was that her very last thought would be of Sylvia. Lorelei grabbed hold of her racing thoughts and—*yes.* She remembered now.

"Coffee," she rasped.

The alp fixed its beady eyes on hers. Some of the pressure eased from her chest. Lorelei took the opportunity to scramble upright and put some distance between them. She pressed up against her headboard, grasping instinctively for the silver chain around her neck.

Gone.

"Coffee?" the alp repeated. There was a spark of interest in its voice. It felt like a whisper against the shell of her ear, an echo in her skull. Even the shape of its body eluded her, shifting in the shadows like light over rippled water. All that was solid was its stupid hat.

"Yes," she wheezed, resisting the urge to tack on something acerbic. "Coffee. You like that, don't you? If you let me go, I'll give you some."

"Lying?" it said, a childish hopefulness tingeing the word.

"No," Lorelei said slowly. She felt perfectly ridiculous, speaking to this beast. "Not lying. Now get out. Once I'm in the hallway, you can follow me."

She felt its delight more than she saw it, a crackle in the air like lightning. By the time she blinked, it had transformed itself into a skein of shadow and slipped out through the keyhole.

Lorelei rested her head on her knees, sucking in greedy lungfuls of air. The dissipating rush in her head and the soreness in her chest made her want to weep from some bizarre combination of stress and relief, but she fought down the impulse. Instead, she focused on the newfound clarity of her mind.

She pulled on her coat, lit a lantern, and surveyed the room. Her window was latched, but her lemon-and-bell chimes lay in a heap on the floor like a discarded toy. It did not take much effort to reconstruct what had happened. One of her dear colleagues had come through the door, torn the wards from the lintel, and lifted the chain from around her neck while she slept her drugged sleep. They had tried to kill her in the most cowardly, indirect way possible. She almost admired it.

As she crossed the room, something on the floor reflected the light. She picked it up and held it up to the lantern. A brass button, abandoned like a glass slipper in a ballroom.

It was too large to have come loose from a gown—and too inelegant to belong to Ludwig. No, she'd seen this many times before on many different people: a button from a military uniform. Lorelei closed her fist around it as a sick sort of triumph slithered through her.

Johann.

He'd been careless. This was hardly enough evidence to convince the others, but now she had a target to pursue. At least for tonight, all that remained was to deal with her unwelcome guest.

She slipped into the hallway. The bells hanging from Sylvia's door—the one just across from her own—glittered through the dark. The sight of her unbroken wards comforted Lorelei more than she cared to admit. She could sense the alp behind her, practically vibrating with excitement, but she caught only a glimpse of its black garment from the corner of her eye. It kept stubbornly to the shadows.

She'd read several of Sylvia's accounts of her run-ins with alps, stories told with far more flourish than necessary. They were, evidently, self-conscious about their appearance. If you looked at them head-on, they turned invisible, feathering themselves into the darkest recesses of a room, or transformed themselves into something more beautiful. Sylvia had a particularly popular tale of how she'd banished one by presenting it with a mirror. Lorelei didn't know exactly how their magic worked, but she knew that they needed their tarnkappe to shape-shift.

She led the alp to the kitchen. It had a ghostly air this late at night, without the cook and the beleaguered servant who brought them their meals. She puttered around, boiling water and rummaging through the cabinets until she found what she needed. She tried her best to replace everything as she had found it, lest Cook think the kitchens haunted (again).

Possessed by a moment of hysteria, she considered asking it how it took its coffee. How had her life so swiftly unraveled? Not two days ago, she was primed to become one of the most respected folklorists in the nation. Now she was providing hospitality to imps.

Once it had brewed, she inhaled the rich, dark aroma and poured the coffee into a mug. Unconsciously, she had chosen Sylvia's favorite, the one with the engraved silver handle and champlevé enameling. She hated that she recognized it. She crouched beside the stirring shadows. The alp's tarnkappe bobbed, red as blood in the darkness. She thought of her dream, of blood unspooling from Aaron's wound, and suppressed a shudder.

"Here," she said, as sweetly as she could muster. "For you."

The alp took the cup from her. Just as its little clawed fingers curled around the handle, she snatched the cap from its head. It shrieked, reeling back. The mug shattered. Porcelain went skittering across the floor, just as the shadows dissipated to reveal a small, loathsome creature covered in coarse fur. Lorelei did not bother trying to hide her revulsion.

"Lying!" it cried, rending its face.

It was all a bit too dramatic to be convincing.

"None of that now. You shall have your coffee and your tarnkappe both if you tell me what you're doing here. Did someone let you in?"

"No one, no one," it whimpered. "Please."

"Think carefully." Lorelei fixed it with a nasty smile. "I'll tear it in two, and where will that leave you?"

She tugged on the seams. A stitch popped, and the alp wept anew.

"What on earth is going on in here?"

Lorelei startled at the sound of Sylvia's voice. She stood in the doorway of the kitchen with an expression caught somewhere between horror and irritation. Her hair hung loose around her shoulders, as wild as flame. Again, Lorelei found herself having to blink against the foolish thought that she looked spectral in the pale moonlight.

"Lower your voice," snarled Lorelei. "What are *you* doing here?"

"You keep sneaking out!" Sylvia spoke in a stage whisper that set Lorelei's teeth on edge. "And it seems I was right to follow you, since I've found you tormenting this poor creature."

"This 'poor creature' tried to kill me in my sleep."

The alp wailed piteously.

"And my wards were broken off the door," she continued. "Someone let it on the ship—the same person, I assume, who murdered Ziegler. It knows something."

"Alps are not loyal," Sylvia said, clearly exasperated. "You have its tarnkappe. If it had the information you want, it would have told you immediately."

"Yes, yes! Know nothing!" The alp nodded, looking beseechingly at Sylvia.

Sylvia shot Lorelei a sharp look that said, *Hand it over.*

Chastised, Lorelei sighed and tossed the cap to the alp. It snatched its tarnkappe with scrabbling claws and pulled it aggressively over its horns. It shot her a downright spiteful look. "Come back someday," it hissed.

"I welcome it."

The shadows whispered over it, and just like that, it vanished with the same gravity of a child slamming a bedroom door.

"Saints," Sylvia muttered. "Quarreling with an *alp* of all things. I would hate to see you encounter something that has a will to match yours."

"I would say you fit the bill."

"Yes, well." Sylvia flushed. After a moment, she fixed Lorelei with a pained look. "Was that meant to be a compliment?"

"Take it as you like." It occurred to her that she was still crouching at Sylvia's feet. Clearing her throat, Lorelei rose to her full height and straightened the high collar of her greatcoat.

Sylvia crossed her arms, her mouth set in a pensive line. "You really believe someone set an alp on you?"

"Are your wards sound?"

"Of course they are! What do you take me for?"

Lorelei winced. Did she have to be so *loud?* "Then it couldn't have gotten into my room without help."

"This is very bad! You told me—emphatically, mind you—that we would be safe so long as we did not investigate. And now you've nearly died from an *alpdrücke*." The way she said it dripped with contempt, as though it were a very ignoble death indeed. Lorelei was almost offended. "How did you escape, anyway?"

"I offered it coffee."

Sylvia fixed her with a very unusual expression. "I don't recall ever discussing alps with you."

"No?" Heat crept into her cheeks. "I'm certain you must have some time or another. Or perhaps I read it somewhere."

"You must have, although I'm only aware of one book that discusses alps' weakness for coffee." A horrible, self-satisfied smile spread across her face. "Lorelei, have you . . . read my books?"

"Of course not," she snapped. "I have better things to do with my time."

"You have!" Sylvia clapped her hands together. "Oh! I hardly know what to say. Did you like them?"

The truth was, Lorelei had read every word Sylvia had ever published.

For the first few months of her tenure at Ruhigburg University, Lorelei had not known her name. She only knew her as the white-haired girl who attended every single visiting scholar's lecture with a clear intent to argue. Her hand shot up constantly—sometimes her entire body, if she felt compelled to argue her point strongly. It was only after a while that someone interrupted her mid-speech and said, *That's enough, Miss von Wolff.*

Von Wolff. She knew that name. Before the First War of Unification, she would have been royalty. Now she lived among her conquerors, all of them watching her for the moment she turned traitor. But most of all, Lorelei knew the shape of the name alongside her own. Ziegler kept a list of every student in the natural sciences department, each of them in order of rank.

Putting a face to the name filled her with a feeling she couldn't entirely describe. Lorelei had always borne a grudging respect for her anonymous rival. She, too, must have understood what it was like to succeed when everyone wanted you to fail. But knowing that she was a bloviating try-hard, a fop with a too-loud voice and a too-easy smile . . . It was almost too much for her pride to bear.

That was the moment she decided to hate Sylvia von Wolff.

Within a year, Sylvia published her first book. Lorelei had devoured it with a vicious hunger—and all the ones that followed. She refused to be uninformed in her hatred.

What could she say about her work? Sylvia sailed in every wind and danced in every stream. It was drivel. And yet it enraptured her. Her tales were *charming*, and they detailed every adventure Lorelei had yearned to have. Her exuberant, heartfelt sincerity was enough to win over even those most suspicious of her. It only made Lorelei's resentment burn brighter.

"Did I *like* them?" Lorelei repeated. "Do you really want me to answer that?"

"On second thought, no." Sylvia deflated. "What should we do?"

"Nothing." Lorelei pressed the heel of her boot into the broken porcelain on the ground. It gave a satisfying *pop*. "We'll be in Albe tomorrow."

"Someone tried to kill you! I can't do *nothing*."

"Well, you will have to manage it!" Lorelei paused, then regarded Sylvia suspiciously. Something had disquieted her that she could not put a finger on. "Is that why you are following me around?"

"Following you?" Sylvia laughed, far too nervously. "I beg your pardon! Why would I—"

"Why would you, indeed? And yet, you are. You found me with—the body." Damn her voice for faltering. "And now, you have found me here."

"Our rooms are very close together, and for some reason, you've made it a habit to go stomping about in the dead of night. I cannot help overhearing."

Lorelei very much resented the suggestion that she *stomped* anywhere. "To do, as you've seen, all sorts of unseemly things. One might begin to wonder at your curiosity."

Sylvia glared at her. "What were you talking to Adelheid about yesterday?"

"Nothing of import," she said defensively. "Can I not speak with Adelheid?"

"You never speak to anyone without a reason."

Lorelei could not argue with that. By way of redirecting her, she asked, "Since you're keeping a full account: I spoke to Ludwig, too. He told me the most interesting story about you and Heike."

"Ludwig," she muttered viciously under her breath. "That is

none of his business, and it is certainly none of yours. I ought to—" She cut herself off with a gasp. "I knew it. You are *snooping*."

"I am not," Lorelei said. "Please, go on."

"You are changing the subject," Sylvia hissed. "Will you not accept help for once in your life?"

"I can assure you there's nothing to help with." Lorelei was teetering on the brink of losing her patience. She could not quite remember why they were arguing. All she knew was that she did not want Sylvia's help. She would ruin all Lorelei's plans with her lack of subtlety, and worse, she would throw herself into danger for no good reason. She'd already demonstrated an alarming lack of self-preservation, if she went chasing both nixies and everything that went bump in the night. "Honestly. I don't understand all this fuss. I imagine you'd be happy if someone succeeded in killing me."

Sylvia stared at her for a long few moments. Her lips parted as though she wanted to say something. In the end, she must have thought better of it. Her jaw snapped shut. "You know, Lorelei, sometimes I think so, too."

With that, she turned on her heel and stormed off. In the heavy darkness, Lorelei was reminded of Sylvia standing by the river. Of the way she had imagined Sylvia's white hair slipping down, down beneath its depths, wavering just out of reach. She was struck by the desire to catch a lock of white between her fingers. Instead, she clenched her hand into a fist and stared down at her own mystified expression, reflected back at her in a puddle of cold coffee.

NINE

OR THE FIRST TIME since they'd left, the sun succeeded in burning away the mist. The landscape had transformed from the dismal marshes that stretched over the central empire to mountain ranges that scraped the bellies of the clouds. They were tall and jagged as a dragon's spine, as if one had folded up its wings and laid down its head to rest. The waters beneath the *Prinzessin*'s hull were a clear, deep green. Light sparkled on its surface, almost blindingly after so long spent on the fathomless dark of the Vereist.

The morning after the Alp Incident, Emma told them the *Prinzessin* would go no farther. Heike's charted course guided them through the tributaries of the Vereist, which spread across Albe like veins on the back of a delicate hand.

"Shallow waters," the captain had said. Her gray eyes were set on some far-off point on the horizon. "You're on your own from here."

They had three sleek rowboats readied for the rest of the journey, each of them loaded up with boxes of scientific instruments and empty wooden crates to carry back any specimens they found. Lorelei picked her way across the deck, dodging through the bustling crew as they prepared to drop anchor.

Sylvia was waiting on the deck already, her bag slung across her shoulders and her arms folded over the railing. Early morning sunlight painted her in a soft warmth as she gazed up at the mountains. *Home.* It was written in the sparkle in her eyes and the gentle smile tugging at the corner of her lips. Lorelei felt as though she were intruding on something private. It stirred up a strange brew of jealousy and wistfulness within her. What must it be like, she wondered, to feel you truly belonged to a place? She did not expect she'd ever find out.

Before she could announce herself, Sylvia turned toward her. "Hello, Lorelei."

"Hello," she said stiffly.

Sylvia regarded her coldly. She supposed she deserved it after their argument last night. All she could think of was the determined fire blazing in Sylvia's silver eyes when she said, *I can't do nothing.*

Strangely, guilt needled at her. So Lorelei found herself saying, "You must be glad to be home."

Sylvia's expression turned suspicious, but she was not angry enough to ignore Lorelei's attempt at conversation. "I am not home just yet. We're in Waldfläche—well-known for its hops, if I'm not mistaken. Still, it's magnificent, isn't it?"

"Its hops?" Lorelei asked skeptically.

Sylvia seemed to be genuinely at a loss for words. "The mountains."

"Ah." Lorelei tilted her head back to look at them, mostly out of courtesy. With some displeasure, she noted that they were crowned in glittering white. If there was still snow this late in the season, perhaps it never melted. Fantastic. If they needed to cross or summit them, it would make their journey unpleasant and far more difficult than it otherwise would be. Someone would likely lose an extremity or two. "Indeed."

It was, apparently, the wrong thing to say. Sylvia sighed unhappily.

Before Lorelei could salvage the conversation, the others arrived. Each of them was dressed for travel in fur-lined cloaks and tweed tucked into calfskin boots. Heike and Ludwig were arm in arm, giggling over something or other. Adelheid approached with

Johann at her side. The very sight of him made her anger flare so hot, her hands began to tremble with the force of it. As if he sensed it, he met her gaze with a challenging glint in his eye. He did not, however, look surprised to see her.

Odd. Had he expected her to survive?

"Are we ready to leave, then?" Sylvia asked.

Each rowboat was meant to hold only two passengers, and they had already paired off. But this posed an opportunity for Lorelei to isolate Johann, one she could not let slip away. She had to be completely certain before she accused him of anything, or else risk the others turning on her.

Grasping for the first excuse that came to mind, Lorelei said, "I cannot ride with von Wolff. We'll capsize the boat."

Sylvia gawped at her, a look of pure outrage in her eyes.

Ludwig smirked, but his tone was all innocence. "I'll go with you, Lorelei."

Heike rounded on him. "Well, I can't ride with her either."

"Must we do this now, of all times?" Sylvia sounded genuinely pained, which admittedly pricked some at Lorelei's conscience. "I am so tired of you making me feel as though I'm—"

"Insignificant? Unwanted?" Heike asked dispassionately. "Imagine that."

"Enough. You're all behaving like children." Adelheid sighed wearily. "Sylvia, come with me."

Adelheid and Heike—rather pointedly, Lorelei thought—did not acknowledge each other. Clearly, their disagreement yesterday had driven some sort of wedge between them. Adelheid rescuing Sylvia from Heike's petty barbs surely would not help matters.

Johann skewered Lorelei with a baleful look. "Let's go."

At least she had gotten what she wanted.

But in all her grand machinations, she had not considered the small issue of their heights. Both she and Johann were almost all legs, and she had to fold herself up just so to keep from spilling out of the boat. Neither of them spoke, but she could practically feel Johann's displeasure pummeling her like a solid wave. Every now and again, he drove his paddle into the water with such force, it sent them veering into the banks.

She considered driving the paddle into the base of his skull but thought better of it. Neither he nor Adelheid would like it, and she did not have a death wish. Instead, she dug her oar into the mud and pushed to right their course.

"Is my company that loathsome to you?"

Johann scoffed but did not reply.

Lorelei pulled up her oar and glared at the back of his head. "I wanted to return something to you."

Johann turned in his seat, looking rather offended that she had spoken to him unprompted. "What have you stolen?"

"I haven't stolen anything."

Lorelei ignored his doubtful expression and pulled the button from her coat pocket. The brass gleamed in the sunlight. Johann took it from her and adjusted his glasses. For a long few moments, he squinted at it in confusion. No flicker of recognition lit his eyes—only a vague curiosity.

"Where did you get this?" he asked.

"I found it—in my room, as a matter of fact." Lorelei could not keep the irritation out of her voice. She had expected some kind of reaction. "It's yours, isn't it?"

"No." Johann frowned and handed it back to her. It honestly surprised her that he surrendered it without any fuss or accusations. Surely, there was some dark ritual she could allegedly perform with a button and a lock of hair. As though remembering who he was speaking to, he made his voice brisk and condescending once again. "Do you see the engraving? It isn't from my battalion."

Lorelei had no way of confirming if that was true. He had to be lying.

"I see," she said.

With a dismissive shake of his head, he turned back around.

When she turned the button over in her fingers, the only thing she could make out was a worn engraving of a dragon. One way or another, she would catch him. She tucked it back into her pocket and took up her paddle again.

The river was strong, frothing white around the rocks jutting from its surface. There was something infinitely reassuring about being able to see the smooth river stones at the bottom, a mosaic of cool blues and grays. Schools of bright silver fish cut through the water, and near the swollen banks, turtles basked on logs draped in thick coats of moss. It was all perfectly lovely—and perfectly ordinary. She detected no glimmers of magic in the water, no strange and fantastical beasts, no unusual plant life. Had she not seen the readings herself, she might have suspected Adelheid was lying.

Lorelei found her attention pulled toward Sylvia. Her boat was a solid ten meters in front of the others, even though she was the only one paddling. Adelheid kept her focus trained on the glass face of her dowsing machine. The sunlight spun her straw-like hair into gold, but her jaw was set and her brows furrowed with concern. Even from a distance, Lorelei could see the muscles in Sylvia's forearms working, the cling of the white fabric of her linen shirt. She had rolled up her sleeves and left her coat draped over the seat beside her.

Lorelei tore her eyes away. What had gotten *into* her lately?

Ludwig and Heike's boat lagged behind. Ludwig paddled in between plucking water lilies from the river's surface and gathering cattails from the banks. They came dripping out of the water and disappeared into the vasculum around his neck. Heike, meanwhile, had her oar slung across her lap and rested her chin primly on the back of her hand, as though she were sitting in a hansom cab. She'd even brought a parasol.

Unaccountably, a shiver passed through Lorelei. The river reflected the trees looming on either side of its banks. They stood tall but at odd angles, like teeth sitting crookedly in gums. The soil beneath them was dark and waterlogged, and the banks of the river looked as though they'd collapsed. All the grass beyond them had died, either trampled or pulled out by the roots. The air hung heavy, like a thick blanket of wool. It dampened all the sound, save for the rush of water.

Lorelei glanced over at Adelheid. The dowsing machine's wire shivered, far more violently than Lorelei had seen before. Then it went terribly still.

The glass cracked.

Adelheid lifted her gaze to Lorelei and said, with impressive calm, "We have a problem."

The current guided them into a wide stretch of the river. It seemed to be carved crudely out of the earth in the shape of an open eye. Many of the trees on its northern side had snapped clean in half like broken bones. Others lay flat to the earth, their bark flayed in long, uneven strips. Standing or felled, many of them were marred with deep gashes that wept sap. Lorelei peered over the side of the boat and nearly lost her balance from vertigo. The water beneath their boats was a pure and startling blue that went down for what seemed like miles.

At the very bottom, Lorelei spotted a fleck of red that shimmered like a coin at the bottom of a well. The image of blood pooling against cobblestones stole into her mind, and her stomach lurched dangerously. She tightened her grip on the oar, focusing on the sound of her leather gloves grinding against wood, on the tremulous rush of her breath.

Sylvia leaned over the edge of her boat and went quite pale. "This is not good."

As if on cue, the water rippled steadily like the pulse of a heart. The splash of crimson at the bottom of the well stirred, and Lorelei swore she saw eyes glowing in the darkness. The image shattered as the water churned beneath them. She could see nothing but a rush of bubbles.

"I suspected something like this might happen." Adelheid held fast to her machine as the waves rocked their boats.

"Perhaps you should save the gloating for another time," Heike hissed.

Before Lorelei could draw another breath, something burst from the depths like coils of rope dredged from the sea. Its head breached first, then its neck, then two massive forelimbs with claws as long as Lorelei was tall. They dug into the earth as the beast hauled itself out of the water, and a nearby tree groaned as it snapped. Water sluiced off its scales in gouts.

A blood-red dragon stared down at them. Its green eyes were mottled with gold. As it blinked, an opalescent film slid diagonally over its eye.

Johann made a quick series of hand gestures Lorelei only vaguely recognized—a religious warding of some sort. He muttered under his breath. The only clear word she could make out was *demon*.

Heike stifled a scream. "What is that thing?"

"That," Sylvia said wanly, "is a lindworm."

The only mention of lindworms in Sylvia's travelogues were the lengths she had gone to avoid them.

Ludwig curled into himself, pressing his forehead to his knees. "We're all going to die, aren't we?"

Sylvia shouted, "If you remain calm—"

The lindworm let out a low, rattling growl from deep within its belly. The surface of the water quivered at the sound. It coiled itself tighter and tighter, readying to strike. Its hungry gaze was fixed on Sylvia. She reached for the saber at her hip but seemed to think better of it.

Why wasn't she doing anything?

All Lorelei could imagine was her pale, terrified face reflected in those terrible eyes. All she could see was her white hair stained red with blood. She did not think. She raised her arms and called on her power.

The aether leapt to answer her, sparks of pale blue shimmering in the air. She gritted her teeth against the weight and force of the river, and in an instant, the thread binding her will to the river's wore thin enough to snap. A trickle of blood ran down her nose and over her lips. *Too much, too soon.* She couldn't do this.

Then, suddenly, it felt weightless.

Beside her, Johann had sprung to his feet to help her lift a wall of water, his face barely flushed from exertion. No doubt he'd trained to handle much more than this. Lorelei dreaded to think what he was truly capable of.

Just as the lindworm surged toward Sylvia and Adelheid's boat, they curled their hands into fists and froze the wall to ice. It shattered on impact, raining chunks of ice like broken glass. Reflexively, Lorelei drew her coat around herself. Sharp slivers of ice sparkled on the floor at her feet.

The beast hissed furiously and dove back into the water. Lorelei struggled to stay balanced as the wake buffeted their boat.

Johann looked at Lorelei as if seeing her for the first time. "You can use magic?"

She realized her mistake too late. A bolt of panic lanced through her, but she kept her voice even as she said, "Perhaps we can discuss it another time."

The dragon cut through the water like an arrow, almost too quickly to track, a flash of red in the deep. Beside them, Sylvia crumpled to a heap at the bottom of the rowboat, her arms caging in her face as though cringing from a blow. Her face was ashen, but worst of all was the haunted look in her eyes. Lorelei recognized it all too well: she was trapped in a time and place far away from here. Adelheid stepped in front of her and settled into a fighting stance.

"Stay focused, Kaskel." Johann's voice was a low growl.

The lindworm surged out of the river. The waves slapped against the boat so violently that Lorelei lost her footing. The floor slipped from beneath her and for a moment, she saw nothing but open air. Her head cracked against the back of the seat, and black burst across her vision.

The lindworm's spined tail arced overhead and smashed into another boat. The sound of splintering wood and screams cut through the haze gumming up her thoughts. She forced herself upright in time to see Adelheid resurface from the river, spitting out a mouthful of water. She grabbed hold of a fragment of the rowboat bobbing in the current.

Where was Sylvia?

"Adelheid?" Johann shouted, his panic obvious.

"I'll manage," she said. "Handle that."

Johann's glare turned murderous as he rounded on the lindworm again. He moved like he was built to fight. It was almost beautiful, the effortlessness with which he pulled water from the river and sharpened it to spears of ice that shattered harmlessly against its scales. With a shout of frustration, he seized upon another wave of water and sent it up. It froze in serrated points.

Johann had clearly lost himself to rage, and Lorelei could see his precision slipping. She could hardly think through the ringing in her skull. With the others incapacitated, it was only the two of them now. The lindworm's translucent eyelid pulled back, and the full brunt of its furious gaze landed on Lorelei. It gave her just enough of a jolt to think clearly.

"Its eye," she snapped.

Johann glanced back at her, his lip still curled in a snarl. "What?"

"Don't waste your time trying to pierce its scales."

After a moment, understanding cut through his bloodlust. He nodded sharply. As the lindworm reared up again to strike, he drew back his arm and launched a thin, wicked spear of ice at it. It struck true, sinking deep into the bright green of its eye.

The beast shrieked, thrashing. The water churned violently,

tossing them on its waves. Its claws dragged into the damp earth of the riverbanks. Sweat beaded on Johann's temples as he clenched his fists tighter, driving the spear deeper into its skull.

With a final cry, the lindworm's body collapsed on the shore. Blood poured off its scales and into the river. Pink froth pooled around its body, and red slowly bloomed across the surface of the water. The sight of its broken body, glittering in its death, almost made Lorelei lose her grip on herself entirely. She slumped against the side of the boat, breathing heavily, and dug her thumbs into her temples. The roiling in her stomach refused to quiet.

"It's unwise to take your eyes off a dying thing, you know," Johann said. "Everything becomes more vicious and more beautiful in its final moments."

Lorelei lifted her gaze to him. He stood in profile, but there was a curve of a self-satisfied smile on his lips as he surveyed what he had done.

"Johann!"

His whole body seemed to slacken at the sound of Adelheid's voice. She stood on the far bank with Sylvia, both of them shivering in their waterlogged cloaks. Lorelei could not read the hard set of her jaw, but a horrible, pleading condemnation burned in her eyes. An entire conversation seemed to pass between the two of them. Johann clenched his fists. Bit by bit, he loosened them and turned them over to stare at his trembling palms. He looked horrified, then ashamed.

As if that could excuse how he'd looked moments before. He'd been wearing the face of a monster.

No, she thought, *a murderer.*

TEN

THEY PULLED THEIR REMAINING BOATS to the shore, tethering them to the banks and covering them as best they could with loose branches and leaves. Sylvia was suspiciously quiet and stood with a very ignoble slouch, as though she could barely hold herself upright. Ludwig slid his arm around her shoulders, and despite her drenched cloak, he let her lean her head into the crook of his neck.

He waved a hand, as though he meant to lift the water from her clothing. He barely managed to wring more than a few drops from it. He flashed her an apologetic smile. "Sorry. That's the best I can do."

Sylvia offered him a wan smile.

Heike eyed them with vague disgust. She cast her eyes around the group as though searching for a target for her annoyance. Predictably, she landed on Lorelei. "So. You can use magic."

Her tone was conversational, but it dripped with sickly sweet poison. Lorelei's stomach twisted as her father's warning rang in her ears. *You must never do that where anyone can see.*

For years, she had been exceedingly careful. One mistake—one foolish act of selflessness—was all it took to jeopardize everything. It was one thing for people to suspect you were a monster. It was another thing entirely to hand them proof.

She could not tear her gaze away from Johann's sword, glinting in the pale moonlight. Her voice kept miraculously steady when she said, "I don't know what you're talking about."

"Oh?" Heike curled her lip. "My eyes deceived me, then."

"I didn't see anything," Ludwig interjected.

"I did. She channeled aether." Johann had removed his glasses and set to drying them with the corner of his shirt. When he replaced them on the bridge of his nose, Lorelei could not read his expression at all. Begrudgingly, he said, "However, her quick thinking likely saved your life."

The force of Lorelei's gratitude startled her. It took a moment for her mind to catch up with the fact that Johann zu Wittelsbach, a supporter of the Hounds, had defended her. "What did you say?"

Heike's mouth hinged open. "Are you feeling quite well? She's—"

"A witch, yes." Johann's mouth pressed into a thin line. "Even so—"

"No, you superstitious *oaf*. She's a liar." Heike advanced a step toward Lorelei and raked her gaze across her face. "Isn't that right, Lori? How terribly convenient for you to let us believe you were the only one who couldn't have killed her."

"Tread carefully," Lorelei replied lowly, "before you say something you regret."

"Can we let this go?" Ludwig sounded uncharacteristically desperate. "At least until we're out of the cold. I'd like to keep all my fingers if possible."

After an agonizing few moments, Heike sighed, and the anger bled out of her. "Fine."

"There's surely a bright side to all this," Ludwig tried. "At least we still have the map?"

"We don't. Or a dowsing machine, for that matter." Heike wrung her wet hair out like a dish towel. With false cheer, she added, "We're well and truly fucked. I hope you're pleased with yourselves."

Adelheid let out an irritated sound. This was the most ruffled Lorelei had ever seen her. Her dress was sodden and mud-stained, and her blond hair hung limp down her back. Still, she looked as imperious as ever. "If only there had been another route we could have taken."

Heike jabbed a finger at her. "Do *not* blame me for this."

"Of course not," Adelheid replied. "You are a victim in this, as you are in all things."

Heike grinned maliciously. "You're one to talk."

"Enough," Lorelei cut in. "I can't think with the two of you squawking in my ear."

A tense silence fell over the group.

She drew in a deep breath and continued, "In every tale, lindworms feed on livestock. There should be a town nearby."

Sylvia's pale eyes were like a brand on her face, but they lacked their usual fire. The emptiness of them unsettled her. "She's right."

Johann gestured to the groove the lindworm's belly had carved out in the earth. It was littered with broken trees and streaks in the torn-up grass that looked disconcertingly like blood. This must have been its path to town. Lorelei could all too easily imagine it slithering back into the water, glutted on hapless cattle. "You're suggesting we follow its trail to town?"

"Unless anyone has any better ideas," Lorelei said, "yes. If nothing else, we can regroup there."

They set off on foot with fog eddying around their ankles. Bit by bit, the night filled up the bowl of the sky like dark waters. The lindworm's trail led them through a dense forest of fir and white-trunked birches. Bone-pale mushrooms unfurled from the bark of trees gone to rot, reaching toward the dappled moonlight.

Lorelei walked alone in the back of the group, her hands shoved deep into the pockets of her greatcoat. Ludwig had an arm slung around Sylvia as they walked. Heike trudged alone just a few paces behind them, radiating a self-pitying misery. Adelheid and Johann followed her, speaking so quietly Lorelei could not make out a word of it. His head was bowed low, as if in prayer—or perhaps awaiting her judgment. After a short pause, Adelheid covered his hand with her own, there and gone in an instant. With that, she went to join Heike. Lorelei watched Heike bristle, then relax as Adelheid talked. Finally, Heike threaded their fingers together.

Apparently, all was forgiven. The ease of it reminded her painfully of arguing with her own sister.

A persistent headache throbbed at the base of Lorelei's skull from some dreadful mixture of stress and exhaustion—one that only worsened when she saw Johann deliberately falling back to match her step for step. Perhaps if she looked sufficiently uninterested, he'd leave her in peace. No such luck. He walked beside her in unsettling silence, his sunken eyes roving over her face.

Reluctantly, she met his gaze. For the first time, she noticed he had scars like Sylvia's, notched into his temples and shining dully in the moonlight. They were fainter, though, and old. He clearly won his duels more often than not.

"I suppose you're expecting gratitude," she said.

"No." His lip curled. "That wasn't for you. Sometimes Heike needs to learn to keep her mouth shut."

"Then what do you want?"

"I want to ask you something." He spoke every word as though he were spitting out a mouthful of glass. "How *did* you gain your powers?"

"The same way you did," she replied icily, "I would imagine."

He narrowed his eyes. Clearly, he did not believe her. "Who taught you, then?"

"Ziegler." The pain that knotted in her chest almost knocked the breath from her. Desperate to steer the conversation into safer waters, she added, "It's reasonably common among my people, but few of us practice magic."

Magic dwelled in water; that much was a scientifically observable phenomenon. Brunnestaaders took great pride in their magical abilities and saw it as an intrinsic link between themselves and the land. Yevani, however, didn't fit neatly into the narrative. *Rootless*, they were called: suited to enterprise and city life. Yevani wielding magic made Brunnestaaders uncomfortable, and discomfort made them violent. Easier to forgo magic entirely than to invite them into the Yevanverte's walls with their stones and torches. Ziegler had always disdained bigotry of that sort. Any institution that sought to bury the truth had no place in her world. And so, she had taught Lorelei to manipulate water as part of her studies.

"With training, you would fight well," he said. "Unless you're holding back. I've heard of Yevani who can manipulate the very blood in your veins."

"Regrettably, I haven't yet found an entity willing to teach me that," she replied sourly. "You're wrong about us."

"I'm not wrong about you." He met her eyes steadily. "You might have defended us today, but that changes nothing. You will turn against us when it suits you."

"So assured," she spat. "How will you be able to live with yourself when you're forced to bow to an Albisch queen?"

Johann suddenly looked exasperated. "If this is about the other night, I spoke in anger. Wilhelm has a strategic mind, and doing what he can to quiet Albisch discontent is a wise move. I fought for him and that dream of his. I can be patient in seeing it realized."

Lorelei was surprised to hear him say it. "And what is that?"

"A united Brunnestaad," he replied, with something like reverence in his voice. "Something pure."

God, she loathed him. She could not keep the disgust out of her voice. "And you believe he'll deliver you that."

"In time." Johann frowned. "Once he has the area fully under his command—and the power of the Ursprung in his hands—he can administrate it as he sees fit. I look forward to it myself. Peacetime is so dull."

"What if he doesn't see fit to do what you want?"

"Herzin is influential," he said coolly. "He will see reason."

Lorelei was not sure what disturbed her more: his vision of a "pure" Brunnestaad or how thoroughly he had upset her expectations. If he was willing to accept Sylvia—and Wilhelm—then he had no motive. Scrambling to regain control of the conversation, she said, "You don't believe one of your own would be better suited to rule?"

He smiled coldly. "Not all of us are as disloyal as you."

Lorelei did not rise to the bait. "I know you're not here for Wilhelm. I heard you were here to fulfill an oath."

"Adelheid told you about that?" He adjusted his glasses, clearly flustered. "I seldom think of it, honestly. Alexander saved my life on the battlefield, yes, but Adelheid has saved it every day since. That's stronger than an oath."

"How romantic," she said dryly. "I almost envy you."

He scoffed. "There's nothing to envy in that regard."

"Then what is it?"

"In Herzin," he said after a long moment, "from the moment you can walk, they take you by the shoulders and point you toward an enemy. They place a sword in your hand and call it purpose. She is the only one who has asked me to set it down. I don't know what you call that."

For a moment, he seemed almost weary. *Human.* Lorelei studied the fang glinting around his neck. "Do you know what a golem is?"

He eyed her almost warily. "No."

"It is a protector," she said. "There are many stories that are told. The most famous one, however, is about a rabbi who saved the Yevanverte from men like you."

He said nothing.

"One day," she continued, "the king threatened to expel all of the Yevani from his city, and so the rabbi went to the banks of the river and built a golem from silt and mud. When he wrote the name of God on a scroll and placed it in the golem's mouth, it came to life."

The golem, it was said, could turn himself invisible and summon the spirits of the dead. Every time the king sent his armies to drive the Yevani out, the golem sent them screaming from the streets. On the day of rest, the rabbi would remove the scroll from the golem's mouth, and he would go dormant.

"And? What happened?"

"It depends who you ask. In some versions of the tale, the king begged the rabbi to destroy the golem in exchange for the Yevani's safety. With one stroke of his pen, he changed the word *truth* to *death* on the golem's scroll. The Yevani lived peacefully in the city, and it is said the golem can be revived again in times of crisis."

He seemed disappointed. "And in the others?"

"The rabbi forgot to remove the scroll, and so the golem went on a rampage outside the Yevanverte's walls. He slaughtered many people before the rabbi could stop him."

"How bleak."

"It is a comforting fantasy for us," Lorelei said, with more heat than she'd intended. "Nonetheless, you remind me of him. It seems to me she takes the scroll from your mouth."

Johann froze as though she had struck him. Lorelei kept walking.

She hated him, yet somehow, she pitied him. Had she not seen the way he'd transformed when he began to fight? Had she not seen the vacant, animal terror in Sylvia's eyes? Lorelei knew what it was like when your mind was still fighting its own wars, ones that had ended long ago for everyone else.

Even as a boy, he was cruel and petty, Adelheid had told her. *His father did not give him much choice in the matter.*

Wilhelm surely knew what he was. It did not surprise her he'd used every weapon, every amusement, at his disposal. Lorelei thought of the yearning in Johann's voice when he spoke of Adelheid, the glimpse of weariness when he described the purpose he'd been given. There was another version of the golem's tale—one in which the rabbi began to fear what he'd created. As he went to remove the scroll from the golem's mouth, it turned on him.

But that did not seem sufficient for murder. Perhaps she'd been wrong about him. And if she had, where did that leave her?

When they crested a hill, the land opened up before them. Tall grass and pastures were silvered with moonlight. In the distance, soft lights bloomed out of the darkness and crept gently up the mountainside.

"A village!" Ludwig cried. "We're going to make it!"

The village was little more than a smattering of wood-paneled cottages with smoke curling from their chimneys. As they passed through, Lorelei took in the wards: iron spikes driven into their doorframes and the silver wind chimes clattering in the breeze. Lorelei could feel the eyes of the villagers on them. The few still outside stopped what they were doing. Others watched from their windows, candles burning on the sills, their gazes narrowed and watchful. Although they'd all dressed for traveling, their clothes were likely finer than anything the townsfolk had seen in years.

"It looks like there's an inn," Heike said. "Thank *God*."

Ludwig and Adelheid exchanged a look.

"Ah . . . about that," Ludwig said. "Lorelei, can I talk to you for a minute?"

His tone filled her with dread. The way he steered her away from the group did nothing to help matters. "What is it?"

"Our instruments are . . . How to put this? Well, half of them are at the bottom of the river, and the other half are in bad shape."

Purchasing their equipment had eaten up more than half Wilhelm's grant. Even if they did have the funds, they could only be repaired by specialists, and somehow, she doubted there was a barometer maker in this yokel town. "Anything else?"

"Most of our money is *also* at the bottom of the river, so . . ." Ludwig cringed. "Um, Lorelei? What are you . . . ?"

After everything that had happened today, she had no energy

left in her to yell. Slowly, Lorelei sat down in the middle of the street. The cold of the cobblestones seeped into her skin, and above her, the stars set into the pitiless black of the sky seemed to be laughing as they twinkled.

I'm ready, she thought. *Just strike me down now.*

God, however, was cruel. Sylvia von Wolff's face appeared in her field of vision instead. "Please get up. People are beginning to stare."

She refrained from pointing out that they had already been staring. "I don't care."

Sylvia sighed, as though Lorelei were being very unreasonable indeed. She supposed she was, but she could not bring herself to care. "I can't do anything about the equipment," Sylvia said, "but I can handle our lodgings."

She extended a hand. Lorelei pushed her arm aside and stood on her own. The stung look on Sylvia's face, she told herself, did not bother her at all.

The inn stood proudly at the end of the road. It was by far the largest building in town, with a quaint, overgrown yard and a wooden fence that had seen better days. Lorelei and Johann both had to duck beneath the low doorframe as they entered.

It looked to be lifted straight from an Albisch woodblock print. The white walls behind the bar were cluttered with portraits of saints, paintings of cows, an impressive collection of cuckoo clocks, and no fewer than five sets of antlers, small enough that Lorelei surmised they belonged to a family of rasselbocken.

Townsfolk clustered around tables near a roaring fire, chattering over glass mugs of ale and plates filled with beets and headcheese. Conversations slowed as people did their best to pretend they weren't staring. Most of them, Lorelei realized after a moment, were eyeing Sylvia as though they were trying to place her.

They were greeted by a middle-aged woman who—after what Lorelei thought an excessive amount of bowing and scraping—introduced herself as Emilia.

"Come in, come in, my lords! I wish I'd known you were coming. I would have had the kitchens prepare better for your arrival." When her starry eyes landed on Lorelei, her smile faltered, as if she'd just noticed a snag in an otherwise perfect tapestry. "What can I do for you?"

"Lodging for the night," said Lorelei.

Emilia recoiled. "Oh."

Oh, she thought. *So it begins.*

She appealed to Johann first. "The Yeva won't be able to stay."

Lorelei bit down on a retort. She had tried for years to scrub the accent off, but it was impossible to do it perfectly—especially when she had gotten carelessly comfortable in Ruhigburg.

"What would you like me to do with her?" Johann asked, clearly amused. "Put her in the stables?"

Sylvia, who still had not fully recovered from the encounter with the lindworm, underwent a sudden and glorious transformation. She smiled, bright enough to dazzle, as she stepped forward and took Emilia's hands in her own. "No intervention will be necessary! I assure you, she won't cause any trouble."

"You can't promise that, milady, as much as you'd like to. They're a scheming type."

"Regardless, she stays with us. She is a valued companion."

Emilia looked as disgusted as Lorelei felt. Still, it surprised Lorelei to hear Sylvia express such a sentiment. Perhaps Sylvia was not as horrid a liar as she'd once believed.

Sylvia's expression grew resigned. "If I may be so bold as to introduce myself, my name is Sylvia von Wolff, and—"

Emilia gasped, stumbling back a few steps. "My sincerest apologies! I didn't recognize you, Mondscheinprinzessin."

Moonlight Princess? Lorelei made a mental note to mock her for it later. Heike coughed to cover a laugh.

"Please, there is no need for formalities." Sylvia laughed uneasily. She lowered her voice, as though she did not want anyone else to overhear. "Allow me to apologize for catching you so off guard.

We were waylaid by a lindworm on our travels. Johann here has dealt with it, but tragically—"

Emilia's voice flattened. "You killed it?"

"Did you want it alive?" asked Ludwig.

"No, milord." Emilia looked ready to throw herself at Johann's feet. "No. It's been picking off our sheep for months."

She turned toward the room and addressed the small crowd—presumably in Brunnisch, although now that she wasn't articulating for their benefit, Lorelei could not make out a single word she said. How hard Sylvia must have worked to make herself understood; these days, Lorelei barely detected her accent.

There was a beat of silence. Then, a cheer went up. They hoisted their glasses in the air, sloshing beer and froth onto the floor. Johann looked as though he wanted to disappear.

"Please, stay as long as you wish," Emilia said. "We must thank you properly."

"That won't be necessary," he said.

"I insist." She smiled at him knowingly. "I know it is provincial compared to what you're used to, but the Feast Day of Saint Bruno is tomorrow. There will be a festival in his honor."

"How lovely," Sylvia said brightly. "We would be honored to stay with you."

"Von Wolff," Lorelei said thinly. "With all due respect, we do not have time for this."

"Lorelei," Sylvia said with equal venom, "Saint Bruno was the first king of Albe, widely fabled to have fallen into the Ursprung. He is a very important figure to us. Surely you understand."

She did, unfortunately. With no map and no equipment, they had to rely on local knowledge. They had gotten this far. Surely someone in this blasted village could give them the final push.

"Very well," she gritted out.

"Besides," Sylvia added, "we need to restock our supplies before going anywhere."

"Wonderful!" Emilia folded her hands. "I'll have someone get a meal for you and show you to your rooms. I trust one of you will watch that one . . ."

Feeling vengeful, Lorelei said, "Surely, it would make everyone the most comfortable if Her Highness were to do it."

Sylvia shot her a downright murderous look. "It would be my pleasure."

They were brought a meal of dumplings stuffed with pork on a bed of cabbage, which Lorelei assumed was intentionally spiteful. She left the dumplings on her plate, which was all the same to her. Her appetite still hadn't returned. Ludwig quietly pushed his cabbage onto her plate and acted confused when she tried to give it back. No one seemed willing to make conversation, and so, they fell into silence and retired for the night.

Lorelei was filled with a prickling dread as she ascended the stairs. Mercifully, however, the room had two beds. They looked as though they would collapse with so much as a sneeze, but there was a fire burning in the hearth and a washbasin full of fresh, clean water. When the door clicked shut behind them, Lorelei said, "I didn't need your intercession back there."

"No? Would you rather I let them run you out of town the next time you are so careless as to open your mouth?" When Lorelei made no immediate reply, Sylvia huffed. "I believe the words you are searching for are *thank you.*"

"Why waste your breath?"

"You make it very difficult to answer that question." Sylvia dropped her bags in a heap. "Fortunately for you, some of us have principles."

"Which you demonstrated so admirably when Heike accused me of murder—and when Johann insisted that I must be a witch." The strangled hurt stubbornly flared within her. It felt like plunging her own hand into a fire when she asked, "Do you agree with them?"

"Of course not," Sylvia said vehemently. "You and I may not get along, but you do not deserve that kind of treatment. I am sorry I said nothing—truly. I was not myself."

To her credit, she looked ashamed. It robbed Lorelei of her well-deserved vindication, but Sylvia's apology pressed sharply against an old wound. Even as a child, Lorelei had not been easy to love. Early on, she'd found it preferable to embrace her unpleasant nature rather than undergo the agony of trying and failing to please. It had served her well while she walked as a stranger in two different worlds. Over the years, Lorelei had been inured to both the baffled mistrust of her own community and the brusque impersonality of her classmates' hatred. But in an instant, Sylvia had pierced through her armor, and the pain felt almost like relief.

Far better to be disliked for who she truly was rather than what she represented.

The expression on her face must have been telling, because Sylvia reached out as though she meant to rest a hand on her forearm. Lorelei withdrew a step, putting a safe distance between them. Her heart thudded far too loudly in her chest.

"At any rate, I suppose it must be nice to throw your weight around in a place where your name means something." With cheerful malice, she added, "*Mondscheinprinzessin.*"

Sylvia groaned in exasperation. "Please don't call me that."

"What does it mean?"

"Nothing. It's an old family story," she said evasively. "Now tell me what that stunt was earlier. You were trying to get Johann alone, weren't you?"

Lorelei set down her own bag and made her way to the washbasin. She stripped off her damp jacket and draped it over the back of an armchair. With any luck, it would dry overnight, but there was little she could do about the silt-and-iron stench of the river. With brisk efficiency, she began to undo the buttons of her waistcoat. "Am I not permitted to speak with Johann either?"

When Lorelei glanced up at her, Sylvia looked away. Her cheeks were tinged red. Lorelei eyed her suspiciously.

Sylvia cleared her throat and said, "I find myself skeptical that you would want to."

Lorelei's fingers stilled on the last button. She did not like the direction this conversation was headed. "Did you get along as children?"

"Most of the time, no. He was a terrible bully and liked to make Ludwig do all sorts of ridiculous things because he was so desperate to fit in. And one time, he conscripted the others to perform an exorcism on me. It was—" She huffed. "You're changing the subject again."

"You surely don't expect me to move past the exorcism so quickly. Did it work?"

"I'm not as dense as you seem to think! Don't you think I can see that suspicious mind of yours at work by now? When you talk to them, you have the same look in your eye as when you're collecting folktales."

"And what look is that?"

"This." Sylvia contorted her features into an exaggerated rictus. "Even the tip of your nose seems to scowl. It's quite impressive. Now, out with it. What have you uncovered?"

"That he is an exceedingly unpleasant man," Lorelei said impatiently. "However, once you are queen, he will not attempt to depose you until it's politically expedient for him to do so. Are you satisfied?"

Sylvia looked as though she meant to argue more, but as Lorelei shrugged off her waistcoat, she suddenly took great interest in the ceiling. Lorelei—rather heroically, she thought—resisted the urge to roll her eyes. There was no need to get so worked up about it. The Albisch and their prudish modesty!

Without dignifying her with a reply, Sylvia collapsed in front of the vanity in the corner of the room. The mirror had gone hazy and spotted with oxidization. She rummaged through her things and lined up a series of crystal bottles on the counter. Then, she began miserably applying various potions (tinctures? serums? It was all beyond Lorelei) to her skin and finger-combing oils through her hair. She looked tragic, like some lovelorn maiden sitting by her window.

The scent traveled through the room. Lorelei had gotten bare whiffs of her perfumes—lemon, bergamot, roses—over the years, whenever she leaned too close or Sylvia swept the mass of her hair over her shoulders. But now the sheer concentration of it was making her feel light-headed. It would haunt even her dreams.

Lorelei tugged the knot of her cravat loose with force. "You're giving me a headache."

"Well, you shall have to cope," Sylvia snapped. "Now . . . look somewhere else."

Obediently, Lorelei turned around. Behind her came the soft sound of Sylvia undoing the buttons of her fine linen shirt, the rustle of fabric as it slid off her shoulders and pooled onto the floor.

Lorelei's mouth suddenly felt quite dry. She fumbled to remove her gloves, but they caught on her skin, damp with river water and sweat. Despite the draft stealing in through the window, it had gotten terribly hot in here, and it was making her irritable. She splashed her face with water from the washbasin.

As quickly as she could, she changed into a sleeping shirt and slid into bed. The covers were thin and scratchy, and they made her painfully aware of every inch of her skin. For a few moments, she lay stiff beneath the linens with her eyes trained on the ceiling.

Footsteps padded lightly against the floorboards. There was a *shush* of breath, followed by a flood of darkness as the candle went out. The creak of springs as Sylvia climbed into bed. Lorelei lay awake, listening to the wild thrum of her own heart, to the slide of sheets over skin. She'd found Sylvia napping in sunny spots in the library and on campus so many times, she knew the exact cadence of her breath as she slept. She listened for it now, the moment she would surrender.

Neither of them slept for several hours.

ELEVEN

LORELEI WOKE TO THE CROW OF A ROOSTER. She nearly launched herself from bed—and then directly into the headboard when she saw Sylvia standing by the window. She had almost forgotten they'd shared a room last night.

The light filtering through their window veiled Sylvia in white. Her hair was a sleek rope draped over her shoulder. It dripped from its ends and stained the starched white of her shirt. Lorelei's stomach twisted itself into a knot as Sylvia tipped her face toward her. The stupid smile on her face evaporated into pity.

"What?" Lorelei bit out. Her voice was raspy with sleep.

"You have nightmares." Sylvia winced as soon as it was out of her mouth, as though she hadn't meant to say it. "Ah, in any case . . . It is a beautiful day!"

Lorelei didn't dignify her with a response. She only rolled her eyes as viciously as she could and flung off the covers. Sylvia von Wolff, looking at *her* with pity. It was an insult too great to bear. Furthermore, it was far earlier in the morning than Lorelei preferred, and she saw little to be so chipper about.

When she rose, she saw the state of the room and made a helpless noise of dismay. It looked as though a gale-force wind had blown through in the night—or perhaps Sylvia had smuggled one of her infernal creatures in with her luggage. The contents of her bags—books, clothing, saber—lay scattered across the floor. "What happened here?"

"I had to get ready," Sylvia said, as if that explained anything at all. Lorelei did not know how she'd slept through such an event if *this* was the result. The saber, Sylvia rescued from the pile of refuse and strapped to her hip. "Emilia mentioned there is a shop down the road. We should be able to restock our supplies there."

Lorelei already felt a headache coming on. "We have no money, in case you've forgotten."

"I am sure Ludwig can help us. Now, hurry up. I have been awake for hours!" This came floating from beyond the door. She had not bothered to finish her sentence before whisking into the hall.

"Ludwig is a merchant's son, not a miracle worker. He already told me the money is—" Lorelei called after her, but the door fell shut.

She sighed. Ludwig could be quite persuasive when he wanted to be. His father had taught him how to haggle and run a business. It did not hurt that there was something sweetly pathetic about his face that made most people go weak in the knees.

When she went downstairs, she found the two of them already waiting by the door. Miraculously, it seemed Ludwig's wardrobe had survived the journey. He wore an impeccably tailored cloak embroidered with cornflowers done in pretty lavender thread and twirled a ring on his littlest finger. Something about it looked vaguely familiar.

"Ready to see a professional at work?" he asked slyly.

"Where did you get such a thing?" Lorelei asked.

"This thing?" He flipped it into the air like a coin and caught it in his fist. The facets of the absurdly large gem refracted light into her eyes. "Oh, Heike gave it to me to pawn. She said she was bored of it."

Sylvia looked quite smug, which Lorelei thought was entirely unwarranted.

Together, they walked into the cool morning light. Beyond the inn's rickety wooden gate, the town unfolded into rows of obnoxiously bright houses, huddled together against the chill. At the end of the road, they found the shop. A crudely painted sign propped up beside the door read:

ENCHANTED GOODS—INQUIRE WITHIN

MILK—1.00

EGGS—0.25 (EACH!!)

NO REFUNDS, NO COMPLAINING

"With that advertising," said Ludwig, "how could we *not* inquire?"

"How curious! The milk is almost certainly produced by a bahkauv. As for the eggs, perhaps an erdhenne?" The interest in Sylvia's voice was unmistakable. "I can only imagine what effects consuming them might have."

"Nothing good," Lorelei snapped. Honestly, she could not fathom how the woman had survived this long.

Bahkauv, although they looked like cows, came armed with sharp fangs, claws, and a priggish hatred for drunks. Sylvia's first book had included a lengthy interlude in which she befriended one living in a fountain outside a pub. It had attacked no fewer than forty men as they attempted to stumble home. As for erdhenne, they were rather skittish creatures, said to have escaped from the coops of more powerful wildeleute. When they took up residence in mortals' barns—and were well cared for, of course—they clucked to alert the household of danger. Her skepticism remained unchanged.

Wildeleute were not mentioned in any Yevanisch dietary laws, which naturally meant that scholars had spent centuries arguing with one another about it. Was a bahkauv kosher if it looked like a cow but hunted men? Could any of the wildeleute be slaughtered without unnecessary suffering? Were they—with their strange, potent magic—containers for the divine? As far as Lorelei was concerned, the justification did not matter. No sensible person would bother with them at all.

"Only one way to find out," Ludwig said as he pushed open the door.

A bell chimed as they entered. Inside, it was warm and cozy and smelled blessedly of coffee. Dried herbs hung from the rafters in thick, fragrant clusters. If she was not mistaken, Lorelei spied a few shards of bone knotted up amid the lavender sprigs. A tight spiral of stairs led up to what Lorelei assumed was the owner's living quarters. A door behind the counter, studded with iron nails, rattled ominously. She caught Sylvia staring at it longingly.

The shopkeeper appeared at the top of the staircase with a shawl drawn over her shoulders. Lorelei absently noted the silver clasp at her throat, engraved with the image of a saint. The woman's shock at seeing Sylvia there was plain, and she narrowly avoided stumbling down the stairs in her eagerness to attend them. "Your Highness, you honor me. What can I do for you?"

"We're collecting supplies for our journey—and stories," Ludwig interjected. "Do you know any about the Ursprung?"

"What do you want children's tales for?"

"We're scholars," Sylvia said brightly.

The shopkeeper's answering expression was entirely bemused—almost pitying, as if she thought them terribly daft. "There'll be a woman at the festival who tells the tale much more prettily than I ever could."

Lorelei filed that information away. With any luck, this detour would not be a complete waste of time.

"Excellent," Ludwig replied. "Now tell us about these enchanted goods of yours."

She was evasive in a practiced sort of way, sharing just enough to remain mysterious. But Ludwig kept up a steady stream of inane chatter as he pointed out what he wanted. Lorelei could hardly track their conversation. It flitted from harvests and rain patterns to business, the wildeleute in the area, a glade just north of the village where a plant that could summon storms grew (at this, Ludwig seemed genuinely intrigued), as well as the many virtues of her six unmarried children. Lorelei almost admired her bald-faced opportunism.

Finally, when she finished wrapping everything in paper, Ludwig laid Heike's ring before her. The sun, evidently sympathetic to their plight, chose that exact moment to lance gloriously through the window. Its rays struck the gemstone and scattered in tiles of multicolored light.

The shopkeeper stared at it as though he had emptied a bag of snakes on the countertop. "That isn't enough."

He whistled. "Well, then. Your prices are considerably higher than I expected. What flexibility do you have?"

"Significantly less now," she groused. "What can I do with a ring that fine?"

Ludwig winked. "It once belonged to the princess of Sorvig, the most beautiful woman in the world. A suitable dowry for one of your children, wouldn't you say?"

"You certainly can't put a price on that," Lorelei said drolly.

The shopkeeper seemed unimpressed. "Throw in ten marks, and it's yours. That's as low as I can go."

"Across the way, I saw a man selling produce for much less." He leaned across the counter and lowered his voice as if sharing a secret. "But I didn't like the look of his wares quite as much, if I'm honest. And he certainly had nothing enchanted."

"And *that*," she said, with no small measure of pride, "is precisely why I charge more."

"But, with our funds as tight as they are . . ." He shook his head with a grave air. "We lost so much to the lindworm, and our Mondscheinprinzessin needs to eat. We'll settle if we must."

Sylvia opened her mouth, clearly ready to object. Lorelei kicked her ankle.

"Fine." The shopkeeper sighed resignedly. "I'll take your trade."

"I'm so glad to hear it. But surely," Ludwig pressed, "you could give us a bit more. Her Highness won't ever forget that sort of kindness."

They left the shop weighed down with food, boots, snowshoes, winter coats, and assorted charms and talismans. In the end, he'd even managed to extract a tray of pastries, balls of deep-fried dough. Some had been dusted in sugar, others glazed with chocolate and marzipan. It seemed to Lorelei a pointless extravagance, but well, that was Ludwig.

Unfortunately, he'd also purchased a pint of milk and a dozen eggs, most likely because he knew it would irritate her. The eggs were disturbingly translucent, frigid to the touch, and contained a glittering black liquid that reminded Lorelei of the Vereist's waters. Even Sylvia was forced to concede they did not look particularly appetizing or salubrious. The milk did not seem terribly out of the ordinary, but Lorelei made a mental note to pour it out before Sylvia could get her hands on it. That no-refund policy existed for a reason.

Once they dropped off their supplies at the inn, Ludwig said, "Why don't we take these pastries and go on a little excursion? I'd like to find that storm-summoning plant she mentioned."

They climbed the switchbacking roads just outside the inn, and when they reached the end of the trail, they slipped through pasture fences. Red-coated cattle lifted their immense heads to watch them pass, silver bells jingling from the ribbons around their necks. Soon, the fields yielded to fragrant pine. Bars of sunlight dappled their path, and overhead, branches framed jagged swatches of sky. Even this late in the morning, frost glittered on the stiff grass.

Ludwig walked with his eyes focused on the ground, the long train of his cloak sweeping the earth behind him. His silence struck Lorelei as unusual. It was almost as though he forgot he was among company, for he looked uncharacteristically pensive.

"Is there something—"

He held out an arm in front of her, halting them. "Watch your step. Irrwurzel."

He pointed it out to her: a plant with delicate feathered fronds.

To her untrained eye, it looked like a common fern. However, she recognized the name from Ludwig's publications. Stepping on it would lead you astray of your path; you'd be cursed to wander aimlessly until the following dawn.

Sylvia peered down at it. "Have you figured out how to collect a sample yet?"

"God, no. I haven't dared try again." He flashed Lorelei a mottled scar on his hand. "Keeping it on you attracts vipers. Who would have thought?"

Sylvia made a sympathetic noise, but she was smiling as if lost in reverie. "It is rather funny in retrospect, isn't it?"

"Funny? I almost died!"

"I did not realize the two of you went on expeditions together," Lorelei said.

"It was nothing so formal. Many years ago, we spent long afternoons roaming the grounds of his country home together." Sylvia stepped around the irrwurzel and onto a fallen log. She walked across it with her arms extended for balance. "Ludwig inspired me to pursue my work."

"Now, I wouldn't go that far. If anything, you had the greater influence." He reached out and took her hand, helping her down from her perch. "You infected me with your recklessness."

They hiked and hiked, and with every passing minute, Lorelei's mood darkened. Cold air flowed down the slopes and pooled in the basins. There was nothing but trees here. Spruce trees and beech trees and fir trees, covered with thick coats of moss. It was unendingly green, so perfectly picturesque as to be mundane. What were they doing here? She'd come no closer to untangling anything, and without their equipment, they had no hope of—

"I think this is the glade the shopkeeper mentioned," Ludwig said.

The interminable trees had thinned out to a clearing carpeted with crocuses. At the far end stood the corpse of what had once been a stately maple. Its trunk was split in twain and blistered with char, and what remained of its branches were skeletal and blackened, clawing at the surrounding greenery. Clearly, it had been felled by lightning. Lorelei liked its stark beauty far more than what had come before.

As Ludwig forged ahead, Sylvia settled herself in a sunny patch of grass. The thin light played in the waves of her hair and illuminated the broad planes of her face. Even the scar on her cheek gleamed like ice. It was unfair, Lorelei thought miserably, that someone could be so effortlessly beautiful.

"You are still in a fine mood, I see."

Lorelei nearly let out an undignified sound of surprise. Sylvia had bitten into one of her pastries, and powdered sugar smudged the tip of her nose. Lorelei focused, perhaps too intently, on the one imperfection she could find in her. After a moment, Sylvia self-consciously ran her thumb along the corner of her mouth, brushing away an invisible crumb. That did not help matters.

"I am still in mourning," Lorelei said, "about our equipment."

"We don't need equipment to find the Ursprung."

Lorelei did not even want to touch that statement. Instead, she said, "We will need it to collect data. Without it—"

"Data cannot give you a complete understanding of something." Sylvia's expression was unreadable, but Lorelei did not like it. It veered too close to pity. "Where is your sense of wonder? Sometimes I think you would sooner let a cyanometer tell you what color the sky is, rather than simply looking up."

Lorelei opened her mouth to protest but promptly shut it again. Sylvia's words oddly stung. Perhaps as a child, she had believed Ziegler's lies: that the world outside the walls of the Yevanverte was full of magic. But she had seen the truth of it time and time again. It was a brutish and violent place—one that had rejected her. If she were to become a naturalist at the end of this, she could do her work with the cold certainty of rationality. There was no need for things like *immersion* and *wonder* to factor into it.

"Well," Lorelei said. "It would certainly give me a more precise shade."

Sylvia laughed, a warm, startled sound that Lorelei felt like a caress against her face. Before she could muster up some snappish retort, Ludwig gave a shout of triumph. He stood on the opposite side of the field, grinning like a fool and holding a fistful of golden flowers aloft.

In an instant, the skies darkened to a surly gray. Dread—more potent than she'd ever felt it—spread through her entire body. All the hair on her arms stood on end, and her fingers tingled with a frenetic energy. Sylvia's hair reached skyward and billowed as though she were underwater. She stared back at Lorelei with a look on her face that suggested they'd arrived at the same conclusion.

Lightning strike.

Ludwig threw the flowers into the woods and bolted toward them.

Everything flashed white. A crash split the world, so loud it felt as though it would crush her skull.

The world stilled. Lorelei lowered her hands from where they'd clamped over her ears and took stock of herself. Her mouth tasted of metal, and the iron chain around her neck was vibrating against her collarbone, but all of her limbs seemed to be attached. Behind the fractal pattern seared onto her retinas, she could see Ludwig and Sylvia coming out of their stupor. The two of them stared at each other for a second. Then, they began to laugh.

"You're both completely mad!" Lorelei cried.

A light rain began to fall through the canopy. Water dripped from the fir boughs like beads of silver and stirred up the sweet, sharp smell of ozone. Her thoughts went quiet as she drank it in. Her heart beat. Her chest expanded with every breath. Somehow, with fear and relief making a muddle of her thoughts, she could not find it in herself to be angry.

By the time they returned to town, the festival had sprung up like a work of fairy magic.

Market stalls lined the streets, bursting with produce: jewel-bright apples and grapes, cartons of strawberries and bundles of green onion, stacks of cabbages and potatoes, vibrant bouquets tied off with twine and arranged in buckets. Children tore down the alleys with wooden swords, others running after them with their arms outstretched like wings. And then there were the cows.

They trundled by in a line that stretched several blocks. Some were crowned in fir boughs and heather, others garlanded in roses and daffodils, others still in bright headdresses embroidered with the images of saints. Mottled cattle dogs darted back and forth along the parade line, barking and nipping at their heels. She could barely hear herself think over the noise.

Only in Albe, she supposed. She could not fathom how such a small village could make such a commotion.

Sylvia's eyes practically sparkled with excitement. "Oh, what fun! Shall we look around? Our springtime festival had all sorts of activities. Carnival booths, eating contests, feats of strength—"

Lorelei leveled her with a flat stare. "What of those things sounds like it would appeal to me?"

"You are just afraid of losing." Sylvia preened. "I suppose that's wise. I *was* the champion tree climber in my village."

Ludwig winked at Lorelei. "I for one would *love* to see that. Maybe they have their own competition here."

"Perhaps they do! I will report back." Sylvia needed no further encouragement.

She vanished into the crowds, leaving Lorelei and Ludwig alone once more. He flashed her an easy smile. "Shall we have a look around?"

Lorelei opened her mouth to say no, but if they'd pinned their hopes on a fairy tale, she supposed she might as well hear it. "If we must."

They passed through the sprawl of market stands, half of them selling some variety of sausage. The stench of woodsmoke and roasting pork was beginning to make her feel vaguely ill. Outside a pub, they'd set up rows and rows of tables, where people sat chattering over their beers. A man had climbed on top of one, hoisting his glass in the air. Another was offering his ale to one of the headdressed cows, who blinked at him with bland, adoring incomprehension.

Then, someone dropped a glass.

Lorelei flinched. Her every sense sharpened, latching on to the smell of spilled beer and sweat, the sound of jeering laughter. Just like that, she was here, a grown woman with her feet firmly planted in Albisch soil, and she was a child again, running blind through the streets of the Yevanverte. Memories crowded in urgently. Teeth bared and glinting in the dark. Raised fists. Blood and shattered glass on the cobblestones. Water drip, drip, dripping from Ziegler's limp fingers and pooling on the floor below.

"Whoa," said Ludwig as he steered her out of the street. "Easy now."

Goddamn it. Not again.

He helped her sit on the grass and sat silently until her breathing evened out and she had worked sensation back into her fingers. Then, he offered a paper bag to her. Inside were roasted almonds, candied and dusted with cinnamon. Her stomach turned. She'd had quite enough sugar for the day.

"No, thank you."

"You're all right?" he asked.

Lorelei bristled with resentment at the pity in his voice. She knew how she must look, with her haunted, vacant eyes. Like someone barely holding herself together.

"Yes, I'm fine," she said, more snappishly than she'd intended. More gently, she added, "The stress must be getting to me."

But she couldn't afford to crumble yet. She had foolishly let this morning slip away from her, and now she was back where she had started. If Johann had not done it, she had to set her sights elsewhere. Her life depended on it.

Across the way, Lorelei spied Adelheid and Heike standing together at a flower stall. Heike was weaving a crown of daffodils into Adelheid's hair; Adelheid endured it nobly. When she finished, a self-satisfied smile curling on her lips, she glanced up and made eye contact with Ludwig.

He waved at her. Immediately, her expression turned chilly. Without acknowledging him, she averted her eyes.

Lorelei couldn't keep the amusement out of her voice. "Did she just give you the cut?"

"I think so," he said cheerfully. "I suppose because I'm consorting with the enemy."

The woman could certainly hold a grudge. Lorelei respected that. "And you genuinely like these people?"

"I do. Most of the time, anyway. It's complicated." She must have looked skeptical because he asked, "Why? Did someone say something?"

He was a terrible bully, Sylvia said of Johann, *and liked to make Ludwig do all sorts of ridiculous things because he was so desperate to fit in.* "No," said Lorelei. "No one said anything."

He seemed to relax some. "Good. Really, most of what you hear is drivel. Wilhelm in particular has a flair for the dramatic, especially when it comes to his war stories. I'm sure you've heard the one where he secured a glorious, bloodless victory during the final battle of his campaign."

Everyone had heard that. Wilhelm, resplendent on the back of his dragonling, had flown over the battlefield. The enemy had laid down their arms in awe, and Brunnestaad was at last unified. "Of course."

"It's true no blood was spilled in combat," Ludwig said offhandedly. "But Imre"—his dragon, Lorelei assumed—"was . . . shall we say, *misbehaved* in his adolescence. A few miles away from the battlefield, he burned an entire village to ashes."

Cold horror prickled along the back of her neck. "Dear God."

"Sylvia and Adelheid were quite cross with him, from what I recall."

"And Johann?"

"He thought it was funny." Ludwig popped an almond into his mouth. "There are a thousand stories like that, but no one wants to hear them. No one wants the truth."

"Which is?"

Ludwig smiled wryly at her. "They're not heroes."

Lorelei frowned at him. Apart from Johann's initial outburst, it was the closest she'd heard one of them come to criticizing Wilhelm on this trip.

"Of course, they're all remarkable people," he added hastily, "and I love them dearly. I'd never speak ill of any of them. Ah. There goes Adelheid."

Sure enough, Adelheid passed by them as she shoved against the current of the crowd. Her drawn expression caught Lorelei off guard. Without thinking, she began following her. Ludwig made a sound of protest but stumbled after her. The dirt-packed roads gave way to mud beneath their boots, still damp from the rain Ludwig had summoned. No one seemed to mind. The farther she pressed into the heart of the village, the more raucous it became. A makeshift stage had been assembled in the square, where Lorelei assumed folk dancers or musicians would give their performances throughout the night.

She wove through revelers in bright-colored gowns until she found Adelheid standing before a cart boasting the largest cabbage of the season. She was glaring at it as though it had personally wronged her.

"Enjoying yourself?" Ludwig asked.

Adelheid startled at their sudden appearance. She looked as

crisp and immaculate as ever in her gown of plain white. Colorful ribbons, which had been curled into ringlets against a knife's edge, tumbled from her flower crown and framed her unsmiling face. "We do not have things like this in Ebul," she said, which Lorelei supposed was answer enough.

"Of course not. Only grim duty and hard work and dirt beneath your nails." His reverent tone somehow gave the impression of an eyeroll.

The displeasure on Adelheid's face deepened, and Lorelei sensed she had stumbled into an old argument. Admittedly, the two of them looked ridiculous side by side: the lavish caricature of a nobleman and a fairy-tale maiden with her austere, downtrodden beauty.

Once, Ebul had been renowned for its tulips and lush vineyards. Now the fields lay in ashes. When Lorelei thought of it, she imagined a countryside salted and burned, an infrastructure buckling under the weight of a surging population. As the easternmost province, it lay between Neide—the royal seat of what was now Brunnestaad—and its age-old rival, Javenor. It had served as their battleground for so long, nearly everyone there spoke both Brunnisch and Javenish.

"Right," Ludwig said, clearing his throat. "Well, I'm going to see if I can watch Sylvia climb a tree."

When he left them, Adelheid sighed. "I imagine you understand. The excess astounds me, but I cannot begrudge these people for celebrating their good fortune. It is no wonder Sylvia is so beloved."

Adelheid nodded toward the gathering crowds behind them. Lorelei turned and blinked into the dwindling sunlight. She spied a flash of snow-white hair. Sylvia had forded the cattle river and was drifting through the festival, stopping to chat with vendors or crouching to speak with the children brave enough to approach her. Lorelei wanted to be disgusted. Truly, she did. But with her head thrown back in laughter and her cheeks pinkened from the alpine cold, Sylvia looked happy in a way Lorelei had rarely seen before.

She forced herself to look away.

"Last harvest season," Adelheid said, "the people called for my father's head."

"And did they get it?"

Adelheid smiled ruefully, but the glint in her eyes was as bright as steel. "No. He fled."

"And is that why you've come on this expedition?" Lorelei pressed. "To hide?"

"No. To hide from my duty would be cowardly." Her voice dripped with disdain. "My father has never protected Ebul's interests, but I will. I have Wilhelm's ear—and once he claims the Ursprung's power, he will stabilize the region. If we stand united, no armies will come to our doorstep again."

Lorelei suppressed a shudder at the fervor in Adelheid's eyes. Like Johann, Adelheid believed in Wilhelm. Years of surviving outside the Yevanverte had dashed the last of Lorelei's optimism. Still, she could only pray Wilhelm would keep his promises to her as well.

"This expedition must mean a great deal to you, then," Lorelei said.

"It does," she replied, "to almost all of us. Some of us, I fear, cannot set aside ambition for the greater good."

"What do you—"

The sound of a horn tore through the festival, and Lorelei swore in surprise. The dogs wailed, and the crowds whooped. Clearly, the performances were about to begin. Lorelei craned her neck to get a view of the square—and saw that an old woman had taken her place on the stage. But the woman held no instrument and wore no costume—only a crocheted shawl wrapped around her narrow shoulders.

"Back in the days when wishes still held power," she began, "a barren woman prayed to God for a son."

The storyteller, then. Lorelei scrambled to produce a pen and her notebook from her bag. She would have to transcribe this tale exactly if she had any hope of extracting something useful from it.

"He listened, and when the child was born with silver hair, it was said he would one day become a great king. And so he grew up much beloved in his village."

Lorelei's hand stilled over the words *silver hair*. A strange, prickling dread crept down her spine.

"Now, in those days, there was a dragon that lived within the bowl of the moon. Once each month, he swept down from his perch and left the sky dark, with nothing but stars to light the way. With his wings, he pulled in the tides, and with his breath, he filled ships' sails with wind. But in exchange for his service, he took a price as well. He gorged himself on sheep and maidens gone out against their mother's wishes, enough to sate him for another month. The village had fallen on hard times, for they could not produce enough lambs or maidens to keep him happy, and no one worthy had emerged to slay him. All who had tried had perished."

Lorelei underlined the word *worthy* after she wrote it. This vague idea of worthiness was a consistent feature of all Ursprung tales. It always chose who would wield its power.

"One night, the silver-haired boy devised a cunning plan. He would climb to the top of the tallest mountain and kill the dragon while he slept." The woman paused. Beyond her shoulder, the jagged mountain range unfolded. As the sky darkened, the fading sunlight limned the tallest peak in bloody red. "He made the treacherous journey with his lance clenched between his teeth, and when he reached the summit, he pierced the moon. The dragon let out a terrible cry, and his blood poured from the sky. It ran like a stream down the mountainside and pooled in the stone's hollow. The boy lost his balance in the dragon's death throes and plummeted toward the earth. He braced himself for death, but he fell into the pool of dragon's blood. When he rose again, however, he found he could pull the tides and bend a river's course to his will.

"So begins the legend of Saint Bruno, the first king of Albe." The old woman smiled. "And today, we are blessed with the presence of his descendant, Miss Sylvia von Wolff."

Lorelei rounded on Adelheid and hissed, "Did you know about this?"

"To a certain extent," Adelheid replied. "I've never heard the story told, but I know it's important to her mother. Sylvia has always hated it."

Apparently only Albisch children grew up on tales of their silver-haired royal family.

"Miss von Wolff," the old woman said, "will you honor us with a few words?"

It felt like some horrible inversion of the evening of the ball. Lorelei standing stock-still, watching the crowds part around Sylvia. There was dirt on her cheek and flowers clumsily woven into her hair, as if done by a child's hand. It truly was no wonder that her people adored her. She was not just benevolent and charming. It wasn't only that she genuinely wanted to know the name of their favorite horse and how many lambs had been born that season. She was a symbol—a fairy tale—come to life.

Mondscheinprinzessin.

"Free Albe!"

The first shout went up—then caught like a flashfire. It spread through the crowd until they were all stoked to a fervor. They all gazed up at the stage as though Sylvia had come to deliver their independence to them herself. Her lips parted in surprise. Lorelei could practically see her mind working as she arranged her features into something resembling composure.

"Thank you for telling the tale so beautifully." She scanned the crowd as if acknowledging each of them. "The strength of a nation lies in its people—the common people. Stories like this shouldn't be forgotten. They teach us about who we are and where we come from."

Sylvia was deluded if she believed her own words. Stories taught them nothing of how they *actually* were. They were like molten steel, ready to be molded into a weapon by one clever enough to wield them.

"I have traveled to many places around the world and across the kingdom. Saint Bruno's story is our own, but many of our folktales are told across Brunnestaad—perhaps not with the same words, but with the same heart."

Murmurs broke out among the crowd.

"I know many of you do not consider yourselves Brunnestader. Some of you may even be older than Brunnestaad itself." She smiled indulgently at the shouts of agreement. "I hear your yearning for the day that Albe will be independent again. Perhaps some of you have even begun planning to fight for that day."

Lorelei could only look on in horror as the murmurs intensified to a steady *yes, yes, yes*. What was she *doing*, encouraging these incipient sparks of rebellion?

"However," Sylvia continued, "the world is changing, and we cannot stand alone."

The crowds fell silent.

"Our enemies beyond our borders are many. I have fought alongside His Majesty King Wilhelm before, and when the time comes that he calls on our might again, I will stand with him. In turn, he will protect us, just as Saint Bruno once did, and I believe he is a worthy successor to his power." She rested a fist over her heart. "Wilhelm is the king of *all* Brunnestaad—the king of Albe. Will you join me?"

There was no more than a beat of silence before the crowd erupted into cheers. Sylvia's expression remained determined, but Lorelei could see the strain behind it.

The greatest threat to Wilhelm's reign is Albe. What if he chooses to charge me with Ziegler's murder?

Lorelei could not imagine how much it cost Sylvia to stand in front of these people and pledge her loyalty to a man she worried might turn on her. Lorelei recognized that desperate fear in her eyes all too well. It was the look of someone with something to prove.

Sylvia stepped off the stage. The crowds parted for her, some people dropping to their knees at her feet, some reaching out to touch the snowy fall of her moonlit hair or catch the hem of her cloak. With utmost grace, she grasped their hands and blessed them with her smiles.

A group of villagers pushed wheelbarrows into the square. Inside were three crude effigies made of bundled straw. One wore a Javenish flag around its neck. The second she thought was meant to be Wilhelm, with his scarlet regalia and a crown woven crudely from branches. The last wore a black coat with a golden ring stitched on the lapel: a Yeva.

Lorelei's stomach curdled. Common enemies, indeed.

Adelheid seized her elbow, and Lorelei could not find it in herself to pull away. "You need to leave."

Two men hoisted Wilhelm's effigy onto their shoulders and began parading him through the square to raucous laughter and chants of *All hail the king of Albe.* Through the chaos unfolding, Lorelei watched a woman raise a torch to the remaining two effigies. Flames ripped up the straw. The sight of that blistering black coat struck Lorelei cold with dread.

"Now, Lorelei," Adelheid said sharply.

"Fuck," Lorelei muttered, feeling oddly dazed. "Right."

But where was she supposed to go? Where *could* she go? The hot press of bodies hemmed them in on all sides, jostling them as they whirled and shouted.

Sylvia's gaze found Lorelei's in an instant, as though drawn to her by a tether. Panic—and regret—knifed its way into her expression. Lorelei could hardly bear to look at her. The fierce, protective determination in her eyes felt in that moment like an unbreakable shield.

Sylvia fought through the crowds, but in the numb haze that had befallen Lorelei, it felt almost as though Sylvia had appeared at her side. The hem of her cloak fluttered behind her as she walked, revealing her hand curled around the hilt of her saber.

"Stay close to me."

What could Lorelei do but obey? All she could see was Sylvia's white hair stained blood red as fire leapt into the darkening sky.

TWELVE

THE MORNING AFTER the Feast Day of Saint Bruno, they set out at first light.

According to the old woman's legend, the Ursprung lay high in the mountains that kept watch over the village: at the peak of the tallest one, which the villagers called Himmelstechen. A gamble, Lorelei supposed, to put all their faith in a fairy tale. But with no equipment—and no Ziegler—it was the only lead they had left.

Their host, Emilia, had all but begged them not to go. If the forest itself (which evidently had a tendency to rearrange itself after dark) did not drive them to madness or kill them, the wildeleute within it almost certainly would. It had become something of a tradition for the bravest and most virtuous in the region to summit Himmelstechen in search of the Ursprung. None had succeeded.

What a waste, Lorelei thought. At this point, surely they'd have adjusted their metric of virtue to account for all the pointless untimely deaths.

But without a doubt, Emilia had concluded, *a descendant of the Saint himself will prove worthy.*

Sylvia had smiled a thin, pained smile at that. The rest of them exchanged looks and were, however briefly, united in their exasperation.

A descendant of the Saint himself. Lorelei still could not fathom why Sylvia never mentioned it before. It seemed the type of thing she would find every occasion to mention. Lorelei could conjure her voice so clearly, full of pomp and undeserved pride. *Why, yes, naturally the von Wolff line can trace its ancestry back to Albe's most important folk hero. That is why I am such a gift to all humanity. Ha, ha!*

Perhaps that last part was uncharitable. Still, her point stood. Humble, Sylvia von Wolff was not. But saintly? In that moment last night—gilded by firelight as she said, *Stay close to me*—Lorelei might have believed it.

No, no, no. Her intervention was nothing more than that hero complex of hers at work again. At any rate, it was far easier to be annoyed with her than to even touch this knot of emotion that had taken up residence inside Lorelei's chest.

Sylvia had set a needlessly grueling pace for their hike. Johann and Adelheid easily kept up with her, but Lorelei—who had never stood in the shadow of a mountain before, much less climbed one—had fallen behind. At one point, Ludwig wandered off alone for upward of ten minutes. Lorelei eventually found him knee-deep and sopping wet in the middle of a stream, clutching a bundle of plant specimens. After that, she left him to his own devices. Heike, it seemed, had given up entirely. Some five kilometers ago, she muttered, "Fuck this," and slowed to an ambling stroll. The rest of them stopped every now and again to let her catch up.

Lorelei glanced over her shoulder to see that Heike had all but collapsed onto the trunk of a downed tree. Once Lorelei had recovered from the shock of the festival last night, she could not stop turning Adelheid's words over: *Some of us, I fear, cannot set aside ambition for the greater good.*

She'd meant Heike.

It made a terrible kind of sense. Heike had always been transparent about protecting her own interests—and the more Lorelei dwelled on it, the more her behavior made sense. She'd been trying to sabotage them from the beginning. They'd taken a detour that nearly killed them, then were stranded in that godforsaken village, all because they'd listened to her. She had been the first to bring up Lorelei's ability to channel aether—almost as though she'd wanted to turn the others against her.

The only thing Lorelei needed to make certain of was her motive.

The thick layer of pine litter muffled the sound of Lorelei's footsteps as she approached. Heike sat clutching her side, her face glistening with sweat and flushed with exertion. Her waterskin lay empty beside her, and her backpack was slumped beneath a tree a few meters back. When she noticed Lorelei, she startled. For just a moment, her eyes shone with alarm. Then, she arranged her features into a sneer and crossed her legs primly, as though she lounged on a throne of her own making.

The distant sounds of burbling water and birdsong filled the silence between them. A narrow stream streaked through the woods just beside them, its surface shining brilliant white beneath the sun. Through rasping breaths, Heike said, "Come to mock me, have you?"

"I've come to make sure you're alive." Lorelei offered her waterskin to Heike, but Heike stared at it as though it were a dead rat Lorelei had dropped at her feet. Lorelei shrugged and took a swig. "Suit yourself."

Heike's eyes flashed warily. "What do you really want?"

Heike did not like her or trust her; that much was abundantly clear. It suited Lorelei fine. She much preferred a direct approach. Now, how best to get her talking?

"I've found myself curious as to why you came on this expedition." Lorelei examined the mud-stained hem of Heike's finely woven walking skirt, then the fat gemstone—one she hadn't grown bored of, evidently—glistering on her thumb. "You rarely went on your own research trips—and the ones you did undertake, you relied on assistants for data collection. Why put yourself through this?"

Heike lifted one elegant shoulder. "Can't a girl do an old friend a favor?"

Evasive, Lorelei noted. Perhaps she'd respond better to provo-
cation. "I find it hard to believe you'd do something without expecting anything in return."

"Ouch, Lori." She touched a hand to her heart. "That hurts my
feelings. I do have them, you know."

"I do know. I sympathize with them, as a matter of fact."

Heike made a derisive noise. "Oh, do you?"

"Or perhaps I've misread you," Lorelei said, "and you're as selfish and sad as you seem, harboring a lifetime of resentment because of a little wound to your pride. Did von Wolff's rejection
sting that badly?"

"Excuse me?" Heike bristled, rising to her feet. "I don't know
where you heard that or what game you're playing, you snake, but
you don't know the first thing about my situation. You don't get to
judge me."

At last, she'd struck a nerve.

*She has always wanted to leave home—by whatever means possi-
ble,* Ludwig had told her. *Sylvia knew that. We all did.*

Lorelei retrieved Heike's backpack from the ground, then held
it out to her by the strap. "That's what I thought. She abandoned
you."

Heike watched her apprehensively, her shoulders coiling tight
with tension. Lorelei could practically see the gears whirring in
Heike's mind as the cornered-prey gleam in her eyes dulled to calculating certainty. Scheming the best way to twist Lorelei's sym-
pathies in her favor, no doubt.

Good, Lorelei thought. Better for Heike to believe that she
could be manipulated.

"If you must know, I *am* here because Wilhelm doesn't trust
anyone but us." Heike snatched the backpack from her and reluctantly slung it over her shoulders. "However, I have been sitting on
a marriage proposal from the prince of Gansland for many years.
He expects an answer when I return."

The prince of Gansland, from what Lorelei understood, was

twice Heike's age—and a widower twice over, at that. After rumors began swirling about what exactly had happened to his young, pretty wives, some had taken to calling him the Prince of Black Doves. A reference, of course, to one of Brunnestaad's crueler tales.

Back in the days when wishes still held power, a peasant girl married a rich and handsome man. As a wedding gift, her mother gave her three messenger doves: a red one to send word she was happy, a white one for when she was ill, and a black one if she ever ran afoul of her husband. Her husband gave her a ring of keys— and free rein of all the rooms in his home, save one. Naturally, when he left on a hunting trip, the intrepid maiden opened the forbidden door—and found eight dead women hanging from his rafters.

Side by side, they began to hike again. Dead leaves crunched underfoot with every step, and overhead, the canopy swayed in the wind. Jagged shadows stirred to life around them.

"Surely, you can decline," said Lorelei.

"I was forbidden from turning him down unless I had a more attractive offer in hand. Mother dearest wouldn't dream of offending him. You know how thorny the relationship between Sorvig and Gansland can be."

Over the centuries, Sorvig had won its independence from Gansland time and time again. Sorvig culture owed a great deal to Gansland: its seafaring, its appreciation for the arts, its cuisine of bread and things atop bread alone. If they wanted to seize Sorvig again, they would have to go to war with Brunnestaad. "Why should that matter?"

"Because my mother must always have an escape route. Besides, many believe Sorvig was better off under Ganish rule," Heike said flatly. "If Wilhelm cannot maintain control of the kingdom, we can run into their arms again. As for me, I am to want nothing. If this pleases her, who am I to disobey?"

Despite herself, Lorelei almost felt a pang of disgust on her behalf.

"After Sylvia turned me down, I *begged* Mother to let me attend university with the others. They like their girls educated in Gansland, after all." Heike scoffed. "I thought I could find another suitable match by the time I finished my degree. I took as long as I possibly could. Alas."

Lorelei refrained from inquiring about Adelheid. She supposed there was little favor to gain in Heike's mother's eyes from the heiress of a crumbling province.

"I thought I couldn't stave him off any longer. Then, the opportunity for this expedition arose. I simply couldn't refuse a request from our king."

The Ursprung being found in Sorvig was her final gambit. And now her options had officially run out. "And if you went against her wishes?"

"I would surrender my inheritance." Heike looked at Lorelei as though she'd well and truly lost her mind. "I would sooner die."

"Is status truly worth more than your life?"

"You wouldn't understand. It *is* my life," Heike said lowly. A wash of sunlight had set her auburn hair ablaze. "I am a princess. Outside my mother's home, that is the only thing that protects me."

But Lorelei did understand.

As Heike stormed ahead of her, all Lorelei could think of was the tale of "The Girl in the Tower"—the story of a beautiful girl locked away in a tower by her cruel, controlling mother. Every evening, the girl let down her long hair, allowing her mother to climb up to her lonely window. It was a wretched, isolated existence—until, of course, a prince happened upon her.

But no prince had come to rescue Heike.

Heike was beautiful, and she had suffered. If the tales her nursemaids told her had any truth to them, that should have been enough. But life was far crueler than stories, and so she'd hatched a plan to rescue herself: sabotage the expedition—and prevent Sylvia from stealing what was rightfully hers.

Now Lorelei had to prove it.

After five days of hiking, morale was low.

The first three days of their efforts had been rewarded with steady upward progress. Over the next two, however, it became clear that they were wandering in circles. No matter how far they walked—even if they walked in one direction, according to Heike's compass—they inevitably found themselves back where they began: a clearing surrounded by a grove of firs.

Lorelei expected to see it again soon enough.

She trudged along at the rear of their grim, single-file line. Everything ached, and at this point in their ascent, the air almost hurt to breathe. Frigid mist poured steadily down the mountainside, and frost glittered in the long shadows the trees cast over the earth. She'd never experienced cold like this before. She could feel it in her *nose*.

The sound of Ludwig's desperate laughter filtered back to her. "Home sweet home!"

"Are you joking?" Heike groused. Then, a few seconds later: "I'm going to scream."

"Have we gone in a circle again?" Apparently, Sylvia's optimism had not yet been crushed; she sounded equally disappointed and surprised. "This is an extraordinarily powerful enchantment. I have never seen anything quite like it."

Johann and Adelheid only exchanged a weary look. Lorelei followed close behind them, ducking beneath a low-hanging branch. Lo and behold, she found herself standing on the edge of their clearing.

Adelheid reached up to pluck a bramble out of Johann's hair. She sighed thinly. "Well, I suppose I'll prepare dinner."

At this rate, they'd run out of food before they reached the summit.

As Johann and Adelheid made a fire, Sylvia set to work warding the area, nailing iron into the ground around the perimeter and hanging bells from the low-hanging branches. Ludwig began unpacking his tent and their cooking supplies. Heike dropped her backpack on the ground and laid her head atop it. Content, as always, to do nothing useful for anyone but herself.

Wind gusted through the clearing, carrying with it the cold, bright scent of sap and evergreen. As it died down, Lorelei could smell woodsmoke wafting from the cooking fire. It might have been pleasant, if not for the unsettling cast of the sky. For days, no matter what time it was, it was dusk-purple and lit with strange stars that sparkled like crushed glass. If Lorelei's pocket watch was to be believed, it was early evening.

She settled herself on a flat stretch of stone and pulled out her notebook. She had checked every night for some detail in a folktale she might have missed, some trick that would free them from this endless loop, but nothing new revealed itself.

Perhaps it was frustration, or perhaps it was despair. But out of some long-forgotten impulse, she began to write to her sister.

Rahel, the youngest of them, had been a sickly child. When Lorelei ran out of books to read to her, she had made up stories to keep her occupied on the days she could not rise from bed. Little tales of adventure and danger, most of them heavily inspired by Ziegler's travelogues—whatever captured the imagination of an antsy, eager child. It did not require much creativity now to describe the exploits of the Ruhigburg Expedition. And yet, the more she wrote, the more certain she grew that she could never send this letter.

At sixteen, the cruelty of this world had not yet touched Rahel. She was too young to remember Aaron, and it wasn't as though Lorelei was in the habit of confiding in her family about the treatment she endured at university.

Sylvia's question haunted her even now. *Where is your sense of wonder?*

Perhaps she had crushed it long ago. The world as she saw it was too ugly and painful to share. Loneliness opened within her chest, too quickly for her to suppress. She could not help thinking of her least favorite of the Ursprung tales, one she had collected from an old Ebulisch woman.

Back in the days when wishes still held power, there was a thief who, while running from his troubles, stumbled and fell into a hole. When he came to, he found himself in total darkness—and face-to-face with a lindworm's glowing eyes. The thief expected to be devoured outright, but to his shock, the beast led him deeper into its lair.

At the heart of an underground cavern was a spring filled with water that shone as bright and golden as the sun. The man feared he would starve before anyone came to rescue him, but as the days went by, he realized that so long as he drank of the spring, he never knew hunger or thirst. For three long years, the thief lived in darkness with no one but his lindworm for company.

Now, there came a day when an earthquake caused the roof of their prison—their home, really, as he'd come to think of it—to collapse. The lindworm stretched toward the sunlight, and the thief climbed the spines along its back to freedom. When they reached the surface, they lay down beneath a copse of trees to rest.

It so happened that a soldier came passing by at that very moment. She had long dreamed of being a hero, and so, seizing her opportunity, she strung heavy iron chains around the sleeping lindworm's neck. The thief awoke at the racket, just in time to see the soldier draw her sword. He considered escaping, for if he was recognized, the soldier might arrest him. But he felt a tender sentiment for the lindworm who had saved his life, and so, he struck down the soldier with a rock and freed the beast from its chains. The lindworm regarded him for only the space of a breath before it crawled back into its cavern. The thief washed the blood from his hands and made the long journey back to his village.

He did not stop even once, for he never grew hungry or tired. But when he arrived at his mother's house, she did not recognize him. His neighbors claimed they'd never seen his face before. His name slipped through their minds like water through their open hands. Distraught, he returned to the one place he knew he still belonged, but the ground over the lindworm's lair had sealed itself shut once more.

Power, even given freely to the worthy, still came at too high a price. Wilhelm was such a fool to want it.

"Lorelei?"

Her pen dragged across the page, bleeding ink all over the illustration she'd absentmindedly begun. The lindworm emerging from its pool of gold now drowned in a sea of black. Perfect.

"Don't sneak up on me," she groused. "What did you say?"

She looked up to find Ludwig perched beside her. He held two bowls in his hands, filled to the brim with a thin stew Adelheid had made of their dwindling supplies: peas and slivers of jerky, from the looks of it. A piece of hardtack rose from its surface like a gravestone. Lorelei was too famished to care.

He passed a bowl to her. "I've been thinking."

Lorelei accepted it and reluctantly closed her notebook. The heat unfurled through her hands, and the steam wafting from its surface warmed her cold-stung cheeks. "That's not good."

"I think I know how to get us out of here."

"Oh?" Lorelei glanced up at him. "And how do you propose to do that?"

"I want to see if it works first before I tell you. It will be so embarrassing if I'm wrong," he said. "Just trust me."

"You saying that makes me trust you considerably less."

"Wilhelm promised me land."

The confession knocked her off guard. "Pardon?"

"I didn't really want to go on this expedition, to be honest, but he bribed me." Ludwig watched her with those clever-fox eyes of his. They were heavy with exhaustion and washed almost red in the firelight. "I'm not self-sabotaging enough to lead us astray. I have too much to lose."

"That," she said, "is exactly why I shouldn't trust you."

He smiled at that.

So Wilhelm intended to follow in his father's footsteps. If anyone challenged him, he would seize the lands of those who turned against him and elevate those who remained loyal. Ludwig had lived among the nobility his entire life, held close but never equal. But at the end of this, he wouldn't just have a courtesy title. He'd have the real thing.

"I cannot believe you'd become one of them," she said, feeling strangely disappointed that he felt the need to—what, demonstrate his loyalty to her? "But I do trust you. You didn't need to convince me."

"I'm touched," he said. "And quite surprised, to be honest. I'd expected some judgment. At least an insult or two."

How could she possibly judge him? She'd clawed her way onto this expedition in some desperate attempt to protect herself. If she were offered a title and land, she would be a fool to decline it. "Don't tempt me."

"No, no. Let's hear it."

"Have some self-respect, you traitor," she said without bite. "Et cetera."

"A little late for that." He folded one knee into his chest and draped his arm over it. "I know you won't like to hear it, but if it helps your investigation, I'm certain Sylvia is innocent."

"I am not—" At his cutting look, she huffed out a sigh. "Fine. Why is that?"

"She wrote to me fairly often during the war. The first letters she sent were about what you'd expect, but toward the end, there was something about them that troubled me. They were . . ." He thumbed his lip pensively, as though the word escaped him or none seemed sufficient. At last, he shrugged. "I was worried about her, so I asked her to stay with me for a few weeks when the fighting ended. I was shocked when she arrived in the state she did. I hadn't seen her in years, but it was like she was a completely different person. Haunted, I suppose."

Lorelei did not need to ask for more details. Although it surprised her, she could imagine it with perfect, horrible clarity. Her moonlit hair disheveled. Her pale silver eyes as empty as her own had been. All of her indefatigable enthusiasm quashed.

Hollowed out by ghosts.

"The only thing that seemed to cheer her up was this pack of kornhunds that lived in the cornfields on my property. She would go outside and watch them for hours after sunset."

Kornhunds were wildeleute who took the form of sight hounds. They ran atop gusts of wind with lightning sparking at their paws, bringing bad luck to anyone who gazed into their eyes. They were driven out of the fields when they were threshed, but during the growing season, they were menaces. They picked off children hunting for cornflowers and tore apart anyone who imitated their howls.

"One night, I looked out my window. It was pitch-dark, so all I could see was her hair and a spark of lightning. One of the hounds had come out of the corn, and Sylvia was crouched there on the edge of the field, waiting for it."

None of this sounded remotely surprising. But she supposed this was Sylvia before she was *Sylvia*. "What happened then?"

He laughed breathlessly. "Well, I grabbed my musket and ran outside, but by the time I got there, she was gone. That's likely for the best. Johann has tried to teach me a thousand times, but I'm a terrible shot.

"I looked for her for hours. And then, come morning, she

stumbled out of the corn. Her eyes were wild, and she was practically shouting in my ear from excitement. I couldn't understand a single thing she said. Because I was so . . . angry."

Lorelei couldn't picture Ludwig angry, but she could picture Sylvia with perfect clarity: tearing barefoot through the fields with a pack of wild dogs at her heels, lightning dancing around her, her hair unfurling into the dark like a war banner Lorelei would follow to her own death.

"I told her she was completely mad. I told her she could've died."

"And what did she say to that?"

"Nothing! She just laughed at me. And when she was finished, she said, *Isn't it beautiful, Ludwig? Isn't life incredible?*"

Lorelei stared straight ahead, unable to meet his eyes. Those infernal creatures had saved Sylvia's life. It brought to mind a lonely young girl in the Yevanverte, collecting bugs from the neighbors' garden and thinking it something like magic.

"And this," she said, "proves her innocence?"

"She isn't capable of killing. Not anymore—and not like that. She refuses to use magic. It upsets her too much."

Lorelei frowned. She supposed now that she thought about it, she had never seen Sylvia wield magic. "Why are you telling me this?"

"Consider it my parting gift," he said lightly. "Someone ought to figure this mess out, and it certainly won't be me."

I have figured it out. She trusted Ludwig, yes—even considered him a friend. But he liked Heike. She refused to drive a wedge between them without proof. Instead, she said, "Don't say things like that."

"Right. Morbid. Sorry," he said. "But really, if I don't come back, you should have that coat of mine you like so much. You remember which one I'm talking about?"

"Yes, yes." Lorelei scowled. "How generous."

For all their sakes, she prayed that his plan—whatever it was—worked.

Later that night, Lorelei slipped into her tent and watched the shadows draw long fingers across the canvas roof. The forest was eerily completely still. She heard no nighttime birds, no insects, no skitter of creatures in the dark. And yet, she could not shake the feeling that someone—or something—was watching them with malicious intent.

THIRTEEN

LORELEI AWOKE TO AN ACHE in her limbs and a cold that had settled into her bones. The first thing that reached her through the fog of her exhaustion was the faint scent of snow.

Now, that would be just their luck.

Outside her tent, that bruised-purple sky awaited her, maddeningly unchanging. The branches over the clearing knitted together like the gnarled, imposing latticework of a wrought-iron gate. No one else had stirred.

Coffee, she decided. It was the only way she could make it through another day of aimless wandering. She grabbed the kettle and walked to the stream that skirted the edge of camp. She knelt by the water and submerged the kettle, letting the current eddy around her wrists. Nothing but the burble of water cut up the silence, but she did not move until her fingers went bone white in the cold. The knot of unease pulled tighter within her. Even now, she couldn't shake the feeling that had chased her into sleep.

Something in this forest was watching them.

After returning to camp, she raked the coals back from the embers of their campfire and boiled water for coffee and oat porridge. They'd tragically run out of raisins yesterday—more accurately, Heike had eaten half of them herself—which left them with nothing but flavorless slop to look forward to.

One by one, the others stirred. Johann first, then Adelheid. They sat side by side, grim and golden-haired. After the most perfunctory of greetings, the three of them sat in silence, which suited

Lorelei fine. She didn't feel compelled to start a conversation with either of them as they brooded by the fire's glow. Within a few moments, a cup of coffee and a bowl of porridge materialized in Adelheid's hands—courtesy of Johann. He fed her before he thought to fix himself a thing.

Heike emerged some twenty minutes later. She let out an exaggerated yawn, but before she could issue a single word of complaint, Adelheid shoved a cup of coffee into her hands. Only a few moments later, Sylvia crawled from her tent. It never failed to amaze Lorelei how wild her hair was—and how incapable she was of managing it. She'd wrangled it into a loose approximation of a chignon at the nape of her neck. It looked more like a knot, with a few stray curls making their bold escape. Lorelei reminded herself to stop staring.

Sylvia paused at the sight of the four of them. "Where is Ludwig?"

Heike took a sip of her coffee. "Still sleeping, I assume. We're out of tea, by the by. Sorry."

She did not sound very sorry at all. Sylvia sighed. "Oh dear. Well, I suppose it's for the best. What we got in town was hardly worth brewing at all."

Adelheid rose from her seat. "I'll check on Ludwig. We've wasted enough time already."

"Good thinking, Addie," Heike said with a lazy wave of her hand. "We cannot be late for our daily exercise in futility."

Adelheid pointedly ignored her.

"It's unwise to make light of evil," Johann said. "There must be some escape from this foul magic."

"Yes, yes, I'm sure we will find one today." Heike rolled her eyes. "You are such a bore sometimes."

Adelheid rustled Ludwig's tent to announce herself. When no answer came, she made quick work of the buttons on the canvas. After a moment, she turned around with a puzzled expression. "He's gone."

Indeed, his tent was completely empty—as though both Ludwig and all his belongings had been spirited away in the night.

Consider it my parting gift, Ludwig had said, all but winking at her.

The memory slammed into her with force. At the time, she'd taken it as a self-deprecating joke, but now she wasn't so sure. Goddamn him. She should have demanded more information from him—or at least asked how long he expected to be gone. All that she knew was that she'd been the last one to speak to him, and that he'd told no one else of his plans. The knot of apprehension within her grew heavy. If they knew he'd gone looking for a way up the mountain, would they accuse her of sabotage?

She did not intend to find out.

"Last night, he told me he was going to look for a night-blooming plant," Lorelei said. "I'm sure he'll be back soon enough."

But by the time they struck camp and passed out their meager ration of dried meat for the afternoon, Ludwig still had not returned. Adelheid and Johann bickered over the remains of their campfire. Heike had taken to doodling in one of her notebooks, her head resting in Adelheid's lap.

Sylvia, however, was pacing restlessly. It was making Lorelei's blood pressure rise. Just as she opened her mouth to tell her to sit down, Sylvia stopped dead. The color of her eyes matched the eerie violet of the skies overhead. "Do you think he got lost?"

Heike did not look up from her sketchbook. When she spoke, her voice dripped with sarcasm. "Oh yes. I definitely think he's lost."

"What are you suggesting?" Adelheid asked wearily.

"Me, suggesting something? Never." Heike set aside her pen and sat upright. "Lori, what was it you said he planned to do?"

"He wanted to find a night-blooming plant." Spitefully, Lorelei added, "Although I believe the word he used was *nocturnal*."

"How fascinating," Heike said. "Which one?"

Her green, catlike eyes gleamed in the twilight. In them, Lorelei saw pure, calculating malice. The other day, Heike had tried to win her over with her sob story. Had she killed anyone but Ziegler, it might have worked. Heike clearly knew it; the only recourse she had left was to turn the others against her.

"I don't know." Lorelei struggled to keep the hostility out of her voice. "He was rather evasive about it, actually."

"Mm." Heike cut her gaze to Johann and Adelheid meaningfully. "And now he's disappeared. What do you make of that?"

"How mysterious," Johann said drolly.

Disappeared seemed rather dramatic, but Lorelei did not like the idea of him alone in these woods. Surely, he wouldn't have tried to summit the mountain alone. He should have returned by now.

"You are only trying to create drama," Sylvia said exasperatedly. "He brought all his things with him, except for his tent. He obviously intended to be back in time to sleep. He's lost—or injured. We need to look for him."

"We need to be strategic about this." Adelheid smoothed her hands over her skirts. "If he returns and finds us gone, he'll go looking for us. We'll never find one another again. It would be wise to divide ourselves into two groups: one to stay here and one to search."

"I'll go," Lorelei said. "But if he's injured, I can't carry him back on my own."

No one volunteered.

Lorelei swept her gaze over the others. Sylvia did not look at her. Unsurprising, she supposed. They hadn't spoken since the day of the festival. The others, huddled by the remains of the fire, had clearly come to some kind of understanding, discussed and decided upon without words. It was a language she'd come to understand well: *us against them*. Lorelei wasn't surprised, only bitterly disappointed. Whatever scrap of power she had been gifted by Wilhelm meant nothing.

She'd been exiled.

Lorelei snatched her backpack from the ground and threw it over her shoulder. She wanted to bear it stoically, but the leering dark between the trees and the serrated ridge of the mountain beyond unnerved her. She'd never braved the wilderness on her own. If anything happened—or if they chose to head back down the mountain without her—she'd be dead. No one would come for her. No one would tell her family what happened.

Then, Sylvia huffed. "Such bravery and selflessness on display. What shining examples of the nobility you all are. I'll go with you."

Once again, that petty, helpless impulse to lash out rose up within her. She wanted to sneer—to reject her help, if only to spite her. She did not want her pity. She did not need it. But she couldn't do this alone.

"Fine," Lorelei said. "Let's go."

To her utter humiliation, she'd failed to keep strangled hurt out of her voice.

Lorelei knew very well they might be marching to their deaths. But outside that damned clearing, she felt oddly lighter. Sylvia, meanwhile, had grown sulky and petulant, dragging her feet as they trudged through the forest's underbrush. Every now and again, she muttered something or other about cowardice and the decay of virtue. For her own sanity, Lorelei let the sound of her voice recede into meaningless noise. If she acknowledged her at all, inevitably they would have to discuss the way Sylvia had leapt to her protection. *Twice.* Lorelei would sooner die.

Bitter cold held the world in its grip, and the air hung heavy and still with the threat of snow. They had wandered this stretch of the woods so many times, it had ceased to be remarkable. And yet, she did not know what to expect anymore; anything seemed possible. Ludwig crumpled on the forest floor. Ludwig emerging from the thicket with his sly, quicksilver grin. Ludwig waiting for them back at camp as though he had never vanished at all.

No, she was not so optimistic as to expect that.

They walked for what felt like hours in grim silence. Lorelei strained to notice anything out of the ordinary, but all around her was interminable green, and overhead was the tangle of pine boughs. God, she couldn't wait to return to the heaving sprawl and noise of the city. Then she remembered that if she did not find the Ursprung—or convincing enough evidence to pin the murder on Heike—she would never go home again.

What am I doing? Walking in circles, looking for a needle in a haystack . . . They would never find him at this rate. All of this was completely, utterly pointless, and—

Something about the tree in front of her caught her eye: an L-shaped mark carved into the trunk. Yesterday, when they'd realized just how lost they were, they'd made a few attempts to record where they'd already been. Johann—to Ludwig's dismay—had slashed a few trees deep enough that they bled sap. But these cuts were careful, shallow, and precise.

Had Ludwig done this?

Lorelei paused to inspect it. Nothing about the tree seemed terribly unusual at first glance. Then, she spotted the mushrooms sprouting from its roots. Their bell-shaped caps looked to be shingled and dripping with liquid aether. It pooled on the earth below, indigo and shimmering.

Sylvia appeared over her shoulder. "Well done, Lorelei!"

Lorelei nearly leapt out of her skin. "Don't scare me like that," she snapped. Her heart was pounding far too loudly. "What am I looking at?"

"A gate," Sylvia said.

"To *what?*"

"Freedom." Her entire being lit up. "As you know, many wildeleute can ensorcell people. Take nixies and their magnetic songs, for example. You will also sometimes find that places with high concentrations of aether become shrouded in a sort of ambient enchantment, often to protect themselves."

Lorelei frowned. "And you think this is such a place?"

"It must be! I don't know why I didn't think of it before. Ludwig was working on a paper many years ago about this phenomenon. He noticed that the bounds of these aetherically charged places are often marked with unusual flora. Oftentimes, the area of effect is quite small: say, the center of a ring of mushrooms or the shade cast by a lone tree in the middle of an empty field. But in this case . . ." Sylvia swept her hand out. "There's a gate. Do you see it?"

To her surprise, she did.

Two narrow trees leaned toward each other, their branches twining elegantly together like a pediment over a doorway. Mushrooms—all of them faintly iridescent in the twilit glow of the woods—carpeted the earth between them.

"Shall we?" Lorelei asked.

Feeling foolish, she squeezed through the narrow gap between the trunks. There was no sudden flood of light, no shiver of magic that passed over her skin. She was almost disappointed. But after a few paces, the landscape began to change. A light dusting of snow glittered on the ground, and delicate icicles dripped from the branches. And there, rising high above the trees, was their destination: the summit, shrouded in a skein of mist as delicate as gossamer. Whatever spell of suspension the woods had imprisoned them in had broken.

Ludwig really had done it.

"How marvelous!" Sylvia's boots crunched in the snowfall as she trailed after Lorelei. "The others will be thrilled to know we've found a way forward—and Ludwig, too, to have another data point for his project." She evidently found Lorelei an inattentive audience, for she asked, with renewed indignation, "Where on earth are we going?"

"Toward the Ursprung."

Sylvia dug her heels in. "What? What about Ludwig?"

Lorelei sighed through her teeth. "He left camp to find a way out of those woods. If that's all he intended to do, he would have come back. I expect he made his way to the summit."

"But you said—"

"Forget what I said!" Her temper flared helplessly at her confusion. "I lied."

The grave disapproval on Sylvia's face rankled her. "I see. Setting that aside for the time being, we cannot just go . . ." She gestured vaguely. ". . . up."

"That is exactly what we are going to do." With that, Lorelei pressed onward in the general direction of the summit.

Sylvia let out a sound of frustration. "You are being stubborn. It's not that simple."

"You have been a great help so far, but—"

"First of all, it's deeply unsettling to hear you compliment me in such an acid tone. Second of all—" Sylvia cut herself off. "Will you stop walking for one moment and listen to me?"

Lorelei stopped so suddenly, they almost collided. "I *am* listening."

"Then look at me!"

Lorelei drew in a deep breath and reluctantly turned around. Sylvia's eyes were as cool as lake water, but they were flung wide and her face was flushed. If Lorelei didn't know better, she'd say she looked almost flustered.

"Thank you." Sylvia huffed out a shaky breath. "As I was saying. Second of all, I refuse to submit to the tyranny of . . . of . . . !"

"Do finish that thought."

Lorelei thought she heard her mutter something to the effect of *a scowling wax bean.* Sylvia threw her hands in the air, exasperated. "You may be the leader of the expedition, but I'm not a knight on a chessboard to be moved around at your pleasure. I have expertise you might find useful if we hope to find Ludwig and make it out of this unharmed."

Sometimes, that obstinate streak of hers was horribly inconvenient. As much as Lorelei wanted to dismiss her, Sylvia had managed to put together what Lorelei had not. Lorelei had no survival skills to speak of and limited knowledge of the creatures that prowled the mountainside. She could not afford to ignore Sylvia.

"Fine," Lorelei snarled. "We'll do it your way."

"And! How do you hope to find— Oh." The anger dropped clean off her face. "You agreed? I'd expected more of a fight."

"Do I want to know what you were going to say?"

"Forests protected by eschenfrau rearrange themselves," Sylvia said, sounding just a little smug. "You'd never make it to the summit without me."

Lorelei might have been impressed were she not so chilled by the thought of being lost in an ever-shifting labyrinth of trees. "And you know how to navigate?"

"If Ziegler's theory is correct, we don't need a dowsing machine to track a source of magic." Sylvia beamed. "The wildeleute can guide us there."

Lorelei felt another headache coming on. "You're joking."

Sylvia's expression soured. "I'm very serious! Of course, if you'd like to try to—"

"We don't have any more time to waste. Don't speak. *Walk*."

To Sylvia's credit, she did.

Although the sky had lightened to lavender as the day wore on, the silence of the forest grew no less oppressive. No birdsong broke the steady crunch of their feet against the snow underfoot. Sylvia walked slightly ahead of her. She'd pinned the wild mass of her chignon in place with a hairpin capped with a red glass bead, as bright as a drop of blood. Lorelei was still considering it when

Sylvia stopped dead, her arm held out in warning. Lorelei nearly crashed into her.

"Ash trees."

A copse of them stood like a group of crones, gnarled and ancient and implacably disapproving. Their branches tangled so thick she could not see the bruising sky or those eerie pinpricks of starlight. Even in this bitter cold, clusters of silver berries, as delicate and shining as ice crystals, hung from their boughs. They were as tempting as the long slivers of bark that curled like fiddleheads, begging to be peeled off. Lorelei had the distinct impression that taking anything would be a fatal mistake.

Sylvia pulled a flask from her bag and approached the tallest of them. Its roots had erupted from the earth and twisted into the shape of a skull. She poured water over it, murmuring softly to herself. "Now I sacrifice so that you do no harm."

The leaves shivered in response. It sounded like a woman sighing.

"Don't touch any of these trees." So that confirmed her suspicion. Sylvia jabbed a finger at Lorelei. "Better yet, do not think about them at all. Do not walk in front of me, either. The eschenfrau are very particular about their offerings."

"Yes, yes, I understand."

Sylvia gave her a considering look before corking her flask. They continued up the mountainside in silence, flanked by rows and rows of ash. It was terrible. On an ordinary day, Lorelei might have celebrated the small victory of managing to stem the flow of Sylvia's unfailing chatter. But the trees' leering presence made her long for one of Sylvia's sparkling-bright moods. She rarely found herself in a position where she needed to start a conversation with Sylvia, and she was hard-pressed to think of a topic that wouldn't devolve into bickering.

"Tell me," she tried. "Where did you acquire all your arcane knowledge about the wildeleute?"

Sylvia glanced over her shoulder. "You really want to know?"

Lorelei leveled her with an impatient look. "I wouldn't have asked otherwise."

Sylvia stopped to pour water over the roots of another tree. The dark, rich smell of damp soil rose around them. "Much of Albe is wild and untamed; we haven't driven our wildeleute out as they have in Ruhigburg. My nursemaids told me all sorts of tales, and I grew up chasing sylphs through the woods outside my home. I saw many wildeleute during the war as well. Many of them fled their natural habitats, but many more were drawn to the carnage. Eventually, I came to understand that even the most fearsome of them can be communicated with, if you care enough to learn how."

"How did you learn?"

"Trial and error, mostly." She smiled almost shyly. "And I suppose I talked to people. My soldiers told me about their lives, about the stories their mothers had told them. I believe that's why I am still alive and so many others are not."

It felt terrible to carry the weight of what Ludwig had told her, to hold on to it alongside this half confession. Lorelei had known the depths of despair and had forged herself on the iron of that pain. She hadn't imagined Sylvia knew something of that, too. Lorelei had once believed her life to be so charmed.

It *was* charmed, she reminded herself. Hardship she had chosen did not undo that. Under no circumstances would she begin to feel sorry for Sylvia von Wolff.

"I see," said Lorelei, more coldly than she had intended.

Sylvia looked stung only for a moment before turning back toward the path. "And you? Do you really know so little about them?"

"I have lived in the city all my life, so I'm afraid I had no opportunity to frolic among them as you did. Yevani used to have house spirits, but most of them haven't survived." Her grandfather, also a shoemaker by trade, apparently had a shretele that would finish any shoes he left out after the workday ended. It never asked for anything in return. "They defended their homes quite fiercely, but there is only so much that can be done."

"I'm sorry." Sylvia sounded earnestly sad. "People are unspeakably cruel."

As they walked, Lorelei could feel the attention of those pale-barked trees on them. It unsettled her, the bark rippling, the knotholes seeming to blink like eyes. Little voices whispered in the flutter of the leaves. Sylvia walked as though she belonged among them, as ethereal as the sylphs she'd followed as a girl.

Something crunched beneath Lorelei's boot. When she glanced down, she saw something glitter with a reflection of the unnatural twilight. She bent down and retrieved a shard of glass. "I found something."

"What is it?" Sylvia grabbed her wrist, startling her, and inspected the glass in her palm. Her face paled, but it took a moment longer than she would have liked for Sylvia to let her go. "This looks like a piece of one of Ludwig's collection vials. Do you think he's . . . ?"

Wind gusted through the trees. Their branches clattered. Their leaves hissed. All at once, they went silent.

A warning.

As storm clouds clawed their way across the sky, darkness closed like a fist around them. And then, cutting through the eerie quiet: a scream.

FOURTEEN

THE SOUND ECHOED THROUGH THE TREES, distorted. It seemed to come from everywhere and nowhere. Sylvia's hand flew to the saber at her hip. "Stay behind me."

Lorelei almost resented the implication that she needed protecting. But with that cry ringing out in the deepening night, she didn't feel much acid behind the insult readied on her tongue. Swallowing it back down, she followed Sylvia into the ash grove. They clambered over the roots and pushed through the curtains of leaves. Lorelei did her best not to shudder at the phantom sensation of tiny hands pulling at her hair and the hem of her coat.

The scream came tearing through the woods again, louder this time.

"It sounds like it's coming from above us." Sylvia pointed at a rocky outcropping. A cascade of water tumbled off its lip and into a narrow stream. "Up there."

A thicket of pine loomed nearly five meters above them. There was no clear path forward; they'd have to climb. With no hesitation, Sylvia hoisted herself up, fitting her boots and hands into small grooves in the rockface. Lorelei kept up as best she could, but the stone was treacherously slick beneath her fingers—and as cold as death. When she looked up, Sylvia had already scaled the cliff. It hardly seemed fair.

Lorelei reached for another handhold, a sharp edge of rock jutting out less than a meter above her. But just as she transferred her weight, it slipped free. It plummeted and clattered to the ground below. Lorelei swore, pressing herself as flat as she could as she struggled to find purchase. Terror had made her woozy, and her fingers ached.

"Lorelei!"

Sylvia's outstretched hand appeared before her. For a moment, Lorelei was stunned at how easily she reached for her. Shifting her balance, Lorelei clasped her forearm and grunted as Sylvia yanked her bodily onto solid ground.

Sylvia flopped onto her back, one hand draped over the labored rise and fall of her chest. Her face was flushed with effort. "Saints, you're heavier than you look."

"I'm carrying a full bag!"

The scream came again, frayed with desperation. Without a word, they shot to their feet and darted into the underbrush. As Lorelei shoved through heavy boughs of pine, she could hear the sound of churning water. She felt imprisoned in that alpdrücke dream: water slipping into her mouth like cold fingers, hands closing around her wrists. She stumbled out into a clearing. Stretched out before them was a shallow pond. At the center, someone thrashed in the water.

No, some*thing*.

At their approach, the movement stopped suddenly. The figure slowly turned toward them. Its mouth was twisted into a merry, wicked grin. Each tooth gleamed, deadly sharp and as yellowed as a sun-bleached bone. It wore a long, hooded cloak that concealed its body and most of its face from view. The garment was roughly woven from reeds and algae, and it glittered with bright-blue sea glass and smooth river stones. As the creature moved, they clattered together, hypnotizingly musical. It made a little sweeping gesture, as if to say *ta-da*.

Sylvia groaned. "Of course."

"What is that thing?" Lorelei asked flatly.

"A schellenrock," she said. "They enjoy making mischief. It must've heard us coming and hoped to sidetrack us."

The schellenrock seemed to wilt a little under Lorelei's impassive glare. "If that was meant to be funny, I'm not laughing."

"Please behave," Sylvia hissed. "They're very easily offended. You don't want to see it angry."

"We don't have time—"

She saw red as Sylvia held up a placating hand. "It may be able to help us. Give me just a moment."

She picked her way slowly toward the pond, stepping carefully around fat white mushrooms. With the same tenderness she'd reserved for the village children, she crouched at the edge of the water and dipped a finger into it. The surface rippled at her touch.

"Good afternoon, sir," she said. "We don't mean to intrude in your territory. We're looking for a friend. A man, just a bit taller than me but shorter than her. Brown hair. Wears a vasculum . . ." Here, she paused and amended, "A tube around his neck. He is always shoving plants into it. Have you seen him pass by?"

The schellenrock seemed unimpressed. From within the recesses of its hood, a set of citrine-yellow eyes blinked slowly. It inspected the hem of its cloak, twirling this way and that as if it were infinitely more interesting than whatever Sylvia was saying. Lorelei wanted to strangle it for its insolence. But Sylvia smiled almost fondly and withdrew a single silver bell from her pocket.

"Fair enough. Well, I brought this bell all the way from Ruhigburg." For effect, she rattled it. It chimed sweetly in the eerie quiet of the woods. "I think this would make a fetching addition to your cloak."

The schellenrock waded closer, its eyes shining with covetous longing.

"You may have it," Sylvia continued, curling her fingers around the bell and clasping it to her heart, "if you would be so kind as to point us in the right direction."

It nodded eagerly. Sylvia beamed, holding her palm flat again. Lorelei could only think of how she'd tricked the alp and threatened it for the information she wanted. But Sylvia allowed the schellenrock to reach out with its small, clawed hands and pocket the bell. It jangled merrily, and although Lorelei could not see the creature's face, an almost childlike happiness radiated from it. It shook the bell as Sylvia had, but the ringing was muffled and discordant from how tightly it clung to it. Her headache pounded in time with the sound.

"Well?" Lorelei demanded.

The schellenrock looked at her, then Sylvia. Slowly, it turned and pointed toward the summit. The tallest peak pierced the sky like a lance. Lorelei thought of the legend the old woman had told. Tomorrow night, when the moon was full, it would scrape against that jagged rock and spill its blood into the alpine lake below.

The Ursprung was nearly within reach.

"You've seen him, then?" Sylvia asked. "He's alive?"

"For now." Its voice brushed the shell of Lorelei's ear, as light as dandelion seeds carried on the wind. "The women of the woods have had their fun with him. I heard them laughing about it."

"The eschenfrau?" Sylvia asked. Lorelei tried to ignore the unease in her tone. When the schellenrock said nothing, Sylvia pressed, "Do you know how to reach the summit?"

It hesitated. With a sigh, Sylvia reached into her pocket and placed another bell on the shoreline. The schellenrock snatched it, and it disappeared into the dark recesses of its cloak. "Follow this stream until you come to a blade. When you cross its edge, you will be there."

"Speak plainly," Lorelei snapped. "What does that mean?"

But as soon as she took a step forward, the schellenrock slipped back beneath the water. A ripple passed over the surface, and then the lake lay as still as a mirror. It reflected the glitter of stars overhead and the grinning shape of the pines.

"You frightened it," Sylvia said sourly.

"It was spouting nonsense! With those directions, we will get even more lost."

"If you have any other ideas . . ."

Lorelei did not. And so, for nearly two hours, they followed the schellenrock's stream like a thread unspooled through a labyrinth. The altitude increased sharply along this path, and by the time the sun set, Lorelei's breaths came shorter and nausea had begun to set in. She had read about mountain sickness before in travel narratives, but she hadn't expected it to hit her so brutally. The headache was a consistent throb in her temples. She did not say anything until a veil of snow draped itself over the mountainside.

"We should stop for the night," Lorelei wheezed.

"Agreed." Sylvia crossed her arms against the chill. The snowfall clung to her pale eyelashes and gathered in her hair. "It's probably best that we share a tent tonight." Lorelei must've made a repulsed face, for Sylvia drew herself up taller with indignation. "Unless, of course, you would prefer to freeze."

"No," Lorelei said through gritted teeth. "That sounds reasonable. Of course."

While Sylvia pitched their tent, Lorelei struggled to coax a fire to life. When they finished eating a meager meal by firelight, Sylvia banked the coals and crawled into the tent. Lorelei reluctantly followed. Inside, it was cramped but surprisingly cozy. A strange lantern burned in the corner, throwing warm light against the walls, and the floor was piled with furs.

"It's so small." Lorelei hadn't intended it as an insult, but her words came out sharply all the same.

Sylvia glowered, her ears burning red as she unfastened the straps on her sleeping bag. "Well, I'm sorry it is not to your standards, but this is all we have."

Lorelei opened the glass door of the lantern and blew. The flame danced over the oil, but it did not extinguish. She tried again—and again—to the same fruitless result. Sylvia watched this unfold with some amusement but said nothing. Lorelei could only conclude it was some work of fairy magic that would lose its charm if explained.

At least it was useful.

In a huff, Lorelei lay down beside her. Sylvia squirmed away, putting as much space between them as possible, and Lorelei tried not to feel stung. She shouldn't be surprised Sylvia would treat her like some sharp thing she couldn't touch, or a venomous snake that would strike given the chance. She had long since destroyed any camaraderie that could exist between them.

As she settled in, she sank deeper into Sylvia's ridiculous collection of furs. Once, Lorelei might have mocked her for it, but at the moment she was incredibly grateful for the warmth. Her fingers were half-frozen inside her gloves, but already some life was beginning to return to them. No matter how she adjusted her position, she could not keep their shoulders from brushing together. It was nearly unbearable. The only mercy was the heat of Sylvia's body bleeding into her.

As Lorelei rolled onto her side, it struck her how vulnerable Sylvia looked like this. In the darkness, her skin was as pale and luminous as frost. Her snowy eyelashes brushed against her cheekbone, and her hair flowed around them like moonlit water. All it would take was a twitch of her hand to twist her finger around one of Sylvia's curls.

As if she sensed Lorelei's thoughts, Sylvia opened her eyes. Lorelei's breath almost caught at how they seemed to glow. She'd surely be ensorcelled if she looked into them a moment longer, and dear *God*, what was happening to her?

"Lorelei?" Sylvia's voice was terribly small when she asked, "Why do you hate me?"

I don't hate you—just what you represent. It surprised her, how easily the answer came to her. But when she opened her mouth, she could not bring herself to say it. Hatred was far too uncomplicated an emotion for Sylvia von Wolff.

"I am no threat to you any longer. You have the position you so desperately wanted," Sylvia persisted. "But even if you didn't, it never needed to be this way. Ziegler played us against each other."

The tight feeling in her chest gave way to grief. "Don't you dare.

You were the one who made this a competition. For years, you were always underfoot, always trying to upstage me. As if you ever needed anything but your name."

Sylvia's lips parted. Anger darkened her cheeks. "The von Wolff name means something, yes. It's the name of Anja von Wolff: the ruler of a rebellious province, a woman always waiting for her opportunity to strike."

Lorelei was startled into silence. She'd heard Sylvia speak exasperatedly about her mother before, but this was the first time she'd sounded almost as though she hated her.

"She is the real reason I enlisted in Wilhelm's army." Her voice trembled. "What else could I have done? When I first began visiting Ruhigburg as a child, people watched me as though I would turn on them like a rabid dog."

"No one thinks that of you anymore," Lorelei said, surprised at her own gentleness.

"Because I have spent my entire life trying to shed that association. But I cannot falter even for a moment, especially when I take over from my mother. You saw what the sentiment was in that village. They are primed for rebellion! I will always have to prove myself."

Lorelei certainly knew what it was like to feel as though she was the ambassador for— No. She would *not* feel sorry for Sylvia von Wolff.

"I'm so terribly sorry about that." Lorelei sneered. "I'm sure I made for a difficult obstacle to overcome."

"I'm so tired of your self-pity!" Sylvia took a deep breath. "And I'm so tired of fighting you. Ziegler could have made enough room for the both of us."

An instinctive shudder tore through Lorelei. They didn't bury her soon enough. They hardly buried her at all. As soon as they turned back, Ziegler's ghost would be there, waiting for her on the waters of the Vereist. "Don't speak ill of the dead."

"I speak the truth of the dead. Death is maybe the only time we get to speak the truth about a person. She wasn't always good. She used us both."

Lorelei closed her eyes. "I don't want to talk about this."

Sylvia made a soft, frustrated sound. "Then how can I ever hope to make amends with you?"

She leveled Sylvia with a flat, impassive stare. "You can't. Our worlds are too far apart."

"You're so dramatic. Do you know that?"

Lorelei laughed bitterly. Coming from *her*, that was rich. "You have no ability for self-reflection. Let me help you, then. Can you honestly say that speech you gave the other day was harmless?"

"They're just stories, Lorelei. Saint Bruno likely didn't exist, but of course my family likes it because—"

"Ah," Lorelei said. "So you do understand. Stories are tools."

"Precisely! Ones that hurt, yes, but ones that could finally bring people together." Sylvia's eyes blazed in the darkness. "You weren't there on the front lines. You did not grow up in a land eager for revolt. You have never seen a day of war. If we can make people understand that we're not so different, then Brunnestaad's soil will never be drenched with blood again."

"Tell me a story, then."

Sylvia seemed startled by the harshness in her voice and the abrupt change of topic. "Very well, then. Which one? Ah, all right." She cleared her throat. "Back in the days when wishes still held power, there was a girl with a red cloak—"

"Not that one. What about 'The Bright Sun Brings All to Light'?"

Sylvia's expression shuttered.

Feeling vindicated, Lorelei said, "What about 'The Yeva in Thorns'?"

"I don't want to tell those," Sylvia said, almost too quietly to hear.

"And do you think I do? Do you know how many times, how many ways, I have heard stories like those? Those stories are who you are, just as much as your red-cloaked girl. I have transcribed them, illustrated them, and sent them to the publisher. I've done this to myself in the hope I might have a chance to do something good."

For the first time in her life, Sylvia didn't have anything to say. She looked utterly overwhelmed, as though she had not thought Lorelei capable of such passion. But Lorelei was too far gone to hold back now.

"I have no place in the Brunnestaad you're building." Her voice trembled. "We Yevani are rootless. We belong in the city, flourishing there like vermin. We're nothing but a blight on this pastoral fantasy your silly little travelogues are helping create. *That* is why I despise you. We would never have been friends. We *will* never be friends. There is no crossing this gulf between us."

"I don't hate you," Sylvia whispered.

Somehow that of all things wrecked her. Raggedly, she whispered, "Liar."

Sylvia smiled wanly. "I thought I was a terrible liar."

Lorelei rolled onto her back again and let out a humorless note of laughter. "You say I know nothing of war, but I do. I've fought one for years. Death haunts me, and I don't know how to banish it."

"Death happens. There's nothing you have done to invite it and nothing you can do to banish it."

Lorelei stared up at the canvas roof of their tent. Branches scraped against it as the wind gnashed its teeth.

"I have found," Sylvia continued tentatively, "that the only thing that closed those wounds was forgiving myself. I can't bring them back, and neither can you. The only thing you can do now is live."

Sylvia would never understand. When you were Yevanisch, you were alive for the dead as much as you were for the living.

Sylvia sighed quietly and turned onto her side. Back-to-back, Lorelei felt an ocean of distance filling the bare centimeters between them. She listened to the unevenness of Sylvia's breathing, the whispering laughter of the eschenfrau in their trees.

Over and over again, she repeated to herself, *I hate you, I hate you, I hate you*. Like an incantation—like a fairy tale—repetition might make it true.

In her dreams, she slipped into cold, dark waters. Her hair and her coat billowed behind her. Her lungs burned. And all around her, suspended, were the pale, haunted faces of the people she had abandoned in their final moments. The people whose souls she had damned to walk the earth forever, barred from the afterlife.

Lorelei opened her eyes to a smothering heat. For a moment, everything around her was hazy, as if she were watching the world from beneath a deep pool of water. Her hair was damp against her temples.

Drowning again.

But then she registered the fur blanket soft against her cheek. The canvas of the tent around her. And then: Sylvia, draped over her like some over-affectionate squid.

It took all her strength not to thrash free. She'd been a child the last time anyone had slept in her bed. Rahel used to crawl into her room whenever a nightmare struck. It wasn't wholly unpleasant, except for the fact that Sylvia was a veritable *furnace*.

Lorelei became too aware of her own breathing, her quickening pulse. This was its own kind of torment, knowing how it felt to have Sylvia pressed against her. It was a cruel vision of something not meant for her.

"Von Wolff," she said quietly.

Sylvia only made a sleepy noise.

"*Von Wolff*," she repeated, more urgently. "Wake up."

Sylvia stirred. When her eyes opened, they were twin full moons bare inches from Lorelei's face. She blinked once, then jerked back with a soft shout of surprise. "Ah! Lorelei! I'm so sorry!"

"It's fine," Lorelei muttered. "Just . . . Get off me."

She disentangled herself, taking her hypnotic warmth with her, and said, "Well. I suppose that is one way to ensure neither of us freeze in the night."

"Thank you for your quick thinking," Lorelei said dryly.

Reluctantly, she crawled out of the tent. Her boots crunched in the snow that had fallen overnight. She was still cloaked in Sylvia's residual warmth, but the cold nipped at her exposed skin. And now that she had risen, the insistent pressure behind her eyes returned in full force. Every breath felt shallow, as though someone were trying to smother her, and she felt exhausted despite the full night's rest.

The sooner they got off this godforsaken mountain, the better.

It occurred to her that she had no idea what time it was. The snow glittered beneath some cold light, but she saw no sign of the sun in the eerie purple sky. For that matter, she had no idea where they were anymore. Nothing looked familiar. As she drank in her surroundings, she became more and more certain that the trees had uprooted and rearranged themselves while they slept. The path they'd been traveling had been stitched shut like a tear in fabric.

Sylvia emerged only a moment later. "I don't like it here."

That, at least, they could agree on.

After they struck camp, they continued to follow the schellenrock's stream. The terrain only grew more brutal—and the air colder. Every now and again, Lorelei swore she felt snow seep into her boots, and when she lifted her foot to inspect the damage, a small hole had begun to wear through the sole. That promised frostbite eventually. Assuming, of course, she didn't keel over from altitude sickness before they reached the summit. Her pace had slowed to a crawl, and her every breath rattled feebly in her chest.

"I thought it would feel different," Sylvia said absently.

"What do you mean?"

"I don't know." Sylvia adjusted the straps of her pack with a preoccupied expression. "Is this really where the Ursprung is? This place is certainly striking. But I expected something more ..."

"Sublime?" Lorelei offered.

"Precisely!" She looked pleased. "If this is truly the origin of all magic in the world, don't you think it should look more, well ... magical?"

"I'm sorry you're disappointed." Lorelei tipped her head. Right now, the sky was perfectly clear: a thin, airy purple threaded with distant stars like a needlepoint canvas. "The perpetual twilight isn't enough for you? Perhaps you would have preferred a ray of light piercing the heavens? The face of God himself peering through the clouds?"

"Oh, leave it," Sylvia muttered. "Perhaps we need to be closer to the summit." Then, she nodded, as if agreeing with her own assessment.

Lorelei was too exhausted to continue to prod at her—especially when her final conversation with Ziegler popped into her head. *Are you sure?*

No, Ziegler had assured Lorelei of her certainty. Lorelei refused to pick open this wound again. Ziegler had been meticulous with her research—and the legend they'd heard in town all but corroborated it. It would be a cruel twist of fate if someone had murdered her over a false conclusion. It was unthinkable that she'd died for nothing.

As they rounded a bend in the stream, a vista stretched out before them. Lorelei stopped dead in her tracks. Soaring above her was the mountain's serrated peak, crowned with snow. It seemed to her both close enough to touch and a thousand worlds away.

She turned back toward the path just as a gust of wind shook the snow loose from the trees. Through the shroud of white, Lorelei could make out a faint smudged shape in the distance. She squinted, and blink by blink, a lean-to materialized. Her heart swelled with such hope, she was certain it had to be another hallucination.

"Do you see that?"

Sylvia gasped. "Yes! I think it's—"

Before she even finished her sentence, Sylvia took off running. Lorelei followed close behind her, then immediately regretted it when her lungs seized. She doubled over to catch her breath, a headache pounding behind her eyes.

"Saints, Lorelei." Sylvia circled back to her. Her tone was exasperated, but Lorelei did not miss the glimmer of concern in her eyes. "Are you drinking enough? Hydration is very important at this height, you know."

"Yes," Lorelei groused. "I'm aware."

Together, they trudged onward. The cold wind sliced through Lorelei's coat, and frost gathered on her eyelashes. Exhaustion weighed down her every step, but she kept her focus trained on the lean-to—and the smoke rising from a dying campfire. Her blood sang with determination. If she could save just one person, perhaps it would be enough.

"Ludwig!" Sylvia called. The wind did its best to snatch her voice away. It tore mercilessly at the canvas tarp.

No motion came from within.

They exchanged a look. Lorelei dropped to her knees and crawled inside. Within, wrapped in no fewer than four coats, was Ludwig. His face was a horrible ghostly white, and his parted lips had turned blue. Her entire being recoiled from the sight.

Why are you doing this to me? Why do I survive when people die all around me?

There was no sense to be made of something so senseless, so—

No, she reminded herself sharply. There was nothing in this universe that was senseless, especially not violence.

She forced herself to look at him. A faint breath whistled out from his nose, ruffling the overlong hair in his face. Thank God. She glanced over her shoulder at Sylvia.

"He's alive," Lorelei said, once she swallowed down the emotion lodged in her throat.

Sylvia let out a sob of relief, crawling in next to her. She slipped off her gloves and rested them on his cheeks. Ludwig groaned. She sucked in a breath and brushed the hair back from his forehead. His blanched skin shone with sweat. "He's running a fever."

"Lorelei? Sylvia?" Ludwig's voice was barely a rasp. With each rattling breath he took, Lorelei felt that low-banked hope within her settle into ashes. It sounded like he was drowning on dry land.

Sylvia rummaged through her bag and procured a waterskin. She held it to his lips and carefully helped him drink. After a few moments, she twisted the cap back on and turned to Lorelei with a troubled expression. "He's been cursed."

"Cursed?"

Sylvia turned over the palm of his hand and pulled back his sleeve. The tracery of veins in his wrist was green and thick against the pressure of her thumb. Roots, Lorelei realized after a moment. Her stomach twisted nauseatingly. Now that she was looking at him closely, she noticed the bark grafted onto his skin. It crept out of his collar and advanced determinedly toward his throat.

"How did this happen?"

"This is eschenfrau sickness. He must've angered them somehow." Sylvia began pawing through his bag. She pulled out a thin strip of pale gray bark: a piece of an ash tree.

"He must have collected it as a sample. That fool."

"I'm not so sure." Sylvia turned the bark over in her hands. "Ludwig is more cautious than that. Besides, he would have put it in his vasculum if he wanted to preserve it."

Dread settled heavily within her at what Sylvia implied. "But if someone else planted it on him, they'd be sick as well, wouldn't they?"

"Unless the eschenfrau gave it freely. They do love mischief."

Lorelei's mood darkened. Ludwig wasn't dead—not yet—but superstition lingered. Best not to discuss this where he could hear it. "Come outside."

Outside, snow continued to fall, but she could hardly feel the cold. She drew it around herself like armor. When Sylvia spoke again, her voice trembled with fury. "Why would they do this to him? It would have been kinder to kill him outright."

"Someone didn't want him to find a way to the summit. They're trying to delay us again," Lorelei said lowly. "We pushed on after Ziegler was murdered, but they knew we couldn't continue if he was this ill."

When they returned to camp, there would be no waiting for the king's paltry justice. She would kill Heike herself. She must've been wearing a particularly murderous expression because Sylvia tentatively rested her hand on her shoulder. "Lorelei . . ."

She shrugged her off. "Stay here and watch him. I'm going to find the Ursprung."

"Oh, no, you're not! He'll die if he's out in the cold much longer, and I can't carry him back by myself."

"Look at him." Lorelei gestured helplessly at Ludwig's crumpled form. "He's not going to make it either way."

"You don't know that! We owe it to him to try."

They were suddenly very close together. Lorelei had not realized she'd moved, but it was practically instinct now to use her height to her advantage. And yet, Sylvia did not budge. She looked as though she was making her last stand before some horrid fairy-tale creature. Lorelei hated it. She stepped closer, until Sylvia's head had to tip back to hold her gaze. Until she could feel the heat of Sylvia's breath against her lips. Until her vision was filled with nothing but Sylvia's defiant, blazing glory. She had half a mind to grab her chin and . . .

Sylvia made a strange noise, but her silver eyes were molten, almost expectant.

Lorelei had to remind herself that Sylvia could not, in fact, read her thoughts. She put some distance between them and drew a slow breath in an effort to compose herself. It felt impossible to get enough air.

"I understand your concern," she said. "However, if we don't find the Ursprung now, we won't get another opportunity. They'll try to stop us again."

Sylvia did not look entirely convinced.

"And perhaps it's our best chance at saving him. None of the tales agree on what it's capable of, but if all magic flows from it, it's possible that all of them are correct. Perhaps the Ursprung has healing properties."

"I . . . I don't know if that syllogism holds," Sylvia said, disoriented.

"We owe it to him to try," Lorelei replied, unable to resist one final jab. "I'll be fine alone."

"But you have no idea what you're up against!" Sylvia protested. "And if you don't return—"

"All the better for you, I suppose."

Sylvia rubbed her temples. "You stubborn fool. I'm coming with you."

FIFTEEN

As they ascended the last stretch of the mountain, guided by the sound of rushing water, the full moon appeared like a seal stamped in shimmering wax. The snow sparkled beneath its glow, and all the world looked inlaid with diamond.

And there, just through the thinning copse of evergreens, they saw it: the first glimpse of the Ursprung. Water thundered down the mountainside and shattered into mist onto the rocks below. Even from here, she could feel it, bitter cold against her cheeks.

"We're almost there!" Sylvia shouted over the noise.

They were. But they'd never make it.

They'd reached the edge of a canyon. On this side, there was nothing but sheer rock and sheets of ice. Without equipment, it would be nearly impossible to scale. On the other, the path to the summit sloped gradually upward. Unless they wanted to descend into the ravine and cross the river, the only way forward was a narrow ledge of rock beneath the curtain of the waterfall.

Sylvia must have noticed it at the same time. With considerably less cheer than before, she said, "This must be the blade."

So the schellenrock's information was good after all. "Great. Just great."

Valiantly struggling to keep the dread out of her voice, Sylvia said, "What is it they say? The only way out is through?"

Lorelei crouched to examine the ledge. It was barely wider than the length of her hand. They'd have to press their backs to the wall and sidle their way to the other side—all while the waterfall buffeted them. She wicked the moisture off her face with a flick of her hand.

Sylvia sat beside her, her feet dangling off the edge of the cliff. Lorelei's stomach flipped just looking at her. "Would you like me to go first?"

Horrible images flickered behind Lorelei's eyelids. Sylvia falling like an angel cast from heaven. Sylvia shattered at the bottom of that ravine. Sylvia's blood pooling around her like a halo of crimson. She'd fret herself sick. Best to go first and plummet to her death unbothered.

"No. I'll go first."

Sylvia smiled at her knowingly. "You're afraid, aren't you?"

Lorelei scowled. "Don't be ridiculous."

"You *are*." She clapped her hands together with delight. "So you really are human."

"Focus, von Wolff. I think you're enjoying this too much."

"Maybe a little. My apologies." Her dueling scar dimpled infuriatingly as she smiled.

Lorelei shrugged off her bag and slipped an empty glass vial into her breast pocket for safekeeping. If nothing else, she could bring a sample back. With that, she took her first step onto the blade. The rock wall jabbed uncomfortably into her spine. Drawing in a deep breath, she slid an inch forward. A pebble skittered off the edge and hurtled nauseatingly into the open air. One misstep, and that would be her. Lorelei swore under her breath.

"Are you *sure* you don't want me to go first? I'm quite experienced with rock climbing! Have I ever told you about the time I came up against an aufhocker—"

"Stop speaking," Lorelei sniped. "If I'm to die, at least let me remember you a bit fondly."

Sylvia's mouth snapped shut.

Lorelei tore her eyes away from Sylvia and focused her attention straight in front of her. It was agonizingly slow going, and with the abyss yawning beneath her, she felt a horrible vertigo. Her chest constricted with every shuffling step, and she could feel her heart pounding in every pulse point in her body. As she neared the waterfall, its hissing drowned out all coherent thought. Unfathomable gouts of water poured down only an arm's breadth away from her. It was so pure it looked to be made of glass.

"I can't see you anymore!" Sylvia's voice sounded impossibly far away.

Lorelei dug her fingers into the rock face to maintain her balance. "I'm fine."

Holding her breath, she continued onward to solid ground. As soon as she made it, she collapsed into a heap and desperately tried not to empty the contents of her stomach. Between altitude sickness and the stress, she felt like death warmed over.

"It's safe," Lorelei called back to Sylvia.

"I'll be right there!"

Don't rush, she wanted to say.

For the first time in weeks, she was alone—truly alone. Under the brightness of the moon, there was enough light to see by but faint enough that the shadows seethed in the corners of her vision. She breathed steadily, fighting back the jagged edges of her fear. There were no ghosts here. No men to strike her dead on the streets of the Yevanverte. Out here, she could almost convince herself she was at peace.

The air felt suddenly glass-like, like the moment of quiet when a hawk's shadow falls over a meadow. A shudder forced its way down her spine.

"Finally," said a familiar voice. "I caught up to you."

It couldn't be.

Lorelei sat bolt upright and turned to face Ludwig. He stood at the tree line, his hands hanging loose by his sides. She couldn't find an emotion to land on as she stared at him. There was something unsettling about the vague shape of him in the dark. He was preternaturally still. Her hair stood on end, and yet, she stubbornly hoped against hope.

"What are you doing here?" she demanded. "And how? You're going to get yourself killed, wandering around in your condition."

"Maybe. But I couldn't miss out on finding the Ursprung."

Ludwig was not quite himself. His light, lilting speech pattern was an almost-perfect imitation, but his face . . .

His smile looked like a painting sitting crooked in its frame. He took an artless, lurching step forward, as though he wasn't quite used to his own proportions. Lorelei suddenly found herself wishing that she'd indulged Sylvia's stupid ego and let her go first.

"You've made an impressive recovery." She'd meant it to come out accusatory, but it was almost pathetically small.

He tilted his head at an unnatural angle. "I honestly thought you'd be a little happier to see me."

"Of course I'm happy to see you're well."

I just don't believe it.

"It may be best for you to stay behind." Lorelei jerked her chin toward the peak. "Unless you're feeling well enough to scale this mountain."

"Oh, it shouldn't be a problem. Say, where's von Wolff?"

Lorelei went very still. Ludwig never called Sylvia by her surname.

It suddenly seemed of vital importance that he knew she wasn't entirely alone. "On the other side of this crossing. She should be here at any moment."

As he came closer, his shadow sprawled long and skinny against the earth. His footsteps tapped out a juddering rhythm.

Lorelei felt the roar of the river, comforting and steady behind her. With a deep inhale, she reached for it and—*there*. As though the current were a thread, she grabbed hold of it. The aether pulled taut against her will. She slid one arm behind her back and curled her fingers beckoningly. A few tendrils of water slithered from the river and curled around her wrist like a serpent.

Ludwig stepped into a pale column of moonlight, looming above her. It was then she saw the bright red cravat knotted around his neck, a shade of rust that was startlingly familiar.

Tarnkappe.

An alp's transformation was always imperfect. His fingers were too long to be natural and jointed quite sickeningly between his first and second knuckles. It gave his hands the impression of claws. She threw her hand forward, and the water slammed into him.

He staggered backward. When he looked up again, water dripped from the ends of his hair. His face was contorted with barely repressed rage. She'd never once seen Ludwig look at anyone like that.

"Now, why did you do that?" he asked lowly.

"I know what you are." Lorelei did her best to sound vicious. "Your transformation is convincing, but the real Ludwig is still too sick to stand."

The alp's lips parted dumbly, as if it hadn't considered that. Its face turned an impressive shade of purple. "I told you I would come back."

"You should have been more patient."

She pulled another stream of water from the river. Clenching her fist, she froze it solid and sent it hurtling toward the alp as a spear of ice. It landed true, embedding deep into the muscle of its shoulder. It howled in mingled pain and fury. Faster than she could track, it leapt at her.

She went down, her back striking the earth with a *thud*. Her lungs emptied painfully, and stars danced in her eyes. Not-Ludwig's fingers locked around her throat, its nails sharpening to deadly points that bit into her skin. She could feel the blood trickling hot down her neck. The smell of copper filled her nose as it bared its teeth.

Von Wolff. Her lips formed the shape of the words, but she couldn't draw a single breath. She couldn't scream. Her vision went black at the edges, and the world blurred into smears of watercolor.

Not like this, she thought. *Not now.*

With a twitch of her fingers, she drove the shard of ice deeper into its shoulder. The alp screamed again, loosening its grip. Air surged into her lungs, and an embarrassing whimper escaped her as reflexive tears welled in her eyes.

Move, she willed her useless body. *Damn you, move.*

The waterfall rushed just within her reach, hissing invitingly. *Viper,* it seemed to say.

With a shout, she called forth a rush of water and knocked the alp back. It gave her just enough of an opening. She threw herself on top of it, digging her knees into its shoulders, and gathered the water like a mask over its face. There was some small part of her that recoiled from her own actions, at just how easy it was to hold Ludwig's likeness under. Bubbles simmered within the water as he struggled against her.

She knew what it meant to hate. She knew it from the moment she saw the depths of it in people's eyes, and she felt it burn through her the night Aaron died. She felt it now, roiling beneath her skin. The alp surfaced enough to pull in a wet gasp of air, but Lorelei forced the water over its mouth again.

"Just die already!" she growled, the desperation roughening her voice.

"Lorelei! What are you doing?"

The sound of Sylvia's voice stilled her. The beast wearing Ludwig's form surged from the water with a broken sob. There was a wild, terrified gleam in its bloodshot eyes.

"Help," he spluttered, clinging desperately to Lorelei's forearm. "Please, help me!"

Sylvia's gaze shifted between them. "Let him go."

How could she be duped so easily? "You can't be serious! It's—"

"Now," Sylvia said, a little impatiently.

Her thumb loosed her saber from its scabbard. Lorelei stared at her uncomprehendingly. And then it dawned on her what Sylvia meant to do. With a show of reluctance, Lorelei let the alp go and scrabbled out of the way.

Sylvia drew her saber with a ringing metallic sound. With a flourish, she lunged and drove it into the alp's abdomen.

It let out an inhuman shriek, clutching at the wound. Blood seeped through its fingers, but it could do nothing for the flesh blackening and sloughing off. Underneath were thick tendrils of shadow, frantically knitting together in an effort to maintain its new shape.

Regret shone in Sylvia's eyes. She rested her blade in the crook of her forefinger and thumb, wiping the blood off in one long stroke, then sheathed it again. Lorelei found it almost alluring— and was too stunned to even scold herself for thinking it at all.

"Silver," the alp hissed. The mask it had made of Ludwig's face continued to melt off in bubbling gouts. "How *dare* you?"

"My apologies!" Sylvia snatched Lorelei's hand with her un-bloodied one and dragged her to her feet. "Run. You can't kill alps, but you can slow them down."

Together, they ran. There was nowhere to go but up the rock face alongside the waterfall. She didn't dare look down, but when it came to pitting one fear against the other, she would take the solidity of the mountain over the murderous rage of an alp any day. She climbed, knocking loose stones and icicles on her way up.

As soon as she pulled herself over the ledge, she curled into a heap to catch her breath. Her bruised throat burned with every pull of air and her stomach threatened to revolt against her, but what lay before her made her panicked mind go quiet.

The plunge pool of a second waterfall stretched out before them. This one, however, burbled gently from its source—*the* source.

The Ursprung.

Ribbons of light danced in the depths of the pool: pure aether, glowing like an aurora against the night sky. Its beauty terrified her.

Sylvia grabbed her elbow and tugged urgently. "We have to go."

Lorelei chanced a look over her shoulder. The alp had recovered enough to pursue them, its eyes blazing with cold fury. Snow swirled around them. There was nowhere left to run.

Before she could think better of it, she dropped her backpack and dove into the pool. The cold punched the air from her lungs immediately and seized every muscle in her body. Twin splashes sounded behind her. She whirled around to see Sylvia swimming toward her.

And then Sylvia was jerked backward. Her eyes flung wide with terror.

The alp had ensnared her by the ankle. Sylvia kicked wildly against it, but the alp held her fast. In an instant, it sank its fangs into the juncture of her neck and shoulder. The air escaped from Sylvia's mouth in a rush of bubbles, and red bloomed in the water. For a moment, Lorelei swore she saw Aaron—his vacant eyes, blood unfurling around his broken skull like a corona—staring back at her.

Her vision blurred with terror. She needed to go up for air. She needed to flee. It would be so simple to let her rival slip beneath the surface. She had imagined this. She had dreamed of this a thousand times before.

She felt Death's presence, spreading his wings above her. The light of the moon filtering from the surface seemed to waver.

No, she thought. *You will not take another from me.*

Lorelei called on her magic, allowing her awareness to unfurl through the pool. She clenched her fists, imagining the molecules compressing. Ice encased the alp's arm first, then spread along its body in jagged crystals. Panicked, it let Sylvia go.

Sylvia drifted limply from its grasp and began to sink toward the bottom. With the last of her strength, Lorelei grabbed her by the elbow and pulled.

The weight of her sodden clothing threatened to drag them both under. Lorelei's head pounded from the strain of her power. At her command, the water guided them upward and toward the shore.

They broke the surface. Lorelei gasped, sucking in a frigid gulp of air. By sheer force of will, she dragged them both out of the water. The bitter cold felt like thousands of needles driven into bones. Her teeth chattered violently, and somewhere in the back of her mind, she knew that they were both going to die from hypothermia, sooner rather than later.

Worry about that later, she decided. For now, she had to get them to the Ursprung.

As best she could, Lorelei hooked her elbows underneath Sylvia's arms and lifted her. She was tiny, but she was dense with muscle—and completely dead weight. Step by step, Lorelei hauled her up the last slope and crumpled at the edge of a spring. At the sight of steam wafting from its surface, Lorelei nearly wept. They would survive this yet.

God. She had almost watched Sylvia die.

She couldn't lose her. If she did nothing, she could still lose her.

Lorelei cradled her jaw and carefully turned her head. The wound at her neck was horrific, but mercifully that vindictive beast had missed her carotid. Her lips were blue with cold, but by some divine mercy, her chest rose and fell.

Alive.

With no fear keeping her afloat, Lorelei lowered herself onto her back. The moon loomed close enough that she swore she could reach out and brush her fingers against its face. By the time she glanced back at Sylvia, her eyelashes had fluttered open. This time, she did not dart her gaze away. They lay forehead to forehead, the cold making delicate plumes of their breath.

In the moonlight, Sylvia was luminous. It hurt to look at her, but it hurt far more to be looked at like this. As though she were a dream come to life. It made her hope too much. Right now, she almost believed that she was something a woman like Sylvia could admire.

Something beautiful.

"You saved me." Sylvia's voice was full of moony wonder. And then, as if remembering the last five years all at once, she said, "You . . . you *saved* me?"

"Ugh." Lorelei draped her elbow over her face. "Must you act so shocked about it?"

"Not twelve hours ago, you told me how much you despised me!"

She had not said that, but even she had the good sense not to belabor the point. "Perhaps some gratitude would be in order."

"Thank you." Sylvia rested her hand over Lorelei's. "Truly."

"You're welcome," she said stiffly. "I would have done the same for anyone."

For a moment, they stared at each other. Lorelei cleared her throat and extricated her hand from Sylvia's. Desperate to focus on something, *anything*, else, she sat up and looked out over the water.

It was a perfect mirror of the sky, serene and glittering with the cold light of a thousand stars. They were so bright, it seemed to Lorelei that there truly were stars submerged here. It would be a simple thing to scoop one out and swallow it whole.

It struck her for the first time that they'd done it. They'd found it.

"It's beautiful," Sylvia said quietly.

It was. But Sylvia was so much more beautiful. Lorelei blinked to clear *that* thought away.

"Indeed," she rasped. "Now let's make camp and dry off. I don't intend to die after all that."

Lorelei began pulling water from the weave of her coat. Droplets floated around her as she worked. This cold would kill them within an hour. She felt more than she saw Sylvia watching her with the rapt attention of a spooked woodland creature.

She refuses to use magic. It upsets her too much.

Rumor had it she'd been quite capable with magic. What must she have seen to swear off it forever? What must she have done herself? Lorelei couldn't imagine Sylvia having a true capacity for cruelty.

Somehow, she found herself asking, "May I do yours?"

"Please." Then, remembering herself, Sylvia added, "If you're offering, it would be rude to say no."

After Lorelei dried their clothes as best she could, they ran to fetch their backpacks, abandoned at the shore of the lake below them. By the time they returned and finished assembling the tent with their clumsy, half-frozen figures, they were both shivering and irritated—but at least they could now change into warmer clothes.

Lorelei emerged first while Sylvia bandaged her wound. Soon, she joined her at the Ursprung's edge.

"How do you think it works?" Lorelei asked. "In all the tales, it grants power to those it's chosen—or to those foolish enough to take it."

"Single-minded as always," Sylvia muttered with unmistakable fondness. "I'm not sure. In the legend, the boy fell into the water. There is only one way to know for certain, of course."

"Don't," she said, perhaps too quickly.

"What, you think I'm not worthy of it?" Sylvia tried for a cocksure smile. "I am no stranger to . . . How have you put it? Headlong rushes into danger?"

"Idiocy," Lorelei amended. The levity evaporated from Sylvia's face. "Still. I cannot ask you to do that."

"It isn't idle curiosity." Her voice grew somber. "I want to know what kind of weapon we're handing Wilhelm. My duty demands that much of me."

Dread sat heavily in Lorelei's stomach. She did not like it. She liked it even less that she could not argue with her. "Shall I push you in, then?"

Sylvia gave a startled laugh. "I'd prefer to go to my doom with some dignity, thank you."

Lorelei could not bear to watch. What would she do if Sylvia's body rejected it? If the life began to bleed out of her, or if she emerged, like the thief from the lindworm's cave, a stranger?

"Don't fret," said Sylvia. "If nothing else, it's warm. See?"

She touched her palm to the surface, and the entire world held its breath. The wind stopped. The snowflakes froze in midair, twinkling in the moonlight. The stars reflected on the Ursprung's surface dulled, until the water shone as black as a moonless night. In this preternatural stillness, it felt as though something un-knowable and ancient had turned its eye toward them.

Sylvia's expression slackened with startled embarrassment, as though she'd spoken out of turn at a dinner party, rather than carelessly *awakened the source of all magic*. If Lorelei were not so terrified of what came next, she might have shouted at her.

A suggestion of a voice skittered through her mind, as elusive as the patter of rainfall or a breeze whispering through an empty field. *Ask your question.*

Lorelei stiffened with surprise. "This isn't the Ursprung."

Sylvia gawped at her. "It must be."

"Back in the days when wishes still held power," she began, her bitter certainty solidifying with every word, "there lived a king whose realm had fallen on hard times. But no matter how poor the harvest or how hostile his enemies, he had one boon: all the waters in his land contained a strange and powerful magic. Of all those waters, the king's greatest treasure was a pool that answered one question of each person who asked."

"Incredible," Sylvia whispered. "What shall I ask it?"

Then, realizing what she'd said, she clapped her hands over her mouth. Too late. That horrible voice hissed, *Your heart's greatest desire.*

Lorelei stared at her in disbelief. It was so absurd, so *stupid*, she could scarcely formulate a coherent thought. All she could manage was "You wasted your question."

"I'm sorry!" Sylvia cried. "I didn't realize that would count."

"You could have asked *anything*, you . . ."

Far too many insults came to mind to choose just one. All of them slipped away as her rage collapsed humiliatingly into despair. If only they had one more question—or perhaps a thousand more. Could it have told her whether any of the decisions she'd made had been the right ones? Could it have pointed her to the perfect piece of evidence to accuse Heike—or told whether Ziegler had ever truly loved her?

Sylvia placed a hand on her shoulder. "Lorelei."

It took Lorelei a few moments to realize how close she'd come to tears. At the plain look of pity in Sylvia's eyes, her fury settled miserably into ashes. Bit by bit, Lorelei pulled herself together. They had come this far; she had to finish what they started. The weight of the spring's anticipation pressed heavily down on her.

"Where is the Ursprung?" she asked.

The air shimmered with aether. Colors swirled through the darkness of the water and slowly, slowly, an image took shape. The full moon skated across its surface, waning as it traveled. When it hung dark in the sky again, another shape bloomed beneath it: an island in the middle of black waters, wreathed in mist. In the distance, Lorelei could make out fields of tulips dusted with ash and villages filled with angry, starving people. As the new moon filled with the thinnest crescent of light, the island shimmered and vanished as if it were a mirage.

Wherever the Ursprung was, it certainly wasn't here.

PART III

The Vanishing Isle

SIXTEEN

ZIEGLER HAD BEEN WRONG.

Lorelei could hardly process it. All of them had given years of their lives to this project. She had rested all of her hopes, her dreams—no, her chance for survival on its success. In the end, they'd been chasing a completely false conclusion. How could Ziegler have made such a terrible mistake? How could she not have *known*?

Ziegler was not a secretive woman by nature, especially when it came to her work. Although Wilhelm had muzzled her in the months leading up to the expedition, it went against her very view of science. She shared her research freely, whenever and with whomever asked: foreign scholars, policymakers, young students. She did her best work when pitted against another mind. *What good is knowledge,* she'd say, *if it can't be improved upon?* If she'd found the Ursprung, she wouldn't have concealed it.

Would she?

No, Lorelei could not dwell on this now; it would break her. The image on the water's surface faded, and the weight of that horrible, unseen stare lifted. The pool glittered with white, celestial light. Through it, all Lorelei saw was the reflection of her own drawn, embittered face.

She could not have received a worse answer to her question.

Not all the folklore Lorelei collected came in the form of neat little fairy tales. In the course of her fieldwork, she'd documented all sorts of artifacts: children's rhymes and clapping games (her least favorite, considering children tended to sense her disdain for them), proverbs, jokes, several types of wedding ceremonies, even the ways people built their homes. And then there were the urban legends, things even stranger than the wildeleute.

One that recurred in almost every region in Brunnestaad was the tale of the Vanishing Isle. It was said that it rose up from the waves on the night of a new moon, shimmering like a mirage. And then, it burned away like mist in the morning light, reappearing somewhere else on the next new moon. In the vision the pool had granted her, Lorelei had seen it rippling in the darkness of the water, exactly as it had been described to her many times before.

The true Ursprung lay somewhere on the Vanishing Isle, and she had only the faintest idea of where it would appear on the night of the next new moon. That was only two weeks from now. She resisted the urge to kick the water out of spite. Coordinates would have been infinitely more helpful.

Sylvia lay on her back, her hair splayed across the stones like a river. The ends pooled in the spring water, and the ghostly white of it had darkened to the steely gray of morning. Like this, with all the starlight reflected in her eyes, she looked almost divine.

Lorelei had a fleeting impulse to brush away the strands of hair plastered to Sylvia's temples, but she clenched her fist around that foolish desire. "Did you recognize the place it showed us?"

"It looked like Ebul."

"*Ebul* hardly narrows it down."

It wasn't particularly heartening, either. They were currently stranded in the middle of Albe, which lay in the southwest of Brunnestaad. Ebul was the eastern borderland. Assuming no more deadly creatures waylaid them—unlikely, given their track record—they would barely make it in time for the night of the new moon. If they missed it, only God knew where it would appear next.

"Adelheid will know if you draw it for her." Sylvia frowned.

"But would it not be wiser to return to Ruhigburg and regroup? This is getting dangerous."

I would like to know who is responsible before you return to Ruhigburg. If you cannot give me that, then I hope you understand that someone must answer for Ziegler's murder. Unity requires sacrifice.

"We can't return to Ruhigburg without the Ursprung."

She tried—and must have failed—to temper the desperation in her voice, for Sylvia stared at her with a strange brew of confusion and concern. But Lorelei could not bring herself to tell Sylvia what Wilhelm had threatened to do. What good would it do Sylvia to burden her with that knowledge? All of them—save Ludwig, perhaps—believed him a good man. Besides, danger would not deter her. Lorelei was no stranger to dooming someone else to save herself.

And deep down, even without Wilhelm's threat, she did not know if she could stop now. Being Yevanisch was about recognizing injustice. She was proud of little in her life, but she was proud of that. She could not rest until she found out what happened to Ziegler.

Grieve her, Adelheid had told her, *but do not let this become an obsession. It will sink you in the end.*

"Think about it," Lorelei continued, more composedly this time. "Wilhelm's position is precarious. If we return empty-handed, it will all but confirm his opponents' view of him as a weak ruler—one desperate enough to chase after fairy tales. Without the Ursprung's power, he cannot hope to stave off a coup."

"Will that be all he does with it?" Sylvia asked quietly.

Lorelei frowned. She had considered it before, of course, that he would look beyond Brunnestaad's borders once more. But with her own death bearing down on her, she could not afford to be so principled. "I don't know. But you will be there to advise him."

Sylvia smiled uncertainly, but when she spoke again, she regained some cheer. "Yes, you're right. For the stability of Brunnestaad, it is our duty to press forward."

"Right. For Brunnestaad." Lorelei paused. "Thank you."

"You're welcome." Sylvia looked bewildered—and a bit frightened. Lorelei filed it away as a future intimidation technique. "We should fetch Ludwig."

"*Now?*" Lorelei very much doubted she could roll down the mountain, much less hike back to Ludwig's makeshift shelter. As much as she hated the idea of leaving him alone in his condition, she refused to risk their lives for his. They'd left him with more blankets, food, and firewood. It would have to be enough. "That is a very stupid idea. You can't save him if you're dead."

"I am not dead yet."

"You look on the brink of it!"

Sylvia only let out a long sigh, one that suggested she was nobly withholding what she really wanted to say.

"Besides," Lorelei continued, mostly to reassure herself. "He could cheat Death himself, if it came down to it."

"He could." She didn't sound entirely convinced.

"We'll leave at dawn. Now go inside. You'll catch your death out here."

"I never knew you fussed so much," Sylvia groused. "Are you certain you're feeling well?"

Lorelei chose to ignore her as they slipped into the tent. Sylvia's enchanted lantern—enspelled to never extinguish, Lorelei assumed—illuminated the small space, but most of it clung to Sylvia. It gilded her hair and filled her pale eyes with fire. It might have been beautiful, had Lorelei not caught a glimpse of blood seeping through Sylvia's coat. For one horrible moment, Lorelei's vision pulsed black with fear.

"Let me look at your wound," Lorelei said.

"Honestly, Lorelei, I'm fine."

She fixed Sylvia with her chilliest glare. Mercifully, the fight bled out of her. With a sigh, Sylvia floundered about in an effort to unbutton her coat one-handed. She pulled her hair over her good shoulder and turned her back to Lorelei, who averted her eyes as Sylvia unfastened the buttons of her shirt. A bright red stain spread across the back, clinging damply to her skin. At last, it fell from her shoulders and pooled around her waist. She'd already bled through her linen bandages.

Carefully, Lorelei unraveled them. The gash underneath looked alarmingly deep—and ripe for infection. Lorelei's stomach bottomed out, her thoughts going to static. Fear nearly pulled her under, but she dug her fingers into her knee and grounded herself.

She could do this.

"I'm going to have to suture it."

Sylvia looked aghast. "Suture? You? You're more suited to taking things apart."

Lorelei gave her a nasty smile. "Unfortunately for you, Johann isn't here. Unless you'd like to take your chances with sepsis, you're going to have to make do with me."

Seemingly cowed, Sylvia kept her mouth shut. The difficult part—getting her to cooperate—was over. All that remained was staying conscious. Lorelei hesitated for a moment, then pulled one glove off. Sylvia took a sharp breath, then turned resolutely away from her as though she'd seen something profane. Lorelei almost wanted to make her look.

No claws, see?

Somehow, it was a vulnerability she couldn't endure. She worked off the other glove and placed them neatly on the ground. They looked unbearably intimate, folded up on Sylvia's makeshift bedclothes, so she focused her attention on getting the rest of her supplies ready.

Lorelei fetched alcohol, needle and thread, and a clean rag from her backpack. She poured the antiseptic over the cloth, then set to cleaning the wound. Sylvia made only a soft sound of protest before setting her jaw, nobly stoic.

Lorelei brandished the needle. It was hooked like a thin crescent moon, glinting eerily in the firelight. "Will this become cursed if I disinfect it in your lantern?"

"I'm sure I don't know what you mean," Sylvia said testily, but there was a note of genuine curiosity in her voice, as if she hadn't entertained the possibility before.

Lorelei scoffed as she heated it in the flame. "Ready?"

"As much as I'll ever be."

Sylvia hardly made a sound as Lorelei stitched the wound shut. The blood seeping out between her fingers made her stomach feel slippery, as though she'd swallowed a fish whole, but she finished as quickly as she could. Tying off the knot, she snipped the thread with a pair of scissors. A cold sweat had broken out across her forehead, but she felt oddly proud of herself. "That should hold."

"Thank you." Sylvia hesitated. "You have a steady hand."

"My father is a cobbler. I apprenticed with him for a year before Ziegler took me in. Skin isn't so different from shoe leathers." She wasn't sure why she'd offered that up—and so easily, as if she were in the habit of making small talk about herself at all.

"Shoe leathers," Sylvia repeated. It sounded almost as if she were smiling. "I'm not sure whether I should be offended or not."

"Take it as you will."

Lorelei's ears burned with embarrassment. She busied herself putting away her supplies while Sylvia produced an improbably ornate comb out of her bag. It had an opal-inlaid handle that gleamed like bone and teeth of silver. From the corner of her eye, Lorelei watched Sylvia struggle with it.

She sighed piteously as she attempted to lift her injured arm. Then, with great effort, she pulled the comb feebly through the snares and tangles with her non-dominant hand. It seemed to Lorelei a pointless vanity, given everything they'd endured tonight, but she was too tired to comment on it. She was too tired to even enjoy her suffering.

"Allow me," said Lorelei.

Sylvia clutched the comb to her chest as if Lorelei had just asked her to hand over her firstborn. "Why?"

"Because this is unspeakably painful to witness. I'm not entirely heartless."

Sylvia reluctantly placed the comb in her outstretched hand. Lorelei knelt behind her, lifted the weight of Sylvia's hair, and let it fall down her back in a wild spill. It was mercifully still damp; Lorelei did not want to imagine the nightmare of wrestling a comb through it dry.

She began to work through the knots from bottom to top. Nothing but the sound of their rasping breaths and metal catching in Sylvia's hair filled the heavy silence between them. Warmth radiated gently from Sylvia's back, and her pulse thrummed in the arch of her pale throat. It was exquisite torture. Lorelei had never touched her hair—never but in her dreams—and she'd so desperately wanted to. It was as luxurious as she'd envisioned. With every stroke of the comb, she swore she smelled rose water.

After a few minutes, she'd managed to pull all the snarls loose until it fell in sleek coils down Sylvia's back. Some part of her was tempted to rifle through Sylvia's things until she found her oils, or perhaps a scrap of ribbon. *Ridiculous,* she thought. She would have to settle for braiding it.

"Where did you learn to do this? Your hair . . ." As if it were taboo to mention, Sylvia lifted her uninjured arm and brushed her fingers along her own jawline.

"I had long hair once. A very long time ago."

Sylvia laughed. "Really? I can't imagine it at all. This style suits you."

Lorelei did not know what to do with such a compliment. "I often braided my sister's hair. She was a sickly child and would lie in bed for days at a time. Someone had to take care of her hair to keep it from matting. I find it rather relaxing, actually."

She realized after a moment that she was babbling—at least by her own standards. Sylvia put her out of her misery quickly. "I didn't know you had a sister."

Lorelei fastened the end of the braid and absently tugged on the loops to loosen it. "Why would you?"

The silence stretched out like a fraying rope. "What is her name?"

"Rahel." Lorelei hesitated. "I also had a brother once. Aaron."

She could see Sylvia fighting to ask more questions, shifting under the weight of her curiosity. "You must be the oldest."

Lorelei considered replying sarcastically but thought better of it. "I am."

Lorelei heard the smile in Sylvia's voice. "I always wanted siblings."

"They're more trouble than they're worth." Satisfied with her handiwork, Lorelei pulled the braid over Sylvia's shoulder. She touched it, as if testing if it were real. "I thought the five of you and Wilhelm were like siblings."

"During the summers, when our families all traveled to Ruhigburg, yes, we were. We met when we were about six years old. Those summers meant everything to me. But the rest of the year, I was quite lonely." Sylvia hesitated, as though uncertain whether she should continue. Lorelei found herself curious.

"Were you?" she prompted.

"It will sound silly, I'm sure." Sylvia settled onto one hip, turning to face Lorelei. The fairy light of her lantern traced the curve of her cheekbone in gold. "My mother showered me with affection— or at least with extravagances. Anything I wanted, I received. But from an early age, I got the sense that all my mother saw when she looked at me was the color of my hair. Her little Mondscheinprinzessin: an Albisch folk hero—a *saint*—born again. Her heir. Her province's future. Hers, hers, hers."

Sylvia tucked a loose strand of her hair behind her ear. "She never truly saw *me*. The few times she did, I do not think she liked what she saw: a girl too silly to see her ambitions realized. And so, she did her very best to reshape me in her image. She impressed upon me the greatness of our family name. She hired me the best tutors. She promised me that I was destined to do incredible things for our people. But I never knew if she truly loved me."

Her voice trembled, and her expression softened with bafflement—surprise, perhaps, at that child's hurt resurfacing so fiercely. Lorelei did not know how to comfort her.

"After she had finished parading me around at court, I was left to my own devices at home. In our estate, there were so many rooms and no one at all to fill them. I didn't know what half of them were for. It was a labyrinth. There were staircases that led to nowhere and all sorts of secret passages. In retrospect, I suppose those were for the servants."

Lorelei was unsurprised to hear it. It was no wonder Sylvia's imagination ran so wild. She could easily see Sylvia as a young girl, tearing through the woods like an imp and chasing sylphs through the meadows. She could easily envision her wandering the halls of her empty estate, spinning stories out of hidden corners. It made her terribly sad. Worse, it made a terrible kind of sense.

She'd spent her entire life trying desperately to be noticed.

The pang of sympathy knocked her off-kilter. For so long, her disdain for Sylvia had grounded her and driven her. But now, as she rifled through her memories, every one of them was knotted hopelessly, inextricably, with wretched fondness. Sylvia and her passionate, too-loud interjections when she argued for what she believed in. Sylvia singing as she brewed tea on the nights they stayed late in the office. Sylvia wading into dangerous waters to protect people she'd never met. Sylvia, always there in the edges of her awareness—and always looking away the moment Lorelei noticed her. Had these tender sentiments always been there, or had they overwritten her resentment with time? Lorelei no longer knew how to orient herself.

"Fascinating." She could muster only a half-hearted attempt at derision. "Would you like to share your favorite color as well?"

"Must you ruin everything?" Sylvia said crossly, although there was little venom in it. "If you must know, it's—"

"Amethyst. I know."

Sylvia blinked at her. "Oh."

What has come over me? It wasn't as though there was any *reason* she'd ferreted away what colors Sylvia favored and which flattered her best. It was impossible not to notice her. She tore through the world like a streak of white lightning.

Before Lorelei could die of humiliation, she said, "At any rate, we should discuss our plan. You and I are outnumbered. And now that you're injured, we're at a disadvantage."

"We?" Sylvia echoed.

"Surely that's not a surprise."

"Oh?" Color rose in Sylvia's cheeks. "Then perhaps I'm misremembering the time you loomed over me like some second-rate opera villain and said, *I have no interest in solving this case.*"

Sylvia had done a very unflattering impression of her, complete with an expression that could only be described as ominous. Lorelei sincerely hoped she didn't sound like *that.* "I lied to you. You were right."

"I'm sorry." Her smile was like daybreak. "Can you repeat that?"

"Get that smug look off your face," Lorelei snapped. Fortunately, all it took to eradicate any tender sentiments was spending five minutes in Sylvia's presence. "I bow down to your power of perception. Besides, I could use your help. You have insight and skills that I don't."

"Please stop complimenting me. It's flustering me."

"I shall restrain myself going forward." Lorelei procured a notebook from Sylvia's bag and flipped it open to a blank page. No small feat, given half the pages were filled with what seemed to be poetry. Her eyes skirted over a few lines about piercing gazes and capacious black cloaks before she decided she really did not want to know.

"So. Our plan."

"Right." Sylvia sprawled out beside her and tapped her chin. "There's a potential hole in your logic that's been troubling me. I will grant that it's likely someone killed Ziegler because the Ursprung was here in Albe. However, you're assuming they acted because they wanted it to be in *their* homeland. What if there was another reason entirely?"

Lorelei readied a retort but found she could not dismiss it out of hand. It was a reasonable enough challenge to her assumption. "Such as?"

Sylvia straightened up as if she had just been called on in lecture. "What if they killed Ziegler on my behalf?"

Any charity she'd felt toward Sylvia instantly evaporated. "And why would they do something like that?"

Sylvia looked affronted. "Because they don't want Wilhelm and me to marry! Perhaps they do not want us to consolidate our power, or . . . or perhaps they love me! Is love not the most powerful motive of all?"

"That is the most ridiculous theory I've ever heard! No one on this expedition is in love with you."

"It is not ridiculous! I'll have you know I have many suitors in Ruhigburg. I simply haven't met anyone worth my time. No one who's bothered to make their interest clear, anyway."

Lorelei could tell there was a specific someone behind that *anyway*. A dark, bilious feeling came over her, and she was immediately disgusted with herself. It shouldn't matter to her that Sylvia had feelings for someone. Why should anything that Sylvia did matter to her? But right now, in the too-close heat inside the tent, it felt terribly urgent. It felt like it would consume her entirely.

My God, she thought with a slow-dawning horror. She was jealous.

"Of course," she said. "No one is good enough for you."

Sylvia flushed with indignation. "Have you been speaking with Heike?"

"Ah, yes. Perhaps it's Heike who's still pining for you."

"Don't mock me," Sylvia said miserably.

"Yes, we should focus." Lorelei returned her attention to the notebook and tapped her pen against her knee. "I believe I have figured this out, but I would like to run my theory by you."

Sylvia sat up straighter, her expression growing serious. "Very well."

Lorelei wrote each expedition member's name in a neat column and explained the interviews she had conducted since the beginning of their voyage. In short: Ludwig lacked a clear motive, especially given the boon Wilhelm had promised him. Adelheid believed Wilhelm would use his power to stabilize Ebul—in no small part because he was in love with her. Johann, while he did have a clear motive and a violent nature, had seemed genuine in his devotion to Wilhelm. Which left, of course—

"Heike?" Sylvia's expression twisted in disbelief.

Lorelei had to admit she was offended. "Yes, Heike. She wants someone who can protect her, and you took that from her. Twice, as a matter of fact. Sabotaging this expedition could be a way of getting back at you—and also getting another chance with Wilhelm."

Sylvia rolled onto her back with a groan—whether humiliated or exasperated, Lorelei could not tell. "Saints," she muttered, "you really have been speaking to her."

"And who do you think it is?"

"Johann."

Again, that note of revulsion—no, she thought, fear—crept into her voice. "Why?"

Sylvia stared at her as though it were obvious. "I have made my career out of observing monsters. Johann is the worst of them. He does not see entire groups of people as people. And even those he does consider human, he enjoys hurting."

Lorelei had seen how ruthlessly he'd taken down that lindworm, how detachedly he'd examined Ziegler's body, and yet . . . "But he's a medic."

"That is precisely why he's a good medic." Sylvia sighed. Her fingertips traced the dueling scar that cut across her cheek. In the lamplight, it gleamed. "Many years ago, he gave me this."

That was no wound inflicted by a wooden practice sword. Lorelei sat up straighter with surprise. "You dueled him?"

"He and I fought in the same battalion. I challenged him because he treated our enemies monstrously—with no dignity." Her voice grew far away. "No mercy."

"And you lost."

She smiled ruefully. "He was always the superior swordsman."

"I still don't see it," said Lorelei. "Heike has the most to lose. She led us into the lindworm's den. She has been the most vocally against me. I just . . . can't prove it yet."

And at this point, she did not know how she would. Ziegler's body had been sunk in the river, her office scrubbed clean. Their last recourse was asking Ludwig if he remembered anything— assuming, of course, he saw anyone before he left camp.

"You've fretted enough for one day," Sylvia said gently. "You and I will figure this out together. I promise."

Together. All these years, Lorelei had been so convinced Sylvia wanted nothing more than to see her crash and burn.

I've misjudged you, she wanted to say. *I'm sorry.*

And yet, all she could manage was "It's late."

As they lay down to sleep, the sound of Sylvia's voice chased Lorelei into dreaming. *I'm so sorry, Lorelei.* That night, as she did every night, she dreamed of drowning. Only this time, in the exquisite and unbearable sweetness of Sylvia von Wolff's eyes.

The next morning, the world seemed far less strange. The sky had returned to a clear and bracing blue. Sunlight sparkled off the snow and glazed Sylvia's whimsical braid, one Lorelei could scarcely believe she'd woven with her own hands the night before.

Lorelei wasn't entirely convinced she hadn't dreamed it. But the evidence of it was laid out before her. It was more than that dam-nable braid. It was the way she found herself strangely . . . empty. No, not empty, exactly. Some fire within her had certainly gone out, but a new one kindled at the center of her chest, warm and insistent and *soft*.

It was horrible.

Sylvia walked ahead of her, humming under her breath. On any other day—any *normal* day—it would have been infuriating, the sound like a splinter beneath her skin. But today, it made her feel . . .

Ugh. She had to put a stop to this at once. With as much acid as she could muster, she said, "You're in an unusually good mood this morning."

"Am I?" Sylvia smiled radiantly, as though Lorelei had paid her a compliment. Her heart stuttered uselessly in response. "I'm sorry. It's only that I'm feeling so inspired, I feel I could write an entire book about our encounters these past few days."

"Your work truly brings you joy."

Sylvia slowed her steps until they walked side by side. Their boots crunched rhythmically in the snow. "Yours doesn't?"

"Not for its own sake. I always wanted to be a naturalist."

Sylvia grabbed her elbow. "Really?"

"Yes." Lorelei yanked her arm away. She could still feel the burn of Sylvia's touch through her sleeve and resisted the urge to shake out her hand. "However, Ziegler thought I would do better as a folklorist."

Sylvia looked as though she wanted to say something but thought better of it. "Well, it doesn't matter much anymore what she thought, does it? Perhaps you'd like to experience it firsthand."

"It," she echoed skeptically.

"Yes! *It.*" Sylvia sprang ahead a step, kicking up a veil of snow. "Being a naturalist. The Absolute. All of it! Don't you want to know what it's like to forget yourself for a time? Don't you want to get lost in the beauty of the world?"

Her sudden enthusiasm was alarming. "No. I have seen quite enough of your methodology to last a lifetime."

"Where's your spirit of adventure? You don't even need to be ensorcelled."

Somehow, that didn't assuage her. "We don't have time for this nonsense. Have you forgotten about poor Ludwig?"

"Of course I haven't! I have an idea. We will reach him even faster this way." Without warning, Sylvia seized her hand and twined their fingers together. Lorelei was certain her heart had stopped entirely, but Sylvia barely spared her a second glance. She touched her as if it were the most natural thing in the world.

Sylvia tugged her through a grove of pines shivering off a shawl of snow. It dusted the shoulders of her coat and clung to her eyelashes. When they broke through the low-hanging boughs, what she saw nearly stole her breath away.

With morning light bleeding over the horizon, she could see the entire world laid out before her: hazy blue mountains feathering toward the horizon, the river set ablaze with sunrise, and somewhere in the distance, turreted white castles.

Sylvia pointed. "Look there."

Only a few feet below them was a stretch of open plateau. A herd of mara stood grazing in the field. At a distance, they could almost be mistaken for ordinary horses. But their eyes burned the same red as a lit coal, and their manes drifted around them like thick plumes of smoke. If you climbed onto a mara's back, your feet would never touch the earth again. It would run and run until the years slipped away from you.

"Let's ride one," Sylvia said, suddenly very close to her ear.

Lorelei whirled to face her. "Absolutely not!"

Sylvia touched a finger to Lorelei's lips to quiet her. The sheer *condescension* of it . . . Lorelei had half a mind to bite her. In a stage whisper, Sylvia said, "You worry far too much. I've done this a thousand times before, and it will make transporting Ludwig much easier—and faster. There is no downside."

Lorelei wanted to say something smart, but all that came out was a sickly groan. This would be a stupid death if there ever was one. What kind of self-destructive fool decided to make a habit of riding mara? She supposed a lesser sort of fool than one who agreed to be taught.

"Fine. Just make it quick."

"Perfect! It will be easy. You will need to be quiet and project an aura of total calm." Lorelei considered herself capable of a great many things, but *projecting an aura of total calm* was not one of them. Sylvia seemed to realize her mistake, for she added, "Ah ... Well, maybe don't follow *too* closely."

Together, they slid down a rocky embankment and into the tall grass. Lorelei stayed as low as she could while still keeping her sights on Sylvia. She winnowed through the field soundlessly, but as she approached, the mara lifted their heads.

The largest of the herd regarded her with those otherworldly crimson eyes, its ears pricked warily forward. Step by step, Sylvia approached it, one hand extended. Lorelei couldn't bear to watch, and yet she couldn't tear her eyes away. That beast had to be twice her size. When at last Sylvia stood within arm's reach, she petted its nose as though it were as docile as a pony.

"You've got to be joking," Lorelei muttered.

The wind carried the soft sound of Sylvia's singing to her. Sylvia slipped her fingers into the mara's diaphanous mane. Without any hesitation, she hoisted herself onto its back.

Lorelei's heart dropped into her stomach. This was it. This time, she truly would watch Sylvia die. One moment ticked away, then another. When nothing catastrophic happened, Lorelei forced herself to breathe again.

Sylvia guided the mara toward Lorelei. When it stood before her, Lorelei stared up at Sylvia with dumbstruck awe. The pale light of the sun haloed her. She was utterly resplendent. She looked like an angel, or perhaps a fairy-tale knight. Neither option was good.

As calmly as she could manage, she said, "That is very dangerous."

"I know." She extended a hand to Lorelei, the picture of gentlewomanly grace. "I'll keep you safe."

Lorelei's heart thudded too fast in her chest. For the first time in five years, Sylvia had said something that shocked her beyond words, beyond derision. She didn't think she'd ever heard those words before in all her life.

I've clearly lost my senses.

Lorelei allowed herself to be pulled into a seat. At once, she hated everything about it. The ground was impossibly far below her. Sylvia was pressed distractingly against her back. And now, a reedy little voice was slithering around her head. It didn't seem to be speaking any language she could discern, but it offered clear suggestions all the same. It made things like *let go* and *surrender* pop unbidden to mind.

When she pointed it out, Sylvia only laughed. "Yes, they do that. Ready?"

"I suppose." Even her voice sounded jaundiced.

"All right," Sylvia said against the back of her neck. She sounded breathlessly giddy. "Hold on!"

Lorelei barely had time to tangle her hands in its mane before the mara took off at a gallop. The world streaked to a blur of color around them.

She screamed, which only made Sylvia laugh harder. Her eyes watered from the sting of the wind on her face. It hissed in her ears, doing nothing to drown out the mara's insistent voice. The iron chain around her neck burned, as though she'd dipped it in fire before fastening it around her neck. Somewhere beneath it all, she thought she might be afraid. But everything—her ghosts, her fears, this entire expedition—felt so far away from her now. They ran so fast, she swore they were one bound from taking flight.

Aaron, if only you could see me now.

When Lorelei glanced back, Sylvia was grinning at her. Her

hair had come loose from the braid and lashed the air behind them. Her excitement was infectious. It was as intoxicating as wine, her stupid smile even more so. Lorelei's own tugged stubbornly at the corner of her lips.

She really had been blind, if she had refused to acknowledge how beautiful Sylvia was before now. The Absolute was much closer than she'd ever believed. It was not in God, not in nature. It was right here before her. Close enough to touch.

Close enough to profane.

You stupid fool, she thought. All those years spent watching Sylvia, dissecting her, envying her ... It left a window open for something else to slip through.

After living among the nobility for so long, it seemed Lorelei had forgotten how vast the gulf between them truly was. There was no world in which this schoolgirl fantasy could be made real. Their stations were too different. They were too different. Sylvia would be cast in Lorelei's shadow, her brilliance dulled. She would tarnish like old silver at her very touch. Lorelei's chest felt painfully tight. This sharp stab of longing was a bittersweet and sorely needed reminder.

If they survived this, they would not be colleagues forever. When the documents detailing the disaster of the Ruhigburg Expedition were filed away in some minister's dusty cabinets, they would go their separate ways.

Lorelei knew the shape of a fairy tale: a prison. She had transcribed hundreds of them herself, written down her sordid end in her own tidy hand. Anything she might have imagined between her and the heiress of Albe had an ending already predetermined, if it was possible to imagine it at all. Maybe she truly was as covetous as these tales led the good people of Brunnestaad to believe.

Some things were not hers to possess.

SEVENTEEN

BY THE TIME THEY MADE IT back down the summit, the sun was a bloody thumbprint against the horizon. Its light stained the snow a livid red. They nearly missed Ludwig's shelter. It was half-buried, protruding from the snowdrifts like the wreckage of a ship.

"Stop!"

Before Sylvia even brought the mara to a halt, Lorelei slid off its back. Almost immediately, she crumpled to her knees with exhaustion. Just how long had they ridden for? It couldn't have been more than a few hours, but she felt as though she'd swum for days without surfacing for air.

"Are you all right?" Sylvia hopped down beside her. She landed soundlessly, with the grace of someone who'd indeed done it a thousand times before.

"Fine," Lorelei snapped. "Hold on to that thing."

The mara looked quite offended, until Sylvia scratched its withers. In the darkness, its eyes glowed like embers.

Swearing under her breath, Lorelei ducked under the tarp of the lean-to. The air within had thickened with the sweet, autumnal smell of decay. Ludwig was propped up against his backpack. His eyes—now a verdant green—roved over her face. Burning within them was a familiar, terrible awe. He looked as though he were staring at the face of someone long dead—or maybe at Death himself. Rahel had often looked at her like that in the throes of her fevers.

"Ludwig? Can you hear me?"

He groaned in reply.

Guilt soured her stomach. She never should have agreed to Sylvia's ridiculous antics. She never should have let herself grow so weak that a smile was all it took to make her abandon all sense. But with night falling like a blade and the exhaustion settling into her bones, the mara might very well save their lives.

Damn you, von Wolff.

Lorelei crouched beside him. The bark had clawed its way to his chin, and a fine layer of moss had grown on his shoulders. She did not know if she had the stomach to check the roots that had begun pushing through his skin like soil. She racked her brain for something that would pass for comfort, but there was little she could offer that wasn't a lie. "Can you stand?"

He hummed noncommittally, which Lorelei decided to take as a no. Which meant they'd have to haul him down this godforsaken mountain. Just her luck. They'd have to abandon his tarp; it was too cumbersome to bother with. It could stand as a grim memorial to this disastrous expedition, for all she cared. His backpack, however, might have something worth salvaging.

Lorelei rifled through its contents, tossing aside empty vials and ones filled with mysterious, half-rotted specimens. The shard of ash tree she removed and carefully set aside. She couldn't be sure if it was a catching curse, and she didn't care to find out.

After pocketing a few medical supplies and rations, she slipped the vasculum from around his neck. It couldn't hurt to see what he'd gathered so far. It was lighter than she expected, a large, sleek cylinder made of iron and painted with ivy. Inside were plants pressed flat between delicate sheets of cloth, gorgeously arranged and painstakingly preserved. As she thumbed through them, she paused over one sheet, which seemed more brittle than the others. When she pulled it out and lifted it to the light, she could do little but stare at it with a hazy sort of disbelief.

It was covered in Ziegler's handwriting.

There was no mistaking it. Ziegler often wrote like a woman possessed, with her tidy scrawl going every which way. You'd need a magnifying glass to fully appreciate its organized chaos: how she would write in both Javenish and Brunnisch, sometimes in the same sentence; how she would cut out and paste passages from other books into her own notes or press leaves into its pages. It was both intimate and staggeringly violent to see a stray page from her journal like this.

All the papers in Ziegler's room and the war room had been destroyed on the night of her murder—or so Lorelei had thought. She'd been certain to check the pages of every book and rummage through every drawer.

"Where did you get this?"

"Found it," he said blearily.

She was not in the mood to play this game. With Ludwig, it was impossible to tell what was a result of delirium and what was him being deliberately obtuse. Grabbing him by the collar, she gave him a shake. "*Where?*"

Sylvia's face appeared beneath the lean-to's opening. "Is everything all right?"

With a growl of frustration, Lorelei thrust the scrap of parchment out to Sylvia. Although she looked bewildered, she took it without question and scanned it. There was nothing especially noteworthy about its contents, but its existence vexed her. Either Ludwig had kept a document from when he'd disposed of her papers, or he'd found a cache of her writings the killer had not. She sorely hoped it was the latter.

"Where did he get this?" Sylvia asked.

"He says he found it."

Sylvia hummed pensively. "I suppose he must have."

Lorelei's life had spiraled entirely out of her control. Her temper spiked impotently in response. "Obviously!"

Sylvia primly folded the page in half. "Yelling isn't going to help anything."

"He deserves to be yelled at," she said spitefully. "I wish he could understand how unimpressed I am with him. Perhaps we should leave him here to die."

"Lorelei!" Sylvia gave a look of pure reproach as she ducked beneath the tarp. Kicking aside the mess Lorelei had made of Ludwig's belongings, she grabbed his arms and pulled. "Get out of the way, please."

Her voice was pinched, and her features were twisted in a grimace. Her wound clearly was bothering her. After everything Lorelei had done to ensure it'd heal properly, her carelessness was an insult. "Put him down before you rip your stitches out, you clod. I'll carry him."

"I'd rather not watch you snap in half. I'm not so fragile that I can't bear half his weight."

Lorelei glared but did not protest. Although she was taller than the both of them, she doubted she could get very far under Ludwig's full dead weight.

They slung his arms over their shoulders and hoisted him to his feet. He moaned in protest, his head lolling against her shoulder. Her legs still trembled with exertion, but she could manage this much. The real challenge would be getting him onto Sylvia's demonic mount.

"He's lucky he is so slight," Sylvia muttered as she struggled to drape him across the mara's back. The beast stomped one hoof in the snow, clearly displeased with the extra burden. Sylvia made a frustrated little sound and glared at Lorelei accusingly. "Are you even helping at all?"

It seemed the best remedy for her ill-advised feelings was the very woman she harbored them for. Lorelei had half a mind to drop him, just to spite her. "Shut up and push."

Once they got him onto the mara's back, they picked their way back down the mountain. Sylvia held fast to the mara's mane with one hand, guiding it on foot. Lorelei walked ahead of her, the enspelled lantern swaying at her side. With the snow reflecting its unearthly light, all the world seemed aglow.

And yet, all she could think of was that scrap of Ziegler's journal. The rest of it had to be somewhere on the ship. Ludwig wouldn't have kept one meaningless sheet of paper and destroyed the rest. There would be no point to it.

Maybe, she thought, *he wanted me to find it.*

And she would, even if she had to tear apart the *Prinzessin* board by board.

In the distance, she spied a fire burning brightly against the night. Three tents stood sentinel over the camp, made imposing in silhouette. By the time they arrived in the clearing, Johann had emerged from his tent to intercept them. His hand rested on the pommel of his sword, and it seemed he did not know who to look at first: Sylvia, in her tattered, bloodstained jacket; Lorelei, sporting a collar of bruises; or Ludwig, unconscious and hanging off a deadly horse like a rag doll.

He looked as though he'd seen a pack of ghosts.

"Don't just stand there gawking," Lorelei snapped. "Tend to him."

The four of them sat around the campfire while they waited for Johann to reemerge, Lorelei and Sylvia on one side, Adelheid and Heike on the other. The flames rose like a solid wall between them, but the *hiss* and *pop* of burning wood and sap filled the silence.

After what felt like an eternity, Johann's tent rustled open.

Sylvia sprang to her feet. "How is he?"

"I've given him medication for the pain, but his survival is entirely up to chance." Johann removed his glasses and rubbed at his bleary eyes. "Either the curse will work its way out of his system, or it will kill him."

"That is all the esteemed Herr Doktor Johann zu Wittelsbach has to say for himself?" Heike's tone was as viciously droll as ever. "Incredible."

"What will you have me do?" He replaced his glasses and leveled her with an impassive stare. "Cutting him open won't do any good at this point. The roots go deep."

"I'm sure you've done all you can," Adelheid interjected with a warning look at Heike.

She rolled her eyes. Turning to Lorelei and Sylvia, she asked, "What took you two so long?"

The question was a trap waiting to be sprung. Although Heike spoke with an eerie calm, the days they'd been gone had not been kind to her. Her hair hung limply around her face, as dull as tarnished copper, and her skin was red and chapped with cold. Even Adelheid watched her like she would a wild animal.

Lorelei had been dreading this. The subject of the Ursprung's location would have to be broached with more delicacy than usually employed.

Sylvia, ever tactful and patient, puffed herself up defensively. "We took a detour to search for the Ursprung."

Lorelei flinched.

"That is not the plan we agreed on." Adelheid's eyes glittered viciously in the firelight. "Your dallying may well cost Ludwig his life."

So much for delicacy, then.

"And what did you three do while we were gone? Play cards? Walk in circles?" When Adelheid said nothing, Lorelei sneered. "That's what I thought. We found Ludwig, and we made it to the summit. The Ursprung isn't here."

Shock extinguished all of Adelheid's outrage. For a moment, she stared at Lorelei with her lips parted. She recovered quickly enough, shaking her head. "That's impossible. All the data we collected led us here."

"As you said before, our data lead us to *a* source of magic, not necessarily *the* source." As she explained what they had found, Lorelei retrieved her sketchbook from her bag. She sketched what the vision had shown her: an island rising from a vast lake, flanked on either side by two isles. "Do you recognize this place?"

Dread wrote itself across Adelheid's face. "Unfortunately, yes."

"Unfortunately?" Sylvia asked.

"That is the lake we call the Little Sea. There are four islands in the center of it. You say you saw a fifth in this vision?"

"I believe it's what I've heard called the Vanishing Isle. It will appear in your Little Sea on the night of the next new moon and disappear again come morning." Lorelei met her eyes. "You're certain that's where it is? We only have one chance at this."

Adelheid frowned as she studied the drawing. "Yes. It's a very accurate likeness. I've only been once before, but it's not a sight one forgets easily. All those islands are completely uninhabited."

Sylvia, evidently unable to resist the promise of danger, perked up. "Why is that?"

"Because the Little Sea is crawling with nixies and shipwrecks. Going there is a death wish."

Lorelei could not have conjured a worse possible location if she tried. "Oh, perfect. Just perfect."

Heike laughed. At first, it was soft. But once she got going, she couldn't stop. She doubled over in full, hiccupping guffaws. "God, you must think we're stupid."

Lorelei bristled. "Your point being?"

"Let me make sure I understand this. You somehow managed to make your way through an enchanted forest with no equipment. You conveniently found Ludwig along the way to the summit, where you had a mystical vision of where the Ursprung is. And it just so happens to be on the other side of the country. Is that right?"

When she laid it out like that, it did sound difficult to believe. "That's correct."

The sulfuric glint in Heike's eyes kindled brighter. Lorelei recognized this kind of hateful desperation well by now. In the face of uncertainty and terror, the one thing that could be counted on was the wickedness of a Yeva. "You really *have* learned how to spin a fairy tale, you snake."

"Bite your tongue!" Sylvia had drawn herself up, as though she could gain another six inches of height by sheer force of will. Lorelei could not look away from the set of her jaw, the broad line of her shoulders. Sylvia stoked into a righteous fury was something to behold.

"Aw," Heike cooed. "Did I strike a nerve?"

"Enough." Adelheid rose to her full height and glared down at Heike. "This behavior is beneath you."

"You cannot be serious!" Heike had the gall to sound betrayed. "Do you believe her?"

"She has never been to the Little Sea. Even if Sylvia described it perfectly, she could not have drawn it so accurately."

"What do you suggest?" Johann asked coldly. "We return to him with nothing?"

"Of course not!"

"Or perhaps lie to him?" Johann continued, stalking in a slow circle around her. His fingers twitched toward the handle of his saber. "Present him with this fake Albisch spring?"

Heike's eyes went round with feigned hurt. "Heavens, no. I'm not suggesting we do anything *seditious*." Her voice hardened. "Now, are you going to get your hand off your sword, or will I have to make your handler command you?"

His lip curled, but he retreated a few paces away from the fire. Even Adelheid regarded her warily. "This is for the greater good, Heike. It is worth the risk."

"Right. The greater good. Our promise. His stupid dream!" The bitterness sharpened with every word. Then, she drew in a shuddering breath and wrapped her arms around herself. For a moment, Lorelei almost believed her sadness was real. *Almost.*

"I'm so tired of this," Heike murmured. "Haven't we done

enough? We can try again, can't we? I just want to go home. Don't you want to go home, Addie?"

"Home." Adelheid's eyes fluttered closed. Lorelei could feel the turn of her thoughts as if they were her own. Blood in the soil. Smoke in the air. The healing, tender fields trampled under soldiers' boots once again. "And if Wilhelm cannot maintain power while we prepare to set out again? Where will my home be at the end of that?"

Heike clasped Adelheid's wrist and pulled her hand into her lap. "With me."

Adelheid pulled her hand from Heike's. When she spoke again, it was with a terrible chill. "Sometimes, you sound just like him."

Heike blinked back unshed tears. Just as quickly as she'd put on airs of plaintive desperation, she tossed them aside. A manipulator to the end. "And if we press forward, another one of us will die!"

Lorelei almost laughed. Was that a promise?

Adelheid composed herself into perfect neutrality once more. With her hair shining golden in the soft moonlight and her broad shoulders determinedly set, she looked like a statue of a warrior-queen stirred to life. "It is your decision, Lorelei."

Lorelei swept her gaze over the group. The firelight cast their faces in harsh shadow, and their haunted eyes were locked on her. She felt as though they were standing in the middle of a lake in midwinter. The ice beneath their feet was crackling, and she didn't know how the fault lines would divide them. All she knew for certain was that all of them would be pitted against one another until the bitter end.

"We've come this far and lost too much to give up now." She prayed she sounded more assured than she felt. Through the delicate scrollwork of branches, the narrowed eye of the waning moon glared down at them. "We will give him the Ursprung, or we will give him nothing. We've no time to waste."

EIGHTEEN

$\mathcal{J}$T TOOK THREE DAYS to reach the *Prinzessin*, where it lay in the river like a sleeping dragon, softly belching smoke. The relief Lorelei had felt upon seeing it vanished the instant she stepped onboard. She'd nearly forgotten the nauseating sway of the floor—and the repressive atmosphere was not helped by the crew, who had stared at Ludwig as though his curse were a catching thing.

Lorelei could not say she blamed them.

As soon as she scrubbed off the grime of the last two weeks in the washbasin, she shut herself in her room. The temptation to collapse into bed was almost too powerful to deny, but she could not afford to fall asleep. Instead, she paced restlessly. Water from her damp hair ran down the back of her neck and slipped into her collar like cold, searching fingers.

She would have to find Ziegler's journal before the others caught on to her—or saw her rummaging through the professor's belongings. She waited until her eyes burned with exhaustion, until she was certain everyone else had fallen asleep. Then, she tucked a tarnished vesta case into her waistcoat's pocket and draped her greatcoat over the back of her chair.

Lorelei cracked open her bedroom door, and cool air sighed into the room. Before she could think too hard about what she was doing, she stepped out onto the balcony.

The dark closed in on her immediately, but the ambient light from the moon above and the crew's lanterns below made it tolerable. She could see the massive paddle wheel dipping into the lightless waters of the Vereist. It turned inexorably, half of it eerily vanishing and reappearing as it churned the water to black froth.

There were two blessings she could count on. One, there was no direct line of sight from the deck. And two, there was no one to disturb her on this side of the ship. In a neat row were her room, then Ziegler's, then Ludwig's, and lastly, her destination: the war room. Through the ringing in her ears, she could make out the low drone of the crew's voices filtering up from below.

Now or never.

The doors leading into the war room were enormous, inlaid with windows that reflected the pitiless black of the night. By some miracle, they were unlocked. As Lorelei slipped inside, the warding bells mounted on the lintel chimed breathlessly. She muffled them with her fist before easing the doors shut again. Just as they settled, Lorelei drew up short at a flicker of movement in the glass.

Ziegler's face loomed just over her shoulder.

Lorelei gasped, whirling around. In her haste, she knocked a book off its perch. It landed with a resonant *thud*. The plush carpet barely muffled the sound.

Nothing was behind her, but she could *feel* Ziegler there, leering at her.

"Fuck," she whispered.

Footsteps echoed just outside the war room. It was enough to rudely jolt Lorelei back into her body. She must have woken someone up. The dregs of her fear rooted her in place, but if she stood here gawking like a fool, she'd be found. She ducked behind the massive writing desk and did her best to quiet her panicked breathing.

The doors to the war room swung open. Lantern light spilled into the room, lapping at the toes of her boots. It was then she realized she'd left the book lying on the ground.

Careless. If she went down like this, she would never forgive herself.

"No, I didn't hear anything at all," Sylvia said, her voice over-loud. As unconvincing as ever. Lorelei could have groaned aloud. "What do you think you heard?"

"It sounded like something fell," Adelheid said skeptically.

A door's hinges creaked as someone began rummaging through the closet on the other side of the room. Footsteps trod softly across the floorboards and stopped just in front of the desk. Lorelei held her breath.

After an agonizing moment, Sylvia said, "Nothing over here," and slid the book underneath the desk with the toe of her boot.

"Strange." Adelheid sounded puzzled. "I suppose it was nothing."

"Perhaps there are ghosts on board," Sylvia said conspiratorially.

Lorelei could practically hear Adelheid's withering glare. "Perhaps."

The latch of the door announced their departure. Lorelei counted ten seconds before she emerged. Complete, smothering darkness awaited her. She pulled the curtains shut over the glass doors, then withdrew her vesta case from its pocket and struck a match. The flame sparked into a long, ghostly taper, then sputtered. It traced the shape of the cluttered bookshelves and lacquered the massive table in the center of the room with a sickly glow. She lit the slumping candles on the desk and shook out her match. Smoke curled around her as she sat in the finely uphol-stered chair behind Ziegler's desk.

I will find what you've kept from me.

Lorelei had known her mentor for the better part of twelve years. Once, she thought she knew Ziegler's mind as well as she knew her own. Clearly, she hadn't been thinking enough like her when she'd first stumbled into this room, blind with grief and ex-haustion. If she hadn't wanted anyone to find something she'd hidden, where would she have put it?

She opened a drawer and ran her gloved fingers along the inside, searching for a false bottom. Nothing. Clicking her tongue, she continued rummaging through the desk. She removed the drawers one by one and turned them over. She shone candlelight into the empty sockets that remained, searching for some sign of a trick door, a hidden compartment. It took only minutes to dissect it completely.

Next, she took to pulling books off the shelves and shaking them out. Her efforts produced little but a shower of pressed flowers and clouds of dust that made her eyes water. Leafing through the pages revealed nothing but a robust collection of texts on the cosmos and botany. By the time she was through with the room, she'd pried every stuffed and mounted beast from the wall, and the closet looked as though it had vomited its contents onto the ornate rug.

This was utterly, infuriatingly pointless.

Lorelei slumped into the desk chair and allowed it to swivel her in a slow circle. If there was nothing in this office, there could still be something in Ziegler's room.

As soon as she set the war room to rights, Lorelei drew the curtains and peered out into the darkness. No lanterns. No sign of Sylvia or Adelheid. She took the opportunity to slip back onto the balcony. It creaked and settled with every footstep as she made her way toward Ziegler's room.

She paused outside the door, but her arm suddenly felt too heavy to lift. Her emotions were already simmering too close to the surface, and the very thought of going in there made her feel ill. She couldn't do this. She couldn't paw through Ziegler's effects like a common thief. How much more disrespect could she pay her? She'd sunk her body in the river, for God's sake. But she had come this far in pursuit of the truth. Perhaps uncovering it was the greatest honor she could pay Ziegler now.

She forced herself to enter.

Lorelei lit the candles. Although she'd never been in Ziegler's quarters before, she found it suspiciously in order. Her mentor had always been a messy person, the chaos of her space a mirror of her mind. Someone—probably Ludwig—had certainly been in here to tidy up.

All the same, there were odds and ends that suggested someone had lived here, even for one night. Her inkpot lay on the desk, along with an open jar of salt and a mug of tea caked with dried leaves. It was as though she'd stepped away in the middle of writing a letter. At any moment, she might step through the door again and smile to see Lorelei standing there.

Lorelei blinked back the humiliating sting of tears and crouched beside the bed. She felt silly as she peered underneath, like a child checking for monsters. When that turned up nothing, she stripped off the sheets and tossed them into a heap in the corner. She lifted the mattress from its frame, then probed the edges for any misplaced stitches.

Nothing.

With a sigh of frustration, Lorelei dismantled the desk with the same harried precision she had the one in the war room. Inside, she found a drafted chapter of the fourth volume of *Kosmos*, Ziegler's latest and most ambitious project, bound in a delicate white ribbon. At least her killer had a modicum of respect, to leave this untouched.

Shutting it back into the drawer, Lorelei flung open the closet door. She was greeted with the unwelcome sight of more outfits than Ziegler possibly could have worn over the course of the expedition. She unceremoniously began tossing garments onto the floor. Silk and finely painted cotton puddled at her feet. At last, she found a coat that struck her as unusually heavy—and was startled to realize that she recognized it. It was the same one Ziegler had worn on the night of the send-off ball. Draped over her arms, it looked like the shed skin of a serpent.

The temperature plummeted. Her breath plumed unsteadily in the cold.

From the darkest corner in the room, Lorelei swore she could feel those horrible eyes boring into her again. Her every muscle seized with primal terror. A wisp of silver slithered across her vision, but when she turned around, the room was still and empty.

"Leave me alone, damn you," she muttered.

She laid the coat on the bed. Something sharp-edged had been stitched underneath the lining. With a sick feeling in her stomach, she retrieved a letter-opener from the desk and slit open the fabric. Nestled inside was a journal, bound in pristine leather and closed around a silk-ribbon bookmark.

This had to be it.

With trembling fingers, she opened the journal. The spine gave a satisfying *crack*, and although Lorelei knew Ziegler had been using it within the last month, it somehow felt ancient, like a fairy-tale witch's spell book.

Upon first inspection, it contained nothing unusual: documentations of supplies Ziegler had requisitioned, reminders to herself on which work to delegate to Lorelei, absent-minded recordings of the weather. It was in the middle of these mundane entries that Lorelei found the jagged edge that fit perfectly against the sheet Ludwig had taken. What had he found so interesting? It was all so . . . ordinary.

Lorelei began thumbing through the pages more urgently. Halfway through the journal, Ziegler's notes abruptly ended. What followed was nothing but blank pages marbled with water stains. The previous entries had been dated weeks prior to their departure, and Ziegler journaled daily. Why had she *stopped*?

Unless she hadn't.

Distantly, Lorelei remembered one of the first "science experiments"—or had she called it a magic trick?—Ziegler had conducted with her. All it required was heat, parchment, and lemon juice. She couldn't possibly have . . .

Lorelei tore out a page and held it above the candle sputtering on the writing desk. Words began to appear on the parchment as though written by a ghostly hand. They glowed the color of burnished gold and blackened around the edges.

"You absolute madwoman," Lorelei muttered, caught somewhere between disbelief and admiration. Ziegler had written all of these entries in invisible ink.

She'd printed each letter absurdly large and with exaggerated care, but her shorthand was barely comprehensible. Eventually, Lorelei managed to translate it: her initial speculations on the Ursprung's location. Every passage was rendered in her trademark style, full of overblown lyricism and yearning.

Lorelei missed her terribly.

She tamped down that thought by ripping another page from the journal. Each one did little to sate her curiosity. They painted a straightforward picture of a woman she already knew, one with a flair for the dramatic and a love for life. She considered feeding them to the fire out of sheer frustration—until a peculiar abbreviation caught her eye.

Spoke again with AvW.

Lorelei waved the candle beneath the page with a newfound determination. With each word that appeared, her heart rate rocketed higher. The candle's wax dribbled onto her gloves as she read.

Data suggest unlikely to find Source in Albe. However, evidence of high aetheric concentration in mountains should be enough to support A's case.

The longer Lorelei stared at the pages, the more she willed it to make sense. Blood roared through her ears, drowning out everything else. Ziegler had known. Ziegler had *known* they were chasing the wrong spring, and she misled them. It was as good as her dying a second time.

After how hard they'd worked, after nearly a year of struggle and preparation, she'd thrown the truth away for the sake of Anja von Wolff's politicking. And with Wilhelm's reign so unstable, she'd all but abandoned the people of Brunnestaad to their fate. It seemed impossible to accept that she'd do something so utterly selfish—and so shortsighted.

But of course she would, Lorelei thought.

Wilhelm had kept her like a monkey on a leash for years. After this expedition, he never would have let her leave his sight again. This was an escape plan, no different from a wolf chewing off its own paw to free itself from a snare. Whether she fooled him or not, it didn't matter. Ziegler had lived in Javenor for most of her life. She had friends and peers who wrote her hundreds upon hundreds of letters a year. If war came to Brunnestaad, the prison she so disdained, she had somewhere to run. What did it matter what happened to the rest of them?

Lorelei threw down the journal. Where there was smoke, there was fire. There was more to it than this.

With a newfound purpose, she tore apart Ziegler's belongings once again. Stitched lovingly into another jacket's lining was a handsome sum of cash, with documents promising more from the von Wolff coffers. Hidden in the sole of her favorite leather boots was a passport with a visa already stamped, valid from this month to the next five years. There was even a deed to a house tucked away in the charming seaside town where her influential Javenish friends lived.

Ziegler was a woman already long gone. In the last months of her life, she had thrown all of her principles away. And in doing so, she'd sealed her own death.

You damn fool.

Piece by piece, Lorelei put together what Ziegler had done. In exchange for Ziegler's placing the fake Ursprung in Albe, Anja would fund her research for the rest of her life. A fair trade, Lorelei supposed, when Ziegler would all but hand Anja a narrative that would justify their rebellion. King Wilhelm, the thieving, conquering outsider, stealing magic from the good people of Albe in order to prop up his feeble reign. Such an insult could not be borne.

Under Ziegler's instruction, Lorelei had sharpened her mind into a blade. Now she felt like a soldier come home from war. Confused and purposeless, with a weapon to turn nowhere but inward. She felt utterly naïve and furious for it. This expedition was never an academic pursuit. It was nothing but a desperate scrabble for survival. Once, Lorelei had believed truth was the most powerful force in the world. Now she understood that none of what they did was as pure as Ziegler had led her to believe.

Seething beneath this pain was another terrible realization. Sylvia didn't know what her mother had done—and now Lorelei had to tell her.

NINETEEN

BEFORE THE SUN HAD RISEN, Lorelei pounded on Sylvia's door. She hadn't even lowered her fist when it swung open.

Sylvia stood there, ethereal in the moonlight, her quartz-silver eyes glowing softly through the gloam. She wore a gauzy nightgown knotted artlessly around her waist, as though she had gotten dressed in a rush. It was maddening, the casual intimacy of her dishevelment. Lorelei's anger crashed hopelessly against it.

Without speaking, she pushed past Sylvia and shut the door behind her. She leaned against it, barring them both inside. Even so, she towered above Sylvia, who looked up at her with an expression caught halfway between indignation and dreamy disbelief.

"I didn't say you could come in."

"I have to tell you something."

Sylvia gave a perplexed little shake of her head, as though Lorelei had spoken Yevanisch. "What could possibly be so urgent?"

Lorelei turned the lock behind her. Its grim, decisive click echoed too loud in the silence. Sylvia's throat bobbed in a swallow. Lorelei couldn't help following it with her eyes before she dragged her gaze back to Sylvia's. "Ziegler and your mother were colluding."

Her words struck Sylvia like a bucket of cold water. The anticipation on her face dissolved into an alarming blankness. "What?"

Lorelei produced the journal entries from her pocket. Sylvia gingerly accepted them from her and began to read. For a long few moments, she was silent. When she finally met Lorelei's gaze again, her expression was anguished. "Tell me you've written this yourself."

At the plainness of her shock, Lorelei's temper cooled to ashes. "I'm sorry."

Sylvia clutched the parchment so tightly, it crumpled. "Why would Ziegler do such a thing?"

"She was ready to cut her losses and flee to Javenor at a moment's notice. I found her passport and her savings—what was left of it, anyway." Not to mention her entire wardrobe, packed to the brim with everything she'd need to stake out her new life. The horrible feeling of betrayal bubbled up within her again. Her mouth tasted like bile.

"She was in quite a bit of debt from her publications. Those expeditions and engravings certainly did not pay for themselves." Lorelei grimaced. "Your mother agreed to pay her debts and fund her research going forward in exchange for placing the Ursprung—or a fake Ursprung—in Albe. The moment Wilhelm claims Albisch magic for himself, she plans to stage a coup."

"That snake," Sylvia muttered. "My mother must have been laying the groundwork for quite some time. I suppose that explains why those villagers were already so riled up against Wilhelm."

Lorelei leaned her head back against the door. "I understand why Ziegler did it, but at the same time, I can't understand it at all. She was willing to doom us all to whatever upheaval she left in her wake."

"I'm sorry, Lorelei," Sylvia said quietly. The candlelight flickering in the corner of the room painted her in achingly lovely hues. "I know it hurts when the people we love disappoint us. But I refuse to believe she would abandon you of all people."

"How can you still insist on seeing the best in her? You read her note."

"I did, yes." Sylvia hesitated. "But she left us the key to finding the true Ursprung. Perhaps that was her last contingency plan: trusting you to know how to use it."

It was a delusion—pure delusion. It might have been a comforting thought, if Lorelei were at all disposed toward forgiveness or optimism. Sylvia was far better than her. "How are you faring?"

"I don't know. How is one supposed to feel when their entire life has been upended? My aspirations, my plans, any illusion I still had of my mother caring for me . . . All of it is shattered." Sylvia's expression turned desolate. "How could she keep me in the dark about this? Did she expect that I would comply—or that I wouldn't? I do not know which is worse. I . . ."

She pressed the heels of her hands against her eyes, and Lorelei struggled to keep the alarm off her face as Sylvia's shoulders began to shake. God, she could not bear it when people cried. She never had been any good at this sort of thing.

"Would you like me to make you some tea?" she asked. "I'm afraid it's the best I can offer, short of seeing her imprisoned when we return to Ruhigburg."

Sylvia let out a startled laugh through her tears. "You're awful."

"I'm aware." With a sigh, Lorelei pulled her handkerchief from her breast pocket and handed it to her. It was a rough scrap of linen, nothing so fine as the embroidered silk ones Sylvia carried, but still, she smiled at Lorelei as though she'd given her something precious.

"I suppose you have a point in that all we can do is move forward." Sylvia held her gaze with a conviction that made Lorelei's mouth go dry. "One way or another, when we return, I will see my mother pay for what she has done. I will claim my rightful title as the duchess of Albe and do what is best for my people."

"Is independence not what's best for them?"

"I meant what I said. I intend to stand with Wilhelm. He is not perfect, but he has not mistreated us. War would see so many lives lost." Sylvia sighed. "For what? The Albisch fear our culture being taken from us. We are proud of it—understandably so. But the way that pride has manifested . . . It unsettles me."

She was clearly thinking of the effigies.

"Beyond that, Wilhelm's reign would not survive an Albisch coup, and God knows there are far worse people than him waiting in the wings. I have seen who Johann keeps company with." Sylvia frowned. "I will have to do my best to maintain order. It will require meeting with my subjects, a thorough review of my mother's correspondence—and, certainly, reconsidering the positions of those she has kept close in court."

"A controversial vision for the new duchess of Albe," Lorelei mused. "You'll be stripped of your title within the year."

Sylvia smiled fondly at her. "I so appreciate your vote of confidence."

"I do have confidence in you." She was surprised to find that she meant it. A strange, bittersweet feeling lodged itself in her throat. "I shall look forward to seeing what you achieve from afar."

"Afar?" Sylvia echoed. "I had hoped . . ."

"What, that I would come with you?"

"If you would like to." She sounded uncharacteristically uncertain. It made Lorelei suspicious.

Lorelei blinked slowly. "Forgive me. I think I might've suffered lasting brain damage from my strangulation."

Sylvia flushed a charming shade of red. "I should have known better than to express a single tender sentiment to the likes of you."

"Don't mistake me," Lorelei said, more bristly than she had intended. Softening her voice, she added, "I appreciate the invitation. I . . . am only confused."

"It is not a trap!" Sylvia protested. "Perhaps you could advise me instead of Wilhelm. Or perhaps you could spend your days skulking about, doing . . . whatever it is you wish to do. It does not matter to me."

Lorelei felt suddenly light-headed. Of all things, it was anger coursing through her. She had not spent her entire life afraid and striving just for Sylvia von Wolff to offer her an escape rope as though it were nothing. "Why would you propose such a thing?"

For a long while, silence thickened around them, until Lorelei could scarcely breathe. She felt wild and out of sorts. It was only when she could no longer bear the weight of it that Sylvia laughed. It was a breathless sound, bewildered and exasperated and somehow wholly relieved. She raked her hands through her hair, pulling apart her waves. Errant strands rose around her like wisps of white fire. "Do you really want me to spell it out for you?"

"Spell out *what?*"

Lorelei was beginning to feel hysterical. She did not know what exactly they were talking about anymore, but she sensed Sylvia working herself up to something. Sylvia stepped closer, and Lorelei's focus narrowed to the precious little space between them. Lorelei could hear Sylvia's shaky breaths. She could feel the press of her body against hers, Sylvia's warmth seeping into the weave of her coat.

"How can you be so smart and so . . . so *stupid!*"

"I beg your pardon!"

"I'm trying to tell you that I care for you, you impossible woman!" Her face flushed. "Are you happy now? Surely you've known for years."

Lorelei opened her mouth, and for the second time tonight, she was speechless. All that came out was a strangled sound, something between a croak and a muffled groan. When she finally recalled their shared language, all she could manage was a weak "I did not know that."

"But you . . . You must have! It was so obvious. The way you would mock me when you caught me looking at you, or . . . the way you . . ." Sylvia trailed off helplessly as she realized she had shared far more than she'd ever planned to. She buried her face in her hands and made a sort of pained, dying sound. And when she dropped her arms and saw Lorelei still standing there, slack-jawed and wild-eyed, it apparently dawned on her that there was no going back from this. "How could you not know I wanted you?"

Never in her life had Lorelei been subjected to so many emotions at once. "How could I have possibly known? If you truly wanted me"—she stumbled over the words—"why have you been such a menace all this time?"

"Because you *despise* me! You think me beneath you. I could see it in your eyes, and I . . . God, I would have done anything to earn your respect, your attention. I just wanted you to look at me." Sylvia floundered for a moment. "When you do, I . . . It's terrifying. It's exhilarating. You're like something out of a nightmare."

Lorelei stared at her as her entire life rearranged around this revelation. So much clicked into horrifying, sickening clarity. Every flush of Sylvia's face she'd misinterpreted as indignation. Every tremor of her voice she'd read as barely leashed anger. The ways their eyes always found one another in a room. The way she always stood too close when they argued.

If she examined her own behavior, she would combust from humiliation. How *had* she been so stupid? To act on this now, when their lives hung in the balance, was madness. To care about anyone but herself was a weakness she couldn't afford. And yet . . .

"I understand, of course, if you want nothing to do with me," Sylvia said. "I won't make a fuss if you deny me. However, I cannot go on this way. I can't pretend anymore that I don't—"

"Sylvia."

The sound of her name drew her up short. It was the first time Lorelei had ever spoken it aloud, and now she feared she might never stop. *Sylvia, Sylvia, Sylvia.* It felt like the rhythm of her own heart. Like something she could not survive without.

Lorelei brushed her fingers against Sylvia's throat, until she cradled her jaw in her palm. She tilted her chin upward until their eyes met. She could feel Sylvia's pulse thundering frantically against her thumb. She applied the barest hint of pressure and felt the answering gasp tear through her like a drug. It pulled every coherent thought from her mind. Distantly, it occurred to her that a good person would not feel so exhilarated at holding a lover's very life in their hands.

You're like something out of a nightmare.

And you, Lorelei thought despairingly, *are resplendent.*

What did someone like Sylvia see in her, loathsome creature that she was? She could not possibly want her as she truly was: the tender, nerve-stricken parts of herself she did not let anyone see. But if she wanted her monstrous—a fantasy—then Lorelei could give her that.

In one motion, she spun Sylvia around and backed her against the door. It rattled in its frame. She bent down until their lips just barely touched, until the air felt as thin as it had on the Himmel-stechen's peak.

Sylvia's breath frayed at the edges. She gazed up at her as though she were a thing stepped from her wildest imaginings. The cool, liquid silver of her hooded eyes was nearly consumed by her blown-wide pupils. Lorelei's stomach dipped low at the sight of her so full of unbridled *wanting.* She'd never thought herself capable of inspiring this sort of desire. It was dizzying, addictive. She could no longer convince herself this wasn't some lurid dream.

When Lorelei kissed her, well and truly, Sylvia let out a moan that nearly undid her. Her lips parted eagerly, and she molded her body against Lorelei's and fisted her hands in her lapels. It felt like a collision—like burning alive. Sylvia kissed like a woman starved. Lorelei almost smiled despite herself. Why had she expected any different? Sylvia von Wolff had never once been able to temper her passions.

She scrabbled desperately at the knot of Lorelei's cravat. At last, with a sound of triumph, she succeeded in unfastening it. Cool air sighed across Lorelei's bared collarbone, and the scrap of silk went sailing into some dark, forgotten corner of the room.

Insatiable, she thought, with only mild disapproval. Of course

Sylvia would rush headlong into this, as she did all things, but Lorelei had imagined this far too many times to let her ruin it with haste.

Lorelei tangled her fingers into Sylvia's hair, and for one moment, she allowed herself to relish the heavy weight of it in her grasp. Then, she pulled hard enough to expose the pale column of her throat. God, Sylvia was so beautiful. Every inch of her begged to be touched. Lorelei could not resist bending down to trace the side of her neck with the barest touch of her lips. Sylvia's skin pebbled, and her breath hitched again.

Sylvia made a soft, frustrated sound. "You impossible, infuriating—"

She cut herself off with a whine—half pleasure, half protest—when Lorelei sucked a bruise onto her skin. This time, Lorelei did smile. If only she'd known sooner how easy it was to silence her.

"Insults will get you nowhere," she murmured against Sylvia's ear. Her voice trembled, just barely.

And her mind went utterly blank when Sylvia shot back, with only a touch of wryness, "Please."

Please. It set her entire body alight. She tightened her grip in Sylvia's hair, anchoring her in place as she kissed her again with redoubled, demanding hunger. Sylvia could easily break free of her hold if she wanted. Instead, Sylvia melted pliantly against her, and Lorelei hooked her arm around her waist to support her weight. The illusion of control tonight—something she might very well never have again—sent a heady rush through her.

For so long, she had yearned to crush Sylvia underfoot, to have her entirely at her mercy. And now that she had her, she hardly knew what to do with this rush of power. She wanted Sylvia desperately, forever, in a thousand different ways. It frightened her, but she didn't know how to stop this.

She didn't want to stop.

Lorelei drew back to catch her breath. Sylvia's lips were wet and parted, and her eyes were dreamy, like she hadn't quite processed what was happening. There was nothing at all noble about her now. What a scandal they would cause should anyone find out.

A bolt of alarm shot through her. Lorelei stumbled a few wary steps back, determined to put some space between them. God, she couldn't think straight with Sylvia looking at her like that. As evenly as she could manage, she said, "I can't do this."

"What?" Sylvia wheezed.

"*You* can't do this."

It took a moment for Sylvia to catch up. Her expression landed somewhere between desperate and murderous. "Why not?"

She was alight with her typical determination. Her hair was a flash of lightning in the dark, and all the candlelight blooming out of the darkness gilded her. She was radiant, as bright as the sun itself. In that moment, it was all Lorelei needed to seal her decision.

She was a weed, drawn helplessly to light she did not deserve. And now she had knowledge she was never meant to have. The sound of her sighed-out name on Sylvia's lips, the taste of her kiss. Now, she would never be able to stop wanting her. Like another fairy-tale curse inflicted upon her, she was struck with a hunger she could never satisfy.

"No one would accept this." It hurt more than she expected to say aloud. No matter what happened, there was no escaping that reality.

The weight of it bloomed between them like ink dropped into water. Sylvia was a princess, and Lorelei was a cobbler's daughter. Some gulfs were too wide to cross. What use would she be as an adviser on matters of governance or—hell—which plates to use when some foreign dignitary came to call on them? The two of them would be the laughingstock of the entire nation. Lorelei couldn't bear to humiliate her.

Tentatively, Sylvia brushed her fingers against Lorelei's face. Lorelei felt each of them like a brand against her skin. "They would have to."

"Don't delude yourself. People like me don't win the princess's heart."

"They're just stories, Lorelei." Sylvia's voice frayed. "You must stop taking them so seriously."

"You and I know very well that they're not."

Their breath mingled. For the first time, Lorelei studied the bruise blossoming on the side of Sylvia's neck. Pride and shame snared together within her.

Careless, she thought. *Mine.*

And yet, she would never truly be hers.

"I meant what I said," Sylvia said. "I can't go back to pretending I don't care for you. Can't we be happy?"

"Happy," Lorelei repeated. The word felt foreign on her tongue. If Sylvia could not be convinced with sense, she would have to hurt her. "And what happiness would a life with you grant me? I would be entirely dependent on you for the rest of my days. I would never see my family or hear my language again. I can't cut off any more pieces of myself. I'm nearly bled dry."

She did not wait for an answer. She fled.

As she walked back to her room, her mind frantically worked. One way or another, Sylvia von Wolff would be the death of her. If she could not find decisive evidence, Wilhelm might very well punish Sylvia for Ziegler's murder instead of Lorelei. It was a neat story. Anja von Wolff and Ziegler had schemed to plant a false Ursprung, and then Sylvia had gotten rid of the loose end.

Perhaps Lorelei could never have Sylvia, but she could still save her. That would have to be enough for this lifetime. One way or another, Lorelei would find proof.

All she needed was the right opportunity.

TWENTY

*T*HE NEXT DAY, her opportunity arose.

Outside the window of the mess hall, the evening was clear save for the haze chuffing from the *Prinzessin*'s smokestacks. It drifted lazily across the sky and veiled the pale face of the waning moon. Its dwindling was like an hourglass: only ten more days until the Vanishing Isle would appear.

Lorelei surveyed the room from her usual corner table, a cup of coffee warming her hands. The ship's crew had filtered in for dinner and spent most of their allotted fifteen minutes casting resentful gazes her way. She did not blame them. To make it to Ebul on time, they needed to work around the clock, and she'd been the one to give the order. God willing, they wouldn't mutiny—and the steam engine wouldn't overheat and blow them all sky-high before they arrived. They'd survived far too much to suffer such a mundane death.

The double doors of the mess swung open to admit Adelheid and Heike—together and *laughing*, to Lorelei's surprise. Evidently, they'd swung back into each other's good graces. The two of them folded themselves into a table, and the kitchen staff leapt to attend to them. With grim efficiency, they laid out flatware and brought two portions of tonight's meal: carp pounded thin, breaded, fried, and laid atop a veritable mountain of boiled potatoes.

Heike inspected her plate for a moment, then primly nudged it to the side. She leaned across the table with her hands folded under her chin, clearly prepared to share a juicy morsel of gossip.

Lorelei strained to listen in out of idle curiosity—but perked up when Heike said, "So, did you hear the big news? Ludwig sat up today."

Adelheid's expression did not change, nor did she glance up from her plate. She was consumed with the task of sawing her carp in half with painstaking care. "Yes, Johann mentioned it to me this morning. It's heartening."

One could always count on Adelheid for a bland appraisal, Lorelei supposed. It was far more than heartening. If he'd recovered enough to sit up, perhaps he was lucid again—lucid enough to tell her what had happened on the night he disappeared from camp.

Heike deflated at Adelheid's non-reaction but pressed onward. "Well? Have you seen him yet?"

Adelheid had moved on from her fish and began cutting her potatoes into tiny cubes. "No. Johann is not allowing visitors until his condition stabilizes."

Heike scoffed. "I've never once seen him show such concern for Ludwig. But if he isn't letting *you* see him . . ." She frowned, preoccupied. "Has Lud said anything yet?"

After swallowing her mouthful, Adelheid said, "Not that I'm aware of. Are you going to eat that?"

Heike sighed exasperatedly and pushed the plate across the table to her.

Of course Heike wanted to see him. If he'd begun improving, then she would want to silence him before he talked—which meant Lorelei had to get to him first.

Damn Johann for making it more difficult than it needed to be. Fortunately, the man was exceedingly predictable; she could practically set her watch to his schedule. At the top of each hour, he gave Ludwig a dose of pain medication. Lorelei consulted her pocket watch. About now, he'd be on his evening walk, circling the deck as though he meant to outpace something trailing hungrily behind him.

Lorelei glanced back up at Adelheid and Heike. By the looks of it, they'd begun bickering over something or another. With any luck, they'd be occupied for another ten, fifteen minutes at most. A narrow window, but if Heike caught her sneaking into the sickroom, she'd ensure Lorelei never got another opportunity to speak to Ludwig alone—or ever again.

She had to go now.

As casually as she could manage, Lorelei rose from her seat and headed for the doors of the mess. She strode out onto the main deck and let the cool night air wash over her. Too late, she noticed the figure careening toward her and nearly collided with—

"Sylvia."

Lorelei steadied her by her shoulders, then all but dragged her into an alcove. A lantern swung above them, scattering light across the deck. In the gloom, she could make out the starlit fall of Sylvia's hair and the alarmed shine of her pale eyes.

"Thank God," Lorelei said.

Some of the wariness slipped off her face. "Oh?"

Lorelei did not know so much hope could be contained in one syllable. She realized, dazedly, that she'd all but backed her against the wall—and that Sylvia was wearing a coat with an unusually high collar. The golden buttons gleamed in the dim lantern light, fastened to conceal her throat and the bruise Lorelei had left behind. Mortification seized her all at once. How could she have—

No, for the greater good, she could set aside her feelings. Slowly, she loosened her hold on Sylvia and took a step back. "I need you to distract Heike for me. She's in the galley."

The tentative hope in Sylvia's expression vanished. Fury and—worse—*hurt* took its place in an instant. Apparently, she could not expect Sylvia to adhere to her same standards of professionalism. "Why?"

"Just do it," Lorelei hissed. "I don't have time to explain."

"You have a lot of nerve, Lorelei Kaskel. Is that really all you want to say to me?"

Sylvia was nowhere near as tall as Lorelei, but she made a valiant effort to rise to the occasion. In retrospect, asking for Sylvia's help mere hours after kissing her—and rejecting any possibility of finding happiness with her—was not her brightest idea. Now she'd left herself open to a discussion of their *relationship*. She could have gagged on the word.

Lorelei raked a hand through her hair. "What is there to say that I haven't already said?"

Sylvia looked stung. "Is that all I'm to expect from you, then? I know you think I'm silly and empty-headed. Perhaps I am. But some of us do have feelings. They're real, and they matter."

Lorelei felt almost dizzy with the accusation, the very same one Sylvia had lobbed at her on the night after Ziegler's murder. *You really are coldhearted.* It struck her harder than she'd anticipated. How desperately she wanted to prove Sylvia right. It would make her life far easier if she truly were as heartless as she wanted everyone to believe.

"I'm sorry," Lorelei gritted out. "Truly. Will that tide you over for now? I need your help. Ludwig was awake today. I need to speak with him without alerting anyone."

Sylvia's expression softened some, but she crossed her arms guardedly. "Fine. But I must remind you that Heike does not *enjoy* my presence. What am I supposed to say to hold her attention?"

"You have known her for the better part of twenty years. Surely you can think of something."

Sylvia seemed to consider it. "Perhaps I will try to apologize to her again. Or perhaps I could suggest my feelings have changed. Yes, that will hold her attention. I will tell her that I have long mourned our broken friendship, but over these past few weeks, I have come to realize that I have been blind to my own ardor. That my capacity for deluding myself extends far beyond—"

"God, no. Don't do that," Lorelei said, without bothering to mask the horror in her voice. "You sound like you're auditioning for the lead in a two-bit melodrama."

Sylvia gasped. "Oh, you insufferable, clueless . . . ! Give me one good reason I should not throw you overboard this instant."

"Because I'm going to save both of our miserable lives."

Sylvia was standing far too close to her again. Even when she was like this—*especially* when she was like this—Lorelei could not help wanting her. It made her sick. It terrified her. It would be so simple to close the gap between them. To shove her against the wall and kiss her until she couldn't remember her own name. To let herself believe in all her wild, impulsive promises. Her expression must have revealed the turn of her thoughts. Color rose high on Sylvia's cheeks. She looked like she wanted to kiss her—or, indeed, throw her overboard.

She did not have time for this. Her window was closing.

"I trust you to handle it," Lorelei said hastily. With that, she turned on her heel and left Sylvia to stew in her indignation.

Never in her life had she felt so self-sabotaging.

The wall sconces illuminated the corridor of the expedition's quarters and winked off the dust swirling through the orbs of light. Lorelei stopped in front of Ludwig's door with her heart lodged firmly in her throat.

At long last, she might have the answers she sought.

When she knocked, the sound reverberated through the empty hallway. No answer came from within. But then, what had she been expecting? No doubt Ludwig had drifted back to sleep. Johann kept him well sedated. Lorelei curled her fingers around the knob and carefully eased it open. She was met with the sweet, rich smell of growing things—and decay. Inside, it was dark, but the narrow window behind the headboard let in the faintest wash of moonlight. A silhouetted figure stood in front of the glass.

Lorelei stumbled backward in surprise. "Fuck."

At first, she could only make out the hulking shape of its shoulders. Then, blink by blink, her eyes adjusted. Johann inclined his head toward her, his medical case open at his feet and a syringe in hand.

"Kaskel," he said, a wary edge to his voice. "What are you doing here?"

When her heart stopped trying to launch itself from her rib cage, she replied, "I thought I would come see him. I heard he sat up."

"He did. But he's sleeping now."

A thin blade of moonlight fell across Ludwig's pallid face. She could still see the faint green lines creeping up his neck. Despite the stubble on his jawline, he still looked boyish and fragile in slumber. Lorelei tore her eyes from him and studied Johann. In truth, he did not look well himself. Exhaustion carved hollows beneath his eyes. Belatedly, it occurred to her that he had not lit any candles. He only leered out of the dark at her, looking for all the world like a child caught with his hand in a biscuit jar.

Her stomach twisted into a knot of dread. "What are *you* doing here?"

Johann flicked his syringe. "I'm administering his pain medication."

"In the pitch-dark?"

"I don't need much light," he replied. "When you've done this as often as I have, it becomes second nature."

As a strange pressure built in her skull, chills erupted across her arms. It was an instinct far beyond rationality—one she had relied on many times before. *Danger.* Looking at Johann now, she could not help thinking of the tale of Godfather Death.

Back in the days when wishes still held power, there was a poor man who searched high and low for a godfather deserving of his son. After rejecting all his family—and God himself—he at last settled on Death, who promised to make his son a rich and powerful man. When the boy came of age, Death came to him in the dead of night and led him into the woods. Eventually, they arrived on the banks of a spring, one that granted the ability to mend any wound or cure any disease.

Once you drink from this spring, you are destined to become the most renowned physician in the world, said Death. *But in exchange, you must grant me my due. I shall appear at your patients' bedsides. If I stand at the head of their bed, you may save them. But if I stand at the foot, their soul belongs to me.*

As Death promised, the boy grew up to be a famous physician—and a scheming, ambitious man who believed he could cheat his godfather. Whenever he wished to save a patient fated to die, he would simply turn them around in their bed so that Death stood at their head. Death, believing his godson no longer worthy of the power he'd been granted, collected his due in the end. The magic turned sour within the physician and rotted him from the inside out.

Lorelei had always thought it a strange tale. The Yevanisch God admired such craftiness in finding loopholes in his laws, and their folklore reflected it. Now, it struck her cold. She swore she could see Death standing dutifully at the head of Ludwig's bed, regarding Johann with his twinkling, familiar eyes. Here was the godson Death deserved: a man willing and eager to cut souls loose too soon.

Frowning, Johann followed Lorelei's gaze to the dark corner of the room. When he saw nothing, his cold blue eyes snapped back to her face.

"I just can't help noticing it's early for his medication."

Johann's expression turned flinty. "I suppose it is."

"What were you going to give him, then?"

"A fatal dose of morphine," he said with unsettling calm. "What do you intend to do now?"

So he wasn't denying it. Her every sense felt alive—sharpened. She'd been so certain he hadn't done it, but she could not bring herself to feel much of anything at all.

"I don't know yet," she said. "I could scream."

"You're welcome to." He set aside the syringe. "Perhaps Sylvia will believe you, but Adelheid certainly won't. Heike already thinks you killed Ziegler. I'm only doing my job. You came in spouting accusations—or perhaps to finish him off yourself."

Cold rage tore through her veins. It took every ounce of strength she possessed to root herself in place. "So it was you. You tried to kill him."

"Not exactly. If I had wanted to kill him, I would have." His spectacles glinted in the moonlight. "I couldn't allow him to lead us out of the woods. This seemed a good way to delay him."

Lorelei let out a humorless laugh. "Why bother? Sentimentality?"

"Something like that," he said flatly. "Unfortunately, he's proven more resilient than I'd expected. It's too much of a risk to let him live any longer. The same goes for you."

Lorelei took a reflexive step backward and hit the door. Slowly, the weight of the situation sank in. Johann was a soldier, easily twice her size in weight. She could not hope to survive against him. Perhaps she could appeal to his prejudices. Play the role he expected: the cowardly, conniving Yeva. "I can keep quiet. Just let me go."

"I don't believe you." Johann smiled ruefully. "You're like Sylvia—a rare example of your kind. Neither of you ever learned when to stay down or mind your own business."

He rose from his seat, nothing but a looming shadow in the dark.

Her mind whirred with terror. Even if she escaped him now, she wouldn't make it long. Adelheid would believe whatever he told her. Heike already thought her guilty. And Sylvia . . . She couldn't stand against the three of them alone. But Johann was right about her. Lorelei had been fighting for too long to roll over and die now. She'd spent too long running from Death.

She felt for the flask around her belt and unstoppered it. Calling on her magic, she threw her arm out in a wide arc. Water burst forth, following the path her hand carved through the air. Cold unfurled within her as she froze it solid and sent two thin daggers of ice hurtling toward him. One smashed against the wall with a brittle sound like shattered glass. The second notched itself into Johann's shoulder—far from any vital point. He let out a startled shout of pain.

For a moment, Johann seemed stunned. He touched the wound and stared at his fingers, slicked red with blood. Then, his eyes locked on hers. A terrible, ravening hunger lit them from within: pure bloodlust.

It said, *You're dead.*

Lorelei slipped through the door and ran blindly. Her heart thundered in her chest, and her frantic breaths sounded far too loud in her own ears. She felt like that terrified girl again, sprinting through the alleyway with blood caked on her boots. She could hear the sound of bone splitting. She could hear jeering laughter and shattering glass.

It took only a few moments for Johann's footsteps to echo behind her. Lorelei dared to glance back. Aether shivered over her skin as the fog gathered over the river poured in through the windows and slipped beneath every door. With a sinuous curl of his fingers, it swirled around him like a wraith summoned to attend him.

Lorelei threw open the doors to the war room and stumbled inside. She shoved a chair beneath the doorknob and all but collapsed to the ground. Her vision pulsed black with terror both urgent and half-remembered. Still, the fog slipped in and bloomed through the room. The air sighed ominously, beading against her face like sweat. It slid an insubstantial finger down her back.

"There's no point in hiding," he called. "No one is coming to save you."

And now she'd trapped herself in here—in the very same room where Ziegler had died. The doorknob twisted threateningly. When it did not give, he threw his weight against the door.

"Think, goddamn you," she muttered. "Get ahold of yourself."

There had to be some trick—something, *anything*, she could do. With trembling hands, she pulled the moisture from the air. If she could get just one good shot . . .

The barricade groaned, then gave way. Lorelei scrabbled backward as the doors flew open. All she could see was his golden hair, loose and wild around his shoulders—and the fog unfurling around him like Death's cloak. It all happened too quickly. Before she could think to move, water crashed toward her in a torrent.

She went sprawling across the ground, the wind knocked out of her on impact. Through the rheum over her vision, she could see the glint of ice—and the cold shine of his eyes as he loomed over her.

"Don't struggle."

A spear of ice burrowed itself into each of her palms. She strangled a scream as he pressed the heel of his boot into one of the shards. Her vision went momentarily black, her lungs seizing with agony.

When she came to, she hardly recognized him. She had seen him miserable and brooding; she had seen him dark and threatening. But this was something else entirely. His eyes were bright, the pupils blown so wide they nearly consumed his entire iris, and his face was split in a wild grin that chilled her. He looked practically giddy.

Although adrenaline had blunted the worst of the pain, the animal part of her wanted to thrash free. "Before you kill me, tell me why. Why did you do it? Why did you kill her?"

He seemed surprised. "I didn't."

Shock had dazed her. She must have misheard him. "What?"

Johann crouched beside her. As he leaned over her, the ends of his hair brushed her cheeks. "I didn't lie to you. I do believe in Wilhelm. But if I must choose between them, I'll choose her every time."

Of course. If he hadn't killed Ziegler, then he was protecting whoever did.

"You . . . You *idiot!*"

What else could she say? She had thought all of them besides the murderer would be allied on this one point: to expose who had done it. But she had failed to take into account all the ways people were flawed.

Johann straightened again, gazing down at her as though she were an insect he could crush underfoot. He raised his hand, and the water obeyed, coiling like a serpent ready to strike. "Spitting venom until your last. I almost admire you."

"Johann!"

Like a puppet with its strings cut, the water dropped.

A pale gray smudge appeared in the threshold of the war room. Through the lattice of curls plastered to her face, Lorelei saw Ziegler's murderer standing there with a cold gleam in her eyes.

Adelheid.

TWENTY-ONE

ADELHEID SEIZED HIS ELBOW, and with fury steeling her voice, she said, "That's quite enough, don't you think?"

The effect was immediate. Johann shuddered violently, then jerked a step back from Lorelei as though he'd only just noticed her there. "She saw me in Ludwig's room. It'll pose too many problems if she's allowed to live."

"What were you doing in his room?" she asked sharply. "I told you to *wait*."

Johann looked chastised. "If he talked—"

Adelheid held up a hand. "We'll do this without more senseless bloodshed. Go. I will deal with Lorelei."

He did not answer her, but Lorelei could feel his shadow pass over her as he left.

Once they were alone, Adelheid knelt on the ground beside her. There was something darkly tender in the way Adelheid looked at her now. With a wave of her hand, the ice pinning Lorelei to the floor melted. It dribbled cold into her wounds and chilled the exposed skin of her wrists. Adelheid touched the hems of her gloves and tugged as if she meant to remove them.

"Don't," Lorelei bit out.

"Don't be a fool. If you don't remove them, your wounds will get infected."

As if that mattered now. Lorelei sprang, knocking her to the ground. With the adrenaline coursing through her, it was a simple thing to pin her to the floor. The pain was excruciating when she locked her mangled hands around Adelheid's throat, but she refused to back down.

"You killed Ziegler."

It wasn't wise to take your eyes off a dying thing. Johann had told her that once. She finally understood what he meant. When you had nothing left to lose, you could afford to be recklessly, violently unpredictable.

Squeezing the life out of Adelheid would perhaps be the most satisfying thing she'd ever done. But having the target of her rage before her made her feel horribly alive, more focused and clear-eyed than she'd felt in weeks. She couldn't kill her without learning why exactly she'd done it.

Adelheid looked remarkably calm. She hardly even struggled, save for the barest application of pressure on Lorelei's wrist. A polite reminder that she was indeed suffocating. Her lips parted wordlessly once or twice before Lorelei finally let up.

She wheezed out a breath. "You want to know why."

Lorelei sneered. "Not more than I want to see you dead."

Adelheid's gaze was flatly disappointed. "Sylvia is injured from your journey up the mountain. You're effectively alone on this ship—and in the capital. You may have her support, but you know as well as I do that Wilhelm isn't interested in the truth of what happened here. When presented with a Yeva, the daughter of his father's greatest enemy, and the woman he loves, who do you suppose he will believe?"

There was no smugness in her voice, no victory. Her matter-of-factness made it all the more painful. Lorelei's wounds pounded in time with the thrumming of her heart. For a moment, she could do nothing but gaze hopelessly at her own blood staining Adelheid's throat. Her eyes fluttered shut. "So what, then? Why have you spared me?"

"I wanted to talk plainly with you," she said. "Viper to viper."

Lorelei's eyes opened wearily. The image of Adelheid's face wavered in front of her as though she lay at the bottom of a pond. "I'm listening."

"Like you, I have done what I must to survive. Like you, I know what true desperation feels like. That is why I killed her. Wilhelm can never be allowed to have the power of the Ursprung."

Lorelei wanted to see it as pure manipulation. It *was* pure manipulation. And yet, the cold determination in Adelheid's voice compelled her. "Why? You told me—"

"I lied to you." She clenched her jaw. "Wilhelm is unfit to rule. Maybe once, I believed he had a vision, but I've come to see it for what it is. Nothing but a fantasy. He is willing to sacrifice many for his own selfish gain. Continuing his father's pointless wars is testament enough to that."

"Once the kingdom is stabilized—"

"There will always be another war." Adelheid spoke with the world-weariness of a woman who'd been burned many times before. "Once he stabilizes his reign, others in the region will see him as a threat—and Ebul is a convenient weak point to target, just as it always has been. He will conscript our people to fight his battles, and then what little harvests we have will rot in the fields with no one left to tend them. And when the dust settles, he will send no aid.

"That," she said flatly, "is what awaits us in a unified Brunnestaad."

Horror unfurled through Lorelei slowly. "Then what do you plan to do?"

Adelheid canted her chin. "I will claim the power of the Ursprung. I will return to Ruhigburg. I will deliver him his murderer: Sylvia. I will marry him. And then, while he sleeps, I will drive my lance through his heart."

It was a scheme befitting a fairy-tale heroine. Lorelei could think only of the tale of the Dragon Prince.

Back in the days when wishes still held power, the queen gave birth to a dragon. When it came time to find a wife for the Dragon Prince, no woman in all the kingdom's vast lands would consider his suit. They were terrified of him, for he was hideous—and the rumors of his cruelty and hunger preceded him. Only one girl, the daughter of a shepherd, was brave enough to offer her hand. Not only was she brave but clever, too, and knew hunger like an old friend. On the day of her wedding, she dressed in every gown she owned—and wore a knife against her breast. When the Dragon Prince took the girl to their marriage bed, he asked her to bare herself to him.

A layer for a layer, my love, she told him. With every gown she shed, he shed his scales. Beneath them all was a beautiful young man.

One without armor or teeth.

"You mean to stage a coup," Lorelei said.

"No." She met her eyes steadily. "As soon as Wilhelm is dead, I intend to return to an independent Ebul. Whoever wishes to squabble over the remains of Brunnestaad may do as they please."

"Does Heike know?"

"No." Her expression shuttered. "She never would have agreed with this course of action. It's too direct. Besides, if I failed, I did not want any of this to touch her."

"And Ludwig?" she asked bitterly.

"Ludwig was a regrettable casualty." Her mouth was set in a grim line. "The curse is unfortunate, but Johann did what he had to."

"What he did was monstrous!"

Adelheid's expression settled back into its usual cool politeness. "Is there anything else you want to know?"

"Why are you telling me all this?"

"Because you and I can work together. What I ask is simple. Look the other way. Help me find the Ursprung. Let Sylvia take the fall."

"If you think I would *ever*—"

"Wilhelm is a snake," Adelheid cut in impatiently. "When his reign is threatened next, do you think he will spare even a moment to give you what you're due? Do you think he would even hesitate to throw the Yevani to the wolves if he thought it would gain him an ounce of public approval? Trusting Wilhelm to protect you is the greatest mistake you will ever make. I will not see someone else fall prey to his lies."

She couldn't deny it. She'd already seen the depths of his ruthlessness when he wrote her that letter. *Unity requires sacrifice.* Anger rolled through her anew. "There's only one thing I don't understand. Why me? Sylvia would be a far more valuable ally."

"Yes," she conceded, "but Sylvia would never resort to something so underhanded. She's too idealistic to believe Wilhelm is a lost cause. Besides, I have something you want."

Lorelei curled her lip. "What do you know about what I want?"

"I will give you—and all your people—your freedom and your safety in Ebul. Your cooperation is all I ask."

Lorelei's breath shuddered out of her. That *was* all she wanted.

If Wilhelm lost control of Brunnestaad, then there was no telling what would happen to the Yevani of Ruhigburg—or those in the other Yevanverten across the kingdom. Sylvia had offered to bring Lorelei with her to Albe, but such generosity could not extend to all of them. Her mother's betrayal would make her position precarious enough. Far safer to throw in her lot with a ruler delivering her people from ruin.

But to allow Sylvia to take the fall? She could not live with herself.

"There has to be someone else. Johann would sacrifice himself for you gladly."

"And lose Herzin's support—and my dearest friend? No."

"Heike, then."

Adelheid only looked at her pityingly.

On some level, Lorelei had always known it would come to this: her survival or Sylvia's. Ever since Wilhelm's letter arrived, she had run from it. She'd thought she could find some way to change her fate, and for a time, Sylvia made her believe she could. Listening to her was like being led by the hand through a dark, enchanted wood.

But she was not so naïve anymore.

Adelheid's fingers closed around her wrist, as if they were two friends sharing confidence. "This is an easy choice. Make it."

Beneath the cold stare of the moon, the room glowed with a cold, spectral light. It glinted off the silver handle of Ziegler's walking stick, leaning against a corner as though waiting for its owner to return. Through the impossible pang of grief, Lorelei could not help thinking that betrayal had been an easy choice for Ziegler to make. Even now, she could not escape the reality of just how thoroughly she'd molded herself in her mentor's image.

For years, she had fought for her own safety and for the safety of her people. And now, she would have it. Any cost was worth that. Sylvia's life was worth nothing against hundreds. It was worth nothing at all. She could not live only for the dead. She had to live for the people she could still save. That meant herself.

"Fine," she said. "I'll do it."

Sober, Lorelei might have felt more dread at the prospect of stabbing Sylvia in the back. But she'd blunted the sharpest edges of it with half a bottle of schnapps she'd nicked from the galley. The whole world seemed wrapped in gauze, which made it difficult to focus on much of anything at all.

She'd laid out her evidence before she asked everyone to meet her in the war room. A half-empty bottle of sleeping draught. A shard of ash. Ziegler's travel documents—and every correspondence she could find from Anja von Wolff, bound in rough twine. Arranged on the altar of Ziegler's desk, it looked like an offering to some darker god.

Heike arrived first, looking rather like herself again. Her auburn hair was arranged in neat ringlets, and she'd donned the armor of her red lipstick. How had Lorelei ever suspected her? She'd never felt more like a fool.

With a vague gesture at her tableau, Heike asked, "What is all *that?*"

"You'll see."

"Huh." Heike snapped open her fan and gave her a very unsubtle once-over. "Good heavens, Lori. You look dreadful. Couldn't sleep?"

Lorelei didn't care to imagine the state she was in. "Something like that."

As if on cue, Sylvia's voice thundered down the hallway. "Where is she? Tell me where she is this instant!"

Heike blew out a thin sigh, as if she wished she could remove herself from the situation. Lorelei was of a similar mind. But she had to face what she had done. There was no stopping what she'd set in motion now.

Johann shoved Sylvia through the open door with Adelheid following close behind them. She stumbled into the room, her hands bound and spitting like a doused cat. Her hair was an unmitigated disaster, and the side of her face was in ruins, caked in dried blood and smeared with bruises. Lorelei's breath caught out of sheer rage. She had not considered that they'd needed to detain her. No doubt, she hadn't gone without a fight. Lorelei allowed herself a private moment of satisfaction to see the bleeding wound on Johann's temple.

"Good God." Heike covered her mouth. Horror shone in her eyes. "Sylvia?"

But Sylvia only looked at Lorelei. "You're unharmed."

Sylvia's whole bearing changed. Her relief was as warm as sunlight, and even the alcohol couldn't dull how much it hurt to see. Even now, Sylvia trusted her.

You romantic fool.

Steeling herself, Lorelei hooked her ankle over her knee and leaned back in her seat. The room lurched sickeningly. "I've cornered you at last, von Wolff."

Sylvia's smile faltered.

Heike slammed her palm flat on the war room table. "Would you care to explain what the hell is going on?"

"The von Wolff family played us all for fools," said Lorelei. "Allow me to read you a passage from Ziegler's journal.

"*The Ursprung is in Ebul; it's indisputable. But Anja von Wolff will not be denied what she wants. However, I believe I have found another spring that will be a convincing enough replacement for her.*" Lorelei flipped the notebook shut decisively and tossed it on the desk. "If you want to read all the documents, be my guest. You'll find there is ample evidence to suggest that Anja colluded with Ziegler. She intended to falsify the findings of the Ruhigburg Expedition for their own political and financial gain. Although it seems von Wolff here did away with their loose end."

"Lorelei, please," Sylvia said breathlessly. "You know I had nothing to do with this."

"No more of your lies," Lorelei replied coldly.

Adelheid was watching her with an intensity that frightened her. All last night, she had turned over every move, had shuffled every chess piece on the board in her mind. But she could not brute-force her way out of this, nor could she contort the evidence into the shape she wanted. All of it pointed to Sylvia. She could do nothing with Adelheid's confession, but she could do something with her protection.

She had seen what happened when men descended on the Yevanverte: broken windows, broken skulls, broken spirits. She couldn't allow it to happen again, even if it meant enduring the look of naked confusion in Sylvia's pale eyes. No, it was far worse.

It was betrayal.

Magic crackled through the room, and the vase of flowers on Ziegler's desk burst into shards. Water coiled around Heike as she fixed Sylvia with a look of open hatred. For a moment, Lorelei was certain she'd strike her. Sylvia took a step back.

"What was last night, then? Some sort of play?" Heike's expression twisted with revulsion. "I thought you . . . Never mind. God. I could kill you for what you did to Ludwig."

"Heike," Adelheid said wearily. "She is the only one among us who knows how to subdue nixies. We'll die crossing the Little Sea without her."

"And how do you think that's going to go?" Heike snapped. "As soon as we're on the island, she'll be free to roam the ship. Who knows what will happen while we're gone?"

"Not if we bring her with us," Lorelei said. "She will be our prisoner."

"And if I refuse?" Even with her arms wrenched behind her back, Sylvia broadened her shoulders defiantly. Lorelei could practically see her fingers itching for her saber.

"You will face the executioner's block one way or another. At least go with the last scrap of your honor intact. No one else needs to die on this expedition."

For a moment, Sylvia stared at her in astonishment. And then she lunged, so quickly that Lorelei flinched. She hated herself for it. Johann grabbed Sylvia's elbow, halting her before she could close the gap between them.

"You can't do this." Her voice was thick with desperation.

"On this ship, I can do whatever I want."

Sylvia's breath shuddered out of her. Her eyes were livid, burning as bright and wild as an open flame. Sparking within them was something Lorelei realized then that she had never seen before, not even when they first met five years ago. It felt as though she'd been struck across the face with the shock of it. She had been a fool if she thought for even one moment she knew what hatred looked like on Sylvia von Wolff's face before now.

"One day," Sylvia said, "you will grow tired of this thing you've made yourself into. One day, all there will be to content you is ghosts."

Good. It made it easier if Sylvia despised her. If she wished this pain on Lorelei, then Lorelei could endure it for her. "Put von Wolff in her room. I don't want to look at her anymore."

Adelheid nodded at Heike. "Come with me."

Together, they led Sylvia out of the war room. Johann lingered by the door, watching Lorelei like she might fly across the room and bite his throat out. It was admittedly a tempting prospect. But with everyone out of the room, without adrenaline pumping through her, she suddenly felt very drunk and very miserable. She rested her forehead on the desk.

"How are your hands?" he asked.

"Oh, fuck you."

When she turned onto her cheek, she saw him smirking down at her. He lifted his medical kit like a white flag between them. "Let me clean your wounds. It's the least I can do."

Lorelei said nothing, only peeled off her gloves with her teeth. The agony of leather pulling against her broken skin whited out her vision. When she blinked the world back into focus, bile rose in her throat. Her palms were such a mess, her mind refused to process it.

"Careful," he said, clearly irritated. "You'll hit your head if you faint."

She hadn't realized she'd nearly pitched forward. "Right."

While her pulse thrummed sickeningly in her fingertips, Johann procured a rag doused in antiseptic. "This will hurt."

He sounded far too pleased about it. "No more than it hurt last night," she said.

With a shrug, Johann dabbed at the wound. He hadn't lied. It stung far worse than she'd anticipated. Every tendon screamed in pain as he manipulated her fingers—at least, what she could feel of them between the troubling spots of numbness.

In the daylight, his features were almost completely transformed. The sun smoothed away all his harsh lines with a gilded brush. His brows were furrowed in a preoccupied little frown as he worked to pack her wound. The pressure of bandages winding around her hands made her head swim. Spots danced across her field of vision.

"Are you afraid of blood?" he asked with a touch of amusement in his voice. "How curious."

"As I've said, I've conducted no blood sacrifices," she muttered. "You're pleasant today. Calmer, at the very least."

When he met her eyes, they were haunted. "Then you understand why I must protect her."

"Because you're a lovesick dolt who's never had an idea of his own."

He tied off the dressing with more force than she thought strictly necessary. "Because when I'm with her, I can almost believe that I really am human."

Lorelei curled her lip in disgust. "You *are* just a man. That's what makes you so despicable."

"And you're just a woman. If there's any justice in the world, you and I will one day get what we deserve." Johann's lips twitched in a thin smile. "How fortunate for us there isn't."

As soon as he left the room, Lorelei flung open the doors to the balcony and promptly emptied the contents of her stomach off the side of the boat. As she draped herself over the railing like a sheet left out to dry, she gazed miserably down at her own pallid reflection. Two faces wavered on the surface beside hers.

Ziegler. Aaron.

Each of them had one hand on her shoulder.

All there will be to content you is ghosts.

By the end of this, maybe she really would get what she deserved.

PART IV

The Source

TWENTY-TWO

EBUL UNFURLED LIKE A WAR BANNER, all sun-scorched hills and gravelly soil. What tenacious blooms remained in the tulip fields waved against dry, golden fields. The few settlements they passed were small, the people hard-eyed and thin as they watched the *Prinzessin* pass. Here, Lorelei thought, was the royal family's legacy.

As they sailed, Adelheid stood at the bow like a figurehead, her eyes set against the rising sun. She cut an imposing silhouette, her broad shoulders draped in a cloak of white and her yellow hair woven severely around her temples like a diadem. Johann trailed her, her ever-present shadow. Heike wandered the ship like a sleepwalker. At the very least, her hostility toward Lorelei had abated. They circled around each other almost apologetically.

According to Johann, Ludwig's fever had broken at last and his breathing came easier. It seemed there was nothing to be done for the bark that had grown on his neck. Each time Johann attempted to chip it off, the wound wept sap and scabbed over with cork. No doubt when he awoke—assuming Adelheid let him off this ship alive—he would delight in conducting some botanical study of himself.

Sylvia, Lorelei had not seen at all. It was better that way.

They dropped anchor where the river opened into the Little Sea. Four islands crested from its waters like the sleek coils of a lindworm. For the first time in nearly two weeks, the engine fell silent and the smokestacks sighed out one last stream of exhaust. By some miracle, they had made it just in time.

Lorelei climbed to the observation deck and waited. Over the hours, the sun died slowly. It bled its light into the sea and stained the sky with striated bands of orange and purple. When it finally dipped beneath the horizon, it left the sky in complete, obliterating darkness. Her breath quickened with anticipation. The new moon hovered above her, outlined faintly in silver.

In the distance, the mist billowed. Then, the fifth island appeared.

She could almost convince herself she'd imagined it. It was a flicker of shadow, then a silhouette, then an imposing mass leering out of the gloom. The Vanishing Isle looked exactly as it had in her vision: like a bad omen.

She curled her fingers around the railing and leaned over the edge. Pain shot through her palms, chased by a crawling numbness along the inside of her arm. Yesterday, she'd dared to ask Johann if the mobility in her hands would recover, and the look he'd given her was almost affronted. *There's no guarantee with injuries like this.*

She had tried to make her peace with it, mostly by refusing to think of it at all. Even if she survived this ordeal, she'd never properly hold a pen again. What that meant for her career did not bear dwelling on. It was a fitting enough punishment for what she'd done.

Dark shapes moved sinuously beneath the water. Every now and again, she caught a glimpse of a finned tail, a flash of iridescent scales, or solid black eyes. None of them had sung, but something about them, weaving in and out of sight, made her consider diving in to pursue them. The others had opted—perhaps wisely—to remain inside, safe behind their wards and thick ashwood doors. Lorelei wore iron around her neck, on her cufflinks, and on all the buttons of her heavy greatcoat. As soon as the ship made landfall, the true danger would begin. Until then, she wanted to feel the wind against her face. She wanted to be alone.

As they drew closer to the Vanishing Isle, her skin prickled with unease. The air hung heavy and impossibly still, as though the entire island began holding its breath the moment they laid eyes on it. The bottom of the boat scraped rock, and the gangplank *thunked* ominously into the muddy shallows.

It was time to finish this.

The remains of their party gathered on the deck, grim-faced and weary in the dark. A group of deckhands worked to drag the *Prinzessin* into the shallows and tether her to the shore. If the legends held true, the island would vanish again in the light of dawn. Lorelei had no doubt they'd be here longer than that, and she did not want to have to swim when they left—or track down a new ship. Assuming, of course, they *could* leave before it reappeared God-knew-where next month. They'd stocked up on supplies in case its magic trapped them here. The weight of Lorelei's heavy pack bit painfully into her shoulders.

"Well, then," Lorelei said. "Let's go."

She led their trudge down the gangplank. As Lorelei made her way onto the shore, faint glimmers in the water snagged at her attention. She resolutely ignored them. Something about the way the water eddied here sounded suspiciously like laughter.

Heike stepped off next, clutching the silver charm around her throat with a white-knuckled pressure. Adelheid followed close behind, surveying their surroundings warily. Last was Johann, dragging Sylvia along like a willful horse.

Her wrists were bound behind her with coarse rope. Lorelei hated it, the unnecessary brutality of that knot. Most of all, she hated how battered Sylvia looked, with her ruined hair and the bruises mottling the side of her face. Despite her wounds, Sylvia carried herself with prideful defiance, her shoulders drawn back and her chin held high. Just then, Sylvia raised her eyes to Lorelei's. The hatred burning within them struck her with force. She tore her gaze away.

Your fault, your fault, your fault.

The chorus of her ghosts' voices were painfully loud and horribly urgent. She bit down on the desire to tell them exactly what she thought of them. She needed no assistance to punish herself.

Heike ducked beneath the heavy limb of a tree with a look of vague disgust. It dripped with round, peculiar fruits that had fissured to reveal a seam of rather noxious blue within. The flesh glittered with concentrated aether. Lorelei hated that her first thought was to wonder what would happen if she took a bite.

God help her. Dead or alive, Sylvia would never let her go.

"So," Heike said. "Where to?"

Sylvia spoke without hesitation. Her voice rasped from disuse—or perhaps overuse. "First, we'll need to find a river. If the Ursprung is here, all we need to do is follow it upstream to its source."

No one objected, and with that, they set off in silence.

Johann and Sylvia headed up the group. He clutched her lead in one hand and her strange fey lantern in the other. They walked until they found a narrow stream, its surface glittering like broken glass in the dark.

This place unsettled Lorelei. It brimmed with magic like a glass overfilled. Aether shivered through the fog and puddled in the water. It unfurled through the veins of every leaf. It sparkled in the air and set the world aglow with its strange, wondrous light. The entire island seemed *aware*, watchful and waiting for their next move.

After what felt like hours, Sylvia stopped dead. "Wait. Look there."

Lorelei strained to see through the dark. No more than a few meters away, those vague, tantalizing shapes Lorelei had seen beneath the Little Sea were rising from the river. Nixies dragged themselves onto rocks to bathe in the light of the stars. One inspected the shine of its lethally pointed nails, while another draped its tail across a sleek river stone, enticing as a woman lying over a chaise lounge. They regarded the group with those horrible reptilian eyes.

Instinctual terror seized hold of Lorelei. "This is far too dangerous. Find another way."

"There *is* no other way," Sylvia replied. "Do you want my help, or don't you?"

"Lorelei has a point," Heike said airily. "Why should we trust you not to drown us?"

"Please," Sylvia muttered, somewhere between exhausted and exasperated. "I don't have a death wish. Even if I made it out of these bonds and incapacitated you, your crew would detain me the moment I stepped foot on the *Prinzessin.*"

Heike hardly seemed appeased.

"It *is* dangerous to follow the river," Sylvia conceded. "However, those nixies don't strike me as aggressive, by their body language. They're curious about us." She took a considering pause. "However, that can change quickly if they perceive us as a threat."

Johann did not take his eyes off the nixies. "Who has silver they can part with?"

Adelheid looked expectantly at Heike, who was wearing a capelet fringed with delicate silver scales.

"Seriously?" Heike groaned. "This is brand-new."

Adelheid's non-expression deepened. With a long-suffering sigh, Heike yanked a few pieces of silver off the hem and placed them in Johann's waiting palm. Her capelet chimed and shimmered with her every movement.

"What do you intend to do with those?" Lorelei asked warily.

He closed his fist around his new cache of silver. "We can purify the water and corral them."

"Don't!" Sylvia's eyes went round. "It's monstrous to treat them that way."

"I, for one, would prefer not to be eaten," Heike countered. She did not look up, too consumed with prodding at the loose thread on her capelet. "Do you have a better plan?"

"It's certainly possible to earn their trust over the course of several days, maybe weeks . . ."

"Do it," Adelheid said impatiently.

Without hesitation, Johann hurled a scale into the water. It tumbled through the air, flashing white and silver, then cut through the surface of the river like a knife. It took only a moment before the nixies recoiled. Their gills flared. They rent at their hair. And then, they shrieked.

The sound scraped against the very marrow of Lorelei's bones. In a frenzy, the nixies dove into the river and swam upstream. As the last one disappeared into the current, it struck Lorelei that they had done something they couldn't take back. She imagined the metal leaching into the water like poison.

Johann watched the scene unfold with a self-satisfied smile and turned away only when Adelheid took him by the shoulder. He was no better than a child burning ants beneath a magnifying glass.

Sylvia's eyes glimmered with anger—and something like sadness, too. When she caught Lorelei looking, her expression shuttered. It stung more than she expected.

"I suppose we are proceeding like brutes, then," Lorelei said. "Shall we?"

Adelheid, Johann, and Heike pulled ahead while Sylvia dragged her feet. Her fraying lead line trailed limply behind her like a sorry wedding train. Lorelei had half a mind to pick it up, if only so she wouldn't trip over it or go on looking like a soldier on a death march. After a moment, she thought better of it. Sylvia would resent it, and Lorelei had no desire to incur any more of her rage. Once, a part of her might have relished how spectacularly low she had fallen—might even have mocked her for it. Now, it felt like watching a hawk with its wings clipped.

They walked side by side in silence. At first, Lorelei thought Sylvia would have enough self-restraint—or spite, perhaps—to remain silent. But in the end, she spoke.

"Why?"

"You'll have to be more specific than that."

"You know very well what I mean. After everything, after . . ."

She trailed off, and what Sylvia left unspoken gutted Lorelei. It hurt to breathe. Too many memories crowded too close to the surface. Snowflakes caught in Sylvia's moonlit hair. Her eyes as molten as quicksilver. The pale blue of her lips when Lorelei pulled her from freezing waters. The exultant delight of her laughter on the back of the mara. Sylvia, for one, glorious moment, entirely hers.

It all seemed so far away now.

Now, Sylvia's eyes shone with unshed tears. "How could you?"

What could she possibly say to that? After all this time, perhaps she'd finally succeeding in becoming what everyone suspected she was. Disloyal and conniving and self-serving. A dog eager to bow and scrape for anyone, so long as it would stave off the blow. "My hands were tied."

Sylvia laughed bitterly, the irony clearly not lost on her. "You're a coward."

Yes, I am. More than you could ever know.

"Not all of us can afford to have principles."

Johann looked back at them with a scowl that said, *I'm watching.*

Lorelei knocked into Sylvia's shoulder as she shoved past her.

The thick moss growing along the riverbank muffled their footsteps, but the burble of the current—and the occasional snapping twig or shrill cry of a bird—offered some respite from the grim silence. Unlike the fathomless dark of the Vereist, the water here was as transparent as glass. Aether settled over its surface like a slick of oil, iridescent and shimmering beneath the glow of their lanterns. Here and there, she caught slivers of the ghosts' haunted eyes: peering out at her through the latticework of leaves and the pebbled depths of the water.

Lorelei shuddered. The sooner they got off this island, the better.

As they walked, Johann tossed whatever iron or silver he could find into the water at every juncture: beads pulled from Heike's gown, coins plucked from his own wallet, even a medal he'd found discarded at the bottom of his pack. Sylvia winced at every *plink* of metal.

They traveled until they were too exhausted to go any farther. Once they set up camp, Lorelei huddled close to the fire. Shrugging off her greatcoat and rolling her shirtsleeves to her elbows made the heat somewhat bearable. It was a humid night, close enough to be smothering, but the light kept the ghosts at bay. They hovered just outside its sphere, the wide moons of their eyes blinking in and out of focus.

Lorelei watched the flames dance until movement on the outskirts of camp caught her attention. Johann had shoved Sylvia to the ground at the gnarled base of a yew tree and was now fastening the ropes binding her around its trunk.

"Must you?" Sylvia asked. "I assure you I'm not plotting my escape."

He did not reply.

"I'm thirsty," Sylvia said, more imperiously than Lorelei might have in her circumstances.

"Are you?" Johann asked with a sharp edge of amusement. He uncorked his waterskin and, with a startling cruelty, poured it onto her head.

Sylvia gasped, blinking through the water running down her face. With that same proud fire in her voice, she gritted out, "Thank you."

Johann stared at the waterskin for a long moment, as if he just realized what he'd done. Without another word, he turned and retired to his tent.

A horrible feeling curdled within Lorelei, and her fingers twitched around some impotent, murderous impulse. God, she despised him. More than anything, she wished she had the power to hurt him in a way that mattered. She had half a mind to shake Adelheid awake and demand she leash her dog. But it wouldn't do Sylvia any good. She sat slumped against the tree with water trickling down her chin. It was pathetic. Lorelei could not leave her there unattended.

She rummaged through her bag until she found her own waterskin. As quietly as she could, she approached Sylvia. The fire barely reached her here. Only the faintest light—and none of its warmth—whispered over the leaves, bathing Sylvia's features in gold.

Lorelei crouched by her side and uncorked her waterskin with her teeth. "Here."

"I won't fall for the same trick twice," Sylvia said sulfurically. "Or perhaps you've poisoned it."

"Don't be ridiculous. If I wanted to kill you, you would not see it coming." Sylvia didn't rise to the bait. It was almost disappointing. The sweat cooled uncomfortably on the back of her neck. "You're cooperative. Johann is being needlessly cruel."

"How reassuring to know you'd aid them the moment I stop being cooperative."

Patience had never been Lorelei's strong suit. Even now, when she knew that she should be groveling at Sylvia's feet for forgiveness, she felt dangerously on the brink of pouring the water down her throat and throttling her with the empty canteen. It would make both their lives easier if she simply accepted her kindness. But when Lorelei drank in the raw hurt in Sylvia's eyes, all her irritation drained from her in a rush. Both of them whittled down to their most vulnerable, their most spiteful . . .

She did not want this anymore. How had she ever wanted it?

"I find I've little spirit left to hurt you," Lorelei said, "unless you asked it of me."

Sylvia's breath caught. "Don't mock me."

"I'm not," Lorelei said quietly. "Just drink it, von Wolff. Your pride isn't worth your life."

It looked like it cost her something when she nodded her assent. Lorelei raised the waterskin to her lips. She drank as if Lorelei would snatch it away from her at any moment. When she drew back, struggling to catch a breath, a rivulet of water ran down the line of her jaw.

Lorelei wanted to dab it away with her handkerchief. She wanted to tend to her wounds, to work the knots from her hair and braid it as she once had on that Albisch mountaintop. She wanted to kiss her again, tenderly first, then with all the hunger she had not yet burned out of herself. She wanted and wanted and wanted, so much and so deeply she feared her greed was boundless when it came to Sylvia von Wolff. And yet, she had ensured she would never have her again. Sometimes, she despised herself. Most of the time, really.

"You could lead everyone astray," Lorelei said. "It would be simple."

"To what end? I meant what I said earlier. If I die, all of you will die with me. That isn't what I want."

"They would deserve it." *Especially me.* She hesitated. "I'm sorry. If I'd seen any other option at the time . . ."

"It is late for that." Sylvia let out a sound somewhere between a sob and a laugh. "But here I am, ready to forgive you. What a fool I am."

It felt like a benediction, one wholly undeserved.

"Let me earn it." The words spilled from her without thinking. "This isn't over yet."

"How can you say that?" Sylvia asked brokenly. "It's hopeless. If you truly mean that you had no choice, then you and I are prisoners. Even if we survive this, Wilhelm will punish me for Ziegler's murder—and Albe for what my mother has done. There's nothing I can do to stop any of it."

If there was anything to be said of Sylvia von Wolff, it was that she was unfailingly, infuriatingly optimistic. Lorelei hardly recognized her now. She looked utterly defeated, battered and curled in on herself. Of all things, it made Lorelei furious. "You disgust me."

Sylvia's eyes turned flinty. "I? Disgust *you?*"

Yes, fight me, she thought. *Fight back.*

"You are Sylvia von Wolff," she hissed. "That name means something, or have you forgotten? Do you really intend to lie here and die like a beaten cur?"

"And what would you have me do? You have taken every option from me." She turned away sharply. "Go away, Lorelei. I want to rest."

Lorelei obeyed, fuming. As much as she craved the oblivion of sleep, it would not come easy with her blood pounding like this. She stalked to the river. Once she finished refilling her canteen and splashing her face with water, she peered down at her wavering reflection. She looked gaunt and exhausted, but for the first time in weeks, she felt truly alive.

Her mind had begun to work again.

As a Yeva, two principles had been instilled in her since birth. On one hand, survival. On the other, justice. When she'd been backed into a corner, they'd seemed irreconcilable. At the time, casting her lot with Adelheid had seemed the prudent decision— the *only* decision. But she had no guarantees in these nobles' games, no leverage, and even if Adelheid kept her word, the power she held over Lorelei would be a poison slowly killing her for the rest of her life. To know her freedom and her mind were not her own was the most agonizing sort of death she could imagine.

She had been enduring it for years already.

The night was staggeringly clear. The water reflected the stars overhead. They unfurled across the surface like glimmering skeins of fabric. Beneath the captured image of the sky, she saw something oddly familiar.

Half-buried beneath smooth river stones was one of Johann's iron coins. Before she could think better of it, she pulled off her glove and plunged her hand into the water. The cold was an agonizing sort of bliss, like pressing ice to a burn. Her fingers clumsily scraped the silt, kicking up clouds of mud in the water. It was a struggle to close her fingers around the coin, and she felt a pathetic sort of triumph when she finally managed to take hold of it. She held it aloft, dripping and gilded in celestial light.

A sleek gray head emerged from the water.

Lorelei's breath stuttered with surprise. The nixie watched her with barely restrained hostility—but when it noticed the coin in her hand, its black eyes softened with reluctant curiosity. Its lips parted to reveal a startling row of serrated teeth.

It would be so very easy for this beast to drown her now. But it remained entirely still, as if waiting to see what Lorelei would do next. She held the nixie's gaze steadily as she tucked the coin into her pocket. The nixie looked almost approving.

No, she thought. *Grateful.*

It slipped beneath the surface and disappeared.

This certainly wasn't over yet. A plan took shape foggily. Sylvia was right. The two of them were effectively prisoners, and as Johann had soundly proven, they were outclassed. Alone, they had no chance at escaping. But there were still allies to be made.

If she had to drag Sylvia kicking and screaming out of despair, she would. She would not allow her to surrender.

TWENTY-THREE

By MID-MORNING THE NEXT DAY, it had grown hot enough that everyone shed their coats. The clouds swelled and blackened until they broke in an ill-tempered fit. The skies drenched them with rain, and all the world was glazed with damp. Magic hummed in the air, and the iron chain around Lorelei's neck burned as the distant song of a nixie rose above the hiss of the storm.

"I hate this," Heike said. "This is by *far* the worst trip we've ever taken."

She trudged glumly in the back of the group. Her hair was slicked against her face, and her fine boots now seemed to be made more of mud than leather. She radiated a powerful misery that was trying the very last of Lorelei's delicate patience.

"Surely there is some data you can collect," Adelheid said flatly. "Make yourself useful instead of complaining."

"On second thought, walking through this wasteland is *great*." As if on cue, the top of Heike's backpack snagged on a low-hanging branch. She wrenched herself violently free with a *snap* of wood. "What is wrong with him?"

Out in front of them, Johann marched like a man pursued. Sylvia stumbled to keep pace with him as he tugged on her tether.

"I can't imagine," Lorelei said dryly.

"Nothing, I am certain." Adelheid shot Lorelei a reproachful look. Her next step landed her in a puddle that soaked her to the knee. Adelheid gave an undignified full-body shudder. She yanked her boot out of the mud with an obscene *squelch*.

Heike snorted.

With an exasperated sigh, Adelheid said, "Right. Tread carefully, then."

They followed the river until they reached a waterfall. It tumbled off the lip of a limestone cliff in a perfect white curtain and emptied into a vast pool. Johann stopped dead in his tracks when it came fully into view. Sylvia collided with his back, letting out an indignant *oof!* It took no more than a moment for Lorelei to realize why.

Rocks jutted from the water in an eerie, circular formation. The sun had broken through the cloud cover and glimmered on the pool's surface like a golden ring. A horde of nixies had installed themselves on the stones, sunbathing and humming and braiding their hair. There were more than she'd ever seen congregated in one place, likely driven upriver by the iron poisoning their water. The chain around her neck burned in warning.

"Brilliant," Heike said sharply. "A great plan, Johann—and flawlessly executed. Now what do we do?"

The nixies turned and regarded them. It was difficult to attribute any human traits to them, but they looked quite displeased to see them. Their gills flared, as did the gauzy fins that fringed the bottoms of their tails. There was nowhere to go, unless they backtracked through the woods.

Adelheid turned to Sylvia. "What would you advise?"

Sylvia, no matter how embittered, apparently could not help offering her knowledge when asked. "Ah, well . . . Last night, I said the nixies didn't look particularly aggressive. However, these ones are presenting much differently."

"Is that right?" Heike asked impatiently. "How would you characterize these ones?"

"Hostile!" Sylvia rounded on her. "If you had listened to me in the first place, we would not be in this predicament at all."

"Then fix it," Heike hissed.

Adelheid interjected with a genteel cough. "Perhaps it would be wise to turn around."

"No," said Lorelei. "Why don't you sing to them, von Wolff?"

Johann looked nauseated at the very suggestion. Sylvia regarded her suspiciously.

"She can speak to them," Lorelei continued. "I have seen it firsthand."

She did not know the extent of Sylvia's . . . *fluency*, if it could be called such, in the nixie tongue. But if she could somehow convince them to distract the others or compel them into stillness, perhaps the two of them could escape.

Lorelei stared at Sylvia with an expression she hoped said, *Go with it.*

Sylvia stared back blankly. Disappointment dropped into Lorelei's gut like a stone. Sylvia hadn't understood—or perhaps she truly had resigned herself to her fate. Then, a smile broke across her face. Glimmering bright in her eyes was something painfully, beautifully familiar: hope.

So she hadn't lost herself yet.

"That," Sylvia said, "is an excellent idea."

"This ought to be good," Heike muttered.

Unease splintered Adelheid's cool mask, but she did not object. The five of them made their way down to the pool. While Sylvia approached the edge of the water, the rest of them huddled a safe distance away. Her wrists were still bound behind her. Lorelei tried not to look too closely at the bruises spreading beneath her pale skin, or the way her fingers swelled from the pressure.

Agreeing to this plan was either staggeringly brave or staggeringly stupid—maybe both. One misstep, and she would be gone, dragged to a watery grave or torn to ribbons. But for perhaps the first time in Lorelei's life, worry seemed a faraway thing. How could she possibly doubt Sylvia? She had watched her defy death time and time again. While Sylvia did not channel aether, she possessed another, more potent sort of magic. Every wildeleute they encountered fell hopelessly under her enchantment. For the longest time, Lorelei could not figure out how she'd managed it. But now, she understood.

Sylvia had opened herself up to wonder.

She loved them.

The nixies bared their pointed teeth at her. Most of them stayed on the rocks, lashing their tails. The boldest of them dove into the water and beached themselves on the shore. Their scales rasped against the rock and scintillated in the sunlight. They propped themselves up on their elbows, their hair pooling in slick knots around them and their gray skin streaked with silt. Sylvia walked into the water until it swallowed her up to her knees.

Then, she began to sing.

She had a horrible voice, truthfully, but she was always one hundred percent committed. Lorelei couldn't find it in herself to be anything but awed.

The nixies, too, watched her raptly. One by one, they joined in chorus with her. A flock of crows overhead took off squawking. Magic prickled along Lorelei's skin like electricity. All her wards vibrated at the onslaught of ensorcellment. The iron chain around her neck nearly scalded her. The sound was *dreadful*, scraping agonizingly against her skull. And yet, there was something compelling about it. The song swilled through her blood like wine.

Sylvia stood with her face tipped toward the sun. One of the nixies curled its fingers around her calf, almost worshipfully. Lorelei couldn't be certain whether she wanted to beat it away from Sylvia or join it at her feet.

"It's beautiful," said Johann.

Startled, Lorelei turned toward him. He had spoken with true feeling in his voice, but his eyes were glassy. When he staggered forward, Adelheid was startled from her stupor. She blinked hard, then grabbed hold of his arm, half to stop him, half to steady herself. "Johann."

He wrenched his arm from her grasp. "I have to go."

"*Johann.*" She took his elbow.

This time, he leveled her with a glare Lorelei never expected he'd turn on Adelheid. Without warning, he knocked her aside—hard enough to send her sprawling across the ground. She sat up after a moment, lips parted in mute shock and clutching the side of her face. Lorelei could see a bruise forming beneath her fingertips. Her yellow hair had come loose from its coronet and hung in front of her eyes.

Heike knelt beside her with a vacant, dreamy smile. "What are you doing, Addie? Don't you hear it? We have to go."

"No. *No.* We are staying right here." Adelheid wound her arms around Heike's shoulders and shot Lorelei a panicked look. "What's wrong with them?"

"Their wards," Lorelei gritted out. "They've been tossing them into the river."

Understanding lit Adelheid's eyes. With slow-dawning horror, she turned her attention to Johann.

"Watch her." She fumbled to free one of the chains around her neck, then looped it around Heike's. "I need to go after him."

"Are you mad?" Lorelei snapped. "Look what he did to you! Those things will kill you if you get much closer."

Adelheid swore. "Johann!"

Johann had already dropped to his knees beside the pool. One of the nixies wound its arm around his neck, another sliding a webbed hand up the inside of his thigh. He bowed closer to them, pliant and eagerly wide-eyed. One of them dragged her palm across his face, leaving a glistening streak from his jaw to his lips. It angled his face toward its own and kissed him. When they broke apart, their mouths were painted red with his blood. It flowed steadily from a bite wound in his lower lip.

The sight of it snapped Lorelei fully from her trance. Her stomach bottomed out as she scrambled to fish the iron coin from her pocket. She squeezed it as best she could, as if that alone could dispel the nixie's enchantment. At the moment, the ragged moan the nixies had drawn from Johann's throat was proving a far more powerful ward.

Disgusting. She had to get to Sylvia before this turned for the worse or she witnessed something she could never unsee. "Sylvia—"

The second nixie pushed itself out of the water, seizing Johann by his cravat. Before Lorelei could even blink, it pulled. Johann went under, smiling deliriously all the while. The water churned and bubbled frantically.

Adelheid screamed, the sound buried somewhere in the chaos.

That snapped the other two out of it. Heike groaned, clutching her head. Sylvia stumbled backward, tripping over her own feet. She fell into the shallows with a splash.

Blood bloomed from the depths of the pool. There was so much of it, and all Lorelei could see was *red, red, red* gushing into the grooves of the cobblestoned street. She heard jeering laughter echoing down the alleyways. The nixies shrieked, circling like a pack of sharks. Lorelei's head swam with terror. It was like *she* had tumbled into those black waters and there was no air, no light. Floating somewhere above herself, Lorelei registered that Adelheid was dragging herself toward the water.

"Adelheid!" Heike grabbed her around the waist. Her voice was raw. "Stop it! There's nothing you can do for him now!"

Adelheid's attention snapped to Sylvia. Tears streaked her face like war paint. "You will pay for this."

The nixies screamed again.

"We're leaving," Heike snapped. "Now."

Reluctantly, Adelheid allowed herself to be dragged into the woods. She and Heike vanished into the underbrush with a rustle of leaves.

"Lorelei!" Sylvia called as she struggled with her bonds. "A little help would be appreciated!"

She crashed back into herself with a gasp. "Can't you make them stop?"

"I'm afraid not!"

Lorelei's hands were trembling violently. She was drenched in cold sweat. She couldn't think. She couldn't go near the water without completely losing her senses, but she couldn't let Sylvia die.

Johann had left his backpack abandoned on the ground. Her hands were utterly *useless*, numb with terror and nerve damage both. With a shout of frustration, she struck them against the earth. Pain shot through her so ruthlessly, her vision whited out.

Still functioning, then.

She fumbled to open the pack, then found a scalpel tucked into his medical kit. She hesitated only a moment before taking Sylvia's confiscated saber as well.

A nixie surged from the depths of the pool, reaching for Sylvia. Lorelei threw an arm out, tugging on the water with all her willpower. She had not accounted for how easy it would be to manipulate water this aether-dense. It leapt to her call like a well-trained hound. A wave burst from the surface, knocking the nixie back from Sylvia with far more force than Lorelei intended. When it resurfaced, it snarled with thwarted rage.

"Incredible," she murmured.

But she didn't have any more time to waste. Lorelei hurried to Sylvia's side and grabbed her elbow. Although it was excruciating to hold the scalpel, she sawed through Sylvia's restraints as quickly as she could. The rope came undone with a *snap* and fell to the ground in a heap. She yanked Sylvia to her feet.

"Come on," Lorelei shouted over the scream of the nixies.

Hand in hand, they ran.

They didn't make it far before Sylvia stumbled on an upturned root. A strangled sound escaped her, and on instinct, Lorelei reached out to catch her. By some miracle, she managed to steady them both. Even through her gloves and layers of linen, the heat of Sylvia's body was searing.

"Be careful," she murmured, if only to fill the fragile silence between them. Her breath stirred the wispy curls around her temples.

For a moment, Sylvia stared dazedly up at her. And then she blinked, and her anger was like a dam breaking. "Don't you dare touch me!"

Once again, Lorelei was confronted with how deeply and utterly she had ruined things between them. Now, she knew, was the time for groveling penitence and heedless self-immolation. And yet, old habits were far harder to quash than she'd ever imagined. Try as she might, she could not take the high road. She could not be wrong with anything resembling grace. Her temper spiked hopelessly, and she dumped Sylvia unceremoniously on the ground. "I suppose I should have left you to die, then!"

Sylvia recovered instantly. Before Lorelei could take a step back, she had sprung to her feet and drawn her saber. The point quivered a bare inch from Lorelei's nose, winking in the dull sunlight. "Maybe you should have. I should kill you for what you've done."

They made a sorry pair. Both of them were breathing heavily, drenched in blood-soaked water. Sylvia's hands were as wrecked as Lorelei's now. Every finger was swollen and mottled blue from the pressure of her restraints, and the wound the alp had given her was weeping again. Her arm trembled with the effort of holding up her blade.

"Do it," Lorelei said.

Sylvia hesitated. The look in her eyes was something like regret—like *pity*. "It's dishonorable to strike an unarmed opponent."

"Fuck you. Fuck honor. Look around you! There is no honor in this world."

"*Excuse* me? How dare you speak to me so crassly?"

"I am not unarmed," Lorelei snarled. With a flick of her hand, water burst from her waterskin—easier to command here than it had ever been before. It spiraled around her menacingly. Never before had she felt as powerful or as wretched. "Once a viper, always a viper. Isn't that right? So kill me. You would be a fool not to. This is how it was always going to end between us."

Sylvia's expression was unreadable. "No."

"Then strike me, at least!"

Punish me. Lorelei couldn't do it herself, not in a way that mattered.

At Sylvia's silence, Lorelei seethed. She wouldn't even do her the honor of a dueling scar. Maybe that was the greatest punishment of all: that after all this, Sylvia found ways to remind her of her station, of all the things she could never have because of it. "Even now, you'd spite me?"

Sylvia's face crumpled. And then she started crying.

"I . . . ah . . ." All of Lorelei's anger extinguished in an instant, replaced instead with an obliterating panic. "What is this? What are you doing?"

"I can't bear it." Sylvia dropped her saber and slumped to the ground again. Burying her face in her hands, she groaned. "I killed Johann."

As though she were approaching a wounded animal, Lorelei knelt beside her. This time, Sylvia didn't pull away. As carefully as she could, Lorelei cradled her face. Deep down, she knew she should not be touching her this way after what she had done. Beneath the mud and exhaustion, Sylvia was pristine. All her scars shone in the light. When Sylvia leaned into her touch, Lorelei indulged the desire to trace the one gashed into her cheek.

"Stop that," she said stiffly. "Look at me."

Sylvia lifted her gaze. Her snowy eyelashes were matted with tears. Lorelei had not been made for comfort, but for Sylvia, she would have to try. "You didn't kill him. The nixies did. Had it been you who fell, he would not be grieving you. You're too softhearted, Sylvia. Save your tears for someone who deserves them."

Sylvia sniffled and hastily smeared away her tears. "Yes. . . . Yes, you're right. I suppose the boy I grew up with died a long time ago. I just . . . I had wished things could be different."

"You did what you had to," Lorelei said. "And you've done a far greater good. Without him, we might actually stand a chance."

Sylvia frowned. "What are you talking about?"

"Johann didn't kill Ziegler. Adelheid did."

"Adelheid?" Sylvia echoed. "No. . . . That can't be right."

"It is." Lorelei had always known Adelheid possessed an iron-clad determination. Now she knew that she was just as ruthless. She explained everything that had happened after she'd asked Sylvia to distract Heike, as well as Adelheid's plan to assassinate Wilhelm and her offer to protect the Yevani in Ebul.

"I thought I was choosing the lesser evil. But I was wrong. I was afraid. I have been afraid all my life, and I fear I always will be." She was babbling like a complete and utter ninny now, but she found she couldn't stop. "I'm as wretched and cowardly a creature as you've always suspected. I am surly and selfish and cruel. But I should have been better than my nature. I should never have betrayed you."

I should have chosen you.

"Saints, Lorelei," Sylvia snapped, and it felt like an absolution. "You are *human*. Do you understand what's happened here? You've acted the part of a villain so well, you've gone and convinced yourself it's who you truly are. You are honestly one of the least self-aware people I have ever met!"

"I am perfectly self-aware! You are brighter than the sun itself. And me . . ."

"Enough." Her voice wobbled. "You've made mistakes, as have we all. But don't you see yourself? You are witty and observant. You are fiercely protective of those you care for—and hopelessly loyal, in your way. I don't believe you've ever once acted completely in your own interest, for better or for worse. I have always admired that about you."

Lorelei did not know what to say. She suddenly felt quite flushed.

"I forgive you." Sylvia smiled beatifically. It felt like sunlight. "Now, then. If I hug you, will I get to keep all my extremities?"

"We shall see."

Sylvia did not need any further encouragement. She crushed Lorelei into a hug. For a moment, Lorelei thought she would be smothered. But once she relaxed into it, it was surprisingly . . . nice, with the damp linen of her shirt and the thrum of her heart against her cheek. Sylvia's fingers twined gently into her hair, holding her steady against her. The simple tenderness of it almost brought tears to her eyes, but she would sooner die than cry in front of Sylvia von Wolff. Old habits died hard, after all.

Lorelei drew back and met Sylvia's gaze. Someday, she would find a way to express all the things she wanted to say. "Thank you."

"Of course. I—"

"We can bring her down together."

Sylvia blinked as though she'd been struck upside the head. "I-indeed? Ah. Yes, of course. Adelheid! Single-minded as always."

"Focus, von Wolff."

Sylvia's expression soured further. But Lorelei was filled with renewed determination—and eager to dance quickly away from the topic of *feelings*. Instead, she imagined the look on Adelheid's face when Johann had slipped beneath the river: the look of a woman who had only one thing left to lose.

"Johann was willing to defend Adelheid to the end," Lorelei said. "But now the playing field is level. Heike is no fighter, and Adelheid will be reckless from grief. If we find the Ursprung first, we can decide what to do with it ourselves."

"And when we return to Ruhigburg? Wilhelm will never see sense when it comes to Adelheid."

"He will have to. Not even he is romantic enough to throw everything he's worked for away for something as ridiculous as love."

"It's not ridiculous!"

Just then, sunlight lanced through the dense canopy. It illuminated the earnest, impassioned indignation burning in Sylvia's wintry eyes. It painted her in soft pastels and danced in her wild hair. She was a work of art. She always had been.

"We shall have to agree to disagree," Lorelei rasped.

Anything else would betray her.

Sylvia's scar dimpled as though she were trying to conceal her smile. "Fine, fine. I suppose we should get moving."

"Oh?" Lorelei raised her eyebrows. "You know where it is, then?"

"Not really," Sylvia said brightly. "But the wildeleute have never steered me wrong before."

Lorelei looked at her incredulously. "And that went so well before."

"Well, we are alive, are we not? I would say that's a small victory."

"Hardly. But I suppose we have to take them where we can." Lorelei sighed. "Lead the way, then."

TWENTY-FOUR

By LATE AFTERNOON, the rain had slowed. Fat pearls of water dangled from leaves and glittered on the fine threads of spiders' webs. All around them echoed the silvery sound of dripping water. The humidity made a pall of the air, a smothering weight that settled heavily over the island.

What little of the sky she could see was the livid purple of a bruise. It reminded Lorelei of the summit of Himmelstechen. Wherever they were, it was no longer the Little Sea.

One problem at a time, she told herself.

As sly evening drew itself across the horizon like a blade across the island's throat, an orb of light winked out of the darkness, then another. They hung suspended between the slender trees, bobbing tantalizingly as if borne on the current of a river. The longer she stared at them, the hotter the chain around her neck burned.

"I've found some wildeleute for you to chase."

"Oh?" The excitement in Sylvia's voice had no right being so endearing.

She stopped and squinted into the underbrush. A dozen ghostly lights pirouetted through the air, merrily circling around one another. Upon closer inspection, Lorelei could make out the faintest shape of a pixie-like figure within each golden aura: limbs, delicate and slender as twigs, and hair like tongues of fire.

"Oh, no," Sylvia said dismissively. "Those are irrlicht. They will lead you astray for the fun of it."

"Ah, of course. Unlike any of the others."

Somewhere in the distance, she could hear the drone of nixie-song.

"We're getting closer," Sylvia offered.

"Fantastic," she said wanly.

The sound of nixies tormented her. Lorelei couldn't banish the image of blood slicked on the surface of the water. She swore she saw Johann in the woods, the looming shape of him traced by the eerie glow of the irrlicht. Another one of the dead had joined her legion. He stood there with a trail of blood blooming from his throat like poppies and his lips bruised. His eyes held an accusation within them.

You killed me.

It was nothing he wouldn't have done to them in turn. She wanted to tell him as much, but it wouldn't do her much good— nor would it be terribly reassuring for Sylvia. If Lorelei were her, she wouldn't want to throw in her lot with someone clearly teetering on the edge of sanity—or, at best, a magnet for wiedergänger, creatures that wore the faces of the dead like masks.

"Lorelei?" Sylvia looked at her with singular concern. "What are you looking at?"

"Nothing," she said dismissively. Not a wiedergänger, then. How disappointing. "I don't do well with death."

"You once told me it haunts you," Sylvia said hesitantly. "What did you mean by that?"

She considered replying tartly, if only to retreat to the safety behind her wall of thorns. But the steadiness of Sylvia's gaze and the compassion in her voice pinned Lorelei in place. *Ugh.* She had wanted to earn her forgiveness. She supposed letting her in—and giving her the truth—was a good enough place to start.

"I see ghosts sometimes," she said begrudgingly.

"Truly?" Sylvia craned her neck to peer into the woods, as though she might catch a glimpse of them as well. "Is it Ziegler?"

"Sometimes," she said. "There are others."

"Your brother?"

"Yes. When we were children . . ." Lorelei had not told anyone this story in years, and she didn't know if she could bear to meet Sylvia's eyes when she did it. Her mind drifted just above her body, allowing the memory to pass without touching her. "I had convinced him to sneak away from the temple with me. I was playing at being a naturalist, when some men from Ruhigburg crossed the gate into the Yevanverte."

There was more she could say here, she supposed. But the exact unfolding of events had always eluded her. How many of them were there, really? What did any of them look like? It was the littlest, most inconsequential details that haunted her.

"They murdered him. It was like a game to them."

"That's . . . that's horrific."

The pain in Sylvia's eyes taunted her. When she knew the whole truth, she would not look at her with such aching tenderness. "He told me to run, and I did. I ran."

"Of course you did—"

"You don't understand. I left him to die. I abandoned him." Her voice broke humiliatingly. "So you see, I have always been a coward. I would sacrifice anyone and anything to survive."

Lorelei closed her eyes. She could not bear to see what she knew would be awaiting her. Reproach. Disgust. Blame. But when she dared look at Sylvia again, her eyes were agonizingly soft.

"What else could you have done?" Sylvia took her elbow in her hand, pulling her closer. "Lorelei, be rational in this, as you are in all other things. You were a child. They would have killed you, too. You're very lucky they didn't."

"I'm not sure I was lucky." The words caught in her throat.

"I didn't think I was, either, in the beginning." Sylvia smiled ruefully. "I did not know Aaron, but if that was his final act, he was incredibly brave and kind. He did not want justice from you, Lorelei. He wanted you to live."

Over her shoulder, she could faintly make Aaron out. Her eternal shadow, her tormenter, her little lamb.

His face was still boyishly round, his frame still gawky. As she forced herself to hold his unblinking stare, she saw it was not as baleful as she always imagined. In fact, she could hardly discern any of his features at all. They were shrouded, as if he lay submerged beneath murky waters. The realization nearly knocked her breathless. He was slipping away from her.

Perhaps she was the one who hadn't let him go.

"Live," she repeated. "I'm not sure I know how anymore."

"For now, just breathe." Sylvia slid her palms up to cradle her jaw. "Focus on me. Stay with me."

I have for years, she might have said. How could she not?

But what came out was a bare exhalation. "I'll try."

The deeper they pressed into the woods, the stranger it became. It felt as though there were a thousand eyes blinking out at them from the darkness. White mushrooms bloomed thick from fallen logs, their gills rippling as they passed. The spores were faintly bioluminescent, twinkling in the gathering dark like fireflies. Everything smelled green, like damp and decay.

Here in her element, Sylvia seemed lighter. She stopped every now and again, rapping lightly on tree trunks as if calling on a neighbor, or crouching to pour water over their roots. Waldschratten emerged in their ragged leaf-cloaks to speak with her in exchange for baubles and scraps of bread. It all felt patently ridiculous, but Lorelei had no choice but to put her faith in Sylvia. She claimed the wildeleute never steered her wrong.

Lorelei supposed Sylvia had never led her astray, either.

She forged ahead of Lorelei to gallantly hold back a branch strung with a tangle of vines. Lorelei had half a mind to scold her for her thoughtfulness, yet she couldn't find it in herself to object. Her palms had spent the past few hours alternating between throbbing agony and blissful numbness. She brushed past Sylvia—only to almost topple headlong into what looked like an enormous hole in the ground.

She scrambled back a step. "Are you trying to kill me?"

"Here we are," Sylvia said with a smug little smile.

Lorelei couldn't see what there was to be proud of. In truth, she did not know what she was looking at. As she leaned over the edge, she realized they were standing beside a karstic spring. The water was mirror-smooth, ringed in impossible shades of blue like a sliver of agate. No power radiated from it. The reflection of her own haggard face stared back at her in bewilderment.

"*This* is the Ursprung?"

"What? No, of course not," Sylvia protested. "This leads to a network of underwater caves. The waldschratten suggested the Ursprung would be somewhere beyond them."

"Caves," Lorelei repeated.

"Yes," Sylvia said brightly. "Nixies tend to make their homes in places like these, so I'm inclined to believe them. We'll have to dive."

"Oh," Lorelei said dryly. "Wonderful."

As if on cue, a dark shape cut across the pool. A nixie.

Lorelei's heart thrummed wildly against her rib cage. All she could see was potential tragedy crystallized over the world. All she could think of was Johann, dragged into churning red waters. Of Sylvia's panicked face, the wild spill of her hair, as the alp dragged her under that alpine lake. She didn't know if she could endure it again.

"Do you trust me?" Sylvia asked.

This time, her answer came without hesitation. "Of course I do."

Sylvia smiled at her. "Then let's go."

"Is that all there is to your plan? Let's go?"

Sylvia ignored her and lowered herself to the ground, letting her feet dangle into the water. Reluctantly, Lorelei joined her. The sweet smell of crushed grass wafted between them. Lorelei shrugged off her jacket and let it pool on the ground behind her. The light refracting off the surface danced across Sylvia's face. Her eyes sparkled with mirth, and Lorelei was once again struck with wretched *fondness*. Everything delighted Sylvia. Even something that might kill them.

Nixie-song burbled up from below them, and magic sparked hot against her wards.

Lorelei did trust Sylvia. She had to.

As if sensing her hesitation, Sylvia rested her hand over Lorelei's. The nixie cut through the water like a knife, then surfaced barely a foot in front of them. Sylvia's fingers tightened against hers as she began to hum. It was a strange thing, to watch them communicate with their call and response. Everything in Lorelei recoiled when the nixie lifted a hand from the water. It placed something on the ground beside Sylvia and then, with an almost mischievous smile, dove once again. A single heart-shaped scale rested in the grass, shining like an opal in the sunlight.

"What is that for?" Lorelei asked impatiently. "What did it say?"

"She didn't *say* anything." Sylvia picked up the scale and turned it over in her fingers. "It's a gift. I'm not sure what it's for, exactly. But I think this means we should have safe passage."

"*I think* and *should* are not reassuring phrases."

"You can't plan for everything, try as you might." Sylvia added, "Do you know how to free dive?"

"Why would I— No, of course not!"

"Ah . . . Well, then you'll want to follow quickly."

Before Lorelei could respond, Sylvia drew in a deep breath, then dove into the water. Lorelei's heart reflexively leapt into her throat. Beneath her, Sylvia was a smear of white against the bottom of the spring. Dark silhouettes circled her. She looked terrifyingly small from above.

Lorelei had well and truly lost her mind to even consider following. And yet, somewhere deep down, she knew she'd never had a chance at remaining *sensible* when it came to Sylvia von Wolff. She'd already lost her heart. What was one more thing?

Lorelei let her inhale swell within her. Before she could talk herself out of it, she plunged into the water. She'd expected her breath to be snatched away by the cold, but it was strangely warm beneath the surface—and impossibly dark. Only a single column of golden light filtered down from above, slicing clean through the murk. Lorelei's hair unfurled around her and reached toward the sun.

As her eyes adjusted to the gloom, she saw they were surrounded by nixies. They lounged in the jaws of rock formations. They swam farther below, skimming the bottom of the pool and kicking up clouds of sand in their wake. They were eerily beautiful, their fins translucent and shimmering with an unearthly glow. Some were golden, others silver, others as brilliant as gemstones. All of them had teeth sharp enough to shred them to ribbons.

Nixie-song reverberated through the water, resonating in the very core of her. On land, its magic was muffled by her wards. But here, it sounded sweeter than any aria. Here, colors seemed more vivid. She could feel every beat of her heart in every pulse point in her body. She was dizzy, with either ecstasy or oxygen deprivation. Maybe the two weren't so different.

Sylvia glanced back at her. Her eyes were as bright as an open flame. She waved a hand as if to say *follow me.* The air burned in Lorelei's lungs, and that was enough to remind her to keep moving. She couldn't afford to drown here like some lovestruck fool. As she swam toward Sylvia, the nixies wove around them, tantalizingly close. She could feel the brush of their webbed hands catching on the billowing fabric of her shirt. Some of them drifted close enough that she feared they meant to brush their lips to hers. They were horrible, but they were beautiful, too. If there was a way to speak with God, to lay eyes upon something sublime, this surely came close.

A few nixies swam through a narrow opening in the rock face of the spring. Without hesitation, Sylvia wedged herself in after them. Lorelei hesitated. If Sylvia's trust in these creatures was the thing to kill her, Lorelei would return as a dybbuk to haunt her. She would never let her hear the end of it. Steeling herself, Lorelei brushed her fingertips against the stone and eased herself inside.

It was narrower than she'd expected. Rocks closed in on her, scraping against her back. Panic threatened to set in, her lungs straining with the effort of holding the breath inside her belly. With a twitch of her fingers, she tugged on the current of the water. It glided past her in a rush, guiding her through and out into open water.

A stream of light filtered down from above. Sylvia swam toward it, her hair billowing around her like smoke from a snuffed candle.

Lorelei's vision went black at the edges. *Just a little farther.*

She couldn't succumb to the urge to draw breath when a lungful of water would sink her like a stone. She kicked desperately toward the surface as her magic buoyed them. Together, they broke the surface, gasping. With the last of her strength, Lorelei pulled herself onto land, spluttering and coughing.

Every pull of air into her lungs burned terribly, as though they were filled with broken glass. Sylvia watched her with something caught between relief and wonder.

"That will teach me to never follow you blindly again," Lorelei groused.

Sylvia began to laugh. "Was that not incredible?"

The longer she looked at Sylvia, the less she could disagree with the sentiment.

Sylvia was practically sparkling, her hair pooled like molten silver around her. Lorelei wanted forever to bask in the light of her smile. She wanted to be carried on the current of her whims. She wanted to argue with her until she was breathless. She wanted to hurt her exquisitely, again and again, for as much time as they had.

The depth of her hunger frightened her.

"I suppose it was," she said huskily.

Sylvia's lips parted. Her eyes were hooded and darkly inviting, as though her thoughts had been following those same delirious loops of *I want, I want, I want.* If she looked at her like that a moment longer, Lorelei was going to kiss her senseless.

"We should get moving," Lorelei said hastily.

"Right," Sylvia said, clearing her throat.

They ventured deeper into the cavern. Mist drifted along the floor, eddying around their knees, but fissures in the stone overhead let in the faintest wash of sunset. Ferns grew stubbornly in the meager light, emanating their own unearthly glow. She supposed the concentration of aether in the water made everything grow just a little strange. Ludwig would have loved it here.

When this is over, Lorelei thought, *he will see a thousand sights as wondrous as this.* No one else she cared for would die on her watch.

Eventually, the cavern opened onto a vast basin of limestone. It let in a perfectly round window of sky, from which a waterfall seemed to tumble from the heavens themselves. The cascade gleamed a frosty silver and emptied into a spring. The soil was warm and alive beneath her feet, and the air itself glimmered, as though crystals floated all around them. A sense of quiet awe struck her then. There was no mistaking it.

This was the Ursprung.

For a long time, neither of them said a thing. Lorelei had always prided herself on her rationality, but the last few weeks had disabused her thoroughly of the notion that natural philosophy could explain the whole of the world. There was something wild and magical about this place, something inexplicable, like the thrill of a nixie's song. Like the sight of Sylvia when—

"We did it!" Lorelei let out a strangled sound of pain as Sylvia grabbed her hand and squeezed. Every one of her tendons screamed, a thousand fires tearing through her arm.

"Oh, Saints!" Sylvia clapped her hands over her mouth. "I'm so sorry!"

"It's fine," Lorelei gritted out while her vision pulsed black. "Just . . . be careful."

If nothing else, it had effectively cleared her thoughts of their moony haze. She felt, for a moment, like the boy in the Albisch Ursprung tale. She could almost imagine a dragon slain above her, its silver blood falling to the earth from a still-open wound. What would power like that feel like coursing through her blood? She would never again need to depend on anyone to protect herself or her people. But even if the Urspung found her worthy of its power, she would be hunted down. She would be reviled.

That alone was far too high a price.

"I'm going to collect a sample," Lorelei said.

"Of course." Sylvia's voice still hummed with reverence.

Lorelei took a vial from her bag and dipped her hands into the water, half expecting them to blister. Mercifully, it didn't seem to know a true Brunnestaader from a Yeva—or perhaps you had to speak the magic words for it to read the contents of your soul. Scoffing, she filled the vial and corked it. It emitted an otherworldly glow, bathing her face in cold gray light. Swirled within it were particles that glittered like diamond, but its waters were a startling, incongruous black. It looked as though she'd bottled the night sky. She stood and tucked it away again.

"Lorelei."

Startled, she whirled around. Sylvia was looking at her with a strange brew of uncertainty and hopefulness and expectancy that she could not entirely make sense of. Her face had taken on a rosy hue. Lorelei considered asking her if she was feeling well. "Yes?"

Sylvia shifted on her feet. "Will you come here a moment?"

"Now?" There were still so many things she ought to do. Change her bandages, for one—and catalogue what remained of her supplies. She did not know what had been lost during their travels. She began rummaging through her pack. "I'm busy."

Sylvia stood there, staring at her with an unreadable expression. After a long few moments, she turned on her heel with a dramatic *hmph!*

It was only after Lorelei had clumsily managed to pry open her inkwell that she realized Sylvia had been staring at her with disappointment. It flew out of her hands and clattered to the ground. Ink sloshed out of the well and bled onto the stone.

You idiot, she scolded herself.

Leaving her bag abandoned by the spring, she chased after Sylvia.

TWENTY-FIVE

SHE FOUND SYLVIA halfway through making camp.

The pieces of their tent were scattered haphazardly across the cavern's floor, as were half of her belongings. Sylvia herself sat perched in a pile of her sleeping furs, fastening her damp hair to the top of her head with a garnet-studded pin. A few stubborn curls bounced in front of her eyes, charmingly disheveled.

"What are you doing?"

Sylvia looked up at her, gasping softly in surprise. She released the hold she had on her hair, and the whole wild mess of it spilled around her shoulders. The pin clanged noisily to the floor, echoing against the stone walls.

"Nothing." There was a touch of self-consciousness in her voice. It was so unlike her, it almost made Lorelei smile. "What are you looking at me that way for?"

"Do I need a reason to look at you?" Then, Lorelei paused, mastering herself. If she could be even-tempered for only once in her life, she needed it to be now. As much as it frightened her, she could not hide behind her snappishness. "I wanted to talk to you."

Sylvia looked quite suspicious now. "Oh?"

"I have been thinking," Lorelei ground out. "Quite a bit."

"Yes. You tend to do that."

Lorelei—in a very noble demonstration of self-restraint—refrained from comment. In matters of love, actions came easy to her. She was not very much in the habit of expressing her affections in pretty words—or at all, if she could help it—and it would require her utmost focus to apply herself to the task.

"Yesterday, you told me I never act in my own self-interest. I suppose you are right, in a way. I often invent misfortune and thwart my own happiness so that I can be disappointed, just as I hold others at a distance so they may never truly know me. I moved through the world with my heart closed to it." She dared to meet Sylvia's eyes. "I lied when I told you I could envision nothing between us."

In the distance, there was the sound of rushing water. She did not think Sylvia was breathing anymore.

"Despite everything that has happened, you have made me believe there is beauty to be found. Your infectious joy, your whimsy, your complete and utter lack of self-preservation . . . You are everything I am not and everything I admire. The thought that I might have you terrified me—the thought I might ruin you even more," she confessed. "There is absolutely nothing I can offer you, save my devotion. But if you will have me, I . . ."

This was complete and utter foolishness. Here they were, stranded, both of them wounded and disgraced. They were dead women walking. But if not now, when could she possibly tell her?

"I am yours," she concluded.

Sylvia smiled with such unguarded happiness, Lorelei's heart gave an answering leap. "That is more than enough. It is all I could ever want. If you will allow me to, I will find a way to ensure your safety—and everyone else's in the Yevanverte. I would stake my life on it."

Lorelei could not believe she'd wasted five years alienating someone who cared for her. Five years trying to ingratiate herself to a man who would discard her the moment it was politically convenient. Five years cutting away enough of herself to make her palatable to the nobles. She'd never please them. But Sylvia had peered into her very soul and did not shy away.

Lorelei laughed, if only to keep herself from weeping. "Would you truly?"

"I would."

"If they came in the night, you would lend me your sword."

"Of course I would."

"If they tried to drive us away, you would—"

"Lorelei, please," she whispered, and the yearning in Sylvia's voice nearly undid her. "You must know that I would do anything you ask of me."

Lorelei dropped to her knees beside her. "How is it possible that you exist? You are something out of a fairy tale."

"So are you. But I am as real as you are." Sylvia's voice dropped lower, and with a honeyed tone, she added, "So will you please get on with it and kiss me?"

Desire snagged like a hook within her. It took a moment to remember how to speak. "As you wish."

Lorelei took one finger of her glove between her teeth and carefully tugged it off, then the other. Sylvia watched her remove them with rapt fascination. Carefully, she unwound her bandages and set them aside. Her wounds had closed, but the scars were still tender, each of them in the jagged shape of a starburst. Sylvia gasped softly at the sight of them. With unbearable tenderness, she grasped one of Lorelei's wrists and pressed a kiss to her palm. Warmth, edged with the barest frisson of pain, suffused her.

"Lorelei—"

"Don't fret." She dragged the pad of her thumb over Sylvia's lower lip. The heat of her mouth was almost too much to bear. She could feel Sylvia's pulse quickening against her touch. As carefully as she could, she threaded her fingers into the hair at the nape of her neck and bent down enough to brush their lips together. Sylvia grabbed the fabric of Lorelei's shirt with such ferocity it pulled her off-balance.

"I swear, if you—"

Whatever protest she made was snatched from her as Sylvia

kissed her again, deep and slow and full of fervor. Suddenly, she could not think much of anything at all. She tasted like lavender— like the river, deep and dark. Sylvia arched against her, as though any space between them was unbearable.

Lorelei hooked an arm around Sylvia's waist and lowered her to the ground, her white hair splaying across the furs like a spill of moonlight. Sylvia reached up to undo the buttons of her waist-coat, but Lorelei caught her wrists and pinned them over her head. The pain that seared through her was immediate and blinding.

"Fuck," she hissed. Then: "Sorry."

Sylvia made to sit up, but Lorelei melted her weight into her and buried her neck in the crook of Sylvia's. Her smothered laughter danced over the shell of Lorelei's ear. "Goodness. Are you all right?"

It *hurt* but not as much as her pride—and her own disappointment. She considered herself a methodical person in all things, even in her hatred. Even in her fantasies. There were so many things she wanted to do to Sylvia. She had spun a thousand encounters, filled with every sordid, desperate desire, all the ways she wanted to make Sylvia suffer and beg and come. She wanted to fuck her until she couldn't remember her own name. She wanted her to think of nothing but her: her hands and mouth on her, how she controlled her pleasure. She had never resented the limitations of her own body more.

When the spots in her vision cleared at last, she said, "I'm afraid I'm a bit limited at the moment."

"There's time." Sylvia cradled her jaw, a fond smile playing at her lips. "I want you however I can have you. I want you brutal, and I want you tender, and I want you at your best and your worst. Saints. I want *you*, Lorelei, and I—"

Lorelei kissed her again, hard enough to bruise. Desire ran through her like a knife, so sharp it was almost painful. When she drew back, they stared at each other, their breaths coming heavy in the dark. Sylvia's pupils were blown wide. Lorelei could see her pulse fluttering wildly in the hollow of her throat. It was a caged, frantic thing.

I want you, *Lorelei.*

Her entire body sang with those words. She wanted all of her. Her every petty barb, every cruelty she could enact, every meager sweetness dripped onto her tongue like honey. Lorelei had not thought herself capable of feeling like this. Passionately, insatiably, recklessly. It terrified her, to have all her control unraveling and slipping away from her, all her walls crumbling. She needed Sylvia to experience even a flicker of what threatened to consume her now.

"Unbutton your shirt," Lorelei said huskily.

Sylvia obeyed without hesitation. Her callused fingers trailed along the column of gleaming mother-of-pearl buttons. Inch by agonizing inch, she bared herself. Lorelei's mouth went dry. She brushed her fingertips down the plane of her stomach, the delicate silver on her cufflinks sliding against her skin, leaving gooseflesh in their wake. Sylvia watched her hungrily, her throat bobbing with anticipation.

She was so breathtaking like this, desirous and entirely hers. Shadowed patterns swam over her skin like lace. Lorelei bent over her, pressing the flat of her tongue to her breastbone and dragging it lower, lower. Sylvia moaned softly as her fingers found purchase in her hair. Lorelei kept her fingers steadily braced against her hip bones.

"You're still wearing too much."

"So are you," Lorelei groused.

Sylvia wriggled free of her trousers and her underclothes with a mercenary efficiency. Had she any of her wits still about her, Lorelei might have teased her for it. Her fine linen shirt was still draped loosely over her shoulders. Lorelei admired the curves of her breasts, but her gaze drifted to the edge of the wound just above her collarbone, imperfectly healed along Lorelei's stitches.

Sylvia caught her looking and righted the sleeve. And when she reached for her waistcoat, this time, Lorelei didn't fight her.

It pooled on the ground behind her with a *shush* of fabric.

Sylvia kissed her, her tongue tracing the seam of her lips. Sylvia's fingers worked desperately to unfasten her cravat, and when she finally tore it away, she dragged her mouth down her throat. She got to work on her shirt next, sliding each ivory button through its eyehole with such tender, reverential precision, it almost embarrassed her. Satisfied, she pulled it from her shoulders, so needily Lorelei feared it would tear. She hooked her fingers into her belt and looked up at Lorelei through heavy-lidded eyes.

"You're so beautiful," she whispered.

"Thank you."

Lorelei's throat constricted embarrassingly. No one had ever told her that before. No one had ever looked at her the way Sylvia did now, breathless and wanting. God, she wanted to give her everything she wanted. She wanted to ruin her. The look Sylvia gave her was molten as she traced a line from her knee to the delicate skin of her inner thigh.

"Tell me," she said. "Do you still think me cruel? Would you like to see the depths of it?"

"Please," Sylvia said breathlessly.

Please. Never had she heard a more beautiful sound.

Lorelei kissed the crease of her hip, then lower. Sylvia's hips rose insistently to meet her touch, and her eyelashes fluttered as she rolled her eyes shut. It took all of Lorelei's control to keep herself collected. But she wasn't sure how she was supposed to keep her composure like this, with the heat of her body and the sound of her name on Sylvia's lips. The desperation lighted her eyes as she denied her again and again. It was almost too much to bear. She never wanted it to end.

She wasn't sure how much time had slipped away from them when Sylvia begged her to put her out of her misery. She shuddered, pulling Sylvia's hair hard enough to hurt, and then went loose against her. Her skin was flushed and covered in a gloss of sweat.

She was a vision, impossibly lovely.

Sylvia smiled at her radiantly. Lorelei hadn't realized she'd said it aloud.

She'd give anything to bask in the light of her love forever. But for now, she kissed her until she felt lit from within, shimmering and warm and safe.

Lorelei woke to a watery dawn light.

Last night had felt entirely unreal, but when Sylvia opened her silver eyes, it sent a thrill through her. How strange it was, to exist in a world where Sylvia von Wolff *smiled* at her. Where they woke at each other's sides as if it were the most natural thing in the world.

"Good morning," Sylvia said blearily.

"Good morning." Lorelei tucked a lock of hair behind her ear. And then, with more regret than she expected to feel, she sat up. She reached for her shirt, but Sylvia caught her wrist.

"Let me."

"I don't need you fussing—"

"I know you don't need it," she said, "but I want to. Don't you want to make me happy?"

Heat clawed up her neck. "More than anything."

"Then it's settled."

Once she was set to rights, they packed up their things and stood lingering by the edge of the Ursprung. Its surface gleamed without warmth, as though it had whiled away the hours drinking in starlight. Lorelei was reluctant to leave their idyll when she so dreaded what came next. Adelheid's words flooded back to her.

Do you think he would even hesitate to throw the Yevani to the wolves if he thought it would gain him an ounce of public approval?

Trusting Wilhelm to protect you is the greatest mistake you will ever make.

Lorelei did not know yet what power the spring would grant, but she did not know if she could hand it over to him in good conscience. "We could tell him we couldn't find it."

The words were out of her mouth before she could stop them. When she dared glance over at Sylvia, she looked less shocked than Lorelei thought she might. She was smiling faintly, but sadness filled her eyes. "I confess, the same thought crossed my mind."

So the incorruptible Sylvia von Wolff had a treasonous thought every now and again. It almost made Lorelei laugh. If she returned without it, she did not know what he would do to her. But if there was another way to keep both him and his caprice in check . . .

Tentatively, Lorelei said, "We could take it for ourselves."

Sylvia's smile dropped. "Oh?"

"If it were convenient for him, he would turn on either one of us."

After everything they'd seen, not even Sylvia could summon an argument in his defense. "Yes, I suppose he would. But protecting him is the best way to ensure stability. Besides, do you truly want to wield that kind of power?"

"I don't. If it is to be one of us, it should be you. It has to be you."

Sylvia shook her head. "Me?"

"You've sworn loyalty to him. With the Ursprung's power, you could protect him. You can be the adviser you always wanted to be. Better yet, you could make him into your puppet. What could he do to you—or to Albe—if he depended on you to keep his enemies at bay?"

Sylvia's gaze drifted to the Ursprung. Its waters twinkled beckoningly. The unearthly glow it emitted filled Lorelei up with a quiet, insuppressible wonder.

"I haven't used magic in years. Not since the war."

Softly, Lorelei said, "I would not press the matter. But you deserve forgiveness."

Sylvia laughed breathlessly, swiping her wrist beneath her eye to catch her tears. "Do you truly think so? I was terrified to touch that spring in Albe, you know. I worried that it would find me wanting. I still worry."

Lorelei could hardly process what she'd said. Here, in this hallowed place, with the light silvering the planes and scars of Sylvia's face, it was the most ridiculous thing she had ever heard in her life. "*You?* Found wanting?"

Sylvia opened her mouth to reply, but Lorelei barreled onward.

"Sylvia von Wolff, the noblest and most compassionate woman I know. Friend to the wildeleute. Full of boundless hope. Open to all joys and magic this miserable world still holds. Who would be more deserving?"

Sylvia did not reply. Suddenly, her hands were warm against Lorelei's jaw, her lips soft and sweet on her own. For a moment, Lorelei could do nothing but stare at her long white eyelashes. Her heart constricted almost painfully with tenderness. Nothing had ever felt so right.

A familiar voice echoed from behind them: Heike. "I knew it."

TWENTY-SIX

DELHEID AND HEIKE STOOD only a few meters behind them, dripping from the ends of their hair. They were dark shapes carved out against the eerie glow of the cavern.

Heike looked different than Lorelei had ever seen her, like something had cracked within her and been clumsily papered over. But through her dishevelment, she burned with steadfast purpose. The look on Adelheid's face, Lorelei recognized all too well. She had worn it herself every day for years. Cold fire smoldered within her green eyes, hollowing them out of everything but her rage. All of them were haunted women. Violence had broken and reforged them, and the sharp edges it left behind made them dangerous.

"Step away from the Ursprung," Adelheid said. "You don't know what that will do to you."

Reluctantly, Lorelei let Sylvia go. "Neither do you."

Adelheid smiled humorlessly.

"How did you get here?" Sylvia asked breathlessly.

"It wasn't so difficult to retrace your steps."

Their arrival shouldn't have been a surprise. Normally, Lorelei would have been more attuned to her surroundings. But her single-mindedness, once her strength, had narrowed the scope of her world. For one precious night, nothing had existed but the two of them. How stupid she'd been.

"This is an impasse," Lorelei said. "You have played the game admirably, Adelheid, but you're out of pawns. It's over."

"This is far from over." Adelheid threw out her arms, and the water in her hair and clothes burst from her in a cloud of mist. It coalesced in front of her, as sharp as a lance, and seethed like a heat shimmer.

Sylvia's jaw tightened. "Adelheid, peace! We can talk through this and be sensible—"

"No. I have heard enough talk to last a lifetime."

It was the only warning she gave them before she launched herself forward. She was a barrage of steel and fury, shaping the water into a whip. It lashed out with the force of a gale, then solidified into ice as it struck Lorelei in the ribs hard enough that she dropped to her knees. It shattered on impact, shards raining down on the stone with a bright, clattering sound.

With a flex of her fingers, the whip reassembled itself, too quickly for Lorelei to regain her bearings. It cut through the air and landed a decisive blow on Sylvia's shoulder, directly over her wound. It was a cheap shot—but effective. Sylvia let out a strangled gasp of pain.

Adelheid took the opportunity to disarm her. Another flick of her wrist, and Sylvia's saber flew out of her hand. It slid end over end across the floor, striking the cavern wall with a bell-like *clang*. Water curled around Adelheid's ankles and flowed into her open palm. Slowly, it crystallized into a pike, which she pointed directly at Sylvia's throat.

"Well fought," she said, without a hint of sarcasm. Her gaze flickered to Lorelei where she lay sprawled on the ground. "Don't move. It would pain me to kill her now, but I will if I must."

Sylvia glared at Adelheid, clutching her shoulder. "Is there finally enough blood on your hands?"

"What is she talking about?" Heike demanded.

Adelheid set her jaw and ignored her.

"You still haven't told her?" Lorelei gritted out. "Do you plan to before or after you run Wilhelm through?"

Heike's mouth opened, then snapped shut again. But a shadow

crossed her expression: doubt. Just enough of a weakness for Lorelei to exploit. "You're lying."

"Adelheid resents Wilhelm for his inaction in Ebul. She plans to take the power of the Ursprung for herself and—"

"I plan to see what power it can offer him," Adelheid replied coolly. "Do not move."

Despite the uncertainty that lit her eyes, Heike lifted her hands as though preparing to channel aether. With that ice blade pressed to the underside of Sylvia's delicate throat, Lorelei did not dare open her mouth again. There was nothing she could do to stop her with brute force. Adelheid was as skilled as Johann had been with magic—and twice as controlled.

Adelheid crouched beside the spring and dipped her cupped hands into it. The water cradled in her palms lay dark and still as she brought it to her lips and drank. For a few moments, she remained where she was, her chin tilted upward and waiting for . . . what, exactly? Some divine parting of the clouds?

Nothing happened.

Lorelei's breath rushed out of her.

Adelheid stood and turned sharply toward them, as though seeking some explanation. Her expression crumpled with confusion. Once again, Lorelei was reminded of why she despised the inconstancy of fairy tales. Perhaps she'd taken too small a dose. Perhaps she needed to submerge herself. Perhaps, like the boy who slayed the dragon, she needed to drown.

Or perhaps it was something simpler.

Lorelei could not help smiling. "You've been found wanting."

Adelheid's face contorted with a cold, quiet rage. "How can that be? My cause is just."

"Your *cause*?" Understanding seemed to dawn slowly on Heike. "They're not lying? *You* did this? All of this?"

Adelheid squeezed her eyes shut. When she reopened them, her cold mask was back in place. "I did this to protect us."

"Us?" Heike echoed. "You dare say this was for *us*? Johann is dead, Adelheid—and Ludwig is well on his way! You won't stop until you've done away with us all—until you kill the one person in this godforsaken kingdom who can save me!"

"Who am I, then? I would have kept you safe," Adelheid pleaded. "Wilhelm would have eaten you alive."

Lorelei averted her eyes. "As touching as this is . . ."

They ignored her. Heike raked her hands through her hair. "God, you're delusional. It's just like all the stories promised. The Ursprung brings nothing but misfortune to those who don't deserve it. All you've wrought is death—all for nothing."

Adelheid bowed her head. "No. Not for nothing. There's still another way."

There was. She could still seize its power—in exchange for a horrible price.

"Don't do it," Lorelei shouted. "It will kill you, you fool!"

Adelheid did not hesitate. She dove, plunging under the water's surface with a splash.

The three of them crowded at the edge of the spring. It was far deeper than it looked. Adelheid sank lower and lower, her hair like a bright vein of gold. The light shimmering on the Ursprung's surface pulsed like a heartbeat. Then, it began to bubble and hiss. Aether crackled through the air like lightning poised to strike.

After what felt like an eternity, the water—and Adelheid—went perfectly still. She settled on the bottom of the spring, her lungs filling up with water like stones in her pockets. Her eyes stared unseeingly up at them, then floated shut. Her lips were parted in something like a smile.

"Help me get her out," Lorelei snapped at Heike. "Now."

For once, Heike did not complain.

Together, with aether buoying her, they brought Adelheid to the surface. Water streaked her face, leaving her cheeks dewy and her lips shining. Her hair clung to her face and floated atop the surface like a halo splayed around her. She almost looked like she was sleeping, like a girl who'd bitten into a poisoned apple.

Heike looked away with a choked sob.

Sylvia paled. "She isn't . . . ?"

As carefully as she could, Lorelei dragged her onto the shore. No breath stirred her body. "I think—"

Adelheid's eyes snapped open.

Lorelei reeled back. Adelheid's eyes were a strange shade of blue, as deep as the ocean at dusk. They glowed faintly, with sparks that mirrored the motes of aether glinting in the air. She looked only half alive—and only half human.

Adelheid coughed and rolled onto her side. Water poured from her mouth—more than Lorelei would have thought possible. As soon as she finished, she collapsed in a heap again, curling in on herself with a soft groan. Her lips parted weakly, slick with water and bloodied spittle. But her eyes were overbright and glassy, drinking in the cavern with a ravenous wonder. She looked as if she were seeing the world for the very first time.

"Adelheid," Sylvia said uncertainly. "Are you . . . all right?"

Adelheid eased herself upright, shuddering. "Yes. I feel . . ."

She lifted her hand in front of her face. She admired the flex of her fingers, the roll of her wrist, as though her own body was some perfect machine. Slowly, the water lifted off her skin in fat droplets. They floated skyward as though gravity had been reversed, each one gleaming like a pearl. The air thickened oppressively with moisture. The ferns dripping from the cavern's slick stone walls curled toward Adelheid as though she were the sun.

Lorelei felt suddenly flushed—and when she looked at her own quickly reddening hands, she realized with horror that her blood was pushing toward the surface of her skin.

"I feel everything."

Adelheid's golden hair lifted from the back of her neck. Water gathered in a cloud above her, thick and angry. Rain began to fall through the cavern's opening, slowly at first—and then in squalls. A hailstone struck Lorelei across the forehead, and she flung up an arm to protect her face. They were standing in the middle of a storm with Adelheid at its center.

"Adelheid," Sylvia shouted, "you don't have to do this. We can all escape this together."

"And let you return to Albe to raise your armies against me? No. Our childhood days are long over, Sylvia."

Sylvia's face hardened with resolve. "Then you leave me no choice."

Adelheid looked at her impassively. "I could boil your blood where I stand."

Lorelei believed it. The pressure in the room made her ears pop. She had never seen anything quite like this, even from the most proficient mages. The only thing keeping her grounded was the sickly pallor of Adelheid's skin. Power like this always came at a price, just as every tale she'd collected promised.

Lorelei curled her lip. "So do it."

Adelheid pinned her with that horrible, inhuman stare. But rather than Lorelei's blood boiling, the water from the spring rose behind Adelheid. It was eerily clear, like a crashing wave preserved in glass, and Adelheid like a goddess beneath it.

She threw her arms forward.

Lorelei braced herself. If Adelheid was flagging, she could deflect it. Drawing in her breath, she focused her will on the wave hurtling toward her. It glanced off uselessly, as though she possessed not a scrap of power. She hardly had a moment to be surprised before the water broke over her and sent her tumbling off her feet. She couldn't catch her bearings. It was as though she'd been dragged out to sea and thrown a thousand leagues down. Lorelei scrabbled against the floor and steadied herself just in time to see Heike's skull hit the limestone wall with a dull *crack*. She slumped onto the ground.

Adelheid studied her with only a flicker of regret. Then, she bolted.

"Stop her!"

If she made it back to the boats first, she would abandon the rest of them here. Lorelei scrambled to her feet. Heike lay dazed on the ground, a trickle of blood oozing from the wound in the back of her head. Lorelei's stomach turned at the sight of it.

Sylvia crouched beside Heike and placed her finger beneath her nose. "She's still breathing, just out cold. Concussed, most likely."

"Good," Lorelei said dispassionately. "Watch her. I'll go after Adelheid."

"What?" Sylvia spluttered. "No! *We* will go after her."

"Heike needs medical attention that we can't give. The next best thing is to monitor her. Secondly . . ."

There was far too much to say and far too little time.

Secondly, I couldn't bear to see harm befall you.

I couldn't exist in a world without you.

What me is there without you?

For so long, Lorelei had existed in spite of Sylvia and because of her. All the words tangled on her tongue. In the end, she settled on "If you die, there will be no one to tell those in Ruhigburg what happened here."

Sylvia scoffed. "I'm not going to die."

"You can't promise me that."

"Neither can you!" Sylvia flushed. God, she was so *stubborn*. "There is so much more to living than fear, Lorelei. For once in your life, let someone worry for you the way you worry for others." Sylvia cupped her cheek and held her gaze steadily. "Let *me* worry about you."

In Sylvia's shining eyes, she saw freedom.

Maybe, just this once, she could be the hero of a story like this. Maybe, just maybe, there was a happily ever after waiting for her on the other side of this nightmare.

"Fine, you impossible fool. What do you propose we do?"

"Exactly what you suggested." Sylvia frowned. "If we hope to survive against her, I will need to use the Ursprung."

"Are you sure?"

Sylvia grinned winningly at her. "You doubt me, then? Do you mean to take back all the kind things you said?"

Lorelei shot her a decidedly unkind look. Sylvia laughed. As they approached the Ursprung, she sobered. Sylvia knelt before it like a penitent before an altar. At both Lorelei's and Adelheid's touch, the water had lain dormant. But when Sylvia dipped her fingers into the spring, the entire cavern seemed to come to life. The air sighed across the back of Lorelei's neck. Every strange, beautiful bloom reached toward Sylvia. Bands of glittering aether swirled around her wrists.

And when she raised the water to her lips and drank, it was as though she swallowed the moon itself. Light bloomed beneath her skin and radiated softly outward. Even her eyes glowed with the spring's strange, wondrous power.

Mondscheinprinzessin.

No, you fool, Lorelei thought. *Just Sylvia.*

And yet, she remained on her knees until Sylvia helped her rise.

TWENTY-SEVEN

THANKS TO ADELHEID, leaving proved far easier than getting there. Rather than swim through nixie-infested waters, she'd carved an exit through the wall of the cavern. Water dripped steadily from the smooth stone walls. Thousands of years of patient erosion, over and done with in a single moment. Lorelei could almost find it in herself to be grateful.

Outside the caverns, the mist had thickened enough to swallow up the woods. It drifted in thick, heavy skeins and twinkled as if imbued with the Ursprung's strange magic. Lorelei could barely see her hand a foot in front of her own nose. When she pushed against the curtain of fog with her magic, it felt like running into a solid wall. Clearly, it answered to only one mistress—or perhaps two.

"Can you do anything about this?"

"Not without considerable effort," Sylvia replied, almost apologetically. Lorelei did not think she'd ever grow accustomed to the eerie, hallowed light that filled Sylvia's eyes. "I'm still getting used to wielding magic again. And it feels like she's holding on to it with all her strength."

Perfect.

"Stay close," Lorelei said. "I don't want to lose you in this."

They moved carefully over snaring roots and water-slicked rocks. Dark shapes—the forked limb of a tree, the drip of lichen—jutted into the gloom every now and again, making monsters of their surroundings. Everything bristled, hostile and watchful as they passed.

A branch snapped.

Sylvia reacted immediately, pressing their backs together and gripping the pommel of her saber. Even now, with all the power in the world at her fingertips, she still reached for the solid comfort of that flimsy silver blade. Lorelei raised her hands, poised to rip the moisture from the air. A moment ticked by, and then another. The forest drew its breath and held it, and that eerie, impossible stillness settled over them again.

Lorelei let her arms fall, feeling foolish for leaping at nothing but shadows. Perhaps Adelheid was already long gone. It would be a simple thing to take the *Prinzessin* and strand them here, cackling all the way to Ruhigburg. It was what Lorelei would have done.

But she knew Adelheid better than that by now; she would take no chances in leaving them alive, and she would want to see Sylvia pay for what she'd done to Johann. The prospect of fighting Adelheid terrified her. She'd flung them about as though they were nothing more than dolls she'd grown bored of. Even if Sylvia—

"Lorelei, there!"

A shard of ice shot from the tree line, a thin needle of moonlight. Before she could even think to react, Sylvia drew her blade and swung. The ice shattered on impact.

Behind Lorelei, magic shivered through the air. She whirled around just in time to see a silhouette appear like a ghost out of the fog. "Behind you!"

Adelheid surged toward them. With a thrust of her hand, a great column erupted from the river and descended on them like a closed fist. With a swear, Sylvia seized hold of it with her magic and redirected it as best she could. Water crashed to the ground— far closer than Lorelei would have liked—and splattered them like blood. The grim reality of their situation set in. No matter how powerful she was, Sylvia still had yet to shake off the rust of five years. Adelheid, meanwhile, was in her prime—and furious.

Adelheid recovered quickly. The puddles around them shivered, then leapt back into Adelheid's hand as a thin sword of ice. Her face contorted with grim purpose, she thrust it at Sylvia's heart. An adept magic user would have melted or vaporized it in an instant. But with a glitter of determined fire in her eyes, Sylvia met Adelheid's blade with her own, bracing the hilt of her saber with both hands. Adelheid's ice sword shattered on impact, and the sound rang out like the clap of thunder. With a shout of frustration, Adelheid drew her own steel.

Lorelei had never truly seen Sylvia in her element, with no reservations holding her back. She moved like the rush of a river, every motion fluid. Adelheid met her blow for blow. Between the two of them, it looked like a perfectly choreographed dance, too fast for her to track. She desperately sought an opening to intervene, but she couldn't risk striking recklessly, or she might very well skewer Sylvia alive.

At last, Sylvia caught Adelheid's sword, locking their blades together. She slid it easily down to the cross guard and, with a flourish, sent it sailing across the clearing. It landed in the river with a dull *plunk*. Adelheid let out a breathless sound of surprise.

"You never were much of a fencer," Sylvia said, with a smile Lorelei would have once found infuriating. Now, it was almost dashing. *Ugh.* Sylvia swung her sword across her body, and water wicked off the end of the blade. "Surrender, Adelheid. Call off this plan, and I will spare your life."

Adelheid smoothed out her expression. With almost bitter amusement, she said, "You're not much of a channeler anymore."

The mist around them funneled like a tornado and clotted into thick, angry clouds. Thunder rolled, and then the sky cleaved open. Rain drenched them in seconds. Sylvia's hair snapped in the wind, and leaves flurried wildly around her. She called on her own power. Judging by the strain on her face, she was battling for control of the storm. The raindrops surrounding her and Adelheid froze in midair, shrouding them in a veil of water. It was as awesome as it was terrible to watch. For a moment, Lorelei believed they might truly be easily matched.

Then, Adelheid's eyes flared with aetheric light. The suspended rainwater dropped like a stone. She launched a column of water directly at Sylvia, who staggered backward at the impact. When the second volley came, Lorelei attempted to divert it, but it felt like the reins of a galloping horse slipping through her fingers. This time, however, Sylvia was ready. She extended her hand just in time to cleave the water rushing toward her; it flowed past her on each side, like a stone in a river's course.

Adelheid did not hesitate to retaliate. Another flex of her hands, and the rainfall overhead solidified to hail. Lorelei held up an arm to shield herself from the renewed gust and gritted her teeth against the cold sting of water in her eyes. Through her blurred vision, she could read the panic plain on Sylvia's face. Where Adelheid's magic was another limb, Sylvia's was a crude weapon whose weight she was still testing. But Adelheid could not go on like this forever. Blood beaded on her temples like sweat and dribbled from one nostril.

Just like the king and his mirror, Lorelei thought bitterly. This power was killing her. Aether always strained its wielder's body. No one could hope to channel this much of it and survive—especially when it had been stolen.

"Why are you doing this?" Sylvia shouted over the howl of the storm.

"There is no other way forward," Adelheid answered. "Wilhelm has sat by idly while our harvests rotted in the fields, while our homes burned, while my family and subjects have starved. And now he plans to sacrifice us all for his own ambitions. I cannot allow it."

"We would have helped you! I would have helped you."

Adelheid curled her lip. "You have always been so naïve, Sylvia. By the time Wilhelm is through, this country will be ruined. Whatever influence you have will be gone. What culture you cherish will be diluted when we are all forced to assimilate. Some of us will be snuffed out entirely." She flung her arm out, as if gesturing over the vast expanse of Brunnestaad. "Open your eyes. We are relics already. Can you bring yourself to hasten our demise?"

Once, all of them had been royalty. This was what he'd reduced them to: dogs fighting for scraps.

"I have brought myself to do many things." Sylvia set her jaw. "I will protect what is mine."

In response, Adelheid lashed out with a whip of water. Immediately, Lorelei focused her attention on the puddle at Sylvia's feet. She brought up a wall of ice to shield Sylvia. Sylvia did not look her way, but she could almost feel her gratitude. Lorelei could never hope to compete with either of their raw power, but she could certainly make a nuisance of herself. If Lorelei could distract Adelheid, perhaps Sylvia could find an opening with her saber.

As Sylvia fought to close the space between her and Adelheid, Lorelei sent chips of ice and bursts of water hurtling toward Adelheid. Even with two opponents and her strength sapped by the Ursprung's curse, she was an automaton of violence, cold and controlled as she swatted aside Lorelei's attacks and launched her own against Sylvia. But one moment of distraction was all she needed for Sylvia to get within range. With inhuman speed, she landed a blow on Adelheid's arm. Blood arced from the wound.

Adelheid reeled back, her eyes gleaming like a cornered animal's as she realized she was losing ground. As Sylvia readied herself to strike again, magic screamed through the air like a riptide. A shudder moved through the earth, and then the river spilled over its banks. The force of the current nearly bowled Lorelei over. She scrabbled up onto a low-hanging branch. Birds were flushed shrieking from their roosts, and branches groaned as they were torn asunder from the trees. She even caught a glimpse of a schellenrock clinging to a shiny shard of sea glass as it was swept, wailing, from its den.

Adelheid would drown them all at this rate.

Against her unbridled power, they didn't stand a chance. Lorelei had to do something—and quickly. But Lorelei had never killed anyone before. She had thought about it in the abstract, of course, but confronted with the possibility, her hands trembled like a frightened child's. She didn't know if she could stomach it. Not the blood and certainly not the guilt.

No. She could not fall prey to sentimentality.

Lorelei knew that look in Adelheid's eye, hollowed-out and bladed. She would cut down any rival who stood in her way. She would make any concession to guarantee her own survival. And Lorelei would die a thousand deaths over to protect Sylvia. The conviction coated her all over with armor. She refused to be afraid, when she had walked in the shadow of Death for so long.

This time, she would fight for what she loved.

But she couldn't be *stupid* about it. She was no gallant fairy-tale knight. But if she could come up with a plan, any sort of plan . . .

Bare inches away from her nose, a pair of citrine eyes blinked out at her. The air itself rippled like a cloak caught in a breeze. Although she couldn't see the shape of its body, she knew immediately what it was.

An alp.

Her alp.

She hardly had time to process it before the beast materialized out of the mist. The crimson of its tarnkappe was as bright as a bloodstain. It smashed the cap down against its head with its tiny claws.

Its hateful voice slithered through her skull. "Came back."

She nearly toppled off the branch. "Now is really not the time!"

It dared to look offended. "Tried to kill me!"

"Consider us even, then!" Oh, she could throttle it. Maybe this time, she really would rend its tarnkappe— No, she had to remain calm.

An idea came to her, slowly at first, then burning as urgent as a flame. Channeling Sylvia as much as she was able, she drew a steadying breath and forced a smile. It flinched. "Right now, you and I share a common enemy."

The alp regarded her suspiciously, clearly recalling her earlier trickery.

The water was still raging below them, frothing and brown as it tore up the earth. Sylvia and Adelheid stood knee-deep in it now. Great gouts of water lashed out at Sylvia like the crack of a whip, only to be held in trembling suspension when she lifted her hands. Her eyes glittered with stalwart determination. Adelheid's shoulders heaved with every breath, and her face was mottled with streaks of blood. It pushed out of her pores and leaked from the corners of her eyes.

Hold on just a little longer.

"That woman," she said, "is going to cause a war. I imagine you are old enough to remember the last time that happened. Armies will come with their machines and their horses, and they will destroy your home without even thinking about it."

Lorelei could not read the alp's expression, but something about its ponderous silence suggested it was remembering some distant loss. It looked quite pathetic, with its matted-down fur and sodden cloak.

"And when all is said and done," she added, with great reluctance, "I do still owe you a cup of coffee in exchange for sparing my life."

"Two," it countered.

"You shall have a whole kettle for all I care." She was too desperate to bargain well—and what did such a small show of generosity cost her, anyway? "Are we agreed?"

It looked spiteful but huffed out a childish "Fine."

Lorelei nearly wilted with relief. "You've been following us, yes? Do you remember the man accompanying us?"

Without a reply, the alp's form swirled into the rain. In the span of a heartbeat, it refashioned itself in the image of . . . well, not quite Johann. It had captured his imposing size well enough, along with the color and texture of his overlong hair, slicked back with rain. It had also somehow mastered the tortured glint in his eyes behind the steel frames of his glasses. But its features were . . . just slightly off, more delicate, more *pretty*, than they actually had been.

At least someone remembered him fondly.

"That's the one," she said. "Now go. Call out to her—and make sure she sees you."

The alp hesitated for only a moment before plunging into the flood.

Lorelei's heart thundered in her chest as she bent the mist around it to give it cover. She rummaged through her pack frantically until she found a knife, then slid off the branch. She landed with a splash. Rain and wind tore at her viciously. The current begged for her to surrender, its pleas bouncing through her head like nixie-song, but she waded in a slow circle to get a better vantage point behind Adelheid.

She had only one shot at this.

The alp had situated itself just over Sylvia's shoulder.

Now or never. Lorelei sliced through the mist. It billowed around not-Johann, shrouding his form with a ghostly pall. From this distance, the only thing betraying him was the tarnkappe, which had taken the form of a crimson cravat. It looked like his torn-open throat.

"Adelheid," the alp called out.

At the sound of her name, her head snapped toward him. Her entire body crumpled—with shock or hope, Lorelei could not be certain. She knew how it felt—that breathless moment when you realized the dead might not truly be dead—but she was beyond pity. Steeling herself, she stood and crept out of the mist, clutching the knife as hard as she dared. It felt impossibly heavy in her hands. It felt like judgment.

As she rose up behind Adelheid, Sylvia's eyes locked on hers. Her gaze was steady and—God help her—forgiving. She could almost imagine Sylvia's fingers encircling her wrist, guiding her true. Floating just beyond her, she could see Aaron there. It was a brutal reminder: *never again*. Never again would she hesitate to use her magic to protect someone. It burned up the last of her hesitation.

"Johann?" Adelheid asked brokenly.

"Seeing ghosts?" Lorelei plunged the knife into Adelheid's back. She almost recoiled in horror. It had gone in so easily—and Adelheid hardly made a sound.

The alp dissolved into a whirl of shadow. Adelheid collapsed to her knees, and the storm dropped like a discarded cloak. The mist lifted. The last of the rain fell in one great, shimmering sheet. Finally, the winds slowed, sweeping a lock of Adelheid's hair over her shoulder before it died with a mournful sigh.

The three of them stood at the center of all the wreckage. The glade was a graveyard of floating branches, snapped like broken bones. Small bodies of wildeleute floated face down in a tangle of leaves. But worst of all was Adelheid, now kneeling at Lorelei's feet with her head bowed. Her hair fell over her face like a death shroud, but through the tangled mess of it, she looked utterly exhausted. Blood vessels had burst in her eyes, and bruises snaked down her arms. Her every breath was shuddering and wet, as though she were breathing through mud.

"I don't want to kill you, Adelheid," Sylvia said quietly. "We can treat this wound, surely. Don't force my hand, I beg of you."

It seemed to Lorelei baseless optimism, but she did not say anything.

"Very well," Adelheid rasped. "I give up."

"Truly?" Sylvia asked breathlessly.

"Yes, truly." Her voice sounded broken. "I will give my family one less thing to be ashamed of. If I cannot protect them, I will at least die with honor in the capital."

The relief on Sylvia's face was immense. "Thank you."

"I want to know one more thing," Lorelei said. "Would you have kept your word to me?"

Adelheid lifted her head slowly. A challenge burned in her eyes. "For as long as it was convenient."

It hardly even stung to hear her admit it. That was the problem with all of them. Not just the expedition, but this whole damn country. They clung to survival, striking like vipers in a mad scramble to the top. Adelheid's reign in Ebul would have been fragile, and she knew it. She would have never rested easy another day in her life. What remained of Brunnestaad would be watching her for any cracks. But her promise to Lorelei was convenient, exactly as Wilhelm's had been. As long as she had a Yeva in her retinue, she had one last recourse.

One more escape route.

"I understand," Lorelei said.

And she did. *Viper to viper.*

Even more, she understood the despair that stole over Adelheid's face. There was something desolate about the resignation in her eyes.

A telltale shiver of the mist lit Lorelei's every nerve.

She followed Adelheid's gaze and saw the moisture in the air solidifying, sharpening. It looked like the blade of a guillotine, glinting in the dismal sunlight. It was aimed directly at Sylvia. There was always a moment of perfect stillness, of suspended breath, when Death spread his wings and drew his scythe. This time, Lorelei didn't hesitate. She pulled on the water around them with all of her strength. And with a clench of her fist, a jagged bolt of ice pierced through Adelheid's chest.

The ice hanging over Sylvia melted suddenly, as if its spirit had fled. It dropped harmlessly onto her head, and she let out a startled cry. Her eyes were flung wide with terror as she stared at Adelheid's slumped body. Blood had splattered Sylvia's face. Her breaths came in quick gasps.

Thank God. Lorelei had been so close to losing her.

She wasn't sure if she would collapse sooner from relief or panic. Adelheid's gaze did not break from hers, even as that horrible alien light dimmed. Her lips were painted scarlet with her blood. Her body hung limp, suspended gruesomely by the spear impaling her. It had begun to melt from the heat of her body, and bloodstained water *drip, drip, drip*ped into the flood. It was horrific. She could not look away.

"You saved me," Sylvia said. "Again."

"You still sound surprised."

Sylvia approached her on fawn's legs. When she drew close enough, she wound her arms around Lorelei's waist and collapsed her weight against her. "Oh, Lorelei. I'm such a fool."

The steadiness of Sylvia's heartbeat against her chest, the soothing warmth of her body, eventually brought Lorelei back down to earth. The film over her vision faded. The feeling in her limbs returned.

"You're not." She drew back just enough to crook a finger beneath Sylvia's chin and tip it up. "You just always see the best in others. I don't."

"Could I have stopped it?" Sylvia whispered.

"No," she said firmly. "You can't walk down that path."

"How can I not?" Sylvia buried her face in the crook of her neck and let out a soft whimper. Lorelei held her closer. The fairy tale Sylvia had clung to all these years—the childhood dream of the six of them, together, on the cusp of a better world—lay dead at her feet as surely as Adelheid. "How can I not despair?"

But all around them, water dripped from the trees, like the first thaw after a long, cold winter. In the distance, birds tentatively resumed their song. She could feel the wild thrum of Sylvia's heart.

"Because life is as bitter as it is sweet," Lorelei said. "It's Yevanisch wisdom I've never believed in. Not until you."

Sylvia met her eyes steadily, disbelief and hope mingled.

"Now, come," Lorelei murmured, brushing away her tears as carefully as she could. "It isn't good to linger where the dead can hear you."

Together, they waded through the floodwaters, arm in arm, as the fog lifted and the sun filtered down again.

TWENTY-EIGHT

They arrived in Ruhigburg not to fanfare but to soldiers.

It was as though the wind carried the news of their arrival, for a battalion in scarlet livery lined up in neat, perfect rows along the docks with their muskets drawn and ready. This, Lorelei supposed, was their welcoming committee. Not that she was expecting festivals in the plaza, but it seemed to her a bit discourteous.

She stood on the observation deck of the *Prinzessin*, the wind dancing along the hem of her greatcoat. Sylvia pressed close to her side, with her arms folded neatly over the railing. Even Heike and Ludwig had emerged from the cabin to watch the city fold in around them. The last week had been fraught, but the four of them had come to a tentative understanding.

Whatever happened, they would vouch for one another.

When Lorelei had envisioned this moment, she'd thought it would be triumphant, in all the ways it mattered and all the ways it didn't. But staring down the gray sprawl of Ruhigburg, she felt only grim resignation.

"I see Wilhelm is feeling as hospitable as ever." Heike sniffed. "Should we be worried? I'm worried."

"Why should we be?" Lorelei gestured vaguely at Sylvia. "We're bringing him what he wanted."

"I don't think this is *exactly* what he wanted," Ludwig said. His voice was still raspy from his brush with death—one of his last lingering symptoms. "No offense intended."

"None taken," Sylvia said wanly.

The two of them made a strange pair: Sylvia with her glowing eyes, and Ludwig with ... well, there was the bark scaling his neck, of course, which had of late sprouted a branch and a few tentative leaves. But his eyes had taken on a green cast, and when you peered into them, you could just make out an ash grove reflected in his pupils. If he was upset by the transformation, he did not share his feelings with Lorelei. But sometimes, she caught him standing on the deck with such stillness, it was as though he'd taken root there. In those moments, he seemed so unknowably lonely, she left him to his brooding.

When they'd told him what had befallen Adelheid and Johann on the Vanishing Isle, he'd said only, *God. What a nightmare.*

He did not care to discuss what happened on the night he vanished. He and Johann had not exactly been close, but the betrayal clearly unsettled him more than he wanted to admit. Lorelei did not push him, partly out of consideration—mostly because Heike radiated sheer malice any time Lorelei so much as looked at him askance. They'd become inseparable since they boarded the *Prinzessin* again.

"At any rate," Sylvia said with forced cheer, "Wilhelm is not an *entirely* unreasonable man. I am sure he will be pleased."

Lorelei hoped she was right.

One week ago, they had left the Vanishing Isle behind. Once they'd oriented themselves and found the nearest town, Lorelei had hired a courier to deliver her report on the expedition, a dossier sealed in navy wax and stamped with Ziegler's signet ring. Inside, she'd enclosed a description of what exactly had unfolded on the Ruhigburg Expedition, as well as Ziegler's journal entries and legal documents: evidence of her and Anja von Wolff's betrayal.

Somehow, that was easier than composing a letter to her family.

Once again, she found herself ill-suited to the task of expressing her sentiments in words. How much of the truth could they handle? How willing was she to pick at her wounds before they'd even had a chance to mend? She'd drafted and shredded no fewer than five iterations before she settled on pragmatism. She would return to them—hale and mostly whole—in a week's time. She could not resist adding, as a postscript:

I love you. I am sorry.

Now, the *Prinzessin* ground to a halt in the harbor, and the dockworkers hauled them in with thick, fraying ropes. The pitch-dark waters of the Vereist lapped eagerly at the hull. After everything, Lorelei had almost missed the bland, marshy climes of Ruhigburg.

Almost.

The four of them made their way down the gangplank and toward the company of soldiers. Behind them, carriages waited like snow globes placed on a shelf, all of them sparkling with wide glass windows. Four, she noted. So Wilhelm was separating them, as if they hadn't had ample time to agree on their story already.

"Lorelei Kaskel, leader of the Ruhigburg Expedition," Lorelei said. "What is the meaning of this?"

One of the soldiers—the highest-ranking of them, if the stars jangling on his shoulders were anything to go by—stepped forward. "We've been sent by His Imperial Majesty to escort the four of you to the palace."

Heike extended an impatient hand. Her bag dangled from her elegant fingertips. She shook it, and all of her instruments clattered menacingly. "Well, what are all of you standing around for, then? If you're going to be so rude, at least make yourselves useful."

As the wheels clattered on the cobblestones, the carriage lurched nauseatingly. Lorelei could hardly form a coherent thought with this godforsaken contraption rattling her skull like a can full of coins. Outside her window, the palace rose up like a leviathan from the black band of the river. It looked even more imposing in the daylight, a cold and precise work of architecture seemingly chiseled from ice. The sun glistered on its spires, bright enough that she had to look away. Unlike the night of the ball, there were no flowers, no laughter, no sweet anticipation to soften its edges. There was only the solid rock of her own dread in her gut and the grim reality of those gaudy black doors.

They had done everything he asked. So why did she feel as though she were about to be punished? The longer she dwelled on it, the hotter her anger sparked. After everything they'd sacrificed for him, how *dare* he treat them like strangers—like prisoners? She sorely regretted not having Sylvia here to vent her spleen on. Or perhaps she'd make Lorelei feel better. No, unlikely. Sylvia's unrelenting cheer—or insulted pride—would do nothing but wind her up tighter.

When her driver opened the carriage door for her, she ignored his hand and thundered up the staircase, the fall of her coat like a skein of shadow behind her. The doors opened for her as if enchanted, but it was only the work of two very startled footmen. Clearly, she was not what either of them had expected.

"Where is Wilhelm?"

One of them silently pointed down a corridor.

The royal palace made the *Prinzessin* look like a cheap toy. The marble was lunar-pale beneath her feet and threaded with gold, and the walls were coated in a layer of water so delicate, it looked like glass. It fell eternally from the ceiling by some work of magic or engineering Lorelei did not have the time or patience to puzzle over.

A second set of footsteps echoed urgently off the walls. Whoever it was breathed in a way Lorelei could describe only as *deliberate*, as if they wanted to let her know they were not at all pleased about having to hurry after her. "Miss Kaskel—"

Lorelei shoved open the doors to the throne room.

"His Majesty will see you in there," the servant pursuing her said limply. The sound of her voice was swallowed when the doors fell shut with an ominous *bang*.

The rest of the expedition already stood before the dais. The first thing Lorelei noticed was Anja von Wolff, perched beside Wilhelm with all the stiff elegance of a statue upon its plinth. She looked like she belonged there, with her regal profile and her practiced look of courtly disdain. But her wrists were shackled, and a set of guards lingered near the door closest to her.

Wilhelm regarded Lorelei with a bone-deep exhaustion. He slouched in his throne as though he were a schoolboy drowsing in his lessons. His cloak was deep indigo, finely woven, and pinned in place with a fat sapphire brooch. His crown, beaten thin in the shape of a wave, was nestled into his dark hair.

"Is that the last of you, then?" he asked. "I see we've had a bit of a retention problem."

Sylvia's temper flared, and she looked for all the world like she was about to fly across the dais and strangle him. "Is that all you have to say to us? Don't you *dare* make light of this!"

"Forgive me," Wilhelm said thinly. "I've found myself at something of a loss for words since I received your briefing. What the *hell* happened out there? How could you fuck this up so spectacularly?"

It was a rhetorical question, of course. Lorelei had detailed *what the hell happened* quite extensively.

"Have we?" she snapped. "You knew the dangers from the outset. This project was doomed from the start."

"Of course I did! But I didn't expect it would be her." His voice faltered. "Goddamn it. I never should have—"

"Regret isn't going to bring her back," Heike said. "Adelheid made her decision—one that *you* made her think was necessary. You'll have to live with it, just like the rest of us."

Color rose in his cheeks. Before he could speak, Heike held up a hand. It was such a quintessentially Adelheid gesture, Wilhelm looked stunned. "No. You do not possibly have anything to say to that."

"Heike is right," Lorelei said. "Adelheid fought valiantly, with every limited resource at her command. She did what she thought was best for her people, in spite of you."

Wilhelm sat slumped in his throne, unmoving. He buried his face in his hands. The seconds ticked by agonizingly. "And what about you, Lud? Would you like to blame me, as well?"

"Me?" He startled. Ludwig was not the first person Lorelei would have chosen to assuage her guilt. His voice sounded like the whisper of dead leaves in the wind—and one could not easily overlook the branch jutting from the base of his neck. "Well . . . Of course not. I wouldn't say it was *entirely*—"

"That's enough." When the king lifted his head again, Lorelei could see the ruin behind his stare. "No, you're right. I'm grateful I can count on my old friends to be honest with me—and new ones as well."

There was something disingenuous and petulant in his words, but they would have to do.

Wilhelm rubbed his temples. "Now, what news of the Ursprung?"

The four survivors of the expedition exchanged glances. Lorelei had written that they'd found it—but decided the news would be best delivered in person. Heike, mercifully, seemed eager to play messenger. With a malicious smile, she said, "I'm afraid you can't have it. It didn't want you."

"And what," he said thinly, "does that mean?"

By now, Wilhelm knew the legends as well as Lorelei did. He knew exactly what it meant; he only wanted to know which one of them had betrayed him.

"It chose von Wolff."

"I see." Wilhelm laughed bitterly. "Seize her."

His guards advanced a step—then froze mid-stride, their eyes flung wide with terror. With a clench of her fists, Sylvia held them fast by their blood. Wilhelm stared at them with a mixture of horror and fascination. Anja looked practically exultant.

"Will you wait a moment?" Sylvia asked impatiently. She relaxed her hands—and her hold on the guards, who flinched back from her. "I am no threat to you. My loyalty remains unchanged. Anyone who opposes you will have to go through me."

"No!" Anja snarled.

"A generous offer. One we will discuss shortly." Wilhelm pursed his lips, clearly displeased. "Well, then. Lorelei?"

She snapped to attention. "Yes, Your Majesty?"

"You're every bit the bastard Ziegler said you were." It had the air of a compliment. "You remind me of her, actually."

"Thank you." The memory of her still stung, but it was a thorny sort of pain, one that made her feel both bitter and tender. "Some people say so."

"Effective immediately, you are granted the status of shutzyeva. You may leave the Yevanverte and live where you please. And tomorrow, if you accept the position, you will report to me as my new chamberlain." He leaned forward in his seat. "I've heard they call you a viper. I'd say the title fits. You've certainly proven adept at flushing out rats, and I'd venture there are a few more in my court."

Lorelei hardly knew what to feel. She nearly keeled over from the shock of it, the thrill of getting what she wanted after five long years. It wasn't exactly happiness. Ziegler had served as Wilhelm's chamberlain and resented every moment of it. It had trapped her, a gilded chain wound tight around her throat. But with this position, Lorelei would have the ear of the most powerful man in Brunnestaad, a man who needed something from her. She could make herself indispensable to him. And with that salary, she would never want for research funds again.

She would be a fool to decline.

"Thank you, Your Majesty." She bowed. "I will serve you as best I can."

Anja laughed, a sharp, mocking sound. "Good luck to you, Wilhelm. Rats have a way of multiplying, especially now that you've invited another one in."

Hatred sparked hot within her. Oh, how satisfying it would be to see Anja's face warp when Lorelei told her she loved her daughter—how she intended to ruin her and how she already had. But before she could say anything regrettable, Wilhelm rescued her. Affably, he said, "I suppose we'll begin with you, Anja. This has been a long time coming."

"Shouldn't I have a say in what happens to her?" Sylvia's voice sliced through the tension like the fall of an axe. The sight of her stole Lorelei's breath away. A sliver of light cut across her face, casting her features in stark shadows. Her eyes burned like cold fire.

Anja stared down at her daughter with her lips pressed into a bloodless line. "Silence, Sylvia."

"I'm listening." Wilhelm hooked an ankle over his knee in the very picture of indolence. "What would you have me do?"

"If you want the support of Albe, it would be wise to leave her alive." Sylvia drew in a steadying breath and met her mother's dispassionate gaze. "I would have you exile her."

The cold detachment slid off Anja's face like a dropped plate. She lurched forward in her chair, straining against her bonds. "What?"

"She has shown utter disregard to Albe and the well-being of its people. She is unfit to rule." Sylvia canted her chin with a touch of that old, haughty defiance Lorelei had once despised. "I will assume the title of duchess, and I will pledge my armies, in addition to the power of the Ursprung, to you."

"You stupid girl, you will ruin us!" Anja snarled. "Everything I've worked for, everything that makes Albe what it is, will be taken from us."

Wilhelm gave a vague wave to one of the guards stationed at the doors. "Remove her."

As the guards dragged Anja from the throne room, Sylvia lowered her gaze to the floor, the muscle in her jaw tick, tick, ticking. "I will quell any sedition in my region. In exchange," she continued, "you will let me go."

Wilhelm hesitated. "What do you mean?"

"I do not know if you intend to uphold your original promise. If you do, know that I will serve you, but I will not marry you. I don't think we are a good match for a number of reasons." She brightened. "Heike, on the other hand—"

"Sylvia," Heike hissed.

Wilhelm blinked, as though he couldn't decide whether to be relieved or insulted. He glanced at the others with a sigh. "Leave us. It seems Sylvia and I have a lot to discuss."

Lorelei bowed low—fortuitous timing, since her eyes were welling with *tears*, of all things. She could not believe it. When was the last time she had cried, especially for something as patently ridiculous as *love*? This is what they'd planned—what Lorelei herself had suggested. And yet, she had not adequately prepared for what Sylvia's new role would entail. Stabilizing Albe—as well as Herzin and Ebul, considering both their heirs had died—could very well take years. More likely than not, it would involve violence.

Sylvia had denied Wilhelm, perhaps, but war was a jealous lover. It could very well take her from Lorelei. When the worst of the spell passed, she straightened to her full height, adjusted the lapels of her greatcoat, and strode out of the throne room.

In the safety of the hallway, Lorelei collapsed against the doors.

"It's going to be fine," said Heike.

And with that, Lorelei found herself crushed into a hug alongside Ludwig. She struggled as if caught in a snare, but it was no use. The air was being squeezed out of her, and her neck was wrenched into an odd angle.

"Um, Heike," Ludwig wheezed. "You're kind of . . ."

Heike let them both go abruptly. She grimaced and dusted off her skirts as though she'd touched something foul. "You're right. That was ... strange. Never again."

"Good," Lorelei groused. "You nearly strangled me."

Ludwig took stock of them. Hesitantly, he said, "Are things really going to be fine?"

"Of course." Heike tweaked his nose as though he were a child. "Sylvia and Wilhelm can handle themselves. So. How about a drink? If he won't throw us a party, we might as well have our own."

"Shouldn't we wait for Sylvia?" Ludwig asked.

Heike shrugged. "She'll find us."

But Lorelei did not see Sylvia again that night. And when she got the news, days later, that Sylvia had returned to Albe, Lorelei began to suspect that she would never see her again.

TWENTY-NINE

$\mathcal{T}$IME SLIPPED AWAY from Lorelei.

In the wake of the Ruhigburg Expedition, once the ink had dried on their degrees and the death certificates, she settled outside the Yevanverte and carved out a meager existence for herself. She took tea with Ludwig every week; predictably, his curse had proven just as much an academic fascination as she expected. She walked the rose gardens with Her Majesty Queen Heike—long may she reign—when both of them could find time in their schedules. She went home, when she could, to see her family and give Rahel the latest court gossip. Mostly, she attended her duties at court. Every now and again, Wilhelm saw fit to bestow on her some update on his dealings with Albe or Sylvia's well-being. It was either kindness or subtle viciousness. Either way, Lorelei downed each morsel like the sweetest poison.

Civil war had come and gone in four months, as short and brutal as life itself. One display of the Ursprung's power, and Wilhelm's opponents had surrendered. For the first time in decades, even the Albisch had been subdued. Apparently, they had taken to calling their new duchess Saint Sylvia.

It infuriated Lorelei to no end. *Saint Sylvia!* She was far from an expert on the subject, but she was fairly certain that one could not be both a saint and alive.

It was far easier to be annoyed at what she had helped set in motion. Sometimes, the weight of responsibility sat on Lorelei so heavily, she couldn't sleep. But for now, the Yevanverte was safe;

she was safe. She clung to that cold comfort on her worst nights. Her ghosts, at least, did not follow her as relentlessly as they once did. And when they did, they were gentler. Aaron's laughter echoing down the alleys outside her father's home. Ziegler's brassy voice carried on the breeze outside the lecture hall. Sometimes, Lorelei thought she saw Adelheid's broad silhouette in an east-facing window that overlooked the river. Although she could not see her eyes, she could feel her gaze. It was melancholy, almost wistful. She had taken to avoiding that part of campus on the occasion she found herself there.

Instead, she dreamed of silver eyes in the shadows, the heat of Sylvia's mouth on hers. It was a torture far worse than any she'd ever conjured for herself: four months without her. Four months without hearing her sing or listening to her prattle on about something or another. Four months without seeing her smile, as bright as sunlight. Lorelei didn't know how she could ever forget her, when everything reminded her of Sylvia.

It was a typical summer afternoon, sticky and languid with heat. Lorelei was, as she always was these days, sorting through the paperwork. Ziegler, it turned out, not only resented her role as chamberlain but was quite bad at it, too. There were thousands upon *thousands* of letters addressed to Ziegler, most of them fawning and simpering. There were hundreds more documents that needed her review that she clearly had not bothered with. Although the entire world knew of her death by now, Lorelei took a perverse joy in replying to the most obsequious of Ziegler's fans to "inform" them of her passing. Ziegler had betrayed her, but Lorelei still loved her best. The rest of these sycophants should know it. Once she'd finished, she began screening the correspondence that passed through her office.

There were, after all, rats to catch.

Sorting the mail was a full-time job all its own. This morning, she'd arrived to a new towering stack. It had slumped over in defeat the moment she closed the door behind her. Lorelei had kicked the bulk of it, scattering it farther across the room, which did make her feel better—at least until she had to gather up the wreckage and organize it again. After a few hours, she plucked an audaciously purple envelope off the floor.

There was a sprig of lavender tied to it with twine. For a moment, Lorelei considered the distinct possibility that it was some sort of assassination attempt—or else a cruel joke. It looked like the kind of letter one would send their lover.

Over the past few months, Lorelei had grown accustomed to the language of courtiers. According to some, lavender meant devotion—but also silence. She wondered which the writer had intended. Lorelei turned it over. She nearly dropped it when she saw the handwriting: unmistakably Sylvia's. Of course she would send documents regarding matters of state that looked like *this*.

But upon closer inspection, Lorelei saw it was addressed to her.

Her hands seized up. The court doctor had done the best he could for her injury, but it was still finicky. There was nothing to be done for her when the weather—or her mood—turned. She spent a few moments working out the knot in her palm, the nerves firing as if in anticipation of some blow. She wanted to tear the letter to bits and cast it into the wind. She wanted to copy down the address and write a scathing reply. But what was there to say? Everything. Nothing.

She could not open it. Sylvia had not written in all this time, and she dreaded to think of what had taken so long. Perhaps her feelings had changed. Perhaps she was too busy enjoying her divinity. Or . . .

The thorns around her heart had withered sometime in those bright days she thought Sylvia was really hers. They'd been replaced now by a horrid, intractable weed. *Hope*. She couldn't cut it down, no matter how desperately she tried.

Lorelei loved her even now.

She had her own signet ring, her own office, her own *life*. So much had changed and yet so little. She was still bitterly unhappy. Lorelei shoved the envelope back in the pile and resumed her work.

On a balmy evening, Lorelei returned to her favorite spot by the river. The Vereist chugged lazily past her, solid black against the sunset. In the gloaming, the world was washed in shades of emerald and gold. Fireflies drifted over the fields racing toward the horizon, reminding her of the irrlicht glowing like lanterns in the woods of the Vanishing Isle.

"They told me I might find you here."

Lorelei choked on a breath.

Sylvia von Wolff was standing behind her. Her hair danced in the wind rising off the river. The fading sun haloed her in soft, golden light. She was—

Lorelei felt—

She'd no words at all. Lorelei rose to her feet. She took a step closer to her, casting her in shadow. Sylvia cranked her neck to meet her gaze, her eyes wide and waiting. She looked exactly as Lorelei remembered—and nothing at all like she remembered. She scoured Sylvia's face for signs of new battle scars but found none. It was only the bone-deep weariness in her face that was new. Even so, hope shone out of her like a beacon.

The branches of the weeping willow clattered and hushed softly in the breeze. It smelled of things beginning to die: a warm, amber smell. They had last stood here a lifetime ago, with the spring mists coiled around them and the expedition hovering over them like a blade. If Lorelei closed her eyes, she could almost imagine the pallid face of a nixie rising out of the water.

"How blessed I am," Lorelei said. "To what do I owe the immense honor of being visited by a saint?"

Sylvia winced. "I did not realize that would reach you here."

"Oh yes. Word of our savior certainly reached me." Lorelei knew she was being unpleasant, but she could not help herself. Hearing Sylvia's voice again lit a spark within her. She felt, for the first time in months, light and incandescent and—and utterly *furious*. "Ruhigburg is not that much of a backwater."

"It is good to see you so unchanged." Somehow, she managed to sound both cross and fond. "How is your family?"

"How is my family? That is all you have to say to me?"

Sylvia winced again.

"They're well, thank you," she spat. "Now, good day to you, Your Grace—or should I say Your Holiness? I know you're very busy. I've seen your calendar, and—"

"Lorelei," she said urgently. "I'm sorry."

"You're *sorry*?" Lorelei felt nearly hysterical now. "I understand, of course, why you did what you did. But after the war was over, I thought . . ." *I thought you would come back for me.* The words caught in her chest like a burr. "You have more responsibilities now, I know. If you didn't want me, you could have said so. If you don't love me—"

"Of course I love you, you impossible, oblivious, self-martyring—"

"You . . ." Lorelei could not even delight in those words she'd yearned to hear for so long. She felt as though she were about to catch flame. "What else was I supposed to think? You never wrote. You didn't even say goodbye. I would have thought you were dead had I not seen your letters for Wilhelm come through, or all the shrines raised to you in the city, so I . . . *What* are you doing?"

Sylvia lowered herself to her knees and took Lorelei's hand. "I tried to write. I did, in fact, many times. But you are a very difficult woman to get ahold of, Lorelei Kaskel. You never replied. I think *I* should be the one who is angry."

Her tone was light, almost teasing. Lorelei couldn't make sense of it. All those letters were for *her*? She'd never bothered to check. Why would she, considering they'd arrived at her *office* and not her flat? God. She had been passing those letters along to Wilhelm for *months*. Why had he not said anything? Knowing Sylvia, they probably contained all manner of . . . of florid declarations and God knew what else. Now that she thought about it, he had occasionally looked at her with a mysterious little smile on his face or—more inexplicably—recited poetry of uncertain provenance and asked her opinion. Poetry! She wanted to lie down and die.

"I've been busy," she croaked.

Twilight darkened the sky, and candlelight bloomed in all the windows of the university's buildings. The nights were arriving sooner and sooner as autumn nipped hungrily at the edges of summer, but they were still warm and humid. The fireflies blinked like stars.

"As have I." Sylvia carefully took Lorelei's wrist in her hand and raised it to her lips. She kissed the heel of her palm, a gesture of courtly grace. The warmth of her lips was blistering, even through Lorelei's gloves. "I have lost count of how many villages I've visited and how many 'miracles' I have been asked to perform. On top of that, we are preparing for the harvest season, and it has been an endless challenge to reach an agreement in my court regarding our relationship with Brunnestaad. However, I think matters have been settled."

Lorelei wasn't quite sure what Sylvia was saying anymore. Her head was spinning. Heike and Wilhelm had married last month, but he had a sister. It made sense, of course, to unite their families. "Congratulations. When is your wedding?"

Sylvia's eyes sparkled. "When would you like it to be?"

"Don't mock me," Lorelei whispered.

"I am being very serious." She sounded a bit cross now. This was not off to a good start. Lorelei opened her mouth, but Sylvia barreled onward with what Lorelei was now convinced was a script she'd prepared. "One word from you, and I shall be the happiest woman in the universe."

"What."

"Not that one," Sylvia said.

"I . . ." Lorelei blinked hard. But when she opened her eyes, Sylvia von Wolff was still kneeling before her. This was a dream there was no waking from. She looked genuinely apprehensive. It did not suit her. "I hope you understand that I will make every day of your life more difficult than the last, more complicated than it otherwise would be."

"I welcome it."

"We . . . We will bicker endlessly, you know. In the court and outside it. This changes nothing."

"I'd expect no different."

"My duties to the king—"

"Can be balanced with *living,* assuming I cannot steal you away for myself." Sylvia smiled at her. "Please, Lorelei. There is so much to do in this one glorious life we were gifted. We can travel. We can write. We can ride mara through open fields and run wild alongside the kornhunds. We can swim with nixies and tame lindworms, and maybe someday, with time, the world will realize there was never anything wrong with someone like me loving someone like you."

"That is a fantasy," Lorelei whispered. "The loveliest fairy tale I have heard in all my life."

"Yes," Sylvia said, with such emphatic tenderness. "But it's ours."

Lorelei could do nothing else but drop to her knees and kiss her. She pushed Sylvia down into the grass. When she pulled back, breathless, Sylvia fixed her with a smile as bright as the sun itself. In all her folktales, never was there an ending so sweet and strange as this.

"Yes. I will marry you, you romantic fool," Lorelei said against her lips. "May we write many more together."

ACKNOWLEDGMENTS

This one goes out to every single person who interacted with me while I planned, wrote, revised, or otherwise spoke about this book. Contrary to common publishing wisdom, my second and even my third novel were relatively kind to me. *A Dark and Drowning Tide* wanted me dead for two straight years. Well, I lived, bitch.

In all seriousness, thank you to Claire Friedman and Jess Mileo, my agents. We've made it to a new age category! You two read a million outlines, assuaged my worries with both humor and practical solutions, and found this book the perfect home. I say it every time, but I really could not ask for better partners.

To Sarah Peed, my editor, who is an absolute joy to work with. Your patience, vision, and enthusiasm mean the absolute world to me—and transformed this book in ways I couldn't have imagined. Thank you for loving this entire cast of weirdos and for providing the insight I needed to bring each of them fully to life. *A Dark and Drowning Tide* truly would not be what it is without you. Thank you as well to Anne Groell, who so warmly welcomed me onto her list and expertly shepherded this book to publication.

To the entire team at Del Rey, whose efforts have gotten this book into readers' hands around the world in such a beautiful package! Thank you to Ashleigh Heaton, Tori Henson, Sabrina Shen on the marketing team; my publicist, Jordan Pace; Rachel Kind and Denise Cronin on the foreign rights team; Lara Kennedy, my copyeditor; and Keith Clayton and Alex Larned in publishing. My eternal gratitude to Audrey Benjaminsen and Ella Laytham for illustrating and designing, respectively, the gloriously gothic masterpiece that is this cover. I might have cried when I first saw it.

To the team at Daphne Press: Davi Lancett, Daphe Tonge, Tori Bovalino, and Caitlin Lomas.

To my friends! Courtney Gould, you made me truly believe there was something here. Audrey Coulthurst, Rebecca Leach, Elisha Walker, and Helen Wiley: I can always count on y'all for commiseration and accountability. A special shoutout to Helen, who, at the last possible moment, descended like an angel from heaven and gave me notes that fixed the whole book. Kali Wallace, thank you for recommending Andrea Wulf's wonderful *The Invention of Nature*, which clarified many things for me as I revised. I owe a life debt to Kat Hillis, Emily Grey, Rachel Morris, Ava Reid, Charlie Lynn Herman, M. K. Lobb, and Alex Huffman, who gave me very early feedback when I was in a pit of despair. Lastly, thank you to the town of Ithaca and Team Claire members Jo Schulte, Ava Wilder, Jenna Voris, and (once again) Courtney Gould for sprinting through the first draft with me in July 2021.

To the artists who worked with me on such stunning illustrations for this book: RiotBones, Ashe Arends, Therese (@warickaart), Jaria Rambaran, Bri (@beforeviolets), Lu Herbert, and Isa Agajanian. Y'all are magic.

Finally, to you, whether you followed me from YA or gave my adult debut a chance. It's because of you that I can pursue my dreams.

ALLISON SAFT is the *New York Times* bestselling author of the romantic young adult fantasies *Down Comes the Night*, *A Far Wilder Magic*, and *A Fragile Enchantment*. After receiving her MA in English literature from Tulane University, she moved from the Gulf Coast to the West Coast, where she spends her time rolling on eight wheels and practicing aerial silks. She lives with her partner and an Italian greyhound named Marzipan.